T0365934

a Collection of SHORT STORIES

WILLIAM STANLEY

ARCHWAY
PUBLISHING

Archway Publishing books may be ordered through booksellers or by contacting:

Archway Publishing
1663 Liberty Drive
Bloomington, IN 47403
www.archwaypublishing.com
844-669-3957

ISBN: 978-1-6657-2472-2 (sc)
ISBN: 978-1-6657-2471-5 (e)

Library of Congress Control Number: 2022910347

Print information available on the last page.

Archway Publishing rev. date: 06/09/2022

DEDICATION

For Christopher and Elijah, may their dreams all come true, and in memory of Pete, my best friend and nephew, who is missed daily.

TABLE OF CONTENTS

WILDERNESS AND NATURE

FICTION

SCIENCE FICTION AND HORROR

FAMILY

WILDERNESS
AND NATURE

THE TRAPPER

CHAPTER ONE

The trapper stood on the shore of Great Slave Lake in the North West Territories watching the float plane that had dropped him off. As it banked sharply and headed away, it left him in silent awe of the great north woods. With his dog at his side as his only companion for the next six months, the enormity of his situation overwhelmed him. His fifteen hundred pounds of supplies lay beside him, ready to be packed away in his cabin and his skinning shed. His dog, which he had named Wolf, was restless; ready to start his routine helping the trapper move his supplies with their homemade cart to his cabin one hundred yards away. However, his priority was checking on his cabin first.

The trapper and Wolf walked the short distance up the path to their cabin. Everything looked in order as the trapper had bear-proofed the building before he had left last April. There were new claw marks and damaged wood where a bear had tried to enter without success. The trapper took his prybar, and upon removing the protection on the door the pair entered the cabin.

Their first order of business was to get a fire going, as it was mid September, and the weather was already beginning to change from fall to winter. They had received snow, but by early October it would be on the ground for the duration of the winter. Wolf loved the snow, as he was a Husky and a registered sled dog that the trapper had bought from a like-minded friend. Wolf was very devoted and protective of the trapper, and a great asset and companion on the trapline.

Soon a fire was roaring in the woodstove and smoke was rolling out of the chimney. The trapper was beginning to relax. The pair made their way to the skinning shed where the cart and winter sled for Wolf were kept. After Wolf was hooked up to the cart, off they went to start the task of moving all the supplies to the homesite.

Their first load was food, and after unloading those items they stopped to eat. The trapper ate a tuna sandwich and Wolf ate dried dog food, the emergency supply when and if they ran out of meat. The trapper enjoyed the bread he brought, but once it was gone there would be no more for the rest of the winter.

It was just coming on dark when they unloaded the last load of supplies and put the cart away, retiring to the cabin for the evening. The oil lamps were lit, and the trapper thanked the Lord for his safe arrival here and asked for His protection for the exceedingly challenging times ahead. He made his bed and collapsed in exhaustion with Wolf beside him. A good sleep was necessary as tomorrow would be the start of his season and work needed to be done.

CHAPTER TWO

The trapper woke with a start. Wolf had heard something also, as a low growl came from the back of his throat. The wolf pack was back. They came every year, usually on the first night, just to let the trapper and his dog know they were here also, and they shared this territory together. In the thirty years the trapper had been coming here, he had never had a negative encounter with the wolves. They sometimes followed him when he was checking his trapline, but never ventured too close. Wolf also did not challenge them, knowing he was no match for their numbers.

The trapper and the wolves had a secret pact. They were given all the leftovers from the deer, moose, and other animals that he or Wolf could not use. These remnants were taken a mile from the cabin and left for the grateful animals. Sometimes the bear that called this territory home beat the wolves to the food, but after a short battle he would be driven away, leaving the wolves to eat their fill and the bear to get their leftovers. Sometimes the hungry bear would make its way to the cabin looking for more food, but one shot from the trapper's gun reminded him this was not a safe place to be.

The trapper rolled out of bed. It was just coming on daylight. He opened the front door checking to see if the wolf pack was still there. They had left, but their prints could be seen in the light snowfall that had fallen during the night. After feeding himself and Wolf a hearty breakfast, they were ready to start their day. They went to the skinning shack, gathering the supplies they needed for cutting wood. The trapper had cut down trees in the spring, letting them dry over the summer. With his chainsaw he cut the trees into woodstove size logs and stacked them to be picked up when the snow was deep enough for Wolf and the sled to retrieve them.

This was the trapper's last winter here. The demand for fur was growing less and less as humans realized that extinction rates for all animals were rising rapidly. This way of life for trappers was also disappearing, as the forest authority was cutting the number of licenses they were giving out by fifty per cent this year and another twenty per cent next year.

Surveying the firewood, the trapper believed that including the wood at the cabin he had enough for the stove and his smoker, which he used to preserve deer and moose meat. The pair headed back to the cabin. The trapper grabbed his gun and went to hunt waterfowl for dinner, leaving Wolf behind. He made his way to the lake, hid in his blind, and waited for any ducks or geese to fly overhead.

Soon the trapper made his way back to the cabin, birds in hand looking forward to a nice dinner. For the next two weeks there would an abundance of water fowl before the lake froze up. The trapper was normally able to stock up and smoke enough goose to last till Christmas. After dinner he worked on repairing traps until well after midnight. He took time to play with Wolf, who was also still awake, and then they both retired to bed. The trapper dreamed about the wolverine stealing and eating animals from his traps. Soon these dreams would be his reality, but for now sleep was what he needed the most.

CHAPTER THREE

Over the next two weeks the trapper worked around the property fixing things in the cabin, his skinning shed, and his underground storage, where he kept his meat during the winter. The weather was getting cold, but they had still not had their first big snowstorm. The lake was starting to freeze, and the trapper had cut a hole in the ice from which his water supply was guaranteed for the winter. He also supplemented his meat supply with the fresh fish caught while ice fishing on the lake. There was an abundant supply of lake trout, whiting, walleye, and various other less desirable fish that Wolf enjoyed. His main concern now was meat for the winter. He had an ample supply of fowl and fish, but he needed a moose.

While working outside on his cabin's windows, making them draft proof, the trapper felt a steady wind at his back which kept blowing stronger. He knew what this meant. The first big snowstorm was approaching. He had to prepare, as these storms could last for days. This meant bringing enough wood, water, and food inside to last for three days. He sealed any cracks in the walls of the cabin that had opened during the summer to keep as much cold air out as possible. It wasn't unusual for the temperatures to go down to minus forty below and stay there for a week, making it too cold for him to venture out for any length of time or check his trap lines.

These were long days for both the trapper and Wolf. Boredom was staved off by reading the books he had gathered over the summer. He had accumulated over five hundred books for his library, some which he had read three times. Isolation was a huge problem for these trappers, as the only companion they had for the six months they spent in the wilderness was usually their dog, and maybe a wild animal or bird that decided to make their cabin a second home, if there was an ample supply of food for them. Some trappers went mad and had to call on their satellite radios for the plane to come get them, many of them never completely regaining their sanity.

Wolf and the trapper ate dinner and listened to the blowing wind outside the cabin. The snowstorm had started earlier in the day, and when it was over the trapper would be able to hook up the sled to Wolf and explore the area. He would check for animal signs and repair the shelters he had constructed long ago along his trap line. The trapper would stay in these buildings when he and Wolf were unable to get back to their cabin. These shelters were primitive, stocked with wood and were placed every two miles along the trapline. They were used only in an emergency.

The trapper fell into a restless sleep wondering how long this storm was going to last and how much snow it would bring. He was anxious to get his season started; the reason he was here. After the storm abated, he planned to hunt for moose, store the meat, and then he would be ready to trap. Nature was now in charge.

CHAPTER FOUR

The trapper woke up to complete silence. After three days of howling wind and blowing snow, the storm was finally over. He looked outside into the approaching dawn and saw a clear sky. This meant that they would finally be able to get work done. The trapper hoped to get his moose today. He had seen signs only a short distance from the cabin before the storm. He ate his breakfast and gathered up his supplies and gun. Leaving Wolf behind in the cabin, he donned his snowshoes and opened the front door to a blinding light. He let his eyes get adjusted to the brightness and with enthusiasm was off.

The landscape was beautiful, snow covering the trees and large rocks. The air was fresh and biting. The trapper loved this. The snow was deep, and the going was hard, but the trapper was used to these challenges. Soon he was in the area where he seen evidence of moose.

The trapper knew that with a sufficient food supply and shelter, a moose would stay in one area for weeks. He slowly approached the trees knowing this was the most likely area where the animal would be found. The trapper stopped and positioned himself out of sight with a good view of the tree line, upwind so a moose would not be able to smell him.

Suddenly a bull moose came out of the trees, smelled the air, and feeling comfortable there was no danger let his guard down long enough for the trapper to take his shot. The moose went down instantly, shot through the heart. The trapper was elated, the moose was less than thirty minutes from the cabin. After a quick examination of the animal, he headed back to get Wolf.

With Wolf hooked up to the sled, off they went to process the moose. The trapper was experienced at butchering moose and deer, but it was still going to be a big job ferrying the meat back to the cabin and storing it in the underground freezer he had built. The sun was just setting when they finished. The wolves were waiting for their share, staying a safe distance away, but this still made Wolf very nervous as he knew the wolves would kill him if given the chance.

Back at the cabin the trapper finished storing the meat, except for a generous amount for dinner. The stove was lit and soon a roaring fire filled the cabin with a warmth they had not felt all day. After a large meal of moose steak and potatoes, which Wolf also enjoyed, they retired to bed for a well-deserved sleep.

CHAPTER FIVE

The next day dawned clear and calm. Today the trapper and Wolf were going to run the trapline, check the shelters, and set snares to catch snowshoe rabbits to add to their food supply. Wolf was excited, he loved to pull the sled through the snow listening to the trapper's encouraging words for him. The trapper treated Wolf well, and in return for this kindness Wolf worked very hard for the trapper.

They soon reached what would be the beginning of the trapline, looking for animal sign along the trail and checking on the emergency shelters. They spent the day doing minor repairs to the structures. They also checked the beaver dam to see if the beaver were still in the area. They found freshly chewed trees, and noticed fresh wood stored nearby. It looked like it was going to be a good season, as there appeared to be a large variety of animals in the vicinity. They started back to the cabin, stopping along the way to set rabbit snares, which they would check tomorrow.

The trapper was ready. Tomorrow they would set out traps, increasing their number daily until all his traps were set. They reached the cabin just before dark, put their supplies and sled away, and retired to the cabin to enjoy the warmth and get dinner. The trapper was very happy with the way things were going and hoped for continued luck for the future. They ate dinner and very shortly thereafter both fell into a deep and satisfying sleep, another busy day awaiting them tomorrow.

CHAPTER SIX

The trapper was up early. He was reviewing the book in which he recorded the number and types of animals he trapped each year, and where the most productive areas were found. Martens, a small fur-bearing animal that have been trapped in the area for over three hundred years, were the most abundant. Fishers and weasels were two other small woodland mammals that were popular on the trapline. Next in line were foxes and bobcats, two of the larger mammals trapped. Beavers were also a prize catch, the trapper using a special trap under the ice for these animals. He took a limited number of beavers, usually only one per lodge, for a total of six per season.

The most elusive and dangerous animal caught on the trapline is the wolverine. He is the trapper's biggest enemy, and the meanest. The wolverine steals animals from the traps to eat and is almost impossible to catch. These viscous animals have been known, when caught, to chew their own leg off to escape. A savage predator, it is known to not back down from any animal in the bush, including the bear, which can be twenty times its size.

The trapper roused Wolf, who had slept in this morning, unlike the trapper who always was awake and up by four a.m. The pair ate breakfast and headed out to the skinning shed to retrieve the supplies and traps that they were to set today. As they approached the shed Wolf became uneasy and soon the trapper saw why. Wolverine tracks! Wolf had picked up the intruder's scent and it made him nervous, as he knew the wolverine could attack out of nowhere, ripping out his throat and killing him instantly. The trapper knew he had to protect Wolf at all costs, because without his dog his season would come to an instant end. This was the first time a wolverine had come to his cabin in five years. The trapper would have to be very cautious about leaving out anything food related. He did not want to make it easy for the wolverine, otherwise this animal would become a regular visitor.

Once the sled was loaded, off they went. The snow was deep, and Wolf ploughed through it breaking a trail. Soon they reached the area where they had set the snares for the rabbits. Out of the twelve snares set, they had caught three nice sized snowshoe hares. This would be a welcome addition to their food supply. They retrieved the snares and set two traps baited with fish in the same area. They continued moving down the trapline, setting the other traps along the trail.

When they had finished setting the traps, they headed for the river. There they cut a hole in the ice and set a trap for the beaver. This was the animal the trapper least liked to capture, but the fur was valuable, and taking a limited number made him feel less guilty. Once finished, and with Wolf leading the way, they headed back to the cabin.

Reaching home just before dark, the trapper unpacked the sled and headed into the cabin, rabbits in hand. Soon the stove was roaring, and supper was cooking. The trapper was tired. He was not a young man anymore and noticed he tired easily, and his bones often ached. He was glad this was his last year at his remote cabin, and he was looking forward to his retirement with Wolf. His brother, a successful banker in Toronto, had died and left him a sizable inheritance which would keep him comfortable for the rest of his life. His love of trapping and the peace and tranquility of the north woods, not the little bit of money made, is what kept him returning to this wilderness. Pleasant memories would follow the trapper forever. Even his dreams were filled with adventure from the bush.

The trapper slept soundly that night, not even hearing the wolverine on the roof, who was searching for a way to get into the cabin when the trapper and Wolf were gone. There was activity in the bush at night that was not acknowledged or seen by humans. Soon the trapper would wake, and another day would begin.

CHAPTER SEVEN

The trapper awoke depressed. The isolation, with no human contact, and thoughts of his situation left him in a state of despair. He took out his satellite radio seriously thinking about ending his season early and starting his retirement. His thoughts turned to a vacation in a warmer climate, like Mexico or Florida. Suddenly he snapped back to reality, putting the radio away. He had to finish, he felt bad thinking about letting Wolf down, who he knew was enjoying the very thing he was bred for. Wolf would love to stay here all year round if he could. He loved the wilderness and adventure the bush provided. The trapper loved and respected his dog, who was up and by his master's side, sensing something was wrong. He was trying to console the man by licking his hand and staying close, until this mood passed.

Today they were to check the traps they had set yesterday and add more along the trail. Hopefully they would bring the first fur of the season back to the cabin to be processed. They loaded up the sled and headed down the trail, Wolf, showing more enthusiasm than normal, helped the trapper get more in tune with what he was doing. The first stop was a success, a marten was in the trap, a mature adult. The trapper removed the animal and reset the trap. They moved along the trail, checking traps, and setting new ones. All the other traps were empty, except the one at the river, which held a beaver.

The beaver was a mature adult, which was too large to fit through the hole in the ice. With axe in hand, the trapper enlarged the hole and pulled the beaver onto the ice. Into the bag the animal went. The beaver was valued not only for his fur, but also for his meat, which was usually made into stew with canned vegetables the trapper had brought just for this occasion.

The duo moved down the river to the next beaver lodge, repeating the trapping process but making the hole in the ice larger and adding a second trap. They got off the river and headed to the closest shelter where they started a fire, getting warm and eating lunch. This was a daily ritual that they practised if they were to be out all day.

The trapper's thoughts turned to the wolverine. He knew that sooner or later he was heading for a confrontation with this animal. When he saw the tracks on the roof, he knew what the vicious animal's intentions were. Before leaving the cabin every day he would have to secure it, like he was leaving it for the summer. If the wolverine gained access to the cabin, he would destroy everything in it. The trapper also knew that sooner or later the wolverine would discover his trapline, and if not stopped would destroy up to half the fur over the course of the season. The trapper's top priority was somehow ending this very serious threat.

Wolf and his partner headed back to the cabin, stopping along the way to set some more rabbit snares where the trapper had seen lots of activity. In addition, he also had to set a large hidden trap near the rabbit snare for the wolverine. If there was a rabbit in the snare, the wolverine would need space to get the rabbit free, stepping into the trap set for him.

Soon the trapper and his dog were back at the cabin enjoying a warm fire and a hot dinner. Tonight, he would process the beaver and marten hides and, in the morning, secure them in a special place where he stored his meat. The trapper relaxed reading a book with Wolf at his feet. After an hour his eyes got heavy, and he fell into a deep sleep dreaming about the wolverine and how he was going to catch him. Tomorrow just might be the day he hoped for.

CHAPTER EIGHT

The trapper looked out into the dawn sky. The stars and moon were still bright, which usually meant a good day on the trapline, as the animals were more active when these conditions existed. He moved around the cabin stepping over a sleeping Wolf to get to his furs that he had worked on the night before. He examined the quality; they looked good. Today he would set the rest of his traps, check the ones he had set, and see if he was lucky enough to catch the wolverine. He had kept one of the rabbits that he had caught previously. Yesterday he had used it to bait the trap, placing it back in the snare and laying its body on the runway, making it look as natural as possible.

Wolf was awake, so they ate breakfast and headed out to the skinning shed to get the supplies that they would need for the day. Travelling down the trail, the trapper noticed evidence of animal activity in the snow. He had a feeling that he was going to collect furs today. His feelings were correct. Trap after trap seemed to hold game, including a bobcat, a prized catch. The only trap that hadn't been triggered was the one for the wolverine. They reached the end of the trapline, ate lunch, and headed back to the cabin to take an inventory of their catch.

Reaching the cabin, they noticed blood and fur on the ground. The trapper examined the scene, concluding that a raptor had caught and eaten a small mammal in his front yard. An inventory of the day's catch revealed he had two martens, two weasels, the bobcat and three more rabbits. This was considered a very good day. He gathered up his furs and took them inside the cabin where they would be safe. Tomorrow he would process all of them.

After a big meal of beaver stew, which was Wolf's favorite, they retired to the spots in the cabin they called their own. The trapper had one daily job to do. He used his satellite phone to check in with the forestry office, updating them as to his status. In return, they let him know about impending large storms heading his way. This was the trapper's only human contact and he enjoyed talking to the rangers even though the contact was brief and business like.

The trapper couldn't sleep, his thoughts were on the wolverine. He had not seen any sign of the animal for two days, but knew it was only a matter of time before he found his trapline. His goal was to catch this menace before the wolverine had a chance to create chaos in his life. The silence of the night soon overtook him, and he fell into a deep sleep dreaming that the wolverine was pulling the sled, while Wolf and the trapper were seated together, both laughing and pointing at him. Tomorrow the pair would stay home, and the skinning shed would be used for the first time to do his furs.

CHAPTER NINE

The trapper awoke early. Today he was planning on taking a break from running the trapline to do some minor repair work on the cabin and skinning shed. He also planned to process his furs and cleanup his cabin inside and out. When those chores were completed, he was going to take Wolf and retrieve the wood he had previously cut. This would also give Wolf exercise. Being a big dog, he tended to get bored and restless when doing nothing.

A crow had taken up residence at the cabin, letting his presence be known by cawing loudly every morning for his breakfast. He enjoyed eating at Wolf's dog food dish and had become the trapper's pet, following him around at the cabin when he was outside doing things. The trapper called him Squawker because he never stopped being noisy, even for a moment. Wolf and Squawker also had become friends and seemed to enjoy playing a game where the bird would swoop over him, landing yards in front of him. Wolf would run fast toward him, and at the last minute the bird would screech loudly, flying to the nearest tree branch and continuing to boldly caw. The trapper got great joy watching these antics from his two friends.

The trapper's least favorite job was doing the hides, but it was the most important. The furs value increased if they had been processed well. He was almost finished when Wolf, who was laying at the doorway, suddenly jumped up, the hair raising on his neck. The trapper sensed trouble, grabbed his gun, and went to investigate. There, fifty yards away, was a bear, the same one that called this territory home. Wolf barked loudly, and the trapper let off a shot, well over the bear's head. The bear ran off, but he and the trapper had an uneasy truce. He could smell the meat when the trapper was working on his hides and knew a meal would soon be coming. The trapper would dispose of the unwanted remains a distance from the cabin but didn't appreciate the bear coming so close.

Wolf and the trapper retired to the cabin for lunch and a nap. The trapper had no sooner closed his eyes when he swore he heard dogs barking, and the barking was growing louder. He left the cabin and could not believe his eyes. Up the lake there was a sled and two dogs coming towards his cabin. Within minutes there was another human holding out his hand in greeting. He was a native American, said his name was Joe, and he had a cabin thirty miles down the lake. He had discovered the trapper's cabin last summer while on an exploratory trip of the area, not realizing that anyone had a camp nearby.

Joe lived here year-round, learning from his father how to be totally self sufficient. He knew the native plants he could eat, the medicine he could derive from them, and he grew various herbs for their healing and nutritional qualities. He believed being healthy helped him keep his sanity and fight off the loneliness of being so isolated.

Together the two men fed and watered the dogs and retired to the cabin, where the trapper prepared a hot meal for Joe, which was greatly appreciated. It was decided that he would spend the night, both men very happy for the company. They talked until after midnight about trapping and hunting, and the trapper told Joe about what was going on in the outside world. They both fell into a deep and satisfying sleep relishing in the fact that their paths had crossed. Joe would leave at dawn as it was a full hard day to get back to his cabin, promising the trapper he would come back to visit before the plane picked him up in the early spring. Their dreams were pleasant, and their sleep was sound, as the tranquility of mother nature enveloped them.

CHAPTER TEN

Joe was up at dawn. The trapper made him a hot breakfast, and with big hugs of gratitude on both sides, Joe was gone. A silence enveloped the trapper as he watched Joe disappear over the horizon. Wolf rubbed up against his master and whined softly trying to console him, as he could sense the sadness coming from his owner. They loaded up the sled and headed down the trail hoping for a good day. A good day it was not going to be.

The first trap held a half-eaten marten. The trapper's fears were realized, the wolverine had found his trapline. They continued down the trail finding another animal that had been eaten. This is what wolverine are known for, destroying the profits for trappers. This would go on until the wolverine was eliminated, a difficult task. A trip to the river brought a moment of happiness, as a beaver had been caught. But even this pelt couldn't stop the trapper from being disappointed, so he decided to go back to his cabin to think about a plan to stop the wolverine, not knowing that nature would take care of this problem for him.

The trapper processed the beaver, the fur being of very good quality. Since this was his last year, he tried to shrug off what had happened. The last time a wolverine had invaded his territory was five years ago. He had finally shot the animal by baiting an area with moose meat, a treat the wolverine could not resist. He had rubbed ripe animal remains over his entire body to mask his odor and sat in a blind he had built a short distance away. He waited patiently for thirty hours before the wolverine made his appearance. The animal was so preoccupied with what he thought was a free meal that he heard nothing. The shot hit him in the head, and he died instantly. The trapper took great pleasure in processing that fur. Now he was faced with the same dilemma, maybe he would have to do the same thing. He would give it one more day and then come up with a plan.

The trapper retired to the cabin with Wolf, had a big supper of moose meat and picked up the book he had been reading. It was about a family in New York that had arrived from Ireland as immigrants and the difficult times they faced adjusting to their new life. The trapper was tired and soon drifted off into a deep sleep, knowing that tomorrow would be another challenging day. Wolf was howling in his sleep, dreaming about chasing and playing with a girlfriend he had just met. This woke the trapper who, when he realized it was only Wolf dreaming, rolled over and fell back to sleep.

CHAPTER ELEVEN

The day dawned bright and sunny. As the trapper and Wolf checked the trapline, the trapper could not get the wolverine off his mind. This menace had to be taken care of, but how? He really did not want to sit in a blind again for such a long time; it was so cold, and his bones ached for days afterwards. Surprisingly, the traps had not been bothered and he had a total of six animals in his sled, his best day yet.

As the pair headed back to the cabin, one of the harness attachments for the sled broke, making it useless. The trapper thought about what he should do. It was getting late in the afternoon and there was no way they could make it to the cabin before dark traveling on foot. He had a re-placement part for the harness with his supplies in the shed, but he would not be able to get it until tomorrow. The decision was made to stay in one of the emergency shelters. Luckily, there was one a short distance away.

After a short walk, the pair arrived. Soon a blazing fire was going in the small woodstove. These stoves were great, providing warmth and a place to cook food. The trapper had stashed smoked moose meat jerky, sealed in a large glass jar, in the shelter for emergencies. This was dinner for him. Wolf ate the meat from one of the animals they had secured that day. The shelter was primitive; he would have to sleep close to Wolf to keep warm, as no amount of wood seemed to make the shelter warm enough. He wound up being awake most of the night stoking the fire.

During one of his wakeful periods, the trapper heard an animal, or animals, outside the shelter. Wolf heard them too. It was the wolf pack; they had probably picked up the scent of the animal from the trapline he had processed for Wolf's dinner. The trapper had to keep Wolf quiet as to not antagonize the wolves, not knowing how hungry they were. Hungry wolves were dangerous wolves. Soon the wolves left, probably picking up the scent of the trapper and knowing that no food was going to be available.

The dawn's light showed a clear sky, they were lucky a storm had not moved in overnight trapping them in the shelter. After a breakfast of jerky for the trapper, and the remnants of dried dog food that had been stored in the shelter for Wolf, they were off. The pair walked to the cabin with the trapper carrying the furs and his rifle. Except for seeing a red fox cross the trail in front of them, their trip was uneventful and after a couple of hours they reached home. The rest of the day was spent resting, finishing the furs, and eating hardily. They would leave at dawn tomorrow with the replacement part, fix the sled, and get back to trapping.

The trapper was tired, turning seventy this year he did not have the energy he used to have. He was looking forward to seeing that plane, knowing he was going to be picked up for the last time. He had told Joe that the cabin and the trapline were his when he left in the spring, as this was his last year here. Joe told the trapper he would probably spend next winter at the cabin. This was a great deal for Joe, as the trapper planned only to take his furs, his gun, and a few personal items with him, leaving everything else behind. Wolf and the trapper retired to bed knowing they had a long walk ahead of them in the morning and they were very tired from their lack of sleep the night before. The trapper hoped it would be a good day tomorrow, unaware a big surprise awaited them. Soon they were both sound asleep, only the great horned owl with its loud hoots breaking the silence of the night.

CHAPTER TWELVE

Dawn always came early for the trapper. He dragged himself out of bed and prepared breakfast for himself and Wolf. It was a two hour walk to the disabled sled, and only took ten minutes to fix the broken harness. They continued checking the trapline hoping for a good catch. Within a short distance they came upon a deer, half eaten, having been taken down by the wolves the day before. The trapper cut a small amount of meat from the body for Wolf for dinner and left the rest for the wolves, knowing they would be back.

The trapline produced little success, only two small martens. The trapper and Wolf headed down to the river to check the beaver traps. Encountering the first trap they noticed a dark shape coming out of the hole. This baffled the trapper. They approached with caution, and as they got closer they realized it was the wolverine, dead. He apparently had been watching them the last time they were here as the trapper broke the ice in the hole to check the trap. The wolverine had come to the hole and while investigating must have fallen in headfirst, wedging his fat body in the hole with his head below the water, causing him to drown. At first the trapper felt bad, it must have been a horrible death for the wolverine. But it was incredible luck for him, as his arch enemy was no more. Now the rest of his trapping season was saved.

The trapper cut the ice from around the head of the wolverine, pulling him out of the hole. Checking the trap, he had also caught a beaver. Within minutes he had two large, valuable animals on the ice. A sense of elation gripped the trapper, he could not believe his luck. Wolf was also very excited knowing he no longer had to fear the wolverine.

The trapper decided to head back to the cabin, checking the rest of the trapline on the way. As they approached where the half-eaten deer had been, they noticed the wolf pack was back feeding on the remains. They gave them a wide berth, not wanting to direct the wolves' attention to themselves. Approaching a wolf pack while eating was a dangerous thing to do, as wolves can become very protective of their kill.

The rest of the trapline did not yield any more furs, so the trapper and Wolf continued towards home. Another surprise awaited them when they got back to the cabin, two game wardens were there. They had arrived by ski plane to check on the trapper's license, and ensure he was following all trapping regulations. The trapper invited them in for coffee, for which they were grateful. The three men sat around the table and the trapper told them about the wolverine. The wardens laughed, telling the trapper they had never heard of such a thing before. After a short visit they left, wishing the trapper good luck and good health for the rest of the season.

It was getting late in the day, so the trapper decided that tomorrow he would take the day off to process his furs and do other small jobs that needed to be completed. The duo retired to the cabin, ate dinner, and at once went to bed.

CHAPTER THIRTEEN

Wolf woke with a start, a low growl coming from his throat. The trapper awoke sensing danger. He could hear activity outside; loud footsteps crunching in the snow, unlike a bear or other large mammal. He grabbed his gun and cautiously went to the window, trying to see who this intruder was. Not seeing or hearing anything more he started to relax, realizing what it was. In the thirty years he had been coming here, this intruder had visited numerous times. It would usually come at night and the only identifying signs it left behind were large human-like foot-prints in the snow. The trapper did not really believe in Bigfoot, a large ape-like mythical creature that supposedly lived in the north woods, but how to explain the footprints? He had never seen this animal, but sometimes while working his trapline he would be overwhelmed by a horrible stench. He knew what it was, it was watching him. He really had no fear, as there was no record of the creature attacking a human, but it still made him nervous.

The trapper went back to bed but was not able to sleep, so he got up, got dressed, and read one of the new books he had bought and saved for just such a time. The dawn light was soon upon him, and he wondered what he should do today after his work was done. He decided on ice fishing, as their stock of fish was very low and it was one of their staples, for both Wolf and him. They ate breakfast, completed the day's tasks, and prepared the fishing supplies. The trapper had an ice auger, one of only two gas powered tools he kept at his cabin, the other being his chainsaw. The auger was used mainly to keep the hole he used to get water clear, but he also used it to cut holes in the ice for fishing.

Because of its isolation, the fishing was very good on Great Slave Lake, as fishermen had little access to it. After an hour of drilling through the thick ice, the trapper had three holes ready for fishing. He dropped the lines in the holes and was immediately catching fish. The catch included lake trout, pickerel, perch, and whiting, an abundant northern fish with a lightly flavored meat, unlike other fish. Soon the bounty was loaded on the sled and the trapper and Wolf headed back to the cabin where he cleaned the fish, keeping the remains for Wolf, a favorite food of huskies bred in the north. It was decided they would eat lake trout for dinner, and afterwards they would decorate for Christmas, which was ten days away.

The trapper would celebrate the holiday as he had in years past, having a Christmas tree adorned with a few decorations he had brought with him years ago. Also, a special dinner was in order, goose being the main dish. Christmas was one of the few days that no work was done, and the trapper enjoyed his bottle of brandy, the only time he drank alcohol all winter.

The days flew by, with the trapper working his trapline, processing his furs, and working around his cabin. The best thing of all was not having to worry about the wolverine, now only a pelt mixed in with all his other furs. Tonight was Christmas Eve, and tomorrow's big event would be calling his only living brother on the satellite phone, an annual ritual. There would be a nice meal and a restful day tomorrow. He and his dog went to bed, the silence of the north immediately putting them into a deep and peaceful sleep.

CHAPTER FOURTEEN

Today was Christmas day, a special day for the trapper. It was a day when he reflected on his accomplishments, his regrets, and his future. His future was retirement, at least from trapping. Before leaving for the winter trapping season, he had been offered a job at the local university to teach a class on the Canadian North. He had taught school for twenty years before he decided that trapping would be his vocation and was unsure if he wanted to return to the field of education.

The first order of the day was setting his satellite radio to a station that played only Christmas music at this time of year. This music was mainly for people like himself, isolated from civilization and alone. Wolf loved the music, sometimes howling along with the lyrics. He seemed to sense this was a special, happy day. The trapper gave Wolf his present, three large beef bones that gave him many happy hours of chewing. The trapper's Christmas present to himself was a bottle of brandy, which over the course of the day he would drink until the bottle was empty. This kept the trapper's mind off the tragedy of losing his wife and son in a terrible car accident after only five years of marriage. He had never remarried and afterward had become somewhat of a recluse, with this tragedy always on his mind.

The trapper got the fire hot in the woodstove. To cook the goose, he had to get the oven hot, and keep it hot, not an easy chore. He still had lots of canned vegetables, which would compliment the meat, but no bread. The music was blaring, and the trapper was drinking, creating a festive mood in the cabin. After a long while, dinner was ready. Wolf and the trapper took their respected places and dug in. The food was delicious, and the trapper gave thanks to the Lord for the meal and their safe season so far.

After dinner the trapper cleaned up, sat in his favorite chair, and called his brother in Winnipeg, a yearly ritual since he started coming here. His brother had health problems, having to have his gallbladder removed recently, but he had recovered and was doing fine. The trapper told him stories about his adventures, including how he caught the wolverine, which his brother thought was very funny. After a long conversation they said their goodbyes. The trapper went ahead and drank his brandy until the bottle was empty and fell into a sound sleep in his chair, where he would remain for the evening. His dreams were of going home and enjoying his car, being able to watch TV, going to the grocery store, and most of all enjoying the gas furnace in his house, which kept him constantly warm with little effort on his part.

The reality was, though, that the trapper was here and had to finish his season, already knowing he would sorely miss this life and all the memories. He would wake tomorrow, and with his companion Wolf, he would continue with his duties until it was time to leave, which he knew would be a very sad time. The trapper slept soundly, helped by all the brandy he had consumed. Tomorrow he would start out groggy, but the cold northern air would almost at once snap him back to his senses. Tomorrow, a surprise awaited him on his trapline, which would help him to have one of the most successful seasons in years. Only the call of the wolf pack pierced the still of the night in the serene wilderness of the great and untamed Canadian north.

CHAPTER FIFTEEN

The trapper awoke, groggy from all the brandy the night before. He slowly rose from his chair, not enthusiastic about starting his day. Wolf also awoke, coming to the trapper, rubbing his body against his master looking for affection. The trapper petted Wolf aggressively and with love, thinking that no one could replace his companionship and reliability. After a hearty breakfast, the trapper hooked up the sled, loaded the supplies and they were off to the trapline.

The first trap, to his surprise, held a red fox, an elusive animal very rarely caught in a trap. The red fox's fur was the most desirable and valuable. The next two traps held nothing, but the next two held marten, the most abundant fur bearing animal in the north, but the one that was the least valuable. They continued along the trapline until they came upon a bobcat, still alive, caught in a trap. The trapper knew what he had to do. He took his gun and with a precision shot, the bobcat was no more. The bobcat was also a valuable fur. Today was turning out to be one of the best days in his trapping history here. The trapper had never caught two such valuable animals in one day before.

Continuing along, they came upon a weasel and another marten in later traps. The trapper had never had such luck, and they were not done yet. They made their way to the river and to their surprise the trap held a beaver. It would take hours to process these furs upon their return to the cabin. After a lunch at one of the shelters, the trapper and Wolf headed back to the homesite with a cold wind increasing at their back. The trapper knew what this meant, another blizzard was on its way.

The pair reached the cabin, the storm ready to unleash its fury upon them. The trapper stocked up on meat from his outdoor underground storage and extra wood from his woodpile. He carried all the animals he had caught on the trapline into the cabin. Because of the storm he would have no access to the skinning shed so the animals would have to be processed inside. The trapper had just finished his preparations when the storm came in. They were lucky to have made it back to the cabin in time, as this storm gave them little warning.

While the storm raged outside over the next three days, the trapper spent his time processing his furs and keeping a roaring fire going in the stove. With the wind blowing, it was hard to keep the cabin warm. Wolf slept and the trapper read his favorite books waiting for the storm to subside. After the third day the winds calmed, and the snow stopped, leaving a bright blue sky and a winter wonderland.

The trapper loved the scenery after the storm; the trees covered in snow, the cleanliness of the landscape, and the fresh animal tracks. Wolf also loved it. Like a child he bounded through the drifts, sticking his head under as if looking for something. He would run fast, snow flying everywhere.

The trapper had also tallied up his catch. So far this season, he had doubled the amount of fur that he had last year. All the profits from the fur went to a children's charity for cancer. He never kept any of the profits for himself. The trapper had been doing this since he had received the inheritance from his brother five years ago. The day went by fast and soon they were eating dinner, and then relaxing by the warm stove. The trapper read for awhile, and then decided to go to bed where he at once fell asleep. His season was getting on and soon he would be home, where all of this would be like a dream.

CHAPTER SIXTEEN

Time was flying by. The weeks were spent checking traplines, doing repair work on the cabin, and processing furs. The supplies were dwindling, but there was a large amount of meat left in the storage area, which Joe would pick up after they left. The trapper had told Joe the date the plane was coming and had spoken to the pilot on the satellite phone to verify it. He was sure Joe would come, even though he had failed to make a return visit before he left. The pilot was coming in a couple of days.

The mood was sullen, as a wave of emotion swept over the trapper as he knew this phase of his life was ending. He was tired and looking forward to living a more modern, easy life in the comforts of his own home.

The next day was spent collecting the traps. The number of animals being caught was getting less and less, which always happened at the end of the season. The last night spent at the cabin was very quiet, the trapper going through a range of emotions. He knew that it was likely that he would never see this place again, which really troubled him.

Finally, the big day was here. The trapper had everything at the lake waiting for the plane when the sound of an engine was heard in the distance. Soon the plane was landing and maneuvering toward the pair. The pilot knew the trapper and Wolf, having flown the old man here for years. They exchanged greetings, loaded the plane, and were soon preparing for takeoff. When the plane was in the air, the trapper asked the pilot if he could make one last pass over the cabin. As the pilot flew over the building, the trapper hugged Wolf tightly, tears welling up in his eyes.

After a ride of about two hours they reached their destination and the plane landed safely. The trapper's friend was there with his truck to pick them up. From here they would drop the furs off, and then his friend would take him home. In a very short time, his life at the cabin would just be a memory and his retirement a reality.

The trapper lived another ten years, but his faithful companion Wolf passed away two years after they had arrived back home, leaving the trapper with just memories. This way of life, trapping, was becoming a thing of the past, as people killing animals for fur had become unacceptable. But most of the old trappers never forgot their past and would often tell their grandchildren stories of their adventures in the north woods.

THE SETTLERS

+ + + + + +

CHAPTER ONE

The man and his wife had just disembarked from the ship which had brought them from England. They were in Montreal, arriving there via the St. Lawrence River. Their destination was Ontario, where they planned to establish a homestead and begin a new life in Canada. The year was eighteen hundred sixty-seven and there had been a mass migration by the English, and other Europeans, to settle this new land. Their friends had come a year earlier and through mail had confirmed they had settled in an area close to a small town called Peterborough. There were grist mills and sawmills that dotted the nearby countryside, providing incentive for small towns to pop up and flourish. The city of York, a fast-growing area on the shores surrounding Lake Ontario, was buying all the lumber they could saw, and all the flour they could mill for a booming population. Jobs were to be had for the strong and able.

Hearing this news, and with assurances from their friends for help getting started, the couple had commenced their journey to settle in this new world. They made their way to the train station, booked their tickets to Peterborough, and soon found themselves sitting in the most comfortable chairs that they had sat in in months. The train left the station with their meager belongings, a large trunk and two suitcases. However, the couple were traveling a sizable amount of money. They hoped to buy property, build a cabin, and farm the land, as the soil was said to be productive for growing grains that could be sold to the mills. He also planned to take a job to earn additional money for the supplies it would take to make this dream come true.

The train made its way through the wilderness. The forest was endless, void of any towns until they got closer to Ontario. The train would stop at these places, pick up passengers and drop off supplies that had been bought in Montreal. After twelve stops, they finally arrived at their destination. Peterborough was a bustling place with industries including textiles, brick factories, clothing stores, places to buy supplies of all sorts, and drinking establishments. But their main concern was to find a hotel and get a good night's sleep. Tomorrow they would hire a wagon to take them to Keene, the small town east of the city where their friends lived. Darkness was upon them as they arrived at their hotel, a coal oil lantern their only light. Sleep came easy after their long journey and their dreams were filled with adventure as their new life unfolded in front of them. Tomorrow would be the start of this life, a new beginning for these early settlers.

CHAPTER TWO

The settlers awoke at dawn, excited but nervous about their future. After a discussion over dinner the night before, they decided to buy a horse and buggy instead of hiring one to get to Keene, as they realized that having future transportation was necessary. A trip to the livery stable would be the first thing on their agenda this morning. After a hearty breakfast at the hotel, they made their way to buy the horse and carriage, surprised at the selection that was offered. They picked a horse and a good used buggy, paid the owner, and were off with a new sense of freedom. After picking up their belongings from the hotel, supplies for their trip, and getting directions from the desk clerk they were off on their journey to Keene.

It was mid-April and because of unusually dry weather the roads were free of muddy making their trip easy. After a six-hour uneventful journey they arrived at their destination. Keene was a small but growing town, boasting a bank, hotel, general store, and much more. Their first order was to go to the bank, open an account, and deposit their life savings where it would be safe. They took the horse and buggy to the livery stable where the horse was fed, watered, and rested. They then checked into the hotel, had a nap, and went downstairs for dinner, hoping that they could get information about their friends' whereabouts.

The newcomers learned that their friends were well known and liked in town, and were living in a small hamlet called Lang, about two miles north of Keene. Lang had a sawmill, called Hope Mill, and a large grist mill, which their friend oversaw. The couple were told their friends had been supplied a house next to the mill, as this was considered an important job and the position required the miller to be on call twenty-four hours a day. After dinner they took a stroll around town, finding the people friendly and helpful. As twilight approached, they made their way back to the hotel, retiring to their room. Discussing the day's events, they decided they had made the right decision coming here, as they felt comfortable in their new surroundings. Soon a deep sleep fell upon them, their dreams of a comfortable life in this new country that they could now call their own. Hopefully tomorrow they would reunite with their friends and get a better understanding of what the future held for them.

CHAPTER THREE

The settlers stirred, the dawn light coming through the window awakening them. They talked about the day ahead and discussed information one of the townsfolk had given them yesterday about a homestead for sale, the note being held by the bank. It was said the family that lived there had decided, after five years of demanding work, to move back to England, not being able to deal with the harsh winters. They had left last summer, leaving the house abandoned for less than one year. Many of the new arrivals had little money, so buying a homestead was not usually an option. But the settlers had the funds and buying a property such as this would save them a lot of labour and time to put a shelter together before winter.

They would investigate this later, because today they were to find their friends for a reunion that was three years in the making. They picked up their horse and buggy from the livery stable, paid the owner and were off to Lang, a short journey from Keene. Upon arrival, they found a quaint little village that had sprung up to house the men and their families who had arrived years earlier to work at the mills. After getting directions to the grist mill, they made their way there, excitement mounting as they thought of the surprise that awaited their friends, who knew they were coming but not when.

Soon a large stone building loomed in front of them. The grist mill was a huge structure built by hand by strong men to harness the power of water to make flour, a much-needed commodity for the settlers and small villages in the area. They parked their horse and buggy and made their way inside where activity and noise greeted their senses. They found their friend, and after a joyous greeting, made their way to his house where his wife had just taken fresh bread from the oven. The settlers joined their friends for lunch, enjoying beef stew and bread, as delicious of a lunch as they had ever had.

After small talk, their friend returned to work and the new arrivals unloaded their possessions from the buggy and took the horse to the barn where he was fed and watered. The house was large, which allowed them to have a bedroom for themselves, a luxury that most new arrivals never got to enjoy. After getting settled, the couple walked over to Hope mill, a sawmill also buzzing with activity that supplied finished lumber and timber to the area's inhabitants.

They stopped a minute and took in the beauty of the river and the wilderness surrounding them. A feeling of peace and calm swept over them as they returned to the house for dinner. Root vegetables, pork and bread were on the menu, followed by bread pudding for dessert. They then retired to the living room where they caught up on all the important events that had happened since their departure from England.

Soon the evening became late, and after wishing each other a good night they retired to their bedrooms. Tomorrow they would ride back to Keene, go to the bank, and inquire about the homestead that was for sale, wishing to get set on their own as soon as possible. Their dreams were now becoming a reality, their luck being uncanny. They soon both drifted off into a deep sleep, enjoying a peace they had not enjoyed in months, dreaming about a tomorrow that would change their lives forever.

CHAPTER FOUR

The next morning the settlers found themselves at the bank, nervously awaiting the arrival of the bank manager, to talk about the sale of the homestead. He soon arrived and ushered them into his office, offering them comfortable chairs to sit in and coffee to drink. He explained to them that the homestead consisted of a one room cabin sitting on thirty acres of land, ten acres of which had been cleared and planted in grain by the previous tenants. It had a small livestock barn, a woodshed, and an implement barn, where the buggy and farm equipment could be stored. A large garden graced the property. It was found on good road halfway between Keene and Lang, and because of its excellent condition it was priced at four hundred fifty dollars. The location was given and the settlers, excited about seeing their probable future home, went on their way.

After a short journey they arrived at the property and were elated to find everything they had been told was correct. The cabin was in fine condition, boasting an excellent fireplace and a good chimney. These were crucial, as it would supply warmth and a place where all the cooking would be done. The furnishings were included, and other than new chinking between the logs, the structure was move-in ready. The woodshed was half full of good firewood, a definite asset. It was demanding work keeping a cabin in enough wood for the winter, so a head start on this was a plus. The implement shed was empty, meaning the couple would have to buy a plough and seeder if they planned to farm the land. The livestock barn was large enough for an oxen team, their horse, and pigs. The fenced outdoor area was next to the barn would give the animals some room to move around, and a chicken coup attached to the barn was also included. The garden was large, and two apple trees would supply an important staple for the settlers. Lilac bushes surrounded the house, supplying a fragrant odour and making the property even more desirable.

A walk on the acreage provided the couple a feel for the land, which was forested with mostly cedar. To their surprise, a river ran through the property, something the bank manager neglected to tell them. This would supply a way to get cedar logs to the mill, another source of income. The ten acres of cleared land would need to be rehabilitated, but the soil was rich and productive looking. The settlers were thrilled with the property and were excited to talk with the bank manager about buying it.

The couple left and headed back to Lang to share the good news with their friends. Upon returning, more good news was in store. One of the men working at the mill was leaving, to concentrate on his farming at home, creating an opening. Working at the mill was back breaking work and the turnover was high, but the settler took the job knowing his savings would not last forever. This would allow him to earn money to get started farming, hopefully the following year. Dinner was served and after small talk they retired to their rooms for a peaceful sleep and hopes for continued luck in conducting their goals.

CHAPTER FIVE

The settlers awoke, excited about what the day would bring. Their plans were to go to Keene and meet with the bank manager about buying the property. After a hearty breakfast and getting a letter of reference confirming his new job, they were off. One hour later they were sitting in the bank office discussing the purchase of their new home. The price they had discussed was agreed upon, four hundred fifty dollars. They would make a cash down payment of two hundred fifty dollars, with the bank holding a note on the remaining two hundred dollars. Payments were to be ten dollars per month. The paperwork was signed, and the settlers were now proud homeowners.

Since the morning was still young, the couple decided to go to their property to get an idea of what their immediate needs were. They then picked up their belongings from their friend's house, planning to spend the night in their new home. A shopping trip was also in order. The general store in Keene was small, but well stocked with household merchandise. A purchase of a coal oil lantern, blankets, cooking utensils, and food was made. In the future, they would go to Peterborough to shop for things they needed but could not buy locally.

With their buggy loaded with supplies, they headed to their new home. Upon arrival the first thing they noticed was the sweet aroma of the lilacs in bloom. It was as if mother nature had put out a welcome mat for them, bringing new life to this once vibrant homestead. A fire was built in the fireplace, as the day had dawned cool and wet, leaving the cabin with an uncomfortable feeling of dampness. Cleaning was the first order, as the cabin had sat empty for a year, allowing dust to accumulate and families of mice to call this home. The crackle of the fireplace caught their attention as a warmth spread throughout, making them feel cozy and comfortable.

After the cleaning was finished, the couple decided to take a walk and then return and cook dinner. The river beckoned, drawing them like a magnet to find a favorite sitting place on a big rock, enjoying the peace and serenity that this new land offered. The future looked bright for these settlers, and they knew with challenging work, they could have a good life in this new land.

His job worked out well, allowing them extra money to buy seed and farming equipment to become a self-sustaining farm. Two children were born, and the settlers spent ten years here, finally selling the property and buying a bigger house and farm in the area.

Not all stories of immigrants migrating to Canada in the eighteen hundreds ended on a happy note, as pioneering life was hard and un-predictable, sending these mostly young and eager people back to their home countries after a short stay. I hope you enjoyed and learned some-thing from this story about early life as a settler in Canada. We forget about the hardships that people went through to survive, as we enjoy all the luxuries of modern life. It was a life of constant hardships, but a satisfying one that could not be duplicated.

THE TRANS CANADA TRAIL

＋ ＋ ＋ ＋ ＋ ＋

The Trans Canada Trail, or the Great Trail as it is called, is a network of walking trails that traverse from Cape Spear, Newfoundland and Labrador to Victoria, British Columbia. These trails extend over fourteen hundred miles, which makes them the longest network of recreational walking trails in the world. The scenery on the trail varies widely as it covers such a large area of the country. This is a description of the portion of the trail that stretches across part of Southeastern Ontario and provides hikers with views of forests, wetlands, creeks, and farmlands.

In the spring, after the snow leaves the trail and the warm sun dries the old railbed, hikers are glad to once again be out of their homes after a long winter and converge on the trail to enjoy nature close-up and personal. The trail is a favorite for dog walkers and bicyclists in the spring and summer. Walking the trail in the spring provides the opportunity to observe the rebirth of life, from the dead brown of winter to a gradual greening of the landscape. This leads to an explosion of growth in late April to early May, marking the start of the wildflower season and the green leaf canopy of the forest trees. The songbirds are back and singing, and the chorus frogs can be heard sending their symphony-like orchestra through the forest wetlands.

A variety of animals can be seen on, or from, these trails including deer, bear, beaver, rabbits, geese, and ducks. Even turtles can be seen crossing the trail to get to water on the other side. Nature aside, the walk offers a sense of solitude and peace away from the everyday hardships and tribulations of modern-day life.

As the spring moves into summer the vegetation thickens, and the forest seems to close in around itself restricting a pleasant view of the surroundings. But things change again in the late fall, as the tree canopies disappear, and the grasses and plants begin their winter hibernation, opening the landscape once again. This time of year offers a different showing of the splendor of nature.

As time progresses into winter, the trail takes on a silence that no one hears except the cross-country skier or hiker out braving the elements of a chilly winter day. But spring will return, and the warm sun will once again beckon people to this special corner of their life. With a sense of happiness, they stroll these trails, never walking by their fellow man without a smile and a happy greeting, a trademark behavior for every hiker.

These trails were built for Canadians to enjoy, providing an outlet for recreational use and fitness. They also allow the opportunity for children to develop a respect for nature. Get out on the trail and enjoy the feeling of being one with nature and the peace of mind that accompanies your adventure. Be thankful we live in a country that affords us this privilege.

THE CREEK

+ + + + + +

The creek is a natural stream of water, smaller than a river, abundant in forests, meadows, and wetlands. In the spring, and after substantial amounts of rainfall, they serve as an important part of nature's drainage system, collecting water from runoff, thus helping to prevent flooding. Some creeks are large, surviving the heat and droughts of summer, but most dry up and will not be seen again until the snows melt, and the runoff begins in the spring.

Creeks are a habitat for insects, like mosquitoes who use them for a breeding ground to hatch their young. Other creatures that use this water are frogs, birds, and fish, which will swim up a smaller creek from a larger stream. However, they will return to the deeper body of water once the water levels drop in this smaller habitat.

Creeks are a mainstay for children's play, being used for multiple purposes. One of these is as a raceway for so called "boats", sticks being a popular choice, as they are followed and helped along for long distances. Following a creek just to see where it goes is another favorite pastime enjoyed by older children.

Only the larger creeks have names, usually those that sustain water year-round. This small waterway, despite its reputation of being unimportant, plays an integral part in how nature balances the environment; not based on the good of humankind, but what is good for nature. Enjoy this body of water. Treat it with respect and appreciate how it brings positive things to our environment and it will remain with us forever.

THE CEDAR TREE

+ + + + + +

As you walk through the cedar bush, a fragrant odour greets the senses, reminding you of Christmases past and peppermint candy canes that adorned the tree. The cedar tree is an evergreen, with species abundant around the world. A prized commodity because of its tendency to never rot, it was used in North America as shingles for the homes of early pioneers, and split rail fences that still stand today, as they did over a hundred years ago. As time went on and wire become cheaper and more available, the cedar post became more prevalent, holding the wire in place to make a strong fence to keep livestock held and property lines separated. Cedar chests were made from the red cedar, its grain a colourful sight and its odour delightful to the senses. This tree was popular as a building material for early homes, and furnishings were also constructed from this wood.

The lure of this tree has not diminished, still being used for the same things as it was at the beginning of the last century. Entire homes constructed from this special wood now dot the countryside. An oil made from the wood has medicinal value, promoting sleep and well-being and as a remedy to help fight skin conditions. This oil is also made into a protective coating for docks and patios, and any other outdoor areas that see abuse from the harsh winter climate.

The cedar bush is nature's provider for important things; supplying food and shelter for animals, including rabbits, skunks, foxes, and deer to name a few. Its evergreen foliage supplies cover for birds, including larger birds like the partridge and the wild turkey.

Let us treat this tree with respect, as its many benefits provide both man and nature with a most useful commodity and will continue to do so for generations to come.

RELIEF

+ +++++ +

As the frigid days of January slowly progress towards the end of the month, there is a sense of relief among the people, knowing that the freezing weather will soon be over, and new life will spring from the frozen ground. The arrival of Groundhog Day in early February, followed by Valentine's Day, combined with it being a short month, makes for a speedy pathway to March. The maple sap will soon run as the days get longer and the daytime temperatures rise above freezing. The snow will slowly melt as the days grow warmer. The early bulbs, such as tulips and daffodils, will be showing us life, their green growth appearing in the cold soil while snow still haunts their surroundings.

The warm sun will bring life back to areas that lay dormant for the winter. The twenty-first of March heralds in a time of year all the weary winter survivors wait for, spring. It is a time of new life blooming everywhere, a transformation and renewal of the spirit as it is realized that the wintry weather is behind us. The warm weather will bring happiness and joy until winter returns.

The relief of knowing that the summer season is coming, brings thoughts of summer vacations and time at the lake. These desirable ideas are made possible by the hot weather, a season most people would prefer to live in all year round. Unfortunately, our position on the Earth promises us many more winters that we cannot avoid; a frozen wonderland enjoyed by some, but not all, in this country we call Canada.

THE ROCKY MOUNTAINS

------ ✦✦✦✦✦✦ ------

Canada's Rocky Mountains are a remarkable sight, a magnificent splendor that is unmatched anywhere in the world. A cascade of emotion greets the senses as beauty overwhelms the viewer. The Rocky Mountains are found west of Calgary, Alberta. Driving west on the Trans Canada highway from Calgary you will first see the foothills, then a smaller swath of large hills, followed by smaller mountains, that eventually get swallowed by their larger cousins.

Arriving in Banff, Alberta, you will notice breath-taking scenery, the town snuggled closely to the mountains as if nature had placed it there herself. Elk visit the parks in town, and sometimes can be seen on the streets. Driving west your next stop will be Lake Louise, a stunning glacial lake, its blue waters mesmerizing. Towering over the lake, the Chateau Lake Louise, a five-star hotel, looms large, a stunning piece of architecture built at the turn of the century.

Driving across the Rockies, your eyes will be treated to unlimited adventure, from mountain sheep on the road, to grizzly bear sightings from your car. Rivers and streams of blue glacial water and cascading waterfalls appease the senses. Glaciers, millions of years old, will be viewed as you drive the seven hundred miles from Calgary to Vancouver, British Columbia. As Canada's largest port city and one of its favorite tourist destinations, it draws visitors from all over the world to see its beauty and friendly people.

This is a trip that cannot be missed, a once in a lifetime venture to search your soul. As the beauty overwhelms you, it makes you feel small in one of nature's most spectacular environments, a showcase of Earth's wonders.

THE TRANSITION

+ + + + + +

As the end of August approaches, the mood changes. Soon the landscape will take on new meaning, the greens turning to a multitude of colours on the trees, signaling a period of dormancy coming that will last until spring. September is a transition month from the hot days and warm nights of summer to the warm days and cooler nights of fall. Waking up one morning, the robins will have left. What switch does nature turn on that tells them its time to leave? That is one of the mysteries man may never solve.

As the nights get cooler, the deciduous trees, knowing its time to sleep, give us a spectacular show. Their leaves turn into a variety of bright colours that slowly fall to the ground, until the trees are bare and look deceased. As time moves on more birds will leave, flying to various parts of the world where they will spend the winter, but they will return in the spring. Is this where humans got the idea of migrating south when the weather gets cold?

Many animals will sleep all winter. This is nature's guarantee of their survival, otherwise they would starve as the availability of food gets scarce. Squirrels are an exception, gathering and storing food for the winter. Living in their nests high in the treetops, they are active on the ground on warmer, sunnier days. Soon the first frost will leave a white blanket over the landscape, turning plants from green to brown. Multiple frosts will kill the plants, and the other vegetation will look dead, but will spring back to life as the warmer months return.

As the days go by, the skies darken, with an almost constant cloud cover. The cold winds blow from the north and soon the snow will fall, putting a blanket over the landscape, creating beautiful scenery, and signifying that the winter season has arrived. Little life can be seen, only humans trying to navigate in the snow either by foot or in vehicles. Winter is a hardship for most, especially the elderly who suffer numerous injuries by slipping on ice and breaking their bones. People who work are also vulnerable, having to scrape windshields, and clear snow just to get their cars out of the driveway.

Humans are adaptable, rarely complaining about winter. They know that eventually the snow will melt, the sun will shine warm and bright again, and life will blossom once more, bringing beauty back to this world in which they live.

THE BLACK SQUIRREL

◆ ◆ ◆ ◆ ◆ ◆ ◆

The black squirrel is a small, tree-dwelling mammal common in both forest and urban settings around the Great Lakes. Because of the abundant food supply stolen from bird feeders, their population has exploded in urban areas. This small animal, with its agility, can find its way into almost any feeder, becoming an annoying pest for homeowners who are unable to stop this invasion. Its acrobatics and stealth cannot be matched by any other tree dwelling inhabitants.

Building their nests in the highest parts of large deciduous trees, like maples, keeps their enemies at bay. Two litters of babies are born in early spring and summer, usually consisting of no more than three newborns per litter. Black squirrels do not hibernate but are active all winter. Only in times of extreme cold will they stay in their nest for a longer time. The nests are well constructed from leaves and sticks. The squirrel, being a master builder at great heights, can build a home durable enough to withstand the strongest of winter storms and come out unscathed.

This little mammal spends most of his time looking for food, living off the seeds and nuts that the trees provide, and food from bird feeders if living in the city. Squirrels store food for the long winter months, acorns from oak trees being their favorite, black walnuts and other nuts being secondary. Their lives are not easy, so the next time you see a squirrel at your bird feeder give him a thumbs up. Without him your feeder would be less interesting, as these acrobats put on a show that cannot be duplicated by any bird. The black squirrel, an annoyance to some, but a friend to nature lovers, will continue to entertain us for generations to come.

FLOWERS

✦✦✦✦✦✦

F lowers, brilliant in colour and character, dominate our planet. If plants and trees did not flower, the Earth would be devoid of any living, natural, bright colour, changing our perception of life on Earth as we know it. Through evolution, the bright colours of flowers attract insects that pollinate the blooms causing them, after death, to produce seeds that drop to the ground and germinate into new life, guaranteeing the survival of this species.

Humans use and view flowers as a stimulant. The abundance of colour from flowers or a tree in bloom creates a feeling of joy that cannot be duplicated in any other way. Millions of people worldwide love and work with plants, growing and using the flowers produced for decorative purposes. However, some flowers are edible, providing food and ingredients for use throughout the globe.

Flowers are everywhere, adorning the homes of the poorest to the richest, bringing colour and happiness to the hearts of the inhabitants. Keeping flowering plants in the home is known to change the mood, creating a more positive and serene environment. Flowers are in abundance at weddings and are used as gifts for special occasions, delighting many women on Valentine's Day, birthdays, or other special events. But on a more somber note, flowers are used in abundance in times of death, decorating funeral homes and churches helping to bring some comfort to mourning family and friends. They are also used to decorate gravesites as a reminder of our love for the deceased.

Imagine what our Earth would be like without the beauty of this special gift from nature; a drab, colourless world that would be detrimental to the human spirit. Let us enjoy this gift nature has given us and use it as we see fit to brighten our lives. When you are out enjoying nature look around, not just straight ahead. Take in the beauty of it all, but especially that special gift we have been given, the flower.

SUMMER

✦✦✦✦✦

Summer is often the favorite of the four seasons; warm temperatures and bright sunshine prevail. Outdoor activities take precedent, camping, fishing, hiking, and barbecues, a few of the favorites. The availability of local produce booms, with people taking advantage of the quality, abundance, and low prices. Farmers' markets and vegetable stands typically run through October, ending with various kinds of squash, including the infamous pumpkin.

Recreational trailers are popular, being used for both mobile and stationary purposes. Trailer parks are abundant. Permanently parked trailers are used mostly by the middle class for weekend getaways, and vacation time. These trailers are seasonal and are typically not used during the winter. The mobile trailers are pulled by trucks or SUVs, able to access any national park, forest, or even small campgrounds in North America.

The farmers are busy cutting hay, planting corn, grains, and soybean. There is a short window to get a lot of work done. The children enjoy the summer the most, and it's nothing but playtime. They enjoy going to the lake, swimming, boating, and campfires, with smores and hotdogs cooked over the fire among their favorites. Summer camps are abundant, giving the kids a week or two of a no parent environment. But most of all, kids just like to hang out with each other having fun with no hidden agendas.

Summertime is all about wearing shorts and tee shirts and enjoying warm evenings out talking to friends. The summer officially ends after Labour Day. The children go back to school, the adults all back to work, and fall is just around the corner. Summer is usually the season that seems to end the fastest. The days are getting shorter, warmer nights are growing colder and some maple trees are starting to show colour. The beginnings of fall are upon us.

ALONE

◆◆◆◆◆◆

The cabin sat alone on the shore of the lake, frozen in time. The summer breezes swept across this untouched wilderness; the air scented with the blossoms of summer. The cabin, once occupied by a native and his wife, sat abandoned, a home now cherished only by the wildlife that lived there. The inhabitants included the family of mice trying to survive after the loss of two members from a snake, the chipmunk who made his home in one of the timbers that had rotted leaving a spacious habitat for this tiny creature to enjoy, the skunk who had burrowed an underground home beneath the log floor providing shelter and a safe place to sleep, and the birds nesting in the remnants of the chimney including a family of squawking babies letting their presence be known. The cabin now provides a second chance to help this group of animals survive their fight for life in a harsh and unforgiving land.

Quiet fell over the cabin, the waves lapping the shore of the lake the only sound to be heard. A predator was approaching; a black bear, hungry, looking for breakfast. Finding nothing he left, leaving the little community in peace. Like a bright star shining over them, their feelings of safety returned. Soon an unusual noise awakened the senses of the little group. A visitor was approaching, and apprehension returned as the unknown threatened their sense of safety.

The inhabitants of the cabin fell silent. The small plane taxied close to shore, its passengers a wildlife photographer and a writer who had come to photograph and document an article on Canada's north, an expanse of pristine wilderness unmatched anywhere on earth. This little piece of history, discovered by a bush pilot would serve them nicely; a natural backdrop for the story they would write, and a setting that would photograph well showing the beauty of it all.

They unloaded the float plane and bid their farewells. The pilot would return at a later date to retrieve them and bring them back to a society they will have forgotten about. The sound of the plane's engines soon disappeared in the distance, leaving a silence that overwhelmed the spirits of the visitors. They stood in awe of their surroundings, the beauty of the moment capturing them, a serene feeling taking their souls to a height never envisioned. They set up their tent by the shore of the lake, their view unobstructed, the water and forest their scenery. The stars shone brightly as night took over the day.

Midnight soon approached, the campfire's coals glowing, signalling an end to the evening, and the sleep that would soon follow. But sleep was not on the agenda of an aware community that was waiting for their visitors to go to bed so they could take full advantage of an opportunity that rarely presented itself, an expedition for food left by the unsuspecting men. The skunk, mice and a racoon from the forest investigated this unusual occurrence after smelling the odor earlier in the evening. The men sleeping soundly in their tent were oblivious to the activity going on outside.

The light of the morning sun shining on the tent and the melody of the songbirds woke the two wilderness enthusiasts, rousing them to get up and light a fire after waking to the cold morning air. The next two weeks the men got to know their hosts, who got quite comfortable sharing their space as long as food was provided. The chickadees and racoon became frequent visitors, along with the inhabitants of the cabin.

The men's time to leave drew near and a sense of sadness prevailed at the thought of this wonderful moment in their lives ending. The journalists left this beautiful setting with memories that would be cherished forever, never to be forgotten.

THE LONELY LAKE

+ + + + + +

The northern lake was alone, a jewel hidden from civilization, an ecosystem left undisturbed. Tim came alone, his grief bottled up inside him, his young wife dead from an accident. The idea for his escape to this isolated spot had come to him while sitting at home, shortly after his wife's tragic death. His father had once told him that he had spent time as a young man at a wilderness lake located in northern British Columbia. Tim had discussed with his father the name and location of this piece of paradise in the wilderness, a beautiful lake surrounded by mountains and alpine forests.

Tim flew into this lake from Terrace, British Columbia, a small city with an airport that was home many bush pilots, who depended on remote fly-ins to these types of lakes for their livelihoods. This was a place of peace that would help Tim through the tragedy of his wife's death. He selected a spot on the shore, his view only of mountains and water. He pitched his tent and set up his campsite. He built a firepit and gathered firewood. His equipment was modern and well-suited for this environment.

Sunset came soon after dinner. Tim started a fire, the air chilled by the mountains. He sat in silence, only the lonely call of the loon reminding him why he was here. He wept, his sobs echoing in the night. His thoughts were solely on his late wife, his heart broken as the loneliness overcame him. Eventually he sat in silence, the crackle of the campfire the only sound to break the serenity of the night. Tim looked up at the sky, a favorite pastime for him and his wife; watching for shooting stars they would make a wish on. Now she was gone, and he was alone.

Tim's time here went quickly, the plane arriving at the agreed upon time to take him on his journey home. The shooting star he saw the night before was a sign from his late wife that a bright light would once again shine in his life as his journey without her would be infinite. His time at this lake brought him closer to his wife's spirit, a remembrance that would be captured in his heart forever.

CLIMATE CHANGE

The earth over millions of years has seen profound changes in its climate that have caused our planet to respond in different ways. In the beginning it was naturally occurring events, but this time it is different, it is man-made. After a hundred years of industrial pollution, coal-fired power plants, poison fumes from cars, trucks, and heavy equipment exhaust, along with other pollution, the earth is in a bind. This planet must follow a strict balance to sustain life, any kind of life. Humans have changed that balance and, in the future, will experience more hardships to survive.

As the climate changes, the oceans grow warmer creating more and larger hurricanes, causing flooding and destruction worldwide. Climate change is also causing severe long-term droughts, destroying millions of acres of arable soil globally. The burning of the rain forest for land clearing and the cutting of the trees for timber, if kept at the current pace, will cause permanent damage to our environment, affecting weather patterns in a negative way globally. Men never viewed, even with warnings, problems that could be detrimental to them in the future, instead ignoring these issues until they became too large to be fixed.

The burning of fossil fuels has pumped carbon dioxide and methane into the atmosphere trapping heat, which in turn is melting polar ice and glaciers worldwide. This change will eventually raise water levels so high that millions of people will be displaced, as their land and homes are taken by the oceans. Large forest fires will sweep the earth spewing more pollutants into the atmosphere, making the problem worse. Humans have created a series of events that are slowly changing our planet, causing a cascade of issues we cannot solve. Eventually the earth will become uninhabitable except for insects. It will go back in time to its beginning of life, where all living things, including humans, were given the same chance to thrive and grow. Now that future will disappear because of mistakes made by the most intelligent life on the planet.

Humans are an undeniable factor in the cause of our planet's problems. Just as a small unseen virus can bring the human species to its knees, our presence has placed our planet in a downward spiral. Neither the planet or humans will come out of this unscathed, but the planet will survive and adapt to changes, as it has done for millions of years. A beginning for new life will advance, and the planet will renew and heal, giving life an avenue to succeed once again.

PLANET EARTH

————— ✦✦✦✦✦✦ —————

Our planet, according to science, is about four and one-half billion years old. In the beginning, it was devoid of life. It was a new world with a bright future. Its progression was slow. Billions of years would pass, as this planet cooled, moving its way forward to its goal; becoming a world where life could exist. This pathway to life has been repeated millions of times in our universe and this pattern will continue for years to come.

Over the course of what we would call infinity, the age of man dawned. The first hominids walked upright and used primitive tools. They started a culture that is recognized today, as our earliest instincts were developed. This period in history began six million years ago leading up to the age of Homo Sapiens, believed to be two hundred thousand years old. The seeds to our modern age had been planted, bringing us to where we are today.

From a non-industrial society two hundred sixty years ago to the highly technology-driven one of today, we have advanced more in the last one hundred fifty years than the previous two hundred thousand. What does this tell us? It tells us that our destiny has been sealed, leaving the age of modern man to be the shortest period in our planet's history. With the passage of time, all traces of human history will be eliminated as the climate shapes the destiny of the earth.

Our lives here on earth are short, rarely lasting one hundred years, never knowing exactly where we came from or why we are here. The future will march on, with or without us. Let us join together as one and try to make this work, ensuring our destiny will be one with a future and not a quick ending.

THE CHORUS FROG

············

I t was springtime, the sun was warm and the frogs that lived in the swamps and woodlands were getting ready to lay their eggs. Frogs lay hundreds of eggs in a gelatin-like mass in the spring. Within two weeks the eggs hatch and turn into tadpoles. These small creatures have little chance of survival. Needing air to breathe they propel themselves to the surface, where they are easily seen by predators who gobble them up like sweet tasting candy. But some do survive and by the end of the summer will reach maturity and join their brethren, filling the swamp with their perfectly synchronized song. Getting to this point in adulthood is challenging because being born the size of a dot, with no parental protection, does not make things safe for these small amphibians. However, survival is meant for many, and as they grow, they undergo an amazing transformation.

From those little dots grows a fat little body and a long tail. When tadpoles are born, they are strictly vegetarian, eating plant and other green matter from the pond. As they grow, their diet changes to insects in the water and even tiny fish. Larger fish, salamanders and birds are the tadpoles' biggest predators, accounting for most of the death experienced by this species. As the tadpoles grow their body takes on a new form. Four little legs suddenly appear, with little webbed feet to help propel them along and eventually give them buoyancy to keep their heads above water. They will also eventually allow them to jump fast enough to escape predators.

As the spring progresses the little tadpoles are no more, having been replaced by the shape of a frog. These little frogs, after their long journey to get here, will soon be able to pull themselves up onto land and bask in the warm sunshine, just like the older members of their species. As the summer grows, so do the newborn frogs, taking on characteristics of an adult. Their diet consists of insects now, either caught airborne or in the water.

As the summer turns into fall, the frogs notice a change in the temperature, indicating their long sleep is near. They hide under logs or other debris and stay there throughout the winter. Chorus frogs can survive freezing, thawing out when spring arrives.

Once again you will know it is truly spring when you hear the chorus of the frogs, including those tiny tadpoles that were born last year. They are now well on their way to becoming egg-laying adults, helping this species procreate and keep its place in the forests and ponds.

If you hear these tiny frogs, enjoy their music, and in times of stress let your mind wander back to their symphony; a change of feelings will prevail, and peace of mind will follow. This is one of God's simple little pleasures put in place for humans to enjoy. Try to find others and your life will take on new meaning, as you become one with nature.

THE BLACK WOLF

◆◆◆◆◆◆

The black wolf surveyed the valley below him looking for any signs of man. Since the bounty on wolves had been raised there had been a significant increase in the slaughter of these animals, which drove the wolves higher into the mountains for their own protection. His first responsibility was to his pack, three females, one young male, and four pups. After he concluded there was no danger, he returned to the pack. They needed to eat, but food was hard to find here, which meant a trip to the valley below.

The black wolf was rare for his species, occurring in only one of every ten thousand births. He was said to have certain instincts and powers that other wolves did not possess. The thought of humans randomly killing for sport and money sickened him. The hunters were even going into the dens and killing the cubs. As the wolves' hunt for food continued, the pack came upon the carcass of a deer, killed by a bear which ate its fill and then left the area. The thankful wolves ate and with bellies full returned up the mountain to feed the cubs.

The black wolf was out for revenge against the humans who invaded their territory and made their lives extremely difficult. He called upon the spirits for help. Sitting upon his rock high above the valley he noticed human activity below. Wolf hunters! The black wolf lifted his head high and howled loudly, catching the attention of the two men below. The men rushed forward toward the black wolf. In their haste one of the men tripped, his gun going off and the bullet striking the other man in the heart killing him instantly. The black wolf's plan was working. He thanked the spirits.

There was activity in the valley that day, but not related to wolf hunting. Word got out about the black wolf and the stories of his supernatural powers spread. Two men from the town thought it all hogwash and were not going to let these rumors stop them from earning easy money by culling members of the pack. Their goal was to kill the black wolf and end the superstitions. The men set out, rifles in hand, thinking they could come up behind the wolves and surprise them. The route to get behind the pack was long and hard, and the one man found it increasingly difficult to climb over the large rocks and rough terrain. The black wolf watched. Suddenly, without warning, the tired man clutched his chest and dropped to the ground dead. He had suffered a massive heart attack.

The black wolf went back to his pack knowing that today he had no worries. This latest incident really spooked the town, making them realize the wolves would be better left alone. The black wolf led his pack, including the cubs, down to the valley where their lives would not be bothered by this evil again. As the years passed, the wolf pack was confident they were safe, as the spirit of the black wolf was always with them.

THE APPLE TREE

+ + + + + +

The apple tree stood alone on the abandoned property. It was a tree with a history for the various families that had occupied this old homestead. It was planted as a seedling years ago to provide nourishment for the family. A variety of products that were derived from it benefited the families that lived there. In early spring the tree came to life, sprouting buds that later turned into bright green foliage. Next came the beautiful white flowers which totally enveloped the tree, giving off a scent that would turn your head when walking by. The buzz of the bees could be heard, as they gathered the sweet sap from the flowers, pollenating the trees, allowing the small fruit to form. Some of this fruit would fall to the ground providing food, mostly for insects, as the fruit decayed in the hot sun. As the fruit grew so did the anticipation of the families who were to harvest it.

A tree full of apples could be used in diverse ways, with the most common being as an edible fruit. If stored properly, these apples would last for what seemed like forever. Next was the cider. The apples, full of juice, nutritious, and sweet, made a favorite beverage for the kids and adults alike. Baking was next. During the harvest, the sweet smell of apple pie and apple crisp was delightful to the senses. Apple salad was also made in a variety of ways, depending on whose grandmother's recipe was used.

In late August, when the apples were maturing, it was time for testing the fruit. The kids would eagerly climb the tree to get to the fruit.

They would pick one or two apples, but no more under their parents' strict rules over the tree. They allowed as little waste as possible as the fruit was an important commodity to the family. In the latter part of the fall, right before harvest time, as the ripening fruit fell from the tree, the yearly visit from the black bear signalled it was harvest time. The sweet apples were a source of food for the bear as it struggled to find enough nourishment to build up its stockpile of fat to get through the long winter's hibernation.

Harvest day was a special event. With ladders the fruit was picked from the upper branches by hand, while the children, to their delight, were sent up into the tree to pick the fruit, and carefully throw it down to the adults below. Not all apples could be reached by hand or ladder, so these apples were retrieved by shaking the tree, allowing the apples to fall to the ground, which usually caused bruising. These bruised apples were mostly used to make cider. Soon the tree was bare, picked clean of its fruit for another year.

As late fall approaches the once vibrant apple tree looks forlorn, having lost all its leaves as it returned to its dormant stage for the winter. It had given up its bountiful harvest for the family to enjoy over the coming months. But now the tree was old and abandoned and was slowly nearing the end of its life. It had given up its glorious past, like the old house that it provided its life sustaining fruit to. Soon the apple tree will die, but even in death it will be seen and remembered for what it once was.

CHICKENS

———— ✦✦✦✦✦ ————

The first hint of daylight was approaching, and the rooster in the chicken coop was ready. He had been waiting, and preparing, to perform this ritual as he had done hundreds of times before. The rooster made his way outside, climbed to the roof of the chicken coop, took his position, stuck his breast out, and raised his head in the air. The sound of the bird's loud voice, a wake-up call for the farmers who used this early morning song as an alarm clock, reminding them that another day was here. The chicken has played a prominent role in its interactions with humans, providing a reliable meat source and fresh eggs to eat. In turn, humans have provided the defenceless chicken with needed protection in the form of small buildings that contain nesting boxes where they can lay their eggs. Wired outside enclosures keep raptors from visiting, and an airtight building provide protection from small mammals like weasels and foxes, two common enemies of the chicken.

The farmer and his wife awaken and eat breakfast. With the dog in tow they go about their daily chores; the man sent to the barn, his wife to the care of the chickens. Feeding, watering, putting new straw down if needed, and collecting the eggs, which are then taken to the farmhouse. The extras eggs will be sold, the money saved and used for Christmas.

Chickens have a reputation as being timid and harmless. This is true only of the female chicken. The male, called a rooster, can be mean and will fight another male to its death. He has no fear of humans, sometimes waiting in ambush so he can chase and bite them. Chickens are common all over the world; where you find them, you will also find man. They have been companions for hundreds of years and they are rarely separated. Pet chickens are common for the children of families who raise them, brought into homes, and treated as family pets. These chickens enjoy a long life compared to the rest of the birds in the chicken coop. Chickens will continue to have a close relationship with humans, providing them with food and an enjoyable hobby to occupy their time, preserving a never-ending tradition of friendship between humans and chickens, a bond that will last forever.

THE TROUT STREAM

t one time in Ontario, Canada trout streams were common. Dotting the countryside, these streams were productive fisheries, providing entertainment and food to the local people who took advantage of this sport called fishing.

Trout are an extremely nervous fish, any movement or noise will send them into hiding immediately, ending any chance of hooking them on a fishing line. Brook trout dominated these streams, a steady fishery that sustained itself for at least fifty years. But not any more, their habitat has been destroyed by bad water management decisions.

Home owners were granted permits to dig private ponds on properties, which have altered these streams. The changed water flow upset the delicate balance needed to sustain this fishery. These sanctuaries have been ruined. This has led to a devastating loss of habitat and population, effectively destroying what once was a thriving ecosystem.

It is rare to catch a brook trout, also called a speckled trout, in these streams today. As a teenager, the trout stream was a favorite destination, providing hours of fun, and usually always fish to bring home. Beating the elusive trout in his own habitat was not an easy thing to do, the fish coming out the winner most of the time. Too damaged for a return to its former glory, all that is left of most trout streams are memories of how they used to be. With future consideration and thought, we should try to maintain things that do not become just memories and share the responsibility to sustain life at all levels, leading to a happier world for everyone.

THE NIGHT SKY

As the sun retreats below the horizon the sky gives up its light and slowly darkens, signifying that nighttime has arrived. The night sky brings with it changes to the way we live. Humans mostly stay indoors where there is light. However, a variety of animals that have remained hidden, having slept all day, awaken, coming out into the darkness to hunt and play. These nocturnal animals, through evolution, prefer the darkness. No reasonable explanation can be given for this. Humans use this time for sleep, rejuvenating the body in preparation of the following day's tasks, which sometimes take a toll if not well rested.

As blackness reigns, the night sky becomes a tapestry of stars, giving us a view that enlightens our mind and soul. For children, stargazing is a popular attraction. There is something quite satisfying about lying on your back in a grassy area and finding the different constellations, like the big and little dipper. On especially dark nights being able to observe the milky way is a special treat. Watching the sky this way has the added benefit of total relaxation of the mind, as you become one with the universe, your spirit joining the stars in exploring space. The call of your mother to come in from the night the only thing that could break this spell.

The night sky is not always dark. Earth's moon, when full, can brighten the night, allowing farmers to continue their harvest until well after sunset. This is called the harvest moon, an especially bright moon that occurs in the fall. But the sky does not always allow you to see its show, as thick cloud cover can obscure your view, acting as a curtain. Like on a stage, this drapery allows nature to control your viewing of this event.

As the night progresses, the darkness starts to lift; the sun making its daily return, bringing light and warmth back to our world. The return of light is often accented by the songbirds singing, reminding us that another day has arrived. This cycle has been repeated for hundreds of thousands of years and will continue to do so until our sun burns out and the night sky will be no more.

On a clear night, take your child and a blanket and enjoy nature's spectacular show, allowing yourself a break from the tribulations of life we face every day. These relaxing moments, enjoyed with your child, cannot be replaced, creating a lifelong memory, never forgotten, of one of nature's most special shows.

PEACE AND TRANQUILLITY

◆◆◆◆◆◆

The full moon shone brightly on the lake, casting a beautiful glow that reflected on the surrounding forest. The quiet was deafening, only the lonely call of the loon and the splash of the waves on the shoreline could be heard. This is Canada, a pristine ecosystem of peace and tranquillity.

The sleeping souls in the tent on the shoreline, their spirits in undisturbed sleep, had become one with nature until their awakening to the sun's morning light and the sounds of the forest. Their canoes lay on the shore beckoning another day of adventure, their blissful minds caught in the moment.

The boys exited the tent, stirred the late-night coals of the campfire, and added wood to warm their bodies after a cool summer night. Silence ensued as they sat around the fire, their spirits becoming one with nature; only the call of the crow and the chatter of the chipmunks changing their thoughts. As the sun warmed the day, their spirits awoke.

Excitement mounted as they prepared to continue on their journey. They loaded their canoes and were soon heading towards their last destination. Only the sound of their paddles and the occasional sound of a fish breaking the surface of the lake disturbed their thoughts. They would soon return to their daily lives, leaving with fond recollections of their time in nature.

Soon these memories would fade as the stresses of modern life returned, leaving them anticipating their return the following summer to join the Creator in the wilderness of Canada's north. This was truly an experience never to be forgotten.

SOLITUDE

✦✦✦✦✦✦

The snow from the previous night covered the trees in a cloak of white. The evergreens, with their boughs laden in snow, stood like giant snowmen in a landscape dominated by blue sky. The man opened his eyes, looking out his bedroom window at a winter wonderland of fresh new snow. The chickadees caught his eye, their acrobatic dips and dives at the feeder entertaining to watch.

He had dissolved his marriage after his wife of many years had betrayed him and squandered family money he had received as an inheritance. Selling his home in Toronto, he bought a winterized cottage on a lake in the Haliburton Highlands, near the small town of Bancroft, about a four-hour drive from the city.

He pulled himself out of bed, going to the kitchen. He looked out the large picture window at the expanse of the frozen lake, the ice and snow like a frigid blanket over the water. The wind-whipped snow, blowing across the surface of the lake like a desert sand storm, caught his eye. On another part of the lake, other movement attracted his attention. He retrieved his binoculars for a better look. It was the wolf pack he had heard but never seen, their howls a common sound in this isolated area. They were feeding on a deer they had chased onto the frozen lake and killed. He would take his snowmobile and drive out to this scene later.

The cold winter air stung his face as he left his cottage. The forest trail beckoned; a two-kilometer trail that wound through the wooded area adjacent to his property. If the weather cooperated, taking a walk was first on his list of things to do after breakfast.

He called it the "loneliness trail" for its ability to bring back memories of days gone by, when the enjoyment of socializing with family and friends took a high priority on his agenda. Time and age had changed things, leading to his decision to move from the city, isolation from the masses now his goal.

The forest trail beckoned, the fresh snow revealing the identity of the mammals that lived in, or were just visiting, this area. A large creek ran through the property, providing habitat for beaver and other wildlife that called this place home.

He was skeptical at first about changing the course of his life but was now sure he had made the right decision. The remainder of his time here on earth would be brought to a happy conclusion by choosing this lifestyle. Like food for the soul, nature provides us with something nothing else can, peace and solitude in what we know as God's country, the land of the Canadian people.

THE RIVER

❖ ✦✦✦✦✦ ❖

T he first light of dawn encompasses the river, starting a series of events that are common in nature. Reacting to the light of day, most life awakens and continues its journey; a complex ecosystem made to work by a mysterious system of checks and balances controlled by nature. As the sun continues to rise, an explosion of activity begins. The mother blackbird, clinging to the sparse branches of the willows, her nest full of babies, sounds a warning to anything that approaches her nesting area. The great blue heron maintains its statue-like position, as it prepares for another day of fishing.

The stillness is interrupted by the sound of an approaching fisherman, his small outboard motor dominating the atmosphere. The river becomes quiet when the man reaches his destination. He sits silent in his boat, alone at his favorite spot, a place where he can reflect on his past, his present, and his future. He listens to the long and distinctive croak of the large bullfrogs that call this place home. The splash of a large fish directs his attention to the shoreline and forces him to focus on why he is here. Under the water, large fish like bass, muskie, and walleye, are feeding on smaller fish for breakfast, a morning ritual enjoyed by these dominate species. A snapping turtle is also hunting for breakfast, looking for carrion left by the larger fish or other water life that have died of natural causes.

The quiet is again broken by the loud splash of a beaver's tail hitting the water, this aquatic animal sounding its warning as he sees the man in his boat, an unnatural sight to this creature. The man readies himself to leave as the sky darkens, and thunder sounds in the distance. A silence overtakes the area as the river prepares for the storm. The passing storm temporarily changes the water, making it easier for the aquatic insects and fish to find food as sediments are stirred up, and nourishment from the riverbanks washes into the water.

The natural activity on the river wanes as the sun returns and morning progresses; man continuing to dominate. Peace and solitude will return as darkness falls, and the river becomes silent, waiting for the morning light, and a return to another day.

The river, if respected, will supply unlimited enjoyment to the variety of life that uses it. It is a vital part of the environment, sustaining the life that depends on it. It provides sustenance and joy to humans and animals alike, asking for nothing in return. Enjoy what it has to offer, admire it, and treat it like the miracle it is.

THE AUTUMN FOREST

———— ✦✦✦✦✦ ————

I t's mid-September and profound changes are taking place. Autumn is here presenting itself in a variety of ways, but the most striking change is what happens in our forests. The trees take on new meaning as the foliage goes from a vibrant green to a cascade of brilliant colours, led by the king of colour, the maple tree. As the month wears on, the maples send a torrent of leaves to the forest floor creating a yellow brick road feeling to the humans that walk the trails of these majestic hardwoods. A never-ending supply of activity by nature is present, including the fascinating display of hundreds of species of fungi growing on the forest floor or covering the downed trees that have decayed and litter the ground like pick-up sticks. All of these fallen trees create a suitable habitat for a variety of species, who use these natural surroundings for life sustaining purposes. The oak trees, another large hardwood, are dropping their acorns, which are a prime food for the squirrels to collect and store for future sustenance.

As you walk the trails of these forests, you experience a profound sense of peace and tranquility. The leaves falling around you and the occasional call of the blue jay are the only sounds to pierce the silence that envelops you. A walk in the autumn forest is a call for your spirit to calm, as life takes on new meaning and allows you to escape the repetitious behaviour of modern life. It beckons. Crossing the paths of other humans creates a feeling of unity with your fellow man not experienced by any other way in the human realm.

The forest is your friend, welcoming you no matter how bad your day, helping to lift your spirits when you are feeling down. The stillness and aromatherapy calm your senses. The forest will always be bigger than you and will still be here after your life on earth is finished. I will never tire of walking the halls of one of nature's greatest creations, one of life's most enjoyable pleasures, a walk through the autumn forest.

SPRINGS ARRIVAL

$\leftrightarrow \diamond \diamond \diamond \diamond \leftrightarrow$

L ike the news of the birth of a child, happiness spreads among the residents of the cold, weary populace of Canada as another long cold season ends. The return of the sunshine wakes the dormant spirit, a result of self-hibernation brought on by the dark, short days of winter. The snow melting and the return of the songbirds usher in a new beginning for life to thrive once again.

The animals that have slept all winter awaken, starting new families that will grow and continue this endless cycle of rebirth. The landscape bursts into beautiful colours, dazzling the mind and spirit of animals and humans alike, which it will continue to do until the return of the snow and cold. By late spring, the flowers dominate the senses, enlightening your spirit, stealing depression from your soul. The cycle of life continues as the trees explode into brilliant green, replacing the barren look of winter with a beautiful landscape, like the painting at the end of an artist's brush.

This cycle will continue until nature is finished with this beautiful season, leaving us to enjoy this creation, however brief it might be. Spring will remain a part of life, never extinguishing the joy it brings after a dormant spirit is awakened. Let us proclaim that nature has the power to control all aspects of life on earth. Therefore total respect for all life should be acknowledged, leaving us to ponder the meaning of the rebirth of our world, in the season we call spring.

A STORY OF FRIENDSHIP

T he dawn light signalled the start of another day. The birds were singing, their early morning melody like an orchestra, bringing a sense of tranquility to the waking souls sleeping in the tent. Their eyes were open, a peace enveloping them as the sounds of nature overwhelmed their spirits.

The boys had been planning this trip after graduation, their college days were ending. The four of them had grown up together in a small town, attending the same high school, playing hockey together, and they were inseparable. Their favorite activities were fishing and camping, which led them to plan this trip before their separation would become permanent. They would soon be off to various parts of the country pursuing the careers they had chosen.

The day of departure soon arrived. One of the boys had borrowed his father's boat and trailer. They had chosen a wilderness lake, which was not popular for camping because of its lack of services that the new breed of campers enjoyed. The boys would have it no other way, their fathers having taught them that this was the only way to genuinely enjoy interacting with the spirit of nature. The drive north was long but uneventful, the last couple of kilometers into the lake was a rough drive; but the four-wheel drive on the truck made it a non-issue.

They reached the lake, a quiet expanse of water. They loaded the boat and traveled to a point of land that one of their fathers had told them about. It was a fine camping spot on level ground with easy access to the boat for loading and unloading supplies. After two hours ferrying supplies to their camping site they were finally done and ready to set up housekeeping. The tent went up first, followed by a small table for their cooking station, and another small tent to be used for storage. They retrieved their camp chairs and sat around the campfire that previous campers had built. The last campers had left a nice pile of firewood beside the firepit, which was a bonus for the boys.

The chattering of a family of chipmunks broke the stillness of the moment, reminding the boys of who really owns this camping spot. A truce would soon become apparent as the mother chipmunk realizes their presence might be a food source, and a place to bring her babies for a free meal. Three of the boys decided to go fishing, while the other individual decided to stay at camp and nap.

The lake was quiet as they made their way across the water. This body of water held many species of fish, lake trout being the most prized, followed by walleye, bass, and northern pike, to name a few. They decided to try their luck trolling for lake trout, hopefully catching enough for dinner. Luck was with them, as within a brief time six fish lay in the bottom of the boat, a nutritious meal for some hungry young men.

Their friend on shore was waiting on their return and helped them dock and unload the boat. The fish were cleaned and cooked for dinner and a feeling of friendship powered their spirits to enjoy the peace the lake and the forest offered. The flames from the campfire were mesmerizing, sending their thoughts back to what the future held for them. The week went by fast, and they soon found themselves back home with a cherished memory that would last forever; a token of friendship that would never end.

FICTION

OMAR

❖❖❖❖❖❖

Omar was one very, lucky donkey. He had the best job in the world, entertaining people at the *Fiesta on the Mountain*, a show that celebrated Mexican culture and hospitality. Every afternoon a bus loaded with people from the city would come up the dusty road and stop in the middle of the square, where all the happy people would disembark. Let the party begin!

Omar watched the people as they tried the different games and activities that were ready for them. He liked it when the kids would gather around him and patiently wait their turn for a ride around the square. Omar felt like a king. He had just received a new saddle and blanket and was proud of his job making children happy.

Omar was also part of the rodeo, where he played games and showed the crowd how fast he could run. The people were always surprised because of donkeys' reputations of being slow and lazy. Omar's friends in the rodeo included the horses, cows, and the mean old bull, which was the least liked animal in the show. After having fun playing games and entertaining the cheering crowd, it was time for the rodeo to end. Everyone, including Omar, were ready eat and rest. Omar was always tired and hungry after the rodeo and looked forward to a meal followed by his afternoon siesta.

Tomorrow another bus load of happy people would come to the fiesta and Omar would be able to do these fun things over again. But for now, Omar ate his dinner of hay and corn, and went to sleep dreaming about his wonderful life at the fiesta.

OMAR LEAVES THE MOUNTAIN

Omar the donkey was excited. Yesterday a man visited the mountain and asked Omar's handler if he thought the donkey would be interested in going down to the city to participate in a petting zoo. When Omar heard this, he was thrilled. He ran around the corral kicking up his back legs and snorting his excitement for everyone to hear. After settling down, he thought what this meant to him. He had never been off the mountain, let alone to the city. It also meant a chance to make new friends and launch a new career. His father would be so proud, as his father worked hard but had never been given such an opportunity.

Omar was excited as he knew today was the big day. He could not eat breakfast thinking about what the day was going to bring. Soon the truck and the trailer that was to take Omar to the city arrived. Omar was ready, his saddle, blankets, reigns, toothbrush, and comb packed. After saying his goodbyes, down the mountain he went. They made their way through the city streets, busy with cars and people. Omar was wide-eyed, taking in the new sights and sounds he was experiencing. Soon the hustle and bustle of the streets lessened, and they turned onto a long driveway leading to a large farm, Omar's new home.

Omar was taken to his place in the barn. The barn was noisy as there were different animals that lived there. Omar's neighbors were a family of goats who had lived on the farm a long time. They offered to give Omar a tour, so off they went to meet the other animals. There was a mother pig and her babies, a miniature pony, a llama, and a sheep close by. In another part of the barn there were rabbits, Guinea pigs, ducks, and chickens. The prettiest animal in the barn was the alpaca. On occasion, other animals would come for a visit, like the baby calf, and at one time a baby camel. Omar had never seen these animals before and would have to learn to have a good relationship with them.

Soon the day was over, which meant dinnertime and bed. After a tasty dinner of hay and oats, Omar said goodnight to the other animals and immediately went to sleep thinking about what tomorrow would bring. This little donkey's life would never be the same.

OMAR AT THE PETTING ZOO

Omar woke with a start; he had hardly slept a wink last night due to his excitement. Today he was going to be in the petting zoo at the local fair. It was still dark outside, but his friends in the barn had shared that on these special days they ate breakfast early, were put on a truck and left for the fair right after dawn. Some of the animals did not like going because of the children who pulled their ears and hair. Omar knew these kids were not being mean, but were excited as they had never been so close to animals and their parents did not always watch them closely. Omar had two jobs at the fair, one was being in the pen where the children could pet him and give him treats, the other was to give rides to them.

After much ado, the animals were on the truck heading down the long driveway towards town. After a short ride they were there. Omar was amazed at the different things at the fair, the mechanical rides, the barns full of animals, the food vendors, and the games. The thing Omar liked best was listening to the horses in the barn next to him stomping their feet, their restless behaviour meaning they were hungry and waiting to be fed. Omar became sad as he realized how he missed all of his friends on the mountain. Someday he would be able to see them again.

Soon everyone was in place and the fair gates opened. Children and parents were everywhere petting the animals, giving them treats and talking nicely to them. Omar was happy, as he loved to see the smiles on the kids' faces and hear their laughter, but some of the children were scared of him. Soon it was time for Omar to give rides, which was his favorite thing to do. After giving rides to happy children, the day was over, and Omar was exhausted and ready to go home. The fair was more fun than he had expected.

The trip back to the farm was quiet, as the animals were tired and looking forward to a restful sleep. Omar was nervous about tomorrow, as he heard that some animals were going to be moved to another farm. He was hoping he was not one of them. He laid his head down and was soon in a deep sleep, dreaming about his past and future adventures.

OMAR LEAVES THE FARM

Omar heard voices in the barn and wondered if these were the men that were going to take him away. They had come yesterday, and he had overheard them talking about moving him to another farm. This made Omar anxious, and he had not slept well worrying about what was in store for him. As the voices drew closer, Omar heard a young girl. She approached Omar and threw her arms around his neck, hugging him tightly. She told Omar she would take care of him, as he was to become her donkey and best friend. Her father took Omar to a waiting trailer, which he entered happily now that he knew good things were in store for him.

After a short journey, they reached their destination and Omar was led to the most beautiful barn he had ever seen. His stall was luxurious. The young girl, whose name was Lucille, had decorated it with streamers and a sign to welcome Omar home. To Omar's surprise, there were also pictures of him and his friends at *Fiesta on the Mountain* hanging on the wall. Lucille had often gone to the fiesta to celebrate special family events and was familiar with Omar. After finding out he had left the fiesta, she went to see him at the fair with her father, who negotiated for Omar to come live at their farm and become his daughter's cherished friend.

Soon Lucille's family and friends were crowded around Omar, remarking on the beautiful makeover Lucille had given him. His ears were adorned with pretty covers her grandmother had made for him. He had a gorgeous blanket her aunt had made and a beautiful saddle and reigns. Omar was one very, lucky donkey!

Lucille took care of Omar, grooming him, taking him for rides around the farm and introducing him to the other animals that lived there. He had the best quality feed and there was always fresh water in his stall, which Omar was not used to.

The days at the farm were filled with fun. When Lucille was at school, Omar went to the corral where he played with his new friends, Taco and Bell, two horses that were brothers and belonged to Lucille's father. They would race around the corral, Omar showing them how fast he could run. The cows outside the fence enjoyed watching, to their great amusement.

One day Lucille came running with exciting news, Omar was getting a girlfriend. Lucille's grandmother had arranged for a sweet lady donkey to come and keep Omar company. Omar would never be lonely again. His head swam with excitement as his thoughts spun out of control. What he needed was a good night's sleep, so he would be ready to meet his new friend with a clear head. Omar was heading for a new adventure, starting a family. He wondered if he was ready.

OMAR AND JULIETTE

Omar waited patiently for the new arrival, dressed in his best outfit, including a new hat. Lucille's family was also waiting. There had been a large party the night before celebrating Lucille's birthday. This morning everyone was waiting on the latest addition to their farm family. Suddenly, a cheer went up as the truck and trailer headed up the long driveway. Omar was so nervous his legs were shaking, and he felt weak, like he was going to faint. He took a large drink of water and turned his attention to the excitement around the trailer which had arrived. Omar stood with Lucille at the back of the trailer. Lucille's father opened the gate and Omar's head exploded with bright red hearts. There in front of him was the most beautiful donkey he had ever laid his eyes on.

Juliette stepped off the trailer, instantly coming to Omar and rubbing her head against his. Omar knew this was a match made in heaven. After much fanfare it was time to show Juliette her new lodgings. The barn had been scrubbed clean anticipating her arrival, and the other animals in the barn were excited for Omar and his new bride. A hush fell over the barn as Juliette took in her new surroundings. Juliette felt lucky to be here, as she had come from a poor family who could barley afford to feed her. The couple retired to their new joint stall where they ate lunch and got to know each other better.

Omar told Juliette about his life on *Fiesta on the Mountain*, and Juliette acknowledged she had heard of him, as he was a famous donkey. She told Omar about her previous home, and how fortunate she was to be here. Soon they both lay down on the thick bed of straw and fell sound asleep. Omar was looking forward to showing his new wife around the farm and introducing Juliette to the other residents. Omar's wife was happy knowing that she, and any future children, would be well taken care of here. Omar and Juliette were already a happy couple.

A BABY IS BORN

Omar was pacing back and forth in the stall. Juliette had been in labor for a long time and the veterinarian had said it might be hours more before she delivered. Omar was excited, this being his first child. He was also very worried, as this was his first baby, and he did not know what to expect. Juliette's pregnancy had been normal, and Omar made sure she ate the right foods and got rest. The doctor said the baby was healthy and would come out kicking. But for Omar it was a nervous waiting game.

Juliette lay comfortably in the straw, telling Omar she thought the time was getting close. Omar heard voices coming; it was the vet, Lucille, and her father. The doctor had decided to administer medicine to speed up the birth process, as Juliette had been in labor for so long. The doctor had Juliette stand up and gave her an injection, saying the baby should be born soon. Omar nestled his nose in Juliette's neck trying to comfort her; this being her first baby, she was scared. Suddenly she felt strange movements and the need to push. In what seemed like only a second, she could hear a low whimpering sound and felt an emptiness in her stomach. The baby had been born.

Omar and Juliette were ecstatic! It was finally over. A huge sense of relief swept over them. The vet examined the baby and gave him a clean bill of health. On wobbly legs, and with a little help from his father, the baby made it over to his mother where he had his first taste of warm milk. He drank his fill and went to sleep with his mother. Omar looked on with a sense of pride in his heart. They knew the baby was a boy, but they had not been able to choose a name for him yet.

The barn was dark and quiet, Omar relieved that everything had gone well. It was time for him to get rest, as tomorrow was going to be busy. He nestled in beside his wife and was immediately sleeping, the day's events temporarily forgotten about. Omar's life had been changed forever.

BABY JACK

After lengthy discussions, and a million names, Omar and Juliette decided to call the new baby Jack. Jack was Omar's oldest brother who had passed away just last year. The baby reminded Omar of Jack, his color and markings identical. After spending two days in the stall, everyone was ready to explore the corral and let Jack get acquainted with the animals that shared the barn. Omar was proud to be a new father and had promised Juliette he would have a big part in raising Jack.

As they left the stall, cheers rang loudly in their ears. Jack kept close to his mother as this noise scared him. Juliette assured Jack he was safe, and this was the animals' way of showing their excitement about his birth. All the animals gathered around Jack, which made him nervous, but after assurances from his mother, Jack calmed down and was ready to meet his housemates.

There were the two horses, his daddy's friends, Taco and Bell and their new baby Burrito. There were goats led by Scruffy and Emma, and there were also sheep with new babies, some only weeks older than Jack. There was the potbellied pig, Petunia, who liked nothing better than to eat and make loud noises, which bothered the other animals, especially when they were trying to sleep. Then there were the cows, Bertha and Harry, and their baby Noah. Last were the geese and their goslings, the ducks, chickens, and the most beautiful, but not modest, Joanne the peacock.

Burrito and Noah offered to take Jack outside and show him their favorite places to play. After coaxing from his mother, Jack threw up his back legs and followed his new friends outside. They met up with their friend Ruffles, the family dog, who often accompanied them on their adventures. Tired from playing, they soon headed back to the barn for lunch, everyone happy they had made new friends. Jack was now comfortable, and knew he was going to enjoy life here at the farm. After a delicious lunch of warm milk, Jack fell asleep snuggled into his mother and was one content baby donkey.

OMAR RETURNS TO THE MOUNTAIN

One morning Lucille came to the barn with wonderful news for Omar. She had made plans to take Omar and his family back to the *Fiesta on the Mountain* for her eighteenth birthday party. Lucille's entire family was coming, aunts, uncles, grandmas, grandpas, cousins, and even Ruffles, the family dog. Omar was excited to be going home for a visit, and able to show Jack where he had been born and raised.

Soon the big day arrived. Everyone loaded into a large caravan of cars and trucks and were soon off. Lucille's father had booked this party as a private event just for his family. After a long drive through the city and up the mountain they arrived in the square. A loud, excited crowd surrounded Omar and his family. The people of the mountain had missed Omar and had been looking forward to meeting Juliette and Jack. They had heard of the donkeys' adventures in the lowlands, entertaining at children's parties, visiting seniors' homes to let the elderly pet and hug them, and being in a show about the history of donkeys in Mexican culture.

Omar introduced his family to all his old friends and took them on a tour of the Fiesta, explaining all they did there. After hours of playing and partying, an announcement was made for the party goers to head to the corral for the rodeo. There the people were entertained with horse tricks, bull riding, and joined in games related to the rodeo.

At the conclusion of the show, it was time to eat dinner. After a short walk Lucille and her family arrived at the dining hall and took their seats. A special area was set for Omar and his family with all the best foods a donkey could eat. After a wonderful meal, the man who ran the Fiesta announced that Jack would be staying to continue on the family tradition of entertaining in the *Fiesta on the Mountain*. Jack was filled with pride as the crowd cheered loudly, and tears flowed down Omar's cheeks. He and Juliette would surely miss their son, but he was older now and would benefit from this safe and educational experience.

Everyone said their good-byes and the caravan went back down the mountain to their farm below. Omar and Juliette were sad that there only son was not returning with them but knew he would be happy on the mountain. It had been a stressful day and Omar and Juliette were happy to be home. They laid down and were quickly sleeping soundly, not even Petunia's snoring keeping them awake.

OMAR RETIRES

The days turned into weeks, the weeks into months, and the months into years. Omar's life had once again taken a sharp turn. He was old. He still loved children, but he could no longer give them rides because his back was not strong. He could not run like he used to, and his bones and joints ached all the time. His wife Juliette had passed away a year ago, after a prolonged illness. Omar missed her greatly.

His son, Jack, had stayed and had a successful career at *Fiesta on the Mountain*. He had a wife named Melony and a beautiful daughter, Rosie, who was gifted dancer. People came from all over Mexico to the *Fiesta on the Mountain* to watch her show.

Omar reflected on his life and was happy with how satisfying it had been. But now it was time to think about his future. No longer able to work, he was going to a donkey sanctuary where he would spend the rest of his life in the company of other donkeys, being well taken care of.

A GHOST STORY

The Murray family was elated. The closing on their new house was imminent and moving out of Toronto was now a reality. The family had bought an old farmhouse in a rural area near Peterborough, Ontario, complete with outbuildings including a barn full of hay, a tractor shed and a woodshed. An apple orchard, a large garden, and flower beds surrounded the property. This dream was realized after Raymond Murray, the father, had won the Ontario lottery, and after consulting with family members, his wife Rhona, and their children Danny, and Becky, they decided to buy and renovate an old farmhouse in the country, and bring it back to its former glory. The house they bought was built in 1898, but what the Murrays did not know was the reputation that came with the house and the reason it had not been lived in for so many years. With the purchase of a mobile home, now placed on the property, the Murrays would have a place to live while the renovations were taking place.

The family arrived at their new property in late May and expected to have renovations completed enough to move in and enjoy Christmas there. The old door creaked as it opened, and the Murrays entered the house, all feeling the emptiness that seemed to seep right to their souls. They wondered about the past, who built the home, the families that had lived here, and their happiness and the sorrows.

The house was full of furniture that had been abandoned, as if tragedy had befallen the last tenants that were here. As they moved through the house their thoughts turned to living here and how different life was going to be. Mrs. Murray thought about her two teenage children, knowing it would be especially hard for them. The enormity of their situation overwhelmed her, and doubts crept into her mind. After exploring the house, they decided to have all the contents removed from the house, saving nothing.

Next, they explored the outbuildings and grounds. The barn was full of hay, the granary full of oats, pigeons nested in the rafters, and barn swallows filled the bottom of the barn. As they were leaving the barn, Danny noticed a box in the rafters. Curious, he retrieved it and inside found an old key. He tucked the box under his arm and followed his family outside, continuing their investigation of the tractor shed. It was empty except for an old carriage that looked as if it had been sitting there for a long time. The woodshed was also empty. Exploring the property there were large flowerbeds that needed to be rejuvenated, and a lot of discarded junk that needed to be cleaned up.

Thankfully, money was not an issue, and help could be hired to clean up and haul away the house contents, and all the debris outside. Satisfied with their investigation, the Murray family retired to their trailer for dinner and a good night's sleep. Tomorrow their first surprise awaited.

Becky woke with a start. She heard what sounded like footsteps outside the trailer. She got up and looked out her window, which was open due to the unseasonably warm weather, but saw nothing. The full moon shone brightly, causing her attention to shift to the old house. In the moonlight the house looked abandoned and forlorn. A creepy feeling passed through her body. She sensed something was not right but decided to keep these feelings to herself, unaware other family members had similar reservations. Becky returned to bed, fell back asleep, and did not wake again till she heard her mother calling her for breakfast.

After eating, everyone went their separate ways to tackle a host of chores. Becky and her mother went into town shopping, while Mr. Murray and his son, Danny, stayed behind to meet with contractors who were going to give estimates on the various jobs that needed to be done. After time passed, they noticed a truck coming up the driveway, it pulled to a stop and the man introduced himself as a nosy neighbor. He had noticed the activity and was curious if he was going to have new neighbors. The man, who introduced himself as Fred Johnson, had lived on, and farmed, the property that abutted the Murray's land for fifty years. Raymond Murray pressed Mr. Johnson for history on the old house, as they retired to the trailer for coffee.

Mr. Johnson said the house was built by a rich American and his wife from New York City, who moved to the area to raise farm animals and provide a safe upbringing for their three children. It was rumoured that this man was wealthy. He never opened an account at the local bank and appeared to have an abundance of cash to pay for everything. About a year after the house was built, tragedy struck. Two men from town, thinking there was a cache of money and valuables there, decided to arm themselves and rob the Americans. The men shot and killed the entire family, the rumored cash and valuables never found.

The house remained empty until the early 1910's, at which time the brother of the original owner sold it to a local investor, who planned to sell it for a profit. This was when the first hint of a haunting occurred. The family that bought the home lasted two months, the paranormal activity driving them out. The old farmhouse had many tenants over the years, but no one ever stayed long, keeping the house mostly abandoned since it had been built. Mr. Murray pondered this development, and decided to keep it quiet from his family, as he did not believe in stories based on hearsay and speculation. Mr. Johnson said his goodbyes and wished Mr. Murray luck as he headed down the long driveway and out of sight

Danny, who had been out exploring came running up, out of breath. Looking shocked and dismayed, he began telling his father he had found a small graveyard close to the house with five headstones in it, all belonging to the same family. His father's heart sank, now he knew that a least part of Mr. Johnson's story was true. How was he going to break this disturbing news to his family? Would all their dreams be gone, and their future put on hold?

In the meantime, the contractors arrived giving a reasonable estimate on cleaning out the house and hauling away the debris left on the property. The women returned loaded down with groceries and supplies, as well as stories from town about the old McGregor house, which it was called. After hearing the local rumors about their new house, Raymond shared the news of the cemetery and Mr. Johnson's story with the family. Dinner was a silent event as everyone pondered the new developments and wondered if they would change their future. The family would sleep on it and make decisions in the morning.

Around the breakfast table, little was eaten as the family engaged in serious conversation. Should they continue with this endeavor or abandon it altogether? Even though they had bought the house and land at an unbelievably low price, they now knew why, and decided too much was at stake to just quit. Their plan was to try to appease the spirit or spirits, and if the paranormal activity proved evil, or detrimental to them, they would be forced to abandon the property.

The family made their way to the cemetery first. It obviously had not been cared for since the burial, and the family decided a cleanup was in order. That would show the spirits the Murrays' intentions were one of respect for the dead. The long grass was cut, the little wooden fence was repaired and painted, and Mrs. Murray went into town and picked up flowers for each gravesite. By the end of the morning the job was done, the cemetery looked great and from here on in would be treated with the utmost respect. Returning to their trailer for lunch, the Murray family felt they had done something positive to improve their situation.

After lunch, the contractor arrived to clean out the house, scheduling the yard clean up for a later date. Mr. Murray and his son would help in the house, observing to see if anything unusual happened over the course of the day. The work was going smoothly, until they got to one of the bedrooms on the second floor. Returning from carrying furniture to the truck, they found the bedroom door closed and hard to open. The workers, certain they had not closed the door, were spooked, as they were aware of the house's reputation. The pace of the work picked up, as there was now an urgency among the work crew to complete the job. After six hours of work the house was empty, and the workers left, feeling they had experienced something unusual. The McGregor house was living up to its reputation.

Dinner was solemn, as the family discussed the major renovations the house was to undergo. It was decided, under the circumstances, the best thing to do was give the house a good cleaning, install a new furnace, rewire the house, check the plumbing, buy furniture, and move in. If the paranormal activity became too intense to deal with, as a last resort they would move back to their house in Toronto, which had not yet been put on the market. Additionally, they would adopt a dog for protection and as an early warning system, having a reputation for being sensitive to supernatural activity. The Murrays would move into the house in about a month, and if everything went well would tackle the major renovations next spring. Bedtime could not come too early, as exhaustion crept in, and the family found themselves all sleeping shortly after dinner.

The next day dawned bright and clear. The Murrays had spent the night awake as severe storms had swept through the area with lightning brightening the night sky and illuminating the old house with an unnatural glow. An uneasiness rested on the family's shoulders, brought on by the series of events of the last few days. Today they planned to pick up their new dog, weed out flower beds, and install new plants. After breakfast they went their separate ways. Mrs. Murray took the kids to pick out a dog, while Mr. Murray stayed behind to discuss the scaled back renovations on the house with the contractor.

Mr. Murray's thoughts turned to the basement of the house, as little attention had been paid to this area and he was curious and wanted to explore. There was rumoured treasure yet to be found. He entered the basement and took in his surroundings. The foundation was made from large stones, the floor was dirt, a large pile of wood that had been used to heat the house was in one corner, and old shelving was next to it. An old door, which led to the outside, graced one corner. Large wolf spiders inhabited the rafters, adding a Halloween feel to this environment. As Raymond was getting ready to leave, he felt as if he was being watched, and the presence of something that did not want him here. He went upstairs, wondering if this was his imagination, or the beginning of a series of unexplained feelings and events.

Looking out the window, Raymond noticed a truck coming up the driveway, the contractor was here. After a brief greeting and small talk, they entered the house and Mr. Murray told him of the new plans. The contractor was fine with everything they discussed and was planning to start the work at once. As the man was leaving, the rest of the Murray family returned from town, bringing with them a beautiful shepherd puppy whom they decided to call Prince. Prince would bring the family joy and help them keep their minds off the circumstances that surrounded them.

After lunch, the Murrays decided to work on cleaning out the gardens and planting flowers that they had bought in town, not knowing the surprise that awaited them. They gathered up garden tools and with Prince at their side went to work on the large bed closest to the house. Shortly after getting started Becky let out a yell, she had dug up what she thought was an old tobacco can. Upon further inspection, she realized it was full of coins. Surprise and curiosity swept over the family as they examined their treasure, a can full of change and one gold coin, dating back to the time the house was built. They soon got back to work and finished their gardening without anything else unusual happening.

Daylight was waning and hunger was being felt, so the family retired to the mobile home to eat supper and more closely examine their find. Tomorrow would be spent working in the house and exploring the barn more closely. The can of coins had influenced the way they felt, bringing a sense of adventure into their lives.

In the morning, the family gathered at the kitchen table, tired from lack of sleep, as Prince had kept them up with his incessant whining and restlessness. The Murrays hoped it was just a matter of him getting use to his new surroundings, and not having anything to do with the old house. After a hearty breakfast they headed to the house to explore. The house had four bedrooms with an eat-in kitchen, dining room, den, living room, attic, basement, one bathroom, and a large back room off the kitchen.

As they drew closer to the house, Prince grew increasingly nervous, pulling at his leash not wanting to go. Danny picked him up and carried him inside. After serious sniffing, Prince settled down and with tail wagging joined the family in their endeavor. The bedrooms were large with huge closets, built like small rooms. Two of the bedrooms were adjoining, separated by a pocket door. Ms. Murry thought these rooms would be perfect for the kids. Moving on they came upon the largest bedroom, which would be the master suite, and a smaller room which would be used as a guest room. Other than needing a good cleaning and a fresh coat of paint, the rooms were in remarkably good condition.

The attic was next, a ladder gave them easy access and they were surprised that none of the items had been removed. Raymond was glad the attic had not been touched as it held a different array of furnishings than the rest of the house, looking like it had belonged to the original owners. As they surveyed their surroundings, an old rocking chair sitting in the corner started to rock on its own sending chills down the spines of the family and making Prince want to leave. Mr. Murray thought they would keep the renovators out of here as much as possible, so as not to disturb the spirit or spirits that called this part of the house home.

Leaving the attic, they made their way downstairs to the kitchen, which had been remodeled but not to their liking. A complete makeover would be needed. The living and dining areas were fine for now, only paint and minor repairs necessary. The back room off the kitchen was used as a storage area for wood and outdoor furniture that needed to be stored for the winter. It was in deplorable condition and would be torn down and replaced.

Making their way outside the house, the family decided to go explore the wooded area behind the home. After a short walk they came upon an unusual mound covered with long grass and brush. Upon further inspection they discovered it to be a bottle dump. Households long ago tended to separate all their bottles from other household trash and keep them together, usually in a place out-of-sight but close to the house. The kid's excitement mounted, as they planned to excavate this area and start their own bottle collections. Fresh spring water could be found in abundance in the woods, leading Raymond and Rhona to believe that adequate well water would not be an issue.

Next was the barn. The barn swallows were busy swooping in and out of the lower part of the barn, busily building their nests and getting ready to raise their families. The upper part of the barn held the hayloft and the grain storage area. The family decided that both the hay and grain could be donated, as the Murrays had no use for it. Upon closer inspection, where the grain was kept there was a small room that doubled as an office, having a small desk and chair, filing cabinet, and one large picture on the wall. They removed the picture to examine it more closely and discovered an area had been cut out of the wall and then replaced, as if someone were trying to conceal something. They placed the picture back on the wall, planning to return and investigate later.

Satisfied, the family returned to their temporary home and decided to all go into town shopping, go out to lunch and discuss their plans, come home, and take the rest of the day off. After a relaxing afternoon and a large supper, it was not long before, one by one the Murrays retired to bed, hoping to get caught up on the sleep that they had missed the night before. Even Prince was much better, and they all would be refreshed and ready for tomorrow.

The day dawned dark and dreary, but the spirits of the family were high, as today they were to solve the mystery of what was behind the picture in the barn. They skipped breakfast, gathered up tools and off they went, anticipation building. Danny removed the picture, used his screwdriver to pry off the wood that covered the hole, and found a metal box with a lock. Danny remembered the key he had found in the rafters of the barn and retrieved it from the trailer hoping it would open the box. It was the perfect fit, but the box was empty. Disappointment washed over the family. It was obvious that at one time this box held valuables, but no more.

They returned to the trailer, now ready to eat breakfast and discuss this mystery. The talk turned to the house and the fact that they would be moving in at the end of next month. They had decided to bring the furniture from their house in Toronto, which would bring familiarity to their new home.

The contractor and his crew began renovations, and over the next month worked diligently every day, completing the job right on time.

The house was now livable and ready for tenants. Not one instance of paranormal activity was reported by the contractor or his crew. Mr. Murray hired a moving company and arranged to have the furniture delivered in a week. This would give them time, to have carpet and window coverings installed. The house had been unusually quiet in the last weeks and the family wondered if it would stay that way.

The moving truck lumbered up the long driveway. Move-in day had arrived and the family, with nervous anticipation, wondered about their first night in the house. Mr. Murray and the moving supervisor entered the house to discuss where the furniture was to be placed. No sooner did they enter, when the chandelier in the hallway started swinging slowly back and forth. Raymond brushed this off as just the wind. The moving men started carrying the furniture in, and it soon became obvious that something was not agreeable with the situation. Lights turned on and off by themselves and doors opened and slammed shut when no one was nearby. This spooked the men, who no longer wanted to enter the house, refusing to work. After a conversation with their boss, it was decided that the movers would unload the furniture and place it all together in the house as quickly as possible. They refused to go upstairs, leaving the Murrays to do the bulk of the work themselves. Soon the truck was empty and heading back to Toronto. As soon as the moving company left, all paranormal activity stopped.

The family got busy, moving furniture and after a hard day's work, finished just as twilight was approaching. They retired exhausted back to their trailer, ate dinner and went to bed for a well-deserved night's sleep. Tomorrow they were to move into the house, hoping the spirits would look kindly upon them, but doubting this would be a reality.

The family awoke to the sound of Prince's howling. The smell of acrid smoke filled the air, and a red glow turned the night sky to light. The old house was engulfed in flames. By the time the fire department arrived, the old McGregor house was no more, laying in ruins; an old home burnt to the ground, its mysteries and secrets lost with it. The family was in disbelief at this tragic turn of events. The cause of the fire would never be proven.

In honor of the murdered family, the remains of the old house were cleaned up and a memorial to the McGregor's built. The land was donated to the township and turned into a park, with the little cemetery becoming the most visited site. The Murrays stayed in the area buying a home in town, their dreams of living in the country were no more.

Years later a county crew, while cutting down a large, rotten tree that was close to the old house, found the lost valuables of the McGregor family. Hidden in the hollow of the tree was a metal box filled with gold coins and paper money valued at a staggering fifty thousand dollars in today's current market. This horde was donated to the Peterborough Museum and Archives, where, along with the story, it has become one of the most interesting exhibits at the museum.

THE GHOST MINE

CHAPTER ONE

Nevada, a U.S. state known for its ghost towns and abandoned mines, had been on the radar of best friends Jamie and Rudy since their high school days. Now, having graduated college, the trip they had been talking about and planning for years was about to become a reality. Being from a small town in Pennsylvania the idea for this adventure had been a fantasy for the boys since ninth grade. A plan had been made that after graduating college they would reunite and use Jamie's dad's camper to drive to Nevada and fulfil their dream of exploring the abandoned mines and ghost towns in the state. Graduating with journalism degrees they thought this trip would be helpful in stimulating their imaginations and creativity. What they did not know was that this trip would send the boys into an adventure that they could never imagine.

After meticulous planning, the boys loaded the camper with the supplies they needed, said goodbye to their families, and left on the greatest adventure of their lifetime. While driving on the interstate, a new-found source of freedom enveloped them. Released from parental grip, they were cast into young adults, able to make their own decisions and plot their own futures. This was first realized when the flashing lights and siren of a state trooper behind them beckoned them to pull over, a tail-light on the camper was burnt out. The officer was not pleasant, issuing them a ticket and requesting to search the truck. Jamie and Rudy had talked about issues they might be facing on this trip, especially with the police, as Rudy was black.

The young men were told to exit the truck, as a K-9 unit was on the way and the police officer was going to do a preliminary search while waiting. His behaviour was deplorable, leaving a huge mess to be cleaned up after the inspection. The police dog arrived, and after finding no indication of contraband, the police left leaving the boys with a feeling that their dignity had been violated by the people who were supposed to protect them. They got back on the road, stopping at the next service centre to reorganize the mess the police had left, and to have a quiet lunch at one of the picnic tables under the shade of the maple trees that dotted the property. Rudy and Jamie talked of this unfortunate incident while enjoying sandwiches and chips, realizing they were on their own. Aside from a major incident, their parents would not be there for them. They decided to keep driving another three hours and stop early at a KOA campground just inside the state line. They would rest and reorganize, starting out with a fresh attitude after the stresses of this day had caught up with them.

Before long, the young men found themselves pulling into the campground enjoying the thought of relaxing their minds and souls, hoping peace and safety would be with them. The boys' early night was punctuated by a restful sleep, and dreams of where this trip would take them. They let their imaginations run wild as life's adventures became the new reality. Calm prevailed as the night sky shone bright with its full moon and millions of shining stars. The boys slept peacefully in the safety of their camper, a new day on the horizon, launching them deeper into this new way of life they had chosen.

CHAPTER TWO

Rudy woke with a start, the pounding rain hitting the camper, thunder and lightning dominating the morning sky. Jamie opened his eyes, his senses taking in the outside activity. Worry crossed his mind, as these violent thunderstorms sometimes spawned tornadoes or straight-line winds that could take down large trees causing destruction and sometimes death to unsuspecting campers. He prayed for the storm to end. Rudy was also apprehensive. They sat in silence waiting for the storm to pass, and as suddenly as it began it ended, the thunder now in the distance. A calm swept over the truck as the stressful situation subsided, allowing the boys to continue their thoughts of the journey upon which they had embarked.

Today their trip would take them across Ohio and into Indiana, where they would spend the night at a college friend's house. A stop would have to made at an auto parts store to pick up a bulb for their burnt-out taillight so as not to repeat yesterday's incident. After breakfast, and in high spirits, they left the park and were soon on the interstate heading west towards Ohio. They crossed the state line, found the bulb they needed, and Rudy changed it in the parking lot of a Walmart store, taking this worry off their minds. After filling the camper with gas, they drove across rolling farmland. The fields contained various grains, corn, soybeans, and hay, already being cut for feed for the animals that lived on the area's farms.

After driving a couple of hundred miles, they decided to stop and eat lunch, not at a rest area but at a fast-food restaurant. Their desire for this food was a leftover from their college days. A Burger King was found, and their cravings were satisfied with a hamburger and French fries. A brief time later, a major slowdown in traffic led them to an overturned tractor trailer carrying chickens. The cages were laying on the ground smashed, and chickens were running everywhere. The state police were trying to lead this chaos to a positive ending. As the boys passed this scene they roared with laughter, an event they would soon not forget.

The rest of the day was uneventful, and they soon found themselves at their friend's house, a one-hundred-acre dairy farm that had been in the family for three generations. Steve, their friend, was overjoyed to see them, giving them a gracious welcome and introducing them to his parents. The plan was to help Steve and his dad do the milking, have dinner, and then go into town for beer and a few games of pool, a popular pastime the boys enjoyed at college. Dinner was a large farm style affair consisting of roast beef, potatoes, fresh vegetables, and hot homemade bread. This was followed up with fresh-baked apple pie, served with vanilla ice cream for dessert. This would prove to be the best meal the boys would eat on their entire journey. They decided after this large dinner they would forgo their trip into town and enjoy the quiet of the porch. They told Steve about their planned adventure and reminisced about their college life. The evening was pleasant and soon it was after midnight, prompting the boys to call it a night. Minutes later they were sleeping, peaceful dreams capturing the quiet of the moment.

CHAPTER THREE

Rudy and Jamie woke early, their goal today was to drive across Indiana and Illinois and stop somewhere in Missouri for the night. They had breakfast with Steve, bid their farewells and were on their way. Travelling on the interstate in Indiana was like driving in Ohio, there was a lot of farmland and wide-open spaces. A silence overtook the campers as the sameness of the landscape and the hum of the truck's engine lulled them into a state of drowsiness. They decided to stop for lunch at a rest area and eat what Steve's mother had made for them just for this occasion. While eating, a small dog approached, obviously very hungry as he immediately assumed a begging position, his owner nowhere to be seen. The boys figured he was either lost or had been abandoned. The thought of leaving him at the rest area alone was disturbing, so they decided to make him a travelling companion, naming him Banjo.

Banjo was overjoyed to be rescued, jumping into the truck with no persuasion, settling into what would become his chair, and immediately going to sleep exhausted from his ordeal of being alone and lost. The decision to rescue Banjo was the right one, providing a new home for the dog, and a companion to break up the boredom of the long drive. A stop was made to pick up needed supplies for the dog, a leash, bowl, toy, and food was purchased. They made their way into Missouri, continuing to drive, deciding to stop when they reached Nebraska. The dog proved to be a good travelling companion, causing no unforeseen problems.

Since it was late, the boys decided to stop and stay in a Walmart parking lot, a service provided by the store at no cost. It was after midnight when they arrived. Pulling into the parking lot a car came speeding by them, almost crashing into their truck. Proceeding further into the parking lot they observed a car with its door open, and a figure not moving in the front seat. They felt it was their duty to stop and render aid if needed. A terrible surprise awaited them, the man had been shot and looked like he was clinging to life.

The police were called, and after what seemed an eternity they arrived with an ambulance. Unfortunately the man died, having a bullet wound to his chest. The boys were devasted by this unpleasant chain of events, never expecting to come upon a scene like this. The police surmised it was a robbery, involving drugs. The boys moved to the far end of the parking lot, hoping to get some rest. However, the image of the deceased man laying in his car haunted their thoughts, their young minds troubled by this experience. It made them realize they were now adults, facing the same world as their parents. A troubled sleep followed, the boys awakening to the daylight when employees arrived to start their workday, oblivious to the events that happened in the parking lot the night before. It was an episode that would never be forgotten by these young travellers.

CHAPTER FOUR

Rudy and Jamie were exhausted, not sleeping well because of the previous night's events. They ate a light breakfast, fed the dog, and took him for a walk. They were soon back on the highway travelling west towards Wyoming. They had decided to drive to Salt Lake City, Utah, find a campground and spend the night. The drive had been quiet until Jamie glanced in his mirror and saw what looked like a wave of motorcycles approaching at a high rate of speed. The bikers soon caught up with them and the boys realized they were Hells Angels, over a hundred in total.

They slowed as they passed the truck, the cyclists looking menacingly at the boys. Suddenly about twenty of the bikes veered in front of the truck, almost causing a collision.

The bikes slowed down causing the truck to do the same. The boys were now surrounded on three sides, the bikers no longer looking at them, only focusing straight ahead. Jamie and Rudy were terrified, not knowing what was going to happen next. After what seemed like an eternity, the bikers sped off knowing they had succeeded in scaring these travellers half to death. With hearts pounding in their chests, the boys exited at the next rest area to calm down, realizing how vulnerable they had been to a different outcome. They walked Banjo and joked about how they would reflect on this event in their journals.

Leaving the rest area, they continued on their adventure and soon found themselves in Wyoming. A most unusual variety of rolling hills and a semi desert landscape greeted them. This state is known for its large cattle ranches and horse farms, going back to the days of settlement. In certain areas it is wide open and treeless. At one time it was Indigenous land, which the natives did not easily or readily surrender. The boys decided to stop in a small town off the interstate, fill up with gas, find a park and eat lunch. Pulling into a locally-owned station, they noticed a small building beside it which housed the station owner's collection of Indigenous artifacts.

Deciding it was of interest, and after paying a small fee, Rudy and Jamie entered the building. It was a fascinating collection of over a thousand pieces, with a good explanation of the artifacts and their dates of origin. The boys were thrilled they had happened upon this exhibit of American history. They ate lunch and continued their journey, driving through a landscape that they had seen only in pictures, making them feel as if they were on another planet. The mood in the truck was happy; they sang songs to the radio that even Banjo joined in on. Tomorrow they would reach their destination, Virginia City, Nevada. A town still alive from its silver mining days, it was surrounded by ghost towns and abandoned mines that beckoned the boys to adventure.

With night coming on they were approaching their campground

outside Salt Lake City. Arriving at dusk, they settled into a spot where they could view the beautiful sunset this region was known for. They walked Banjo, ate a hearty dinner, and played cards till their eye lids became heavy. Retiring to bed, the pair were excited about what tomorrow would bring. The real adventure was about to begin.

CHAPTER FIVE

The boys left early, eager to reach their destination, Virginia City, Nevada in the early afternoon. This city had been established by the prospectors who flooded the area seeking their fortunes, prospecting the substantial amounts of silver that had been discovered here. Resuming their journey, the boys soon found themselves at the Nevada Welcome Center, where they had decided to stop for an early lunch and to walk Banjo. However, the dog had plans of his own. As soon as the door of the truck was opened, he jumped out and did not stop running until he was out of sight, disappearing into the wooded area behind the plaza. Jamie and Rudy were baffled, not understanding why he had done this. They knew he was gone, now just a memory from their past. They ate lunch hoping for his return, but he never came back.

The pair left the plaza with heavy hearts, already missing Banjo as they continued to Virginia City, arriving in the afternoon as planned. Once a boom town for the silver mining industry, it was now a small tourist town promoting the past of Nevada's rich history. Original buildings from the era dotted the main street as the boys walked the wooden sidewalk exploring the past culture of the people that called this area home. They ate an early dinner in the old saloon and played the slot machines that had been brought in for the tourist's enjoyment.

Rudy and Jamie had made reservations at a private campground outside of town where they would stay for the duration of the trip. After a short drive they arrived, a non-descript place void of shade, in a desert setting. They realized now how lucky they had been to plan this trip early in the year and not during the summer, as the heat then would be unbearable. They chose a site and prepared for their stay, leaving their departure date open. The awning on the truck proved to be a good cover from the sun, and with a picnic table placed under it they had a pleasant place to sit outside and enjoy the fresh air. The boys were happy with this arrangement and would enjoy dinners outdoors during this endeavor. They had rented a jeep but were not able to take possession of it until tomorrow, when the previous renters were to return it. This jeep would make it easier to get into areas where the terrain was known to be rough, allowing them to explore more secluded mine sites, and small abandoned ghost towns.

The evening was pleasant, the quiet of the desert and the sky with its millions of shining stars brought a calmness and peace to their souls they had not experienced before. Excitement mounted as the thought of exploring things from the past awaited them. Little did they know that some things are better left alone, and adventures can sometimes turn out to be not as expected. The boys retired to their bunks, looking forward to what tomorrow would bring, their dreams a prophecy of events that were to come.

CHAPTER SIX

The boys awoke to the sound of the cell phone ringing, it was the car rental company saying their jeep was ready to be picked up. Rousing themselves awake they had a light breakfast and were on their way, eager to start exploring. The plan was to pick up the jeep, drop the truck off at the campground, and drive to their first ghost town. There they would find a suitable campsite, and with the camping supplies they had brought with them they would tent camp for the night. All ghost towns had some sort of legend, and the town they had selected had experienced an unspoken tragedy, the loss of twenty townspeople killed during a mine cave in, their bodies never recovered. Soon after this accident, the remaining residents left, not wanting to continue to work the mine where such a catastrophe had unfolded. It was said the mournful souls of the dead miners could be heard, crying out for help. The town, called Silver Springs, was also said to be haunted, the restless souls of the dead left searching for their loved ones on moonlit nights.

The site was an hour's drive from Virginia City over rough terrain, being accessible only by vehicles with four-wheel drive and large tires, keeping this ghost town available to only the most devoted explorers. The boys packed their jeep and set out on their adventure, anxious to get to their destination. For the first half of the trip the road was good, but the turn off from the main road was challenging, being an old wagon trail used to transport supplies during its history as a mining town. They now understood why it was said that few people visited. After what seemed an eternity, old buildings came into view, a general store, a saloon, a barber shop, and abandoned houses. It was a surreal setting in a desert landscape, not to be duplicated by the hand of man, a process that took nature over a hundred years to create.

The old mine sat abandoned near the edge of town, sealed up with a wooden barrier. Trapped in time, twenty skeletons interred inside being its only friend. After surveying the area, the boys decided on a camping spot close to the old mine, hoping to hear the cries of the dead that legend described. After their camp was set up, they would hike the area around the town, but leave the exploration of the town and mine for tomorrow. Their tent went up, and their meager supplies were unpacked, including wood they had brought for a campfire.

Jamie and Rudy set out for their walk, but soon ran into a problem they were not expecting. There were rattle snakes that inhabited the area, making their hike slow and treacherous. Getting bit out here meant certain death, as help was far away. On the lighter side they saw a roadrunner, a bird native to the area, and unusual looking lizards. They found the spring that the town was named after, still providing fresh water, a testament to nature's resilience to stand up to such adverse conditions. They returned to camp, had dinner of cold fried chicken and salads purchased in Virginia City and kept in a cooler they had packed in with them. After darkness came, they lit their campfire, enjoyed s'mores and drank the fresh spring water nature had provided them. They retired to their tent, tired from their long day, not expecting their sleep to be interrupted by sheer terror, which would make them believers of the legend of Silver Springs.

CHAPTER SEVEN

Jamie woke with a start, a sense of terror gripping him. He woke Rudy and told him to be quiet. The mournful cries of the dead pierced the stillness of the night, the boys lay in silence as absolute terror gripped them. The legend of Silver Springs, which the boys had written off as fantasy and superstition, was now their reality. After a short while the cries stopped, leaving the silence of the night seem even more threatening. They turned the lantern on in the tent, hoping the light would alleviate of the anxiety they were feeling.

Then it started again, an inhumane wailing, the souls of the dead miners crying out for help, never finding the peace they sought from their sudden deaths. The boys felt trapped, now wishing they had never embarked on such a crazy adventure. The cries were intermittent, but kept the boys awake till the first signs of light beckoned them to go outside. The silence and isolation no longer embraced, replaced by a feeling of dread and escape from this paranormal hell. The ghost town beckoned, now an extension of the mine, drawing the boys like a magnet to explore the buildings of the miner's past.

An uneasy silence gripped the adventure seekers as they thought about their next move. They decided on staying an extra night, a moonlit night that was said to bring out the spirits of the dead to roam the town of Silver Springs. A daylight investigation was in order first, exploring both the mine and the town. They had agreed to stand tall against this paranormal activity. Being journalists, they felt they had a duty to bring truth to this tragedy.

They made their way to the mine first; the wood had been stripped away from the entrance allowing them easy entry. They had brought headlamps and powerful flashlights for this venture. Entering the mine, they felt a sense of profound sadness, the spirits of the dead dominating the atmosphere making it feel like a tomb. Their thoughts of sharing this environment with the spirits was unnerving. They followed the mine for a short distance until they encountered a wall of rock. They felt this was where the cave-in had occurred. Behind this wall of rock were the skeletons of the miners, a tragedy of their own making. The boys were silent wondering about the chaos this had brought to the people of Silver Springs, the sadness of the families that had lost loved ones in this tragedy. They turned and made their way back to the entrance, the light of the day healing their spirit as they exited this tomb of the dead.

The pair made their way into town to explore the empty buildings that once brought life to this isolated community. The buildings, stripped of their furnishings and their identities, now lay in ruin. As they explored the buildings, they marvelled at the thought that these structures once held hope and promise to the people that lived here, and that a tragedy would destroy those hopes and the town would be abandoned. Finding nothing of interest, they decided to return to camp to get some sleep and ready themselves for their night-time adventure; confronting the spirits that inhabited these buildings, searching for their loved ones they would never find. Much-needed rest was in order to prepare them for an experience they would not soon forget, giving them an insight into a spiritual world they would someday join, a destiny for all humans when their time came.

CHAPTER EIGHT

After a short nap, the boys awoke to the realization that their night-time adventure to the ghost town was only hours away. Eating canned tuna, beans, and bread for dinner, their food supplies were exhausted, meaning they would have to leave tomorrow. They built a fire using the rest of the wood they brought, planning to investigate the town after midnight. The moon shone brightly giving the town an eerie glow, the silence overwhelming the boys' imaginations of what they would encounter. The clock struck midnight as the boys readied themselves to find the truth, making their way into the town.

Upon arriving, the first thing they noticed were orbs of light everywhere, usually signalling paranormal energy. Dark shadows moved about as the boys shone powerful lights in and around the buildings. Jamie and Rudy were scared but did not let this overwhelming fear control their behavior. The slamming of the saloon doors caught their attention. Moving closer they could see the outline of a man, dressed in mining gear, standing by the building. The pair entered the saloon, apprehensive at what they would find. Suddenly, a loud crash caused the boys to run out of the building, fear gripping their souls.

The town was alive with paranormal activity; ghostly shadows everywhere, the stench of death overtaking the senses. The boys had seen enough, they decided to make their exit and return to camp, an overwhelming fear suddenly taking charge of their lives. They retired to their only refuge away from this horror, their tent. The night passed, sleeping was not possible. The boys waited for the un-earthly cries from the mine, which never came. Daylight could not come soon enough as they planned their exit from this hell in the desert, anxious to get back to their truck and some sense of normality.

The appearance of light drove the boys into action. The camp was quickly packed up and the boys left, knowing that their tale would be nothing but a delightful story to the people they told it to. They soon found themselves back at the main road, a sense of relief that they were returning to reality, this experience more like a nightmare that would not soon be forgotten. They reached their campsite without incident, and were soon in the comfort of the truck, an uneasy sleep taking over their tired souls.

The rest of their vacation was just that, a vacation; the remainder of their time here was spent visiting tourist sites, not ghost towns. The boys left Nevada with memories that would never be forgotten, their belief in the supernatural now a fact. A book was written of their adventure, fiction to the readers, but truth to the boys who experienced it, and to the souls of the dead who would never stop searching for the peace they deserved; a mirage in the desert, not ready to give up its secrets in its eternal search for answers, creating a mystery that will never be solved.

THE PLANTATION

‹ ✦✦✦✦✦ ›

CHAPTER ONE

Mary Bottoms, heir to her father's fortune made in New York real estate and construction, would never do without the finer things in life. She hated the cold of New York, opting to move south to New Orleans, a booming southern town. Being a young, hard-driven woman with good business sense, she decided to move to Louisiana, buy a plantation, and start a new life. What she never considered were the responsibilities of being a slave owner. These people, kidnapped from Africa and sold into slavery, worked the cotton fields around New Orleans. They were housed in squalid quarters away from the main house and not well-fed. They survived on their love for each other, their worth measured by the work they could accomplish.

Mary left New York by train and two weeks later she was in an opulent hotel in New Orleans. She contacted a real estate agent to arrange a showing of a working plantation in the morning. Tonight, she hired a carriage and enjoyed the nightlife of New Orleans. She loved the music, food, and excitement of the gambling establishment she visited. Mary enjoyed the evening and met Franklin, a wealthy business owner, with whom she would spend her future. He was smitten with Mary and accepted her invitation to accompany her on her property search. As his family had plantations in the area, and he owned the cotton brokerage houses in town, his input would be invaluable.

The next day Franklin picked up Mary in his buggy. He was familiar with the plantation she was going to see, and after a lengthy drive they arrived at their destination. The long winding laneway was lined by large southern oaks, their branches full of Spanish moss. Mary fell in love with the charm these trees brought to the plantation.

Mary also realized she was beginning to fall in love with Franklin, who felt the same way. In time, their love would blossom propelling them into an unexpected union. Mary surveyed the scenery and was sure she was going to buy the property. However, the end result of this decision might make her wish she had never left New York.

CHAPTER TWO

Franklin and Mary entered the plantation house, which exuded Southern charm. The rooms were furnished with period pieces, which had been shipped from abroad, and cabinets built by the best craftsman in New Orleans. Slaves worked in the home, attending to the owners' needs. The house staff were selected from slaves who demonstrated devotion to their owners, acceptance of their situation, a neat appearance and un-wavering obedience. Working in the house provided them with a better life, including improved quarters, healthier food, and an escape from the unbearable heat of the fields.

After a tour of the inside, Mary and Franklin retreated outside to inspect the grounds. Beautiful flowers and trees graced the property, meticulously cared for by the gardeners. They toured the fields, watching the slaves harvesting the cotton, which would be sent to Franklin's brokerage houses and then on to the mills. An inspection of the Negroes dwellings found a collection of wooden shacks in disrepair. The state of these homes indicated the current owners did not take proper care of their property. There were numerous owners who gave their slaves little, rarely providing needed medical care or life's basic necessities. If they died, the slaves were buried in the nearby cemetery. The owners hired handlers to oversee the laborers in the fields, who were often treated with cruelty and received harsh punishment if they did not follow orders.

Mary thought this property would be a sound investment and, with Franklin's encouragement, she planned to contact an attorney to begin the purchase process when she returned to town. The pair headed back to the city, visiting Franklin's horse ranch outside of New Orleans on the way. Franklin was wealthy, having capitalized on his family's ties to the area. He started his own brokerage house, proved himself to be a successful business owner and soon became the dominate cotton broker in New Orleans. He had been married, but three months after the wedding his wife had died in a carriage accident.

Arriving at Franklin's house, lunch was prepared for the couple. Franklin wanted to show Mary his property, asking if she would like to view it from horseback. Mary was obliged, and they headed to the corral, picked two horses, and were on their way. After a two-hour ride, they were back at the stables. Franklin returned Mary to her hotel saying he would see her tomorrow, giving her a small kiss on the forehead before leaving. Mary felt lucky to have met Franklin, but she knew little about him. For now, the only thing that mattered was the strong attraction she felt toward him.

CHAPTER THREE

The next day Franklin called for Mary, telling her they would be taking a ride on one of the paddle-wheeled steamships docked in town. These boats offered all-day outings on the Mississippi River, with food and gambling being the main attractions. Mary had never been on one of these boats and was looking forward to the experience. After a short ride they reached the waterfront, tethered their carriage, and joined the crowd that had gathered to board. A short blast from the horn on the boat indicated boarding would begin shortly. Franklin had reserved a stateroom, where they deposited their belongings and then made their way to the deck to watch the boat leave.

With a blast from the whistle, huge columns of black smoke rose from the smokestacks as the ship pulled away from the dock and headed into the river, maneuvering around the boats waiting for dock space. New Orleans was a busy trade port, with goods arriving from cities upriver, as well as overseas.

Franklin and Mary headed to the restaurant, where platters of delicious, southern-style fare were offered. After dining, they walked hand-in-hand along the outside deck enjoying the sunshine and scenery. Mary was surprised at the amount of activity on the water. Boats of every shape and size passed by, with people waving to one another.

Inside the ship a live band began playing; Franklin took Mary's hand and led her to the dancefloor. They spent the next half-hour dancing and getting to know each other. Afterwards they entered the casino, trying their luck at the roulette wheel and baccarat tables. Mary watched as Franklin played his favorite poker game, seven-card stud. In what seemed like no time, it was announced that the boat would soon be returning to port.

The couple decided to return to their stateroom to wait for the boat to dock. There was a flurry of activity onboard as the people prepared to return to New Orleans. In the stateroom the couple discussed the meeting with the plantation owners and their lawyers about the sale of the plantation, which was scheduled for tomorrow. Within a brief time, they were back in port collecting their buggy, and heading to Franklin's place to spend the rest of the day.

Mary had loved the boat, as much as she loved spending time with Franklin. She was surprised when he informed her his mother was coming for a visit this afternoon. They went to the stables, where Mary watched him care for the horses, while they waited for his mother. Upon her arrival, they went indoors for tea. Mary found Franklin's mother to be outgoing and charming, and a friendship was born.

Franklin soon took Mary back to her hotel, telling her he would see her tomorrow. She retired to her room where she spent the evening reading and thinking of Franklin. This was Mary's first meaningful relationship with a man, and she hoped she could manage it responsibly.

CHAPTER FOUR

The morning found Mary at the lawyer's office; Franklin, the plantation owners, and their lawyer were also present. They reviewed the plantation's financial statements for the last five years and discussed the transfer of ownership of the slaves. Mary, having her father's business acumen, had her lawyer offer a cash deal twenty per cent lower than market value. With little thought, the owners accepted the offer knowing another opportunity might be a long time coming. Tomorrow they would meet at the Bank of New Orleans to complete the transaction.

Franklin offered Mary the use of his guest cottage until she took possession of her new property. She happily accepted and the couple returned to the hotel to pick up her belongings. That afternoon Mary found herself in Franklin's guest house, with her own servant to take care of her needs. Mary was pleasantly surprised with the young Black girl who was well-spoken and polite. Franklin had to go to his office to deal with things his managers could not oversee. He had a few contracts to negotiate, needed to sign documents, and see if any emergencies had arisen.

At dinner that evening, Mary told Franklin she was fond of her attendant and was instantly chastised for her feelings. He informed Mary the number one rule of being a slave owner was not to befriend the slaves, as trusting them could lead them to take advantage of you. Mary was disappointed to hear this, but understood what Franklin was telling her.

The following morning the papers for the plantation purchase were signed and a bank draft was issued to the previous owners. Mary was now the proud owner of the cotton plantation. All the furnishings had been included in the sale, as the owners were moving to California. Mary was to take possession of the property in a week. The news of the sale created anxiety among the slaves who feared the changes a new owner inevitably makes. Sometimes this transition causes a peak in slaves running away as they fear the worse.

Mary spent the next week with Franklin, helping around the ranch, riding horses, and enjoying the nightlife in New Orleans most evenings.

They had fallen in love, and Mary wondered if it were going to lead to marriage, as she knew Franklin could help, and protect, her as she began her new venture.

CHAPTER FIVE

Mary's move to the plantation was unsettling for the slaves; knowing little about their new owner created panic among them. The night before Mary moved into the plantation house a slave ran away. The earlier owners informed Mary of the situation. They told her the handlers were searching for him, but if the bloodhounds were not successful, she should consider placing a bounty on his head. This turmoil was not what Mary was expecting. Instead of the smooth transition Mary hoped for, she was thrust into something more sinister, human slavery.

Following Franklin's advice, they met with the slaves in the morning. Mary introduced herself and Franklin and assured those gathered no radical changes were planned. Against Franklin's wishes, she ordered a feast prepared for the slaves as a gesture of good will. She then toured their decrepit homes and ordered building materials for repairs, hoping to bring a bit of happiness into their community. Franklin hated what he was seeing but said nothing, he would wait until he had control over the plantation, at which time he would put a stop to this nonsense of being kind to the slaves.

A week later, over dinner at one of New Orleans' finest restaurants, Franklin proposed, and Mary accepted. They agreed to become equal partners in the plantation, with Franklin reimbursing Mary for half the cost of the property. He would sell his ranch and keep his horses at the plantation, where a new barn would be built to accommodate them. Since this was his second marriage, and Mary had no family nearby, they decided a small wedding at the plantation would be appropriate. Their wedding day soon arrived, with a small gathering of twenty people seeing the ceremony and celebrating the marriage with a bountiful dinner.

Franklin completed his transaction regarding the plantation, which gave Mary a sense of relief knowing she had someone with experience helping run the business. Franklin had realized his own dream, owning a plantation and the slaves that came with it. In truth, Franklin was a devious and cruel man, something he hid well from Mary. He planned to cheat her by lowballing the amount of cotton harvested, pocketing the ill-gotten gains for himself.

Franklin treated Mary well at first, but over the following weeks she noticed a change in his behaviour. He became controlling, angered easily, and was disrespectful when he addressed her. Mary was concerned, as she had heard that some men transform after marriage, becoming abusive and domineering. She feared things could get physical in time. Mary's dream was turning into her nightmare, one she had no idea how to escape.

CHAPTER SIX

Mary felt she was losing control of her say in the plantation, as Franklin was no longer asking her opinion, making all decisions on his own. He gave her no information about the finances and tried to keep her away from the slaves. She had befriended them, which Franklin viewed as a threat to his control. Rumours circulated about Franklin's cruelty, dishing out undeserved punishments for perceived infractions, using the tip of his whip on slaves who he felt were not working hard enough.

Mary's most trusted servant pulled her aside and told her that Franklin had been raping the female slaves, including one as young as thirteen. He had told the slaves if his wife found out, he would start hanging them until the person who let out his secret stepped forward and took the blame. Mary was appalled that this was happening without her knowledge. She did not know what to do. If she confronted Franklin, he would deny it, accusing her of believing the slaves over him. He was already calling her "slave lover" for the empathy she showed towards them, which he hated. There was no authority to report this to, as the abuse of a slave was not a crime.

Mary's love for Franklin had been replaced by hatred. She now realized how evil he was, and how easily he had manipulated her. Getting involved with this man had been a huge mistake. She feared for her own life, knowing dropping her would solve all of his problems. She had to be smart and continue living with this man, pretending to not know the truth, while she sought a solution to the problem.

Fate was already catching up to Franklin. The male slaves, their lives becoming unbearable under Franklin's tyranny, and having admiration for Mary, decided to take matters into their own hands. They formed a plan which would result in the sacrifice of two lives in exchange for improving the lives of the other slaves. Franklin's brutality had to stop, even if it meant his death.

The plan was to grab Franklin and hang him from the same tree he was continually threatening to use to punish them. Franklin was a scrawny man who would not put up much of a fight. After they hung him, they would run, using two of Franklin's horses. They hoped to not get caught but knew if captured they would be killed for their crime. This plan would have to be conducted soon for fear that it might be exposed. Change was coming to Mary's life, a change she deserved but was not expecting.

CHAPTER SEVEN

The rope in the tree swayed in the wind, ready for its newest victim. Franklin left the house at his usual time to complete a slave count, making sure no one had run during the night. Two men were ready, waiting in ambush, nervous as they thought about the task ahead of them. Franklin, whip in hand, was angry. One of the slaves had been less than cooperative yesterday, and he was about to teach him a lesson. He had waited to mete out the punishment this morning, planning to whip him and send him out to the fields. Franklin took pleasure in knowing sweat in the slave's open wounds would intensify the pain he felt.

As Franklin neared the slaves' quarters the two men jumped him, threw a burlap sack over his head, and wrestled him to the ground. Franklin never saw them coming. He struggled but the men being larger and stronger made his efforts futile. As soon as the men tied Franklin's hands behind his back, he knew what was coming. He pleaded for his life, offering them whatever they wanted to let him go. The slaves knew better than to listen to his lies, removed the burlap sack and gagged him. They drug him to the tree, a look of terror on his face. Franklin was about to pay dearly for the crimes he had committed against these defenseless people. They slid the noose over his head and soon it was over. Franklin was dead, hanging at the end of the rope.

The slaves congregated around the tree, as word spread that someone had been hung. They expected to see one of their own, never their master swinging in the wind. A gasp of horror went through the crowd, as they now wondered what the punishment would be. The men that ambushed Franklin had quietly left the scene, retrieved two horses, and were now on their way to New Orleans. They would ditch the horses as they got closer to town, and mingle with the people, allowing them time to make their next move. New Orleans had freed slaves, but they had to carry papers, which these men did not have.

Franklin was found hanging by the field supervisors when they arrived for work. He was cut down and authorities were called. Mary was shocked when she learned of Franklin's death, but thought his murder was justified. Two days later the escaped slaves had not been found. The horses were recovered and returned. A fugitive hunt was ongoing, as white people sought revenge for Franklin's death. If captured, the slaves would be hung in the town square, to the delight of cheering spectators.

CHAPTER EIGHT

Franklin had not been well-liked nor trusted by his family or the business community. His days of dishonesty were over, and many in the community felt he got what he deserved. His brokerage firm was left to Mary, a change he had made to his will to gain Mary's trust before they married. However, he had no intention of actually leaving his assets to her. The sale of this business was immediate, as Mary had no interest in running it herself.

Mary, enriched by this sale, gave up the cotton business and freed her slaves. The ones that chose to stay were treated well. Years passed and eventually the freed slaves moved on, finding their own way in life. Mary, unable to sell the plantation abandoned it, and moved to New York with her long-term servant, as the rumours of civil war gripped the country.

The two slaves that had hung Franklin had been taken in by freed slaves who hid them. With Mary's financial help they were able to make it to Kentucky, where with the help of the underground railroad they made it to Canada.

Months after Mary's arrival in New York civil war broke out. The war over slavery was brutal, killing hundreds of thousands of Americans on both sides, with the North being the eventual victor and slaves being emancipated. When the North captured New Orleans, soldiers ransacked and burned Mary's plantation, cementing an end to her misguided venture.

Mary died at the age of ninety. She left her property and money to her caretaker, who had come from New Orleans with her. The end of slavery started a new chapter in the nation's history. Black people had gained their freedom, but were still discriminated against and treated poorly, which continues to be a problem today.

THE ISLAND

✦ ✦ ✦ ✦ ✦ ✦ ✦

CHAPTER ONE

The Katie Ann, a small sailboat, made its way through the warm
Atlantic waters. Annette and Bob had purchased the boat in
Ft. Lauderdale, Florida. Their first trip in their retirement was
going to be exploring the Bahamas. Located east of Florida, this chain of
islands spreads over hundreds of miles and has a history of untold adventure; a spot for pirates trying to find a safe place to hide their ill-gotten
gains, as well as a destination for the slave ships, arriving from across the
Atlantic on their way to the Americas with their loads of human cargo,
to anchor. Now the islands' allure is its beautiful year-round tropical
climate; its warm waters and gorgeous beaches enjoyed by boaters and
tourists from all over the world.

The first part of the couple's trip was to explore the more popular
islands, Abaco, Grand Bahama, and New Providence. They then sailed
to the more remote islands, uninhabited and rarely visited by boaters,
leaving a pristine environment, undisturbed except by the hands of
nature. The sailboat rode the small waves, like a bobber on the end of a
fishing line, its size small, compared to the breadth of the ocean it had
become part of. The couple enjoyed the sunshine and the warm winds
blowing the sails on the boat. The seabirds circled, hoping for food, as a
sea turtle surfaced curious as to what was disturbing its habitat.

They headed to an island they had found from satellite pictures taken off the internet, its coordinates carefully recorded. They were soon coming upon it, a grain of sand compared to the ocean that surrounded it. The island came into view, a beautiful tropical oasis; palm trees swayed in the wind and a, sheltered lagoon where they could anchor their sailboat came into view. As they approached the island, a sudden grinding sound and an abrupt stop threw the couple forward. The sound of water running into the boat could be heard coming from below, causing the young couple to panic. The trip had turned from being idyllic into now what looked like a disaster.

The boat had hit a reef, unmarked on their chart, leaving a small gash in the hull. They were lucky it was low tide, as they had time to salvage items from the boat before it went below the waves. The small dinghy, kept on the sailboat for such emergencies, was put to use. They had just completed their second trip to shore when the tide took the sailboat underwater, leaving only the mast sticking above the surface, a permanent reminder of the situation they were in. Annette and Bob sat on the beach. They were alone, stranded on this island which would provide them with enough food so they would not go hungry. The tranquility and beauty of the moment captured their hearts. Fatigue overtook them as their unexpected adventure had left them exhausted. Tomorrow they would decide their next step forward, an extended stay on this island could be expected, the new Robinson Crusoe they would be.

CHAPTER TWO

The couple stirred, the sun coming up over the horizon and the crashing of the waves on the beach reminded them where they were and why. The warm tropical air caressed their faces as they sat up taking in their surroundings. The ocean looked endless, making them feel small in this giant world of water that surrounded them. Bob looked up; coconut trees loaded with fruit surrounded them. The inside of these nuts. when ripe, would provide a food source and liquid if no fresh water could be found. They decided to explore the area and look for a more permanent place to build a shelter.

They first walked around the island, a sandy beach allowing them easy access to any areas they wanted to explore. They noticed iguanas everywhere, sunning themselves in the hot tropical sun. Curly tailed lizards were also plentiful, helping to keep the bug population down. The interior of the island was heavily treed with thick vegetation; the fruit and banana trees would keep them from going hungry. With the dinghy they could fish, their fishing equipment salvaged from the now sunken sailboat. They decided the lagoon where they had landed was the best area to build a more permanent shelter, and a good place to keep the dinghy.

Upon further investigation the couple discovered the island had caves, a product of the geology this area had been blessed with. They thought that moving into one of these caves until an outside shelter could be built was the best way forward. They had no way of communicating, as their satellite phone was under water shortly after hitting the reef, making it unusable. To the outside world they were two people lost on a sailboat in a vast water-world that takes no prisoners, their existence unknown to family and friends.

They took stock of the supplies they had salvaged; a stove and propane, a good supply of lighters, lamps, blankets, and assorted other important things they would use in the future. Today they would assess their situation. They knew their only option was to wait, in the hope that a boat would come close enough to answer their SOS for help. A large bonfire would be built on the beach to try to attract attention to their desperate situation, but hope was not on their side, as no one was looking for them. They had picked this island for one reason, because of its isolation, so being found by happenstance was unlikely, they were here for the long haul.

Annette and Bob decided a Ficus, a mammoth of a tree, would make a good place to build a treehouse, getting them up off the ground. This would also give them a better view of the ocean, the tree being on the edge of the treeline that bordered the beach. They would use lumber salvaged from the boat at low tide, and materials found on the island to make this construction possible. A plan was coming together, making them feel a little more confident that this might work out. They knew they had to make a new life here until they were rescued, only fate would know what their future held.

CHAPTER THREE

The fury of the wind and the loud thunder woke the couple from their sleep. They had decided to move into a large cave for shelter until the treehouse was built, providing them with a place to keep dry and to store their belongings. The intensity of the lightning put on a spectacular show, lighting up the surrounding area, bringing the island to life, creating an almost supernatural atmosphere. These storms are common in the Caribbean and would become an important source of rain water for the couple, as there was little hope of finding a fresh water spring. The rumble of the thunder became distant as the storm moved on, leaving a steamy sauna in its wake, the hot tropical sun and humidity creating a fog like mist as it evaporated the water from the vegetation.

Bob and Annette decided to re-enact their teenage years; stripping naked they jumped into the cooling water of the lagoon, splashing, and playing like two children enjoying their youth again. They retrieved their snorkeling gear, salvaged from the sailboat, and enjoyed looking at the colourful tropical fish swimming below them; the fish occasionally brushing against their feet tickling their toes. After an hour of fun it was time to get to work. They would ready a large bonfire on the beach to light if a passing boat were spotted, a chance to show their presence on this lonely uninhabited island, and the miracle of a rescue to take place.

Tomorrow if the weather was calm they would take the dinghy, return to the sailboat, and see if they could salvage additional items they could use in the future. There was a large amount of bamboo on the island, a great construction material for the frame of the treehouse. This structure would then be covered in palm fronds, which would keep out the hot sun and rain. A floor would be built from lumber salvaged from the boat. Large natural crotches in the tree made it easier for this construction to be a success.

They retrieved their fishing gear, readied the dinghy and were soon out into the blue waters of the lagoon catching a variety of fish, most edible. Bob was familiar with the different species that called this water home. They cooked the fish for lunch and then laid down together, snuggling, comfort washing over them. They dreamed of being rescued, joined again with family and friends in Florida in their own comfortable home, with all the necessities of life set before them. But dreams they were, as reality was quick to return upon awakening.

The couple needed to accept the situation they were in, prepare for a prolonged stay, and hope someday to be rescued. Bob and Annette gathered fruit and with a blanket retired to the beach to watch the sunset and enjoy the company they provided each other. They held hands, her head on his shoulder, as the sun dipped below the horizon, signalling the end of another day. The night sky, its stars lighting the beach, the full moon casting its light on the water, and the waves splashing the shoreline created a smorgasbord for the senses enjoying this island paradise, capturing spirits that might not ever want to leave. A place in heaven they had found.

CHAPTER FOUR

The couple awoke with a mystery on their hands. Around midnight they thought they heard singing and loud voices coming from the area where the beach was located. Dismissing this as hopeful thinking, they blamed the incident on the wind blowing through the trees.

Bob and Annette were still eating the food they had recovered from the boat, supplemented by an abundance of fresh fruit from the island. They needed meat in their diet, and the only thing they had seen here that resembled that were the iguanas that were everywhere.

They readied the dinghy and were soon at the sailboat, its deck above water for a brief time everyday at low tide. They retrieved some more items that were salvageable, including containers which they hoped to use to capture rain water. A lack of proper tools kept them from being able to harvest wood from the boat, so a different material would have to be found to build the floor on the treehouse. They made their way back to land, deciding to do a more in-depth study of the island. This could result in them changing their plans, depending on what they found.

The land area was not that big; when they walked the beach they had estimated it to be about three miles long and two miles wide. They crossed the island near its middle, to see if there was anything they could find that would make their stay here more comfortable. The first thing they came across of interest was the remnants of a shovel, an old shovel. They wondered where it came from and what it had been used for. Another mystery to ponder.

Moving into the island's interior they were shocked, but excited, by what they found. They went to examine an unusual pile of rocks which appeared as if they had been placed there. Upon drawing closer they heard the gurgling of water. It was a fresh water spring, a find as rare as gold and much more important; a commodity they needed to stay alive.

A system of caves dotted the area and signs of use, from a long time ago, were everywhere. White bleached bones left in old firepits, remnants of meat brought from the boats to cook and eat after making the trek to the water source were found. People spent the night here partying, as containers had been left, their necks sticking out of the sand. The couple thought this island had been a hideout for pirates to escape their enemies. Knowing and keeping this water source a secret would give no one an excuse to want to come here, but would have provided the scofflaws with a commodity that could make their stay long if needed.

The pair decided they would come back at a later date to explore the caves further to see if they could identify the people that had left all the clues to their presence behind. The found shovel came to mind. If they had been pirates, what else might they have left behind? The thought of plundered treasure from ships plying the ocean buried here became a real possibility. The chances of finding this gold unlikely, but a dream they could think about, and a hobby they could pursue as they found their situation changing. Their new dreams realized as this lifestyle took hold of them, keeping them here forever, their destiny sealed.

CHAPTER FIVE

Nights on a tropical island are paradise, the quiet disturbed only by a strong breeze whispering through the palm fronds and the sound of the warm waters of the gulf meeting the shoreline. Bob lay awake, his eyes open. He looked over at Annette, who was asleep, grateful that she was with him and glad he was not having to deal with this situation by himself. Bob had been thinking about their plans to build a treehouse, unrealistic because of their lack of having the right tools to do the job. They had tried to cut a piece of bamboo with the hand saw they had retrieved from the boat, but it was no match for the dense wood of this tropical plant. They would abandon this idea, instead choosing a cave as their new homestead. This would provide a safer shelter from the storms and even the occasional hurricane that were known to frequent this area. Like house hunters they would go look at caves, finding the perfect one that would suit their needs.

Early morning swims were the norm, a chance to cool off and refresh from the steamy humid climate they were living in, the cool breezes off the water their saviour. They retrieved the dinghy and went fishing; the fish they caught were turned into lunch, cooked on the beach. Occasionally they saw a speck on the water, a distant boat too far away to realize their plight, their rescue not easy. The spring they had come across was somewhat of a miracle. Almost all of these small islands harbored no fresh water, this one being an anomaly and a well-kept secret to the people who had used it in the past.

After a discussion they decided to stay in the cave they were in. Its proximity to the lagoon, the only one on the island, and its location minutes from the beach, made it the most sensible location to pick. The days seemed endless as monotony set in, similarity taking over their lives. They hoped rescue would come soon.

The full moon shone bright. The couple were awakened by the sound of singing and boisterous voices, much louder and clearer than the last incident. They looked at each other in disbelief at the thought that they were not alone. They decided to investigate. Making their way toward the beach, the singing grew louder. They were not ready for what they saw, panic rising in their chests as they tried to understand. In front of them was the illusion of a band of pirates with shovels and a treasure chest, digging a large hole and merrily singing. The leader of this group turned to the approaching young couple, raised his arms, and said, "This can be yours. Look carefully at this chest of gold, silver, and jewels. It is hidden on this island for you to find." This apparition then vanished, leaving only the stillness of the night to reign.

This encounter left Annette and Bob bewildered, but excited, at the prospect of this new adventure now facing them. The thoughts of pirate gold dominated their dreams. A chest to be found, a pirate's secret about to be given up; the hunt would soon begin, the end game not certain. The quest for gold was theirs.

CHAPTER SIX

The storm raged outside, the palm trees swaying in the wind, the coconuts falling to the ground, their loosened fronds littering the island creating a carpet-like setting. The hurricane had come up quickly catching Bob and Annette by surprise. The morning after their encounter at the beach, the skies had darkened, the winds changed direction, and the feeling of an ominous threat filled the air. They knew they were in an area that was susceptible to hurricanes and living in South Florida made them realize the similarities of this weather event. They prepared by bringing everything inside the cave that would blow away. They retrieved fresh water from the spring, and collected fruit to eat, not knowing how long this ordeal was going to last. They moved all of their possessions from near the entrance to an area in the back of the cave. They had no way of knowing how strong the winds were going to be.

The storm raged on for hours, finally the eye of the hurricane crossed over the island, creating a deceiving calm before the second half of the storm would return, bringing the hurricane back to its former glory, a power not to be reckoned with. Finally the winds calmed, and the couple ventured outside. Except for trees uprooted, and an endless supply of palm fronds and coconuts littering the ground, there seemed to be minor damage. The couple walked toward the beach and upon arriving were shocked at what they saw. Their sailboat was in dry dock, sitting entirely on shore; the storm surge returning their boat to them. This was a windfall for the castaways, as much could be salvaged from it now that it was on land.

The events of the last twenty-four hours had pushed their encounter on the beach with the supernatural to the back of their minds. It was now taking center stage again as they remembered the unimaginable incident that occurred. They realized the island they were shipwrecked on had been a hangout and hideaway for pirates, whose souls decided to haunt this favorite place of theirs forever. The couple decided to beachcomb the island to see if the ocean had given up any secret's worth keeping. They also felt this would be a suitable time to talk about the pirates' treasure hidden somewhere on the island and how they were going to find it.

The first, and most logical, place to look was in the area of the spring that they had found, where it seemed there had been human activity. That adventure would come later. For now the couple held hands as they walked in the sand. After the storm, the breeze was cooler, and the moment captured a feeling of never wanting to return to their past life. A sense of peace not felt elsewhere gripped their spirit, making them feel as one with their surroundings; an acceptance by nature to allow their survival and enjoy God's creation with no interference. They walked the beach, their next adventure around the corner, in what was shaping up to be an unexpected life on this not so boring island.

CHAPTER SEVEN

The day was beautiful, a bright blue sky and warm southerly breezes dominated the day, making the young couple appreciate this new life they had been given. All the necessities for survival could be harvested here, varieties of fruit, fish, nutritious coconut milk, and fresh water. An unlimited meat source, iguana, a large edible lizard which natives of these Caribbean islands consider a healthy meal, was also available. They had yet to eat one of these reptiles but would try the meat at a later date.

A number of sea shells had washed up on the beach, different varieties, including large conch full of delicious meat. Bob and Annette had discussed building a tiki hut with all the downed palm fronds, a place to enjoy outside, out of the sun. They would use these large colorful shells for decoration in this new structure. Except for seaweed, there was not much else new littering the beach. They walked in silence, their thoughts turning to their new life, a stress-free environment away from all the chaos that has swept over our planet. Theses surroundings had brought a peace to their souls that grew each day, just like their love for one another, which was growing stronger.

Walking farther the pair came upon a small pile of debris, pieces of old wood, a pewter mug and shockingly, a solid gold chain. These items came from a ship wrecked hundreds of years ago, blown onto the reef that lays off this secluded island and deposited on the beach by the churning seas. They continued on their way until they were back at their starting point, never expecting the surprise, the gold chain that they had found.

They took the dinghy out fishing. They enjoyed using this small boat for recreation also, missing the feel of water underneath them and the warm ocean breezes blowing through their hair as they plied the waters with their sailboat, an independence that was now in their past. What was in their future was the tiki hut they were going to build. They started by gathering palm fronds that the hurricane had blown off the trees. These dead fronds had been used by the natives of different cultures to build shelters from the rain and sun. If built properly, these huts provide one hundred per cent protection against these elements.

Annette and Bob also collected the downed coconuts, a source of liquid and fresh food. They gathered conch, and with the fish they caught planned a fresh seafood dinner this evening. They examined their boat which had been fished out of the ocean by the hurricane and deposited on the beach. It could now be inspected more closely, further salvaging possible. The boat was dirty, full of seaweed and sand. The couple would decide at a later date what their plans would be regarding the boat. A delicious dinner that rivaled those found in the best restaurants in Florida was served picnic style on the beach. They enjoyed this gift of food given up for their survival, a gift that would keep on giving as long as they made this island home.

CHAPTER EIGHT

There were many species of birds on the island, all of which were singing at the same time, waking Bob and Annette from a deep early morning sleep. They lay awake, eyes open, listening. The soft music of the birds' song brought back memories of growing up in Wisconsin, the early summer mornings awash in music from a bird population eager to find a mate and raise a family. Bob wondered if they would ever see home again. The amount of time that had passed since their reported disappearance, had led authorities to believe their sailboat had sunk, and they had drowned. Rescue would only be by happenstance; a couple like themselves looking for a secluded place to explore and enjoy in private would find them and be their ticket home.

Further discussion had led to a change of plans again. Instead of building a new structure, the tiki hut, Bob and Annette had decided to spend their energy cleaning up the boat, turning the interior into a livable space they could use like a cottage. This was going to be done under the assumption another hurricane would not take the boat to its final resting place, on the bottom of the ocean. They would use the palm fronds to enclose the deck and make a roof, which would help block the hot sun and keep excessive rainwater off their heads. A plan was shaping up. They might as well make the best of it because being found anytime soon did not seem to be in their future.

Curiosity concerning the pirate's treasure had never left Bob's and Annette's minds. They decided to go back and start checking caves that were located near the fresh water spring. They left after lunch, later finding themselves at the spring, refreshing themselves with the water after a hot walk in the afternoon sun. They carefully combed the area looking for anything old or unusual. Finding nothing outside they entered a large spacious cave. They had a propane lantern which worked well to give them light. They had salvaged two boxes of propane cylinders from the boat, assuring them of light and fuel to cook with for a long time.

They slowly made their way deeper into the cave, the light illuminating an empty space barren of any sign of human activity. The stillness of the cave brought back memories of the ghostly encounter with the pirates at the beach on that moonlit night not too long ago. A sound startled them. The wind was blowing in, a storm raging outside; a lightning flash brought the cave to life. The couple both had the sense that some one was watching them, so they exited out into the storm, no longer feeling safe. They went home resigned to the fact that finding the pirates' gold would not be an easy task unless luck was on their side. Tomorrow they would start working on cleaning up their sailboat, making it serve a purpose again as their quest for gold started to dominate their thoughts. Were the pirates really ready to give up their booty, or was this just a cruel trick? Only time would solve this mystery as their new life unfolded in front of them, a future untold.

CHAPTER NINE

The night sky shone with the light of a million stars. Bob and Annette laid on the beach, looking skyward, mesmerized by the constellations that could be seen. Their imaginations stimulated, they would travel the universe, discovering new worlds, sharing their stories of earth with the civilizations they discovered. Like waking from a dream, the sudden sound of a rogue wave hitting the shoreline brought them back to a reality, their real world cast upon them.

The days were spent preparing the boat for its new purpose, a beach house. The downstairs was readied for sleeping and relaxing, the top deck for sunbathing and enjoying the atmosphere, the ocean and its breezes appreciated on a hot humid day. After days of work the interior of the boat was finished. They moved their belongings from the cave, glad to have a shelter where they felt secure. They now had a hatch that locked down if needed, to keep them dry and safe during the severe storms they would encounter being so close to the beach.

Their first night in their new home was peaceful, the only sound being the ocean, always making them aware of where they were. Sometimes on a beautiful night they would move to the top deck, the night sky always a pleasure to enjoy. The warm breeze and the ocean lulling the couple into an undisturbed sleep, till the first rays of sunlight would wake them, the early morning light signalling another day. With the boat being finished, they could now concentrate on the treasure, a story not to be believed by any sensible individual. The pirates were an illusion, the product of an unexplained happening, a not uncommon event on this mysterious planet we live on.

The dream of returning to Florida was now a daily part of Bob and Annette's life. The reality was they were castaways trapped on this island prison, a paradise only if you are free to leave. Many boats could be seen on the horizon, small objects on a vast ocean, never straying close enough to acknowledge their presence. Small planes flew over, never noticing their cries for help printed in the sand. They had written an account of their adventure, hoping someday they would be rescued and could share their story with the unsuspecting world.

This morning was warm and pleasant, so the couple decided to take the dinghy and travel to the reef. Enjoying the serene feeling of being on the water, they travelled the short distance and anchored the boat offshore of where they had found the gold chain. They had brought snorkelling gear with them to see if they could find anything else of value under the water. The ocean had given up one treasure, the rest they would have to find themselves. Two hours went by, the beautiful coral and fish were the only treasures to be found. They returned home, a feeling of peace capturing their souls, their island life again desired, the feeling capturing the moment, a desire to stay forever.

CHAPTER TEN

The caves on the island were many; the land was sitting on limestone, a porous rock found on the islands in the Bahamas. Over the course of millions of years the water eroded large holes in the limestone leaving vast openings in the rocks that we call caves. In one of these caves Annette and Bob suspected there were valuables beyond belief, a pirate treasure worth a fortune. They readied the supplies they would need for this adventure and left.

After a brief time they reached the area they wished to explore, a large cave with passages they had briefly looked at during an earlier visit. They lit their lanterns and entered. The cave was damp and cooler than outside. A feeling of unease swept over them, knowing the pirates were watching. As they moved to the back of the cave toward one of the passages, a sudden glint caught their eyes. They recoiled in fear. Looking up they were greeted by a shiny white human skull looking down at them, as if to challenge them to enter this unknown realm of pirate territory.

They made their way forward, the passage empty, the silence deafening. They soon found themselves in another large open area. Suddenly the silence was broken by the sound of song. The pirates, not to be seen, were singing, their voices filling the sizable cavern with sound. The couple stood in awe trying not to be fearful. Then all the sound stopped, leaving total silence. An orb appeared as if leading the way, guiding the pair down another unknown passage. They trusted that they were not being led to a bad outcome; lost, dying in the cave, their bones joining the pile of other deceived individuals who had put their trust in these spirits.

They would not be fooled; they turned and made their way back to the last cavern, deciding to choose their own way forward. Shining a lantern against the limestone walls revealed a painting of a skull and cross bones on a black background. It was a replica of the pirate flag that once graced the buccaneers' ships as they plundered merchant vessels coming and going from the new world. The couple inspected the room, coming upon a small opening only large enough to crawl through. They entered and after a short crawl found themselves in another large open cavern. There they found the remnants of a party, empty bottles littered the floor along with forgotten mugs, a tobacco pipe, a broken knife, and the remains of an eye patch. Further investigation led to no surprises. They could go no farther this way, so they made their way back, deciding to head home and return another day to continue on this hunt. This quest may be nothing more than a cruel adventure, perpetuated by these spirits, who had a history of being mean and deceiving.

Bob and Annette reached the boat as a thunderstorm approached, a common occurrence in this tropical setting, leaving the air steamy as the hot sun evaporated the cool rain. The night sky shone bright, the moon bathing the ocean and shore with a soft light, a permanent memory forever etched in the couple's minds as their spirits slumbered off to sleep, only peace enveloping their soul.

CHAPTER ELEVEN

Annette lay on the deck of the sailboat enjoying the sun's warm rays shining down on her. She lay with her eyes closed, memories of her childhood dominating her thoughts; family vacations and Christmases past were all pleasant memories left to ponder. They had built a makeshift roof over the deck of the boat, using materials salvaged from the storm. With ingenuity and time, they were able to construct a secure covering of palm fronds over the vessel, which blocked the hot sun and kept their living quarters cooler. It also inhibited the rain from getting them wet while sitting on the deck. They had left an area at the bow of the boat for Annette and Bob to sunbathe, completing the renovations they had planned for the vessel.

As the days wore on the couple's thoughts turned back to the hidden treasure. They discussed the steps they were going to take to continue their hunt. One cave Bob had in mind to explore was secluded, sitting alone, more in the interior of the island. They had stumbled across it by accident while investigating their new home, right after they were shipwrecked here. Bob had forgotten about this cave but remembered it again while sunbathing with Annette on the top deck of the boat. To Bob it seemed like a logical place to hide something, away from the eyes of the other men, a secret only the captain and trusted aides might have known about. Bob explained his plan to Annette who agreed, a wave of excitement overwhelming them as this thought brought a sense of hope back into their endeavour that had been unsuccessful so far. They decided tomorrow they would try again to unlock the mystery that had evolved around this island.

When they arrived at the cave, they noticed a shaft that went deep very quickly. They carefully made their way down, reaching the bottom without incident. The shaft led to a large open room. Bob took the lead, his light shining brightly in the darkness of this underground world they had now became a part of. Annette strayed from Bob to investigate the room better. She stumbled across a broken shovel and a bucket, both rotten, a time capsule left by men to show they had once been here. There was one passage they could follow, an area that had obviously been made wider, the excess rocks piled in the first room they had encountered. These events were leading to something.

As they moved forward the sound of water could be heard, a bubbling spring and a reservoir of fresh water ran like a mountain stream, disappearing into the earth like a snake retreating to its lair. Bob sensed they were close to the pirate loot. He looked around for a clue and noticed something that did not look right. Where the stream disappeared into the rocks there was obvious signs of human activity; the entrance had been blocked, but not well. In excitement they tore away the rocks from the opening leaving a hole large enough to crawl through. Bob entered a large cavern-like room. He waited for Annette and with both lanterns shining they were rewarded with a sight not to be believed. As if in a dream the answer to their questions, a mystery solved, the island giving up its most precious secret.

CHAPTER TWELVE

Bob and Annette stared in disbelief at the amount of riches that surrounded them. Gold, silver, and every imaginable precious stone could be found. They walked amongst the treasure wondering about the series of events that led up to the seizure of all this wealth, and the lives that were lost in the battles over these riches of ill-gotten gains. Bob adorned his wife with precious gems and jewellery, choosing only a solid gold ring for himself. They left the cave, a sense of wonderment at their discovery and the different paths it would lead them on if they were rescued.

The couple returned to the boat, removed their clothes, and went swimming in the lagoon, enjoying the cooling water after their adventures in the cave, a hot and dirty ordeal. They decided to take the dinghy and go out to the reef, where an unlimited supply of conch and lobster could be harvested using snorkeling gear. Their diet consisted of food harvested from the ocean, and fresh fruit from the island's trees. The only meat available were the iguanas, but the thought of killing, cleaning, and cooking one did not seem like a palatable undertaking to the couple.

They frolicked in the warm waters, splashing, and playing like two young children in a bathtub as their mother gets them ready for bed, their childish whims taking over for the moment. They finished their swim, retrieved the dinghy and their gear, planning on a dinner cooked on the beach under an expected full moon. Bob had selected a beautiful gold necklace adorned with precious stones from the treasure they found in the cave when Annette was not looking. This special seaside dinner was to celebrate their fortieth wedding anniversary and Bob was going to give her the necklace as a gift in celebration.

The full moon shone down casting a warm glow over the party, the only sound to disturb the night was the happy laughter of the couple and the popping of the cork on the bottle of wine they had saved for this special occasion. Bob presented Annette with his gift, placing it around her neck. She wept, hugging him tightly, releasing pent up emotions she had been collecting since their arrival. Bob let her cry, knowing how difficult this whole experience had been for her. The uncertainty of what the future held for them and the thoughts that this island could become their permanent dwelling rested in their minds.

The sky suddenly came alive with shooting stars, an unknown meteor shower to entertain them and an unexpected gift to add to their celebration. The coals in the fire soon grew dark, the activity in the sky dwindled, and a sudden fatigue set in, sending the couple to bed. They slept undisturbed till morning, their dreams taking over where real life left off. The sound of an approaching storm could be heard, its thunder echoing in the distance, the lightning illuminating the night sky. The couple slept soundly; their dreams of rescue not steeped in reality but in their thoughts only. Would tomorrow bring the changes they were looking for? Only time would have that answer.

CHAPTER THIRTEEN

The couple awoke to the sound of a small plane flying overhead, low in the sky, its engine loud. They rushed to the top deck watching it as it flew low over the ocean, finally disappearing on the distant horizon. Their hopes dashed, they returned to their living quarters and discussed the day's plans. They had decided to return to the cave that contained the pirate's gold with more lanterns. They wanted to investigate the treasure and adjoining caves with more light, in the hopes of finding further surprises. But not all surprises are good, as they would soon find out.

After a short walk they reached the cave entrance. A cool breeze made itself known, coming from within, causing an uneasy feeling. Bob and Annette entered the cave, their lanterns' light leading the way, the treasure trove soon in their gaze. What they had not noticed before was the skeleton watching over the treasure; a full set of bones bleached white, with a smile crooked and rotten. Tattered clothes hung from the body, an empty bottle of rum at his feet. With his crooked smile he warned the mortals away, the treasure not theirs to claim. But only a warning he could give, as his soul, no longer in physical form, was incapable of enforcing his own rules.

The couple moved to an unnoticed corridor, making their way into another large room and an underground river with access to the ocean at high tide. The pirates would have used a small boat to ferry valuables from the large ship to here, where they hid their stolen goods in the nearby cave. The skeleton was that of a captain from one of the plundered ships, left to die a slow death, his tortured soul left to guard the treasure forever.

They walked to the water's edge, gold and silver coins littered the river's banks, having fallen from the spoils, never to be retrieved, never missed. The pair followed the water and after a short distance they found themselves in a small hidden cove, the entrance to the underground river not noticeable unless one was searching for it. They returned home surprised at the new discoveries they had come upon, adding a new twist to this adventure.

The summer days passed, the daytime sun hot, the night time breezes cooler. The deck had become their new sleeping area, as the downstairs was confined and stuffy. One evening around midnight Bob and Annette were awakened by the sound of men's voices and the creaking of the oarlocks of a wooden boat. They froze not knowing how to react, the sound slowly faded as the boat distanced itself from their beach. The couple jumped out of bed, running after the boat, wondering what the purpose of this visit was, so late and in the dark.

Silence returned, only the sound of the waves could be heard splashing against the shore. Was it the pirates going to check on their treasure concealed in the cave, only them knowing the whereabouts of this secret stash that they could never recover? It had become a mystery that kept sliding deeper into darkness; unexplained events testing the sanity of the couple's minds. Spirit Island, as it was known by the natives, would take no prisoners.

CHAPTER FOURTEEN

The island lay alone surrounded by a landscape of water; its history unknown but to a few. The spirits of the pirates dominate, their favorite cave full of treasure, their secret given up to mortals.

A small boat approached, entering the lagoon, the occupants shouting out a greeting to the elated couple on the beach, who waved in disbelief at this sudden change of events. The couple on the boat had also found this island using satellite data, as it was not shown on any maps. They were looking for an isolated spot they could explore and use the beach as their own. They never expected to discover this missing couple who had been shipwrecked and left to fend for themselves on this tropical oasis. A paradise lost if you are unable to leave, the situation Bob and Annette had found themselves in.

The Coast Guard was called and hours later the sound of a chopper could be heard as the helicopter drew near, landing on the sand near the beached sailboat. Annette and Bob grabbed some personal belongings, said goodbye to their rescuers and boarded the helicopter, their escape from the island now certain. They returned to Florida, their family and friends shocked at the revelation that the lost couple had been found. The miracle of life snatched from the hands of death, their fate.

The secret of the treasure was never revealed. The few things Bob and Annette had taken from the pirates' cache they kept. The rest of the riches they left, fearing the pirates might haunt their dreams forever if they absconded with their valuables, a matter better to be left alone. The couple never shared their story of finding the hidden treasure and their encounters with the pirates of long ago. A quiet lifestyle was now their plan; a retirement they looked forward to, buying an island only in their dreams.

As the memories faded so did the couple's health, the treasure never found. Bob and Annette spent their final years in a nursing home, old age eventually taking command, ending their dreams forever. Their paradise was lost but found again in the afterlife, as the allure of Spirit Island captured their souls, returning them to their sailboat and the island of their dreams; a new life, never to be forgotten.

A LONG AND LONELY ROAD

✦✦✦✦✦✦

INTRODUCTION

The expectant mother lay in the hospital bed ready to give birth. God had promised her if she tried to get pregnant she would be successful, and she was, delivering a baby boy. A new life has now entered our world, a planet full of chaos and turmoil not seen through a baby's eyes. The newborn, leaving a safe comfortable environment has now been cast into this new world, his survival dependent on his caregiver.

Disease and cruelty reign as humans struggle to survive unforgiving and relentless attacks from various sources, including from each other. Every baby will experience a different life depending on the parents it was born to. Most parents are loving and nurturing, but some are not. The path to adulthood is made up of a series of unforeseen events which, depending on luck, will send this child in a direction of its own choosing. His struggles through life will be daily as he tries to follow the rules, while others that are working beside him break them. This is the story of that child, and his long journey through life ending in his death, a story that may seem similar to your own.

THE BIRTH

The delivery room was abuzz with excitement as a new birth was about to take place. The young husband held his wife's hand, providing comfort to his loved one, who was worried about the safe delivery of their new baby. The soon to be grandparents were anxiously waiting for news, praying for a happy ending for this couple starting out in life. A sudden flurry of excitement and then cries, as the child entered its new world. The father was mesmerized as he watched the birth of his son, a miracle sent by God.

The baby's eyes opened wide taking in its new surroundings, a look of shock on its face as it realized it was no longer being protected by the mother's womb. A sudden feeling of helplessness and dependency took over the baby's spirit, until placed in his mother's arms where an instant bonding between mother and child took place. It was a love that would last a lifetime, never waning in its power to keep mother and child together, a lifetime commitment agreed upon at the birth of the child.

The baby was born healthy and took to nursing right away, resulting in a short hospital stay. The grandparents waited patiently for the arrival of the baby at its new home, where the nursery had been readied by the parents in anticipation of the arrival of this new life. The child would have advantages, being born into money on both sides of the family, guaranteeing him a life of privilege, never having to do without the necessities of life.

Immense joy abounded in the household as the new baby took center stage, its name soon to be revealed to the waiting grandparents. The newborn was fed and put in his crib to sleep while the adults had lunch. A discussion ensued as the reality of being new parents captured the young couple's thoughts. Bernie was the chosen name for the baby, a family name from the father's side of the family, a name this child would live with for life, a word weak in character and not a good fit for this future accomplished citizen.

The grandparents left and the mother took the now awake baby into her bedroom to feed and nurture him. Hopefully afterwards the new parents could have a much-needed nap of their own. A feeling of peace swept over the couple as the weight of carrying the baby to birth was now done, relieving them of great stress brought on by this life changing decision that they had made. The family slept peacefully knowing their journey was at the beginning, a lifetime of change now awaited them, the new baby showing them the way. But for now calm prevailed as their dreams showed a peace and love they would shower upon this new life; a miracle that only God could understand.

THE EARLY YEARS

Tasha, the mother of the new baby, had been up all night. Bernie had started to run a fever after dinner which even with medicine would not break. He would not eat, or drink and his mother was afraid he would become dehydrated, a serious condition to affect a young child. A doctor's visit would be in order tomorrow. The baby's father, Albert, was concerned about his young son who had just turned two months old. This was the first time the new parents had had to deal with a sickness of this magnitude, and it worried them both.

The morning came with no change in the baby's health. They were able to get an early appointment and soon found themselves in the doctor's office with Bernie being examined. An ear infection was the diagnosis, a painful condition caused by a build up of fluid in the ear, usually created by the common cold. The doctor put him on antibiotics and told Tasha how important it was to try to get fluids in him. The parents took him home relieved by the diagnosis and knew, with the medicine, he would soon be better.

Recover he did, and as the months went by Bernie grew. Soon he was crawling everywhere, starting to pull himself up into a standing position by hanging onto furniture. Tasha and Albert knew in a short time he would be walking, and further childproofing of the house would be necessary. Bernie kept on growing, walking at ten months and was soon ready to celebrate his first birthday, a milestone for both baby and parents.

The early years with Bernie passed quickly. Being an only child he was spoiled to the core, his possessions rivaling that of any child in the neighborhood. Tasha was a stay-at-home mom, but soon Bernie would be old enough for school and she planned to go back to work, if things worked out. The first day of kindergarten was traumatic for the mother and child. The bond that had held for five years was about to be broken, an emotional ordeal for both Bernie and Tasha. Time would heal the wounds of separation suffered by both.

Tasha returned to her husband's office, helping him run the large hardware business his father had started, which now provided them with a good income. Bernie did well in school, excelling in math and science, becoming a nerd when it came to inventing new things related to science. First in his class with grades, and a popular student amongst his peers, his future seemed bright.

The early years came and went in a flash, Bernie was no longer a child but now a pre-teen about to enter high school; another profound change experienced by mother and child as Bernie quietly moved toward becoming an adult. His mother was no longer the most significant person in his life; a love that will never die but will become less important as Bernie grows into a man. His mother will be a treasured memory in a locket that he will carry in his heart forever.

THE TEEN YEARS

Bernie was ready to enter a new phase; a slow march toward adulthood would take place, creating a new perspective on life, viewed through the eyes of a teenager. His entry into high school came with challenges he learned to defeat, as his short life began to unfold. Bernie kept an honorable and respectable relationship with his parents, which was rewarded with responsibilities, like a driver's licence and a car at age sixteen.

He excelled at school, taking classes rich in math and science. He was not sports inclined, sticking more to clubs and other opportunities that would help enhance his education. By the end of grade ten he had gained the reputation as a leader and top student in the school. This honor did not go unnoticed by other students that had neither the smarts nor the manners to be a success in life like Bernie. Because of this, he was constantly harassed and teased by other students who were jealous of his success and the attention it garnered him. Bernie would suffer from harassment throughout his life, as people viewed his achievements as unearned, their jealousy and own inadequacies not part of the equation.

Bernie was smart, able to brush off the negativity as he was constantly accosted by people less intelligent than himself. As a teenager he belonged to the boy scouts, was an active camper and angler, the outdoors being his favorite playground. He enjoyed family vacations with his parents and ended up being an only child, God not wanting him to have a sibling. After a family discussion, it was agreed that Bernie would not work at the family hardware store. Wanting more independence, he chose his own path in life, disappointing to his parents but understandable. In his last year of high school Bernie fell in love, a common occurrence for young men. Her name was Grace, and her interests were similar to Bernie's, science and math being the focus in her life. They spent hours together but ended up planning to attend different colleges.

Grace often joined Bernie in his makeshift science lab that had been constructed in part of the garage for him. They lived in a world of fantasy, discovering cures to solve mankind's misfortunes and mysteries. During his senior year of high school, plans were made for college. Due to his educational success, Bernie had options as to which school he would attend. He chose Harvard, with the eventual goal of becoming a nuclear scientist, a career choice for only the brightest and best minds on the planet.

High school graduation was special for Bernie and his parents, with tears shed by his mother who realized that shortly Bernie would no longer be living at home, a change they would both have to get use to. His march forward was now in his own hands, and hopefully the decisions made would be the right ones as he continued on his path to becoming a man and all the responsibilities that come with it. This was a learning process that Bernie would have to master as he entered into this new stage in his life, to him a challenge he was ready for.

THE COLLEGE YEARS

The drive to Cambridge, Massachusetts to Harvard University was very emotional for Bernie. He was leaving his place of birth, the security of the family home, and the close emotional support his parents provided him. He would be on his own, carving out his own path in life, a responsibility that he was now ready to face. His parents had rented him an apartment off campus. It was a short walk to the school, exactly what Bernie wanted, rather than living in a dorm, which he thought would be too distracting. The apartment was large enough to have a roommate if he desired company.

Bernie adapted well to his new surroundings, he studied hard and avoided the party scene, earning a spot on the honour roll, a feat accomplished by few. His relationship with Grace ended as the study and distance took a toll on their connection, which saddened Bernie greatly. He chose to put one hundred percent into his studies, which left him little time to make friends. His social time was spent communicating with his parents, who would also drive up to see him every two weeks.

Bernie joined a club at the urging of his parents, who felt he would benefit from the social contact. He was studying to be a nuclear physicist and hoped to get a job working for NASA in the space program upon graduation. He joined a group interested in his field of study, which is where he met his future wife. Bernie was intelligent but lacked sorely in the field of looks and body strength. He was a nerd, just like Roberta his newfound love. It was an instant attraction, the couple hoping it would result in a lifelong marriage and children. They found their interests were identical and they had even shared classes together. These classes, however, had been large and impersonable, denying them the chance to meet.

Bernie's parents approved of this new relationship, having hoped this would happen someday. Roberta spent time at Bernie's apartment, and they had decided when her lease was up she would move in. They figured they could help each other with their studies and provide friendship and support for one another. They knew this relationship would work well for both, and as the years went by their love grew. They planned on graduating at the same time, and prior to completing their senior year, were offered jobs at the Houston Space Center.

Graduation day came, the proud parents of these two successful scholars meeting for the first time. The happy students both graduated with high honors, showing the courage and stamina they had displayed to reach this lofty goal. The young graduates spent a couple of weeks with their respective parents and then met in Houston, where a house had already been purchased for them as a graduation present given by both families. A new life for this couple propelled them into an adult world they had a hard time understanding. Experience and learning were the best teacher, as they enjoyed the privileges of being an adult, and the responsibilities that came with it; a new life, a new beginning for both of them.

THE ROAD TO HEAVEN

The couple woke in their new home. Last night their neighbour, while drinking, came over uninvited and made lewd comments to Roberta. Bernie said nothing, not knowing the best way to deal with this problem. The neighbor eventually left, making the couple realize they had a problem regarding him. A problem that would be difficult to solve.

Bernie and Roberta pushed this incident to the back of their minds as preparations were made to attend their first day of work. Feelings of apprehension and insecurity gnawed at their souls. It would be one of their first life experiences, working and trying to find their way to a successful future, a lifelong event.

Blocks from work, a man who had just left a house where he had been drinking and using other drugs all night was getting into his car, oblivious as to where he was going. He had been asked to leave after an argument with a resident of the home had turned ugly. He was mad and not in control of his emotions. His foot went down to the floor on the gas pedal, the car roaring off at a high rate of speed. Upon entering an intersection on a red light, he slammed into a car, cutting it in half, killing the two occupants inside.

The young couple that died in this tragic accident were Roberta and Bernie, only two blocks from their new workplace. The couple's dreams and challenging work now passe, a memory only for the survivors. Life would go on, as these two lives were but one story among billions. This tragic accident was an important event only to family and friends. The lesson learned is life is not a planned event, but one that can end at a moment's notice, changing the course of people's lives forever.

EPILOGUE

On impact, death instantly took the couple. A bright light from heaven shone on their souls, as the angels, sent by the Lord, came to take them to heaven. They looked down at the crash scene and their mangled earthly bodies, feeling no emotion. The couple's souls were joined for eternity. Their hearts as one, they will enjoy an afterlife of peace, a reward for the good will they had spread while on Earth.

Screams of agony greeted the paramedics as they tried to treat the impaired man that caused the accident, his death following shortly. Satan came to collect his soul, leaving with it, taking it where it would spend an eternity in hell. This was a suitable sentence for a monster, sent to a place where he would suffer for the atrocities he committed in life, a world of pain and suffering he rightly deserved.

There never seems to be a happy conclusion to a sorrowful tale, only a sad ending to a sad story; a part of life humans can not avoid, as they try to answer the question, why are we here?

CABIN CREEK

‧ ✦✦✦✦✦ ‧

INTRODUCTION

Cabin Creek was a legend, a collection of stories, many true, some myth, about an old way station found in the Sedona desert, in the state of Arizona. With a colourful history of legends and adventure it served as a layover for stagecoaches and travellers alike. A place where sometimes a meal could be had, depending on the proprietor, and his mood for the day. It served as a resting place for everyone, including Mexican bandits, train and bank robbers, and men running from the law. Many men who ran these stations lost their lives to these sometimes ruthless outlaws. Tales of treasure hidden in the area were common, the spoils left by men who lost their lives in shootouts with law enforcement, sometimes surprising them as their paths crossed. Cabin Creek was special, the remnants still standing, a never-ending tale of stories surrounding it. These stories from the past will now be shared, tales of adventure that happened at this old retreat in the desert, stories from the past brought to life in imagination only.

CHAPTER ONE

The old cowboy sat alone, the campfire his only friend. He had just worked a cattle drive and was returning to Phoenix, stopping in the desert for the night. Tomorrow he hoped to reach Cabin Creek, a waystation where he could get a hot meal and a warm bed to sleep in. He laid down beside the fire, the night quiet, the howl of the coyotes the only sound to break the silence. His sleep was restless as his thoughts turned to the uncertain future he was facing. He was a drifter, going where the jobs would take him. His hope was, that he could get a job as a cowhand when he arrived in the Phoenix area.

The night was cool, the sun peeping over the horizon, not yet warming up the morning air. A small desert lizard lay motionless, the warm sun the only thing to bring him back to life, a reptile that does not fare well in the cold. The drifter packed up his stuff and left, having no food to eat and little water to drink. His horse would need water, so his hopes were of running into some on his way to the station. He made the trip without incident and found himself riding into Cabin Creek before dark, a ramshackle place with a big history.

The proprietor was friendly, always happy to see a new customer come through the door. He made the drifter dinner, the first food he had eaten in two days. His accommodations would be a straw bed on the floor, in a large room he would share with other people. He would leave in the morning, rested after his long journey through the desert to this little outpost that has saved lives, a rare spot of hope in this ocean of sand. Tomorrow would bring excitement to this area, common for Cabin Creek as its past has revealed, sometimes resulting in an undesirable outcome.

CHAPTER TWO

The rodent came out of hiding, the morning dawn a deception to its safety. The snake was waiting, its early morning meal in sight. With a quick movement the mammal became food for this desert predator. The land was unforgiving, the heat and lack of arable soil and potable water made it a refuge only for hiding outlaws, and a route for travellers passing through.

The camp was set up in a cluster of rocks, hidden from view. The five outlaws were waiting patiently for orders from their boss. The train they were to rob was rumoured to have a substantial amount of paper money and gold on board. The order was given, and the men rode off; they would hijack the train as it slowed for a sharp turn in the track, boarding and killing anyone who got in their way. The trap was set, the train billowing clouds of smoke from its coal-fired engine approached the turn. The men came out of hiding, three of them boarded the train to complete the robbery, while the others took care of the horses and any unforeseen events that might happen on the ground.

There were two guards on the train, unaware of what was about to happen. The outlaws boarded the train without incident, making their way to where the money was located. The guards, caught unaware, were killed in a brief gunfight; the valuables were stolen and put in saddlebags. The men made their way to the front where the engineer was made to stop the train. The rest of the men on the ground needed to catch up. No one on board dared to challenge this well-armed gang of thugs as they regrouped and successfully escaped into the desert, where they would hide out till things calmed down.

They rode to Cabin Creek hoping to eat a meal and pick up any supplies that were available before news of the train robbery leaked out. The men arrived at the way station, their horses in need of water. The proprietor was instantly suspicious of these men. He fed them, watered their horses, sold them canned food, and in a hurry, they left, to the relief of the old man who ran this desert outpost. The men rode hard, going deeper into the desert knowing a posse was now being organized and would soon be looking for them. Cabin Creek would become a flurry of activity as the posse used it as a staging area for men coming and going while looking for these outlaws and the money they stole.

The gang rode to a pre-determined location, a well-hidden area with a good water supply for the men and the horses. The saddlebags with the valuables were now causing friction between the men. They decided to split up the money and each man could make his own decision as to what he wanted to do. One man decided to go it alone, while the others paired up into two man teams. They left the security of their hideout, bid farewell, the gang disbanding and going their separate ways.

Only the lone gunman escaped, making his way to Phoenix where he was able to spend his ill-gotten gains. The other train robbers were not so lucky, giving up their freedom in the desert that was meant to protect them. Two of these men were killed in a shootout, while the other two were captured and hung for their crimes. The money and gold were hidden in the desert and never recovered, adding more stories and legends to be solved. The land rarely yielded its secrets, only to the most devoted who were trying to solve these mysteries, most times resulting in just a happy story but never a good ending.

CHAPTER THREE

The rattler bathed in the warm morning sun, bringing life back to its cold lethargic state after a night in the desert cold. The wagon train on its way to California lumbered by, causing a feeling of caution to course through the now warming body of the snake. This was life in the desert, a constant emotional drama for people travelling through, with no idea what might lie ahead.

The company of soldiers left their outpost in Phoenix, their mission was to search for a small band of native Americans that had broken from the tribe, the current truce with the white man considered invalid. They were robbing small wagon trains and travelers, stripping them of their valuables; food, water, and guns being the most important finds. Destroying their possessions, the natives left their victims in the hot desert to die a slow painful death. The soldiers headed west as these bandits had become active in the area of Cabin Creek, the soldiers' first destination. A small regimen would be left to protect this important outpost, not wanting it burnt down in an attack by the Indians.

The soldiers arrived at the way station without incident. They set up camp, using this small station as their staging area. Cabin Creek became a flurry of activity as soldiers searched the area, returning at night on most occasions. The native Americans knowing the land, had seemed to disappear into the landscape. A lone traveller stopping for a hot meal and a comfortable bed changed the equation. He had spotted smoke coming from a rock outcropping when he took a short cut he knew, being a regular on the trail as a Pony Express rider he had learned to pay attention to details. He drew the soldiers a map, not being able to disrupt the mail by going with them.

The following morning a large contingent of soldiers left Cabin Creek hoping to surprise the Indians, surrounding them, leaving them no avenue of escape. They reached the area without incident and set their plan into action. A firefight ensued. Both soldiers and Indians died, but in the end, numbers won, handing the enemy a sounding defeat.

The wounded, including two native Americans were brought back to Cabin Creek to be treated by army medics, and were later transferred to Phoenix. The soldiers left and normalcy returned, a quiet descending on the way station only the proprietor knew. The most recent threat to its existence had been extinguished. Tomorrow another adventure at Cabin Creek would unfold, a never-ending series of events, some not to be taken lightly. The sagebrush blew by as the wind picked up the sand, obscuring the view and making the little settlement invisible, just an illusion in the desert but a jewel to a weary traveller looking for a safe place to sleep.

CHAPTER FOUR

The sandstorm was relentless, blowing with a fury not seen in years. The stagecoach had arrived at Cabin Creek just before the storm hit. They would seek refuge here until the winds abated, and the sand quit blowing. They were thankful they got to this shelter before the storm, as getting caught in the open desert with the horses could have turned out to be a disaster. Men have died when caught in these storms, their horses running off in panic, leaving the rider to perish alone, fine sand filling his lungs.

There were six people on the stagecoach, the driver and his guard, a couple from California travelling to Phoenix to visit family, and a sheriff and his prisoner who he was taking to the state penitentiary for murder. Now they sat together at Cabin Creek, an unease in the room noticeable, as the shackled man tried to cause trouble, making suggestive comments to the only lady present. Her husband, a small weak man, said nothing, letting the sheriff do his job.

The storm raged outside, stranding the stagecoach, forcing an overnight stay. The proprietor was a big jolly man, injecting his spirit into this room of rejection by announcing dinner, a hearty beef stew and fresh baked bread. The smell of the food sent feelings of hunger through the weary travellers, who would appreciate a meal. As they finished dinner, the storm began to ease, a quiet descending on the desert. The couple would have their own room to sleep in, a privilege given so they could enjoy privacy. The sheriff would stay downstairs with his prisoner, while the rest of the men would sleep upstairs, sharing a communal room with beds on the floor. The night was quiet, and the travellers slept well.

The morning sun rose early, the smell of breakfast permeating the inn as the travellers awoke and came down for breakfast. Soon thereafter they were boarding the stagecoach and saying goodbye as they continued on their journey to their destinations. This was when the proprietor would sigh with relief, as his company left, leaving Cabin Creek a silent, peaceful place. He fed the coyote who had made this place home, the animal forming a trusting bond with this man, like that of a dog. Few friends were made in the desert, so this was a welcome distraction for the proprietor.

The stagecoach made its way toward Phoenix, a trap waiting a few miles past the outpost. Two outlaws, one the brother of the prisoner in the stagecoach, tried desperately to give the captive his freedom. The plan failed, resulting in the deaths of the two outlaws in their misguided plan, their bodies left for the buzzards to pick clean. The stagecoach arrived at its destination with the passengers intact, having tales to share of their adventures in the desert.

The reputation of Cabin Creek lived on, providing stories of adventure and sometimes sadness at this lonely place. It was a bastion of hope for the downtrodden and weary to rest their spirits and souls, their feelings of anguish temporarily removed as peace settled over them, the desert now in control.

CHAPTER FIVE

The old prospector worked the silver mine he had dug on his claim. His luck had not been good, earning him only enough money to meet his expenses and eat. The old man was up at dawn daily, working the mine hoping for a rich vein of silver to show itself. Unfortunately, he usually went home disappointed, the hard earth not giving up its treasures so easily. His obsession with finding silver, enough to become wealthy, controlled his life. It made him careless working in the mine, easily distracted he was an accident waiting to happen. He had planned to use the rest of his dynamite, in a last-ditch effort to find what he had spent years looking for, a vein of silver more common than not in this area of the Arizona desert. The dynamite was detonated and the unfortunate prospector was crushed under falling rock he had not been smart enough to distance himself from. His tomb was sealed, where he lay was where he would stay, until his bones were found the following spring by another prospector who had taken over his claim.

Cabin Creek was quiet, one lone cowboy passing through, stopping long enough to water and feed his horse and enjoy a bowl of beef stew, the station's special served all day and night to any hungry traveller who might come along looking for a meal. The proprietor of this hotel and rest area would take the quiet time and use it to do needed repairs on all parts of the property. Anything could happen here, from drunken cowboys breaking things, to fighting off Indian attacks, leaving an almost impossible task of keeping the place from falling down. These major repairs would never get done, so a series of temporary fixes were always in order.

The old man loved his job, the colourful characters he met, and the stories he was told about the mysteries that happened in the desert. These included the disappearance of men and the sighting of strange lights, uncommon in that era, not so unusual. He loved the desert nights, especially when alone, the quiet only broken by the howling of the coyote that called this place home.

Quiet at Cabin Creek was always temporary, most times were busy with people passing through. A lumbering wagon pulled by two large mules pulled up to the inn. It was the medicine man, who went from town to town selling his snake oil for every ailment that afflicted man. The proprietor knew this man and liked him, finding his stories, which he knew were all lies, entertaining and funny. Why he really liked this man was because he would bring a bottle of whiskey which he would trade for the night's accommodation. Then the two men would drink it until drunkenness caused them both to pass out, heads down on the table not to move until the morning.

The coyote barking at the door wondering why his breakfast was late awoke the men. Their heads ached and their stomachs were nauseous from the moonshine the medicine man had picked up in his travels, a not so wise decision that luckily did not lead to their poisoning. The man left, hoping to make it to the next town before dark so he could sell his wares and then head to the saloon for gambling and drinking, the man's favorite pastimes. Darkness settled over Cabin Creek, the stars and moon shining brightly, promising a new day tomorrow, with more adventure on the way.

CHAPTER SIX

The desert can be beautiful. An explosion of color can be seen after significant rainfall during the monsoon season. While short lived, it provided a respite from the boredom of seeing sand, rock, and cactus, the three ingredients that make up this part of the Arizona desert.

The lone cowboy pulled himself up, the sun now well above the horizon. He had spent the night in a small outcropping of rocks, hidden from sight. In this environment man was his biggest enemy. Many bad people called this place home. Men running from the law, psychotic humans with nowhere to go, loners who displayed odd characteristics, the desert had them all. The cowboy walked around the outcropping; a small area of large rocks interspaced with smaller ones in a large group. The reflection of the sun's glare caught his eye, a piece of metal on the straps of a saddlebag half buried in the sand were now exposed, brought to the surface by the heavy rain that was experienced here earlier. The cowboy could not believe his eyes. He knew what was in those bags, the ill-gotten gains from a robbery that some outlaw had committed and never retrieved, after being shot dead by the posse sent looking for him.

He picked up the bag, visibly shaken by this incident. The straps were loosened, and the bag exposed its contents, paper money, which now belonged to him. A found treasure was a secret not to be revealed, only known to the finder so as not to cause trouble, which could lead the finder to lose his treasure. The man's hands were shaking as he counted the money. There was a sizable amount. What was he to do with it?

He returned the money to the saddle bag and packed up his belongings. He would go to Cabin Creek today and spend the night, continuing to Phoenix the following day. His plans had changed. Instead of finding a job as a ranch hand or working in one of the mines that dotted the area, he had better options now that he had wealth. However, better choices do not always lead to better decisions, as the man squandered the money in drunken episodes of gambling and loose women. He ended up in jail unable to pay for the damages he had caused to a saloon after a brawl started over a woman that had deserted him because he ran out of money. Enraged he went after this woman's next victim, who proceeded to give the cowboy a good licking, leaving the sheriff to drag the cowboy's unconscious body back to a jail cell.

The evil of money had captured this man's soul, destroying his life, which now would be hard to put back together. Fortunes come and go, the lure of money causing hardships beyond belief, as bad decisions are made, which can result in the death or imprisonment of the guilty party. Life in the desert would continue, turning boys into men, and men into outlaws, the most common inhabitants of this desolate place, a place they call their own.

CHAPTER SEVEN

The western U.S. was still being settled. Wagon trains left daily from cities in the east, heading to California, a promised paradise of milk and honey, a deception experienced by newcomers to this new land they would call home. The man awoke, a sharp pain shooting through his leg. He had been bitten by a scorpion who was unhappy with the sleeping arrangements. When the insect tried to share the man's bed, he was almost crushed when he got rolled on, causing him to strike out for his own protection.

Scorpion stings are not deadly but very painful, the man would be deprived of sleep for the rest of the night. He was part of a small wagon train that had left Missouri, and through trials and tribulations had made it to Arizona. They were now stopped at a way station called Cabin Creek, a desert outpost meant to give weary travellers a meal and a safe place to sleep. It was also a campground for wagon trains because of the spacious open territory that surrounded it. It was the last piece of civilization that these pioneers would see until their desert crossing was completed.

As dusk approached, a man from the wagon train saw a coyote sniffing around one of the wagons. Unbeknownst to him, this was the proprietor's coyote, who he had befriended and made a pet out of. Fearing for the safety of the people in his company, the man shot and killed the animal. This often happens when a wild animal befriends humans. The animal usually ends up dead through neglect or killed because of a stigma that has been attached to it. The innkeeper understood the man's mistake.

Many of the men from the wagon train spent the evening playing cards inside the inn. The proprietor allowed no gambling or drinking on the premises, as in the past this had led to fights, including a murder. After a quiet night, the wagon train left in the morning with a damaged wheel that had been repaired. Hopefully, this wagon would take them across the desert to a place where they could buy a replacement.

Cabin Creek was quiet that day, only the express rider dropping by with mail for the proprietor, which was unusual. Wells Fargo, the company that ran the stagecoach line, was adding a new stop, changing when the coach would be arriving at Cabin Creek. The letter the owner received was to inform him of these revisions.

The evening was approaching as a troop of soldiers arrived. The

men set up camp and went into the inn, treating themselves to the famous Cabin Creek beef stew, a dish known all over the territory to fill
a hungry man's stomach at a cheap cost. If you were broke, it was free.
The soldiers were here on a routine patrol, they rode the trails looking
for disabled wagons and other unfortunate individuals who might find
themselves in trouble. The sergeant of the company also had good news
for the proprietor. The governor of Arizona had declared Cabin Creek
a necessary structure that needed to be taken care of. A grant had been
established and repair work would begin shortly, the labor provided by
the U.S. army with materials bought in Phoenix. The work would change
the look of the building, but the character of Cabin Creek would stay the
same, a reputation a long time in the making, not soon to be forgotten.

CHAPTER EIGHT

The army patrol left early; their mule loaded for an overnight stay in
the desert. Extra horses also accompanied them, to move any injured
or stranded individuals to safety. Finding bodies was common as men
succumbed to the wrath of mother nature, who made it hard to survive
in the hot, waterless environment; getting lost in the desert being the
main cause of death.

The patrol made its way through the rocky outcroppings, the landscape devoid of vegetation except for the cactus, the desert's only friend.
Two hours after leaving Cabin Creek the patrol found their first body.
A skeleton lay with the bones of his faithful dog who had died beside
him, a testament to the devotion of this animal toward its owner. Any
remains discovered were buried in the desert, ending an identity that
began in a mother's womb. The final trace of the individual interred in
an unmarked grave, leaving a family wondering for life what happened.
Their next encounter was with a broken-down wagon on its way to
Phoenix. With the knowledge of the men in the company, repairs were
made, and the family was sent on their way.

The day wore on, the hot sun beating down on the men, causing
mirages and images that were not there, playing tricks on the minds of

those who dared to challenge this creation of God, the desert. Their next episode was with a coyote. The animal, sick from mange, starvation, and lack of water was shot by the soldiers, hastening a death that was imminent. The animal was left where it lay as the men did not want to handle the diseased body. The afternoon wore on, the company planned to set up their camp near a known spring, as life-saving water was hard to find in this dry environment for the livestock and men alike. The spring was found, the horses were watered, and the soldiers camp was set up nearby. They camped in a clearing amongst rocks that loomed large over these men. The bright stars shining with an almost full moon helped light up the dark night, nature's way of supplying light when it could not supply wood.

The men slept peacefully as the chilly night air caused them to pull their blankets tightly around them for the extra warmth they would provide. The morning came early, the sun shining brightly, causing the men to awaken and prepare for another day. They would make their way back to Cabin Creek, taking a different route than the one they came on. Hoping for no unpleasant surprises, those thoughts were dashed when they came upon a man delirious from lack of water. They tended to his situation the best they could, put him on a horse and took him to Cabin Creek for further rest and recover.

The desert patrol had been successful in saving a life. They reached their destination, no other events happening along the way. More stories would be shared around the card table, as the soldiers told their tales to strangers, the only people who would listen. The legends at Cabin Creek would continue to be told, as the mysteries of the desert continued to unfold, creating stories that would never be forgotten in this land of solitude, in an oasis of peace.

CHAPTER NINE

The desert's allure was gripping, the breathtaking sunsets mesmerizing, taking one's thoughts to a new level of consciousness and joy. These moments were deceiving, as the true meaning of the desert is something else, a harsh environment few species can survive in. Lizards and snakes rule this land of sand and cactus. Phoenix, a city that sits on this sand, is a shining jewel in an otherwise forlorn place. It serves as a stopping off point for wagon trains and cowboys heading west, a place to resupply before crossing the desert.

The cowboy arrived in Phoenix looking for a new life. His wife and child were killed in an Indian attack, their home set ablaze and their possessions destroyed. He left in despair, a broken man, bitter at the events that had changed his life. He had little money but had been promised a job at a large cattle ranch outside of town. His throat was dry, the saloon beckoned, so he treated himself to a beer. He met a man who seemed flush with cash. After buying the cowboy drinks, the stranger made a proposition to him. He was an outlaw, new to town and looking for a partner who would join him in his illegal endeavors. The man promised easy money with little chance of getting caught, robbing helpless victims in their homes of their valuables, leaving them unscathed but poorer.

The cowboy had changed since losing his wife and child, his life no longer having any meaning to him. He felt he had nothing to lose by accepting this offer. These types of robberies were new, now known as home invasions, where one enters the home uninvited by the homeowner, terrorizing and robbing him with a weapon, the person usually a wealthy man of the community.

Their first victim was the owner of a mining company that worked silver mines in the area. He was caught in his sleep, rudely awoken by the outlaws who threatened him if he did not give up his valuables. The man, afraid for his life, obliged, leading them to a safe with cash and coin in it. He told the men to take it all, begging to be spared from harm. The outlaws tied up the man and left, heading for the desert where they planned to stay at a place called Cabin Creek for a couple of days, posing as cowboys just passing through.

The proprietor of this desert inn was instantly suspicious of these two men and their story upon arrival. Being a good judge of character he sensed something was wrong. He fed the two men and showed them their sleeping arrangements. Other people arrived later and soon the inn was full, now a hub of activity as it filled with colourful characters, each with a story to tell anyone willing to listen. The outlaws were nervous, they sensed the proprietor's concerns and hoped no law enforcement would drop by. Using Cabin Creek as a hideout was not a well thought out idea and they decided leaving in the morning would be a good plan as they no longer felt comfortable here. The men now felt they were on the run. Tomorrow's events would lead to another chapter in the history of the inn, a continuous saga of drama not to be outdone by the realities of life, an outpost with a life of its own.

CHAPTER TEN

The outlaws were up at dawn. They packed their saddlebags, retrieved their horses, and made their escape into the desert. This was their idea, to make it look like they were riding in one direction, but the actual plan was to circle back and go to Tucson, which was in the opposite direction. It was a long journey but there would be stops along the way where they could replenish supplies. If they could reach Tucson, they felt their safety would be ensured. Their journey would not be strictly in the desert, but would include more wooded areas, which would provide opportunity to shoot game they could eat.

Cabin Creek was abuzz with activity. The posse from Phoenix had arrived around noon, hoping the now wanted men had travelled this way, knowing they would stop here if they had. The proprietor confirmed their presence telling the sheriff he had been suspicious of the men. He steered the posse in the direction the outlaws were last seen heading. There had been a delay in organizing the posse, as the mine owner lay bound in his house and was not found for twenty-four hours.

The day was sunny and warm. The winter months which they were enjoying were cooler, allowing the men to make their perceived escape more tolerable, as they did not have to endure the extreme heat of the summer. Unfortunately for the outlaws, the miner had hired a tracker well known in Phoenix as the best of his kind. He was not easily fooled and soon was able to figure out their plan, even suggesting the outlaws were headed to Tucson.

Dusk drew near as the bandits looked for a safe place to camp. The rabbit they had crossed paths with on the way here would be cooked for dinner. They found a secluded area they felt was secure, gathered wood, and soon had a fire burning that would provide warmth against the cool desert night. The men relaxed, feeling safe from people they knew would be now looking for them. The rabbit, cooked over the fire, sent an aroma that made the men's stomachs yearn for nourishment.

The posse had also set up camp, their haste allowing them to come close to the unsuspecting men. The sound of a lone coyote howling broke the silence of the early morning sunrise, waking the wanted men from their dreams of escape and freedom; now realizing their home robbery had been a mistake. They would soon experience bad luck that would change the whole course of their endeavor.

The man first noticed his horse struggling with one of his front legs, a limp that got worse as the day wore on, leading to the horse laying down not able to get back up. Panic spread through the men, as they realized their escape was impossible with one horse. The more seasoned outlaw knew what he was up against, betraying his less experienced partner in this game of survival. Pulling his gun, he stripped the man of his valuables, leaving him behind to be found by the posse. The former cowboy learned about outlaw trust the hard way. His choices were few, either continuing to try to escape or turn himself in, which would certainly end in a long jail term. His decision would be made tomorrow.

CHAPTER ELEVEN

The cowboy turned outlaw waited, he decided he had no choice but to surrender to the posse and take his punishment. He had no gun to protect himself, so if a situation arose that put his life in danger he would die. He had no food, and just a canteen of water, making it hopeless to think he could survive by evading his captors. A slow death from exposure and dehydration would be the end result if he chose not to surrender.

Serving time in jail seemed a better choice than dying alone in the hot sun. He spent the night hungry, not able to sleep, now looking forward to his surrender. The following day the posse caught up to him. They fed him and turned him over to the sheriff for questioning. It was decided that they would not pursue the other man any further since their supplies were so low. They would take this rogue cowboy back to Phoenix and dish out his punishment.

The other outlaw, after the breakup with his partner, now felt he had a better chance of escaping; being alone he had no one to look out for but himself. He knew the posse would only go so far, and with the capture of his ex-partner he hoped they would turn around and return to Phoenix, which they did. After a day's travel, he reached a small town with which he was familiar. He took his horse to the stable, rented a room at the hotel, paid for a bath, then treated himself to a meal in the hotel dining room. Afterwards he went to the saloon to enjoy a drink, being careful not to overindulge and get caught in a situation that could brand him a troublemaker from out-of- town, resulting in him being thrown in jail. The saloon girl was his company, the first woman he had spent time with in months. Some of his ill-gotten gains were spent on this woman, as she entertained him in her room. This made the outlaw happy.

The man rode out of town the following morning. His next stop was the Superstition Mountains, an area known for the mysterious disappearance of men searching for legendary riches, never to be seen again, and sightings of unexplained lights and lone people walking through the rocks, disappearing when called. The outlaw did not believe any of it, he had travelled through this area many times and had never had any issues or witnessed strange happenings. He reached his destination, where he planned to stay for the night, beside a mountain stream of fresh, clean water. He lit a campfire, enjoying smoked meat and canned food he had bought in town.

The night was starless, as dark storm clouds filled the sky, making the outlaw uneasy about having no shelter. This would turn out to be the least of his worries. The morning sun was just rising when the man felt a sharp pain in his leg, followed by the sound of a rattle. He knew what it was. He threw back the blanket, exposing the reptile that was sharing his bed, a six-foot rattle snake that had already bitten him once. In a panic he tried to escape, startling the snake, causing him to strike, biting the man a second time, delivering a death sentence. The man died from the poison, no way to save himself. He had escaped a jail sentence but received the death penalty, from a snake he had planned to have no contact with.

CHAPTER TWELVE

The stagecoach pulled into Cabin Creek on its way from Phoenix. They had brought goods for the proprietor, a weekly stop, to resupply this important outpost in the desert. They were always rewarded with a large bowl of stew and fresh baked bread for performing this important task. Next, the mailman arrived, giving the owner a piece a mail with an update on the plans for the renovations that were to be done on the building. The proprietor invited his company in to eat, which they accepted with gratitude.

The stage coach driver told the eager listeners gathered around the table about a gang of outlaws that had been robbing stagecoaches, the passengers, who often carried valuables, their main target. The robberies had been committed recently, and a search of the area by the sheriff and his posse had yielded no results. The bandits were smart, robbing coaches on different lines, making it hard for law enforcement to place them in a certain location. The proprietor would be more aware of the men that came to use Cabin Creek for an overnight stay.

An old prospector, with a donkey in tow, was the next visitor. He was giving up his claim, his hard work having yielded few rewards. He offered to sell the donkey for a cut rate price, having no money to feed him once he reached Phoenix. The proprietor bought the donkey, knowing he could sell it later for a profit. The old man ate, his body gaunt from lack of nutrition. He purchased a ticket on the next stage and would be sent on his way tomorrow, with wishes of goodwill and luck, all the innkeeper could offer this man.

Four outlaws were hiding amongst the rocks, watching the stage-coach approach, the dust obscuring their view. They pulled their masks over their faces and took off after the slower horses. These robberies were mostly bloodless, as the passengers' safety was the lines main concern. The men approached the carriage at a high rate of speed, firing their guns over their heads. The coach stopped and the passengers were escorted outside. The terrified riders were threatened with death if they did not hand over their valuables to these dangerous men. The men rode off with cash, silver, gold coins, watches, and jewellery. It was a good haul for these thieves, who deserved to be caught and thrown in prison for a long time.

The bandits rode fast and hard to one of the three hideouts they had. They planned to commit a couple more robberies in this area and then move to a different location, reducing their chances of getting caught. Unfortunately for the bandits that dream would never be realized. One of the outlaws, who had too much to drink in the saloon, let the location of one of their hideouts slip. A man who overheard this, suspected this character might be connected to the recent stagecoach robberies and because of the sizable reward being offered, he reported this to the sheriff.

Desperate to stop these robberies, every lead was followed up on. The sheriff took a posse and found the camp, which showed recent activity. The lawmen hid and waited. The unsuspecting bandits, returning from their most recent robbery, were ambushed. Without a shot fired by these men, they all lay dead, mortally wounded in a barrage of gunfire from the sheriff and his posse. The men, unidentified, were buried in the desert. The stolen loot was recovered and returned to its rightful owners when they could be found. This harsh environment had taken more lives, their spirits now in a better place, a peaceful end to a tragic event.

CHAPTER THIRTEEN

The high winds and blowing sand signalled a storm on the way. Within an hour a dust storm raged outside Cabin Creek, the wind howling, the dust blocking out the sun, creating a surreal atmosphere in this already odd environment. The proprietor was always wary of these storms, his worry being that the high winds could damage this old building even further. He would be glad when the upgrades were completed, relieving him of unneeded stress created by this issue.

Within an hour the storm had subsided, leaving a calm only the most seasoned desert residents could fully appreciate. The little inn had survived to see another day. It would continue to provide food and comfort to the down trodden and weary, and provide an avenue for communications to spread throughout the area. Soon more adventure would unfold as a series of events would throw Cabin Creek into a crisis it might not survive.

It started with a tired cowboy arriving looking for a bed and a meal. The proprietor's intuition told him something was wrong with this man's story, about who he was or where he came from. His demeanor and silent attitude worried him. The cowboy left the following morning saying he was going to Phoenix where he had been promised a job by a family member. The proprietor did not believe his story.

The following day a group of men arrived, looking for the man who had previously stayed here. The group were outlaws, not happy with what their fellow gang member had done to them. The proprietor found himself in what could be a dangerous situation. These outlaws were mad at the betrayal their friend had enacted on them, absconding with all the money this band of thieves had stolen. However, the outlaws behaved and left the following morning, following the trail of their rouge ex-companion.

The next visitors to the inn were a company of army soldiers, looking for the gang of outlaws who had just stayed here. They had robbed a stagecoach of a government payroll, sparking a response by the state to send an army troop to find the money and return it to its rightful owners, the government. They left at once after learning the outlaws had made their presence here. Cabin Creek was finally quiet, but the peace was short lived.

The outlaws returned. They had had a confrontation with the army soldiers, and one of their own was killed. The other three, with the soldiers in hot pursuit, decided to make their last stand at Cabin Creek, using the proprietor as a hostage. They burst into the building, taking up positions, waiting for their adversaries to arrive.

The soldiers advanced slowly, not wanting to get caught in a trap of gunfire and death. The outlaws were scared and hopefully could be talked into giving themselves up. A voice rang out asking for their surrender, pleading for no more bloodshed. The outlaws, knowing there was no escape, only death if they chose to fight it out, decided their best option was life and facing their punishment. The proprietor, who figured he was a dead man, was relieved with this outcome. The bad men were taken into custody and Cabin Creek survived another disaster that could have threatened its existence. The inn fell quiet as the desert slept, preparing itself for another day, the challenges never ending.

CHAPTER FOURTEEN

The Mexican woman was a ranch hand, a breed of woman used to the hard life the desert offered. She worked for a large landowner in Mexico who raised and sold cattle. She came to Arizona on a cattle drive, the men she worked with protecting her like a sister but treating her like a brother. While scouting the area ahead for water, she noticed buildings taking up space in the desert. It was Cabin Creek. She rode her horse closer, at first thinking that the place was abandoned. She then noticed a wisp of smoke coming from the chimney. She tied up her horse at the water trough and entered the building.

The proprietor was surprised to see a woman cowboy on his premises, an unusual occurrence. He studied the woman. She was middle aged, attractive, and in good physical condition. She told the proprietor she was on a cattle drive from Mexico. They were planning on camping nearby, and she wanted to know if he had a comfortable bed to sleep in for a night. He told her for a special lady he had a private bedroom, his deluxe room at the inn. She accepted his offer and told him she would be back shortly.

She informed her party that a spring fed pond for the cattle and as much drinking water as they needed, would be provided by the proprietor at the inn for a small fee. The cowhands moved the herd towards the waystation to spend the night. The man felt a fondness for this woman and unbeknownst to him, the feeling was mutual. She was looking forward to talking with him more. She had been searching for a way out of the type of life she was living, and this might just be the opportunity for her to escape the poverty in her home country for a future in that shining star called America.

Upon her return to Cabin Creek an instant karma developed between the innkeeper and herself, it was truly a case of love at first sight. The proprietor was overjoyed, as this was the first woman he had fallen in love with in his life. She quickly accepted his offer to join him here, leaving her life in Mexico and starting a new life with a gringo, a nickname the Mexican people used for Americans. Her dreams were being realized, lucky to have found her ticket out of Mexico.

She finished the cattle drive and returned to the proprietor and her new home, Cabin Creek. Their relationship was loving and emotionally rewarding. The help from this industrious woman was appreciated. She brought a warmth to Cabin Creek, bringing a woman's touch to areas of the business. The proprietor had grown to love this woman very much and asked for her hand in marriage. She accepted, lovingly hugging, and kissing her future husband. Another tale of adventure and intrigue gripped this little place, as changes loomed on the horizon for this lonely way station in the desert, now a love nest for a happy couple.

CHAPTER FIFTEEN

The wedding date was set. The ceremony was being held inside the inn to avoid any incidents such as the hot sun and blowing sand, common events in a desert setting. A wide range of guests would be attending, including the stage coach driver and the sheriff from Phoenix. The preacher who would marry them also came from there.

Cabin creek was abuzz with activity, a large fire pit was built outside to cook the beef they had purchased for dinner. People who knew the proprietor volunteered their time to help with this endeavor. Anticipation grew as the wedding day drew near. New clothing was purchased for both the man and his future wife for this special day. A joyous feeling spread through the inn as guests arrived and mingled, catching up on the latest gossip and other more serious events that affected their lives.

The preacher soon made his appearance, and everyone went inside to watch the ceremony. The happy couple walked to the front of the room where the minister was standing. A silence enveloped the room as the preacher began speaking. The sound of "I now pronounce you man and wife" sent a happy murmur through the crowd, leading to a more jubilant celebration as the couple left the inn to go outside, where the guests would gather to socialize. The party went well, and the dinner was delicious, enjoyed by the twenty guests in attendance. After dinner, the room was cleared, and a dance was had by the happy couple, who were then joined by their guests. The proprietor had hired musicians from Phoenix to play for the celebration. The night wore on and the guests soon tired and found a place to sleep, where they stayed till morning.

As the sun was rising, a mass exodus of people left Cabin Creek, most returning to Phoenix where they lived. The wedding celebration had been a success, but the newly married couple were glad it was over and hoped that normality would return to their lives. Unfortunately, there was no such thing as normal when it came to Cabin Creek, as a series of events usually happened daily, bringing surprises to bear. The proprietor and his new wife were still tired from the wedding, which had created much excitement and was an emotional event; They were in the mood for quiet, not surprises, but surprises it would be.

Shortly after everyone left, a lone man rode in, a bloodied bandage covering his shoulder. The couple helped him off his horse and he was asked about his wound. He explained he had been drinking and gambling in a saloon in Phoenix and had an altercation with a man who had accused him of cheating when he lost all of his money. This resulted in him getting shot and making a quick exit from town. After an examination of the wound found it to be superficial, bloody but not serious, he was cleaned up, fed a large bowl of stew, and sent on his way. Finally a calm settled over Cabin Creek, a reprieve from the hectic activities of the last two days. The popular desert retreat never losing its allure, a beacon of hope in a desert of sand.

CHAPTER SIXTEEN

The wagons arrived, full of construction materials, with soldiers on horseback following. The long-awaited repairs on the building were about to begin. The proprietor and his wife were happy, the deplorable condition of the premises sometimes made them worry about their own safety.

The men set up camp, expecting the job to be completed in three days. The sound of hammers and saws filled the air as a transformation was being made to the structure. The men worked hard, and right on schedule they finished the job. They stayed one more night and then left, returning to their outpost.

Life at Cabin Creek would continue, the adventures never ending. Five years after the repairs were made, the proprietor died suddenly, the cause never to be known. His death led to the closing of the establishment. His wife returned to Mexico and the property went into disrepair, a new tenant never to be found. The stories of Cabin Creek are now just memories, where only the remains of a structure now stand, leaving a by-gone era whose reputation will forever be with us.

BOBBY

+ ✦ ✦ ✦ ✦ +

Once upon a time, in a long-forgotten age, there was a troll named Bobby, who lived under a wooden bridge and who was very unhappy. He had no friends and the children from town would come daily to torment him, throwing rocks and insulting comments his way. The children viewed Bobby as being different because of his appearance, but Bobby was not different, he had the same feelings and emotions other children had.

The children realized this one day when an errant rock, thrown by one of the children, hit Bobby in the head, causing his head to bleed and making him cry. The children felt guilty, realizing they were bullies and offered to help Bobby. After this incident, the children started to talk to Bobby instead of tormenting him. This led the children to understand that he really was no different on the inside, he only looked different on the outside. This new realization led to friendships, which was to everyone's benefit, especially Bobby. Because of the children's new feelings, he now had friends he could call his own, making him a very happy troll.

As children we tend to stigmatize other children as different if they do not look just like us. It is our duty, as adults, to teach children to be respectful and kind to these individuals they do not understand, creating a happier world for all.

A SAD STORY

⟨✦✦✦✦✦⟩

The elderly woman sat staring out her kitchen window. It was something she did daily, mourning the death of her husband of sixty years who had died suddenly beside her in bed. She had found him deceased when waking a year ago. This tragic moment was thought about daily and would never be forgotten. She was now alone, depression overwhelming her spirit, her will to live diminishing daily. Her daughter tried to help her but to no avail, her mother's grief could not be taken away from her.

She had lived a good life, but tragedy had struck early taking the life of their first born at birth. They continued to have children, bringing four new lives into their family. The years passed quickly, the children growing into adults, and leaving the parental nest to start their own lives. They were all now married, having given the woman the joy of grandchildren, who were now adults themselves.

The old woman's purpose in life was completed, and she realized she would be joining her husband soon. She sensed his spirit beckoning her to join him. One evening she summoned her daughter to be with her, as she knew her spirit would be leaving its earthly existence soon to join her husband in the afterlife. Her passing was peaceful, her sorrow no more, leaving her children with only memories of days gone past. A cycle of life that ends, but also goes on forever.

WHERE EVIL LURKS

+ + + + + +

The burning of the church and the desecration of the cemetery behind it, deeply saddened the residents of the small town. The church, which was built in the late 1800's, was a landmark in the community, and was still being used as a gathering place and a house of worship. Now it was gone, leaving only disbelief and shock that evil had invaded their quiet community.

The call to the fire department came in at 2 a.m., and upon their arrival they found this sacred church completely engulfed in flames. After the fire was extinguished, their attention turned to the cemetery, which had been vandalized. Many of the tombstones had been destroyed or knocked over, cementing the fact that this was no accident. The town mourned the loss of their church, built long ago by the men of this small-town taking root on the Indian River. The investigation by the fire marshal confirmed their suspicions, a combustible liquid, probably gas, was used to start the fire. The investigation that followed found no clues as to the identity of the culprit involved, leaving the town with the realization that Satan had successfully infiltrated this sacred place of worship.

During the clean up of the debris, a small metal box was discovered concealed in one of the walls, undamaged by the fire. When opened, it held a historical record of the founding of the town, the building of the grist mill and their beloved church, as well as other documents related to the early development of this small hamlet. Satan had destroyed the calm that surrounded this area, but God had provided them with something they could treasure from this tragedy, their history, a respite from the fact that their sanctuary had been destroyed.

A new church rose from the ashes, which brought the townspeople a sense of peace, a renewed faith that God was back in charge, and a symbol that the evil that had come to this town had been vanquished. The culprit was never found, but he was forgiven. The people knew evil was a powerful force that sometimes the human spirit can not overcome, ending in tragedies such as this.

As the years went by the memories faded but were never forgotten. The people's faith strengthened, their resolve to let this pass and harbor no ill-will towards the perpetrator an example of facing challenges with grace. Other small towns will experience similar tragedies, whether accidental or intentional, testing their beliefs, but in the end a much stronger faith will endure.

PARADISE

✦ ✦ ✦ ✦ ✦ ✦

The warm tropical breeze blew through the palm fronds of the coconut tree, its clump of nuts hanging, not ready to drop to the ground till ripe. The sounds of nature were the only music that could be heard, the lapping of the waves as they met land ending their long journey across the ocean, and the call of an errant seabird who had lost his way. This little piece of Bahamian land was special.

Sitting alone, it was a piece of paradise that had been discovered by few. Its sand, beaches, and fauna were undisturbed; a spit of land enjoyed by nature only, a pristine unspoiled part of the world untouched by the hand of man. Except for a visit long ago by Blackbeard the Pirate, who hid on the island while being chased by the English, no one had been here.

The British were determined to catch the scofflaw who had been preying on their ships, robbing, and plundering them. Blackbeard took no survivors, except the ships' captains, who were used as entertainment; being forced to walk the plank while the pirates watched in glory and celebration as the captured men were ripped apart and eaten by sharks. This idyllic island protected the pirate, but he only stayed as long as necessary, making his escape as soon as possible.

The putter of a small outboard motor pierced the quiet air as they searched for a piece of land suitable for docking their small boat. A large yacht sat offshore, signalling the presence of a rich American looking to buy a small island he could call his own. He wanted a piece of paradise where he could escape the hectic life he lived in Miami. Unable to find a safe landing spot, the men left, the island undisturbed.

The island would stay the same until climate change took its life, giving it the underwater burial God had planned for it. It was a paradise lost, never meant to be found.

RUBY

+ ++++ +

Ruby Smith was a wretched soul. Standing at just four foot ten inches in height, she had been born with a birth defect that had left her leg twisted. At three-years-old she was taught to use her first cane. The cane became a focal point of her life, never leaving her side. It also became a defining point as to how people reacted and felt about Ruby.

Ruby's house was in a small town at the end of a long street. Her neighbors had abandoned her years ago and their houses were never lived in again. Ruby was so hateful and mean that no one, including her own daughter, who had been born out of wedlock and had been unwanted by both Ruby and her boyfriend would have any contact with her. Ruby knew no love, nor was taught any manners or social skills as a child. Her parents were raging alcoholics who were consumed by their addiction.

To say the inside of Ruby's house was ramshackle is an understatement. Her yard was a mess also, neither seeing any work in years. If any one approached her house, Ruby would come out in a rage, swinging her cane, and yelling and screaming threats about what she would do to them. Over the years, people in town had reached out to her, but to no avail. Ruby just wanted to be left alone, simmering in her anger and hatred of her fellow humans.

When Ruby made her weekly walk into town, even the dogs knew enough to stay away, as many of them had felt the end of her cane if they got too close. The store keepers in town dreaded to see her coming, swinging her cane and muttering unkind words under her breath. When she entered the shops, a deadly silence of uneasy and negative feelings would overtake the room. Ruby loved the feelings she created. She loved making people feel little and worthless. After doing her shopping, she made her way home, to the relief of the shopkeepers who had no idea how to deal with this problem they called Ruby.

One week it was unusually quiet in town. Nobody had seen Ruby, who always made her presence known. People sensed something was wrong but were afraid to investigate. This had happened before and when someone gathered the courage to enter Ruby's house to check on her, she was waiting with her cane and administered a beating while accusing the person of coming to rob her. But this time felt different. The police had to be called.

In the past, if the townspeople asked the police to visit Ruby's house, she would fly into a rage and make life even more miserable for everyone. She was in control. The nearest law enforcement officers were thirty miles away; the town too small to pay for its own force. However, someone made the call and after a long wait, the police finally arrived. They carefully made their way inside the house, aware of this woman's reputation. The town's people waited patiently outside, expecting an outbreak of violence at any time. But there was nothing but silence.

After what seemed like an eternity, the police came out and said that Ruby was no more. They had found her at the bottom of the stairs, her cane thrown across the room as she fell to her death. Ruby would not be missed. Would there be a place in heaven for Ruby or would her wretched soul burn in hell for all the misdeeds and hatred she expressed while on earth? You decide.

THE RABID DOG

King was the family dog. He was allowed to freely roam the forests that surrounded the farm where he lived. He would sometimes not be seen all day, only returning home to feed his hungry belly at dinnertime. During these outings he would chase the squirrels and chipmunks, or any other small animal that he crossed paths with. He had a girlfriend the next farm over that he would visit. She was always glad to see him. After his visit he would find a large clearing in the forest, where he would lay down and let the sun warm him while he napped.

One morning the family noticed that King was not himself. He was lethargic, he walked with a stagger, and he acted angry. In the nineteen fifties rabies was always on your radar if you lived in a rural area. If your dog exhibited unusual behaviour, like King was displaying, he would be isolated and monitored. If the condition progressed to frothing at the mouth, and it looked like the dog was losing his mind, it was usually rabies.

Unfortunately for King, he had chased the wrong animal, been bitten, and contracted this incurable disease. The sentence for these actions was his funeral. The dog was buried on the family farm, missed dearly by his owners and his girlfriend who lived on the neighboring farm.

Even when life seems perfect, your world can change in seconds. Unfortunately, this is what happened to King.

THE MYSTERIOUS WILL

·✦✦✦✦✦·

G randpa was old, reaching the age of ninety on his next birthday. He had come from a poor family that valued a dollar. This
led Grandpa to believe the same way. He was known to family
and friends as the cheapest man alive. Little did they know about the
vast wealth he had created in his lifetime. His frugal lifestyle had fooled
everyone. Even when Grandma died, he had claimed poverty, expecting
the family to chip in and help pay her funeral expenses. After her death,
things changed for Grandpa, he became sad and lonely, withdrew from
family and friends, and became a recluse. No matter what was said or
done, nothing seemed to help, leading the family to eventually leave
Grandpa alone.

Family and friends had often thought Grandpa was up to something, but no one knew the truth. Grandma had kept the secret well,
taking it to her grave. Grandpa was the largest seller of "as seen on TV"
merchandise, which brought him immense wealth. He was obsessed
with becoming even wealthier, spending his days inventing gadgets to
be sold on television. He had created and sold over a hundred products
under assumed names to keep his business a secret. But in his old age his
health was failing. He was almost blind, his heart was bad, and he had
recently experienced a stroke that kept him in the hospital for a week.
He started thinking about death and how fast his life could be taken
from him. It was time to get his affairs in order, time to launch his plan.

Grandpa loved his family dearly, but his money was not going to be handed out without stipulations. There were three families, including sons, a daughter, and grandchildren that were to share his inheritance. Grandpa's biggest surprise was that no one knew about the money, and his children were probably thinking they would have to foot the bill for his service and burial when he died.

Grandpa shut down his business, collected his assets in one place, and drafted his will. He directed each family, before receiving any monies, would be required to travel to every country in the world at Grandpa's expense. They would then be required to write a five-hundred-word essay on the most important event that happened during their visit. They had two years to accomplish this task, and when successfully completed, their inheritance would be released. Failure to comply meant the loss of the money. His lawyers would be monitoring carefully.

One morning Grandpa woke up abruptly with pains in his chest. He knew it was his time to go and his wish to die peacefully at home in his sleep would be granted. Grandpa took a sleeping aid and was soon in heaven with Grandma. As expected by his family members, they paid the cost of his funeral. However, two weeks later everything changed with the reading of the will.

The entire family could not believe he had been able to keep this secret for so many years. His children were all able to complete the travel challenge and fulfill Grandpa's wishes; not a day goes by without Grandma and Grandpa being in their thoughts. Perhaps this was Grandpa's plan, having his children remember him in a positive light long after his death.

THE CUTHBERTSON HOUSE

+ + + + + +

T he old farm lay abandoned, once a cornerstone of this small farming community, it now lay in ruins, age and neglect taking its toll. The children in the family had no interest in keeping this a working farm, instead choosing college, and moving to the city to work. Three generations of the Cuthbertson family had farmed this land and established their name in the area. Their two sons wanted to sell the farm as is, with all contents included, after the sudden death of both parents. Very few of their family's personal belongings were removed from the home.

The farm came to his attention through a family friend. This friend had known the Cuthbertson's, including the two sons, whom he knew were getting ready to sell. Arrangements were made to look at the property, and he soon found himself the proud owner of a nice piece of land in the country, a dream come true. After taking possession and entering the house for the first time as the new owner, he was overwhelmed by the fact that everything had been left as it was before the parents died. Furnishings, in the family for a hundred years, remained, left like garbage to be discarded later. This represented someone's life who no longer existed; the material belongings accumulated during their life on earth. Of no value to them now, their lives changing from a physical existence to a spiritual one.

The investigation of the attic proved to be interesting. A trunk revealed old clothing that had belonged to the previous owner's grandmother, a picture album of days gone by on the farm, and a box of costume jewelry that was old and valuable. He kept exploring, finding Grandpa's fishing collection; a large assortment of plugs, in like-new condition, and a collection of old fishing poles included in his find. Moving to the basement he was surprised to find other family heirlooms, including an old butter churn and a wringer washer. Preserves sat on a table in the corner, still edible, left with the intention they would be enjoyed at a future meal.

The outbuildings included two large barns, their grey boards showing their age. Farm equipment of all kinds filled one of the barns, while the other held everything needed to milk cows, even the milk cooler still there. After careful consideration, the new owner produced a plan. He would have a large farm auction and donate the proceeds to the town, which was raising funds for a new park and playground equipment.

The auction went well. He met the local people who welcomed him and wished him luck. The money earned paid for the playground equipment and was well received. As a token of the town's appreciation a plaque was installed at the new playground in gratitude. He was made to feel welcomed to the neighborhood. A welcome he would keep, living his life in the community until his sudden death twenty years later. His presence in the area not forgotten, the little plaque in his honor remembering him for the good man he was.

THE VAMPIRE AND
THE SCARECROW

❖❖❖❖❖

The deserted mansion stood on the hill. It was abandoned a hundred years ago by a man who now lived in a secret room in the basement. He was a vampire, and his bed was a casket. He was very lonely, the bats that lived in the attic were his only friends. After dark he would raise himself up from his casket and wander the grounds of the old mansion, looking for comfort from the fact that this life would be eternal.

On one of his nightly wanderings, he noticed something different. A garden had been planted, and guarding it was a scarecrow. The vampire moved closer for a better look, examining the scarecrow's red plaid shirt, his coveralls, and his big floppy hat. He was stuffed with straw that mice loved to make their home in. The scarecrow's face lit up as he saw this potential friend come closer. He thought he would be alone here with only the birds he was to keep away. The scarecrow reached his hand out in a greeting, the vampire obliged, extending his hand also.

This started a friendship between the vampire and the scarecrow that lasted long after the garden was harvested. The vampire visited nightly, until one evening during the winter, a blizzard took the life of the scarecrow, scattering his remains over the snowy landscape. The vampire had lost his friend and was deeply saddened, the only comfort he now had was his casket, and pleasant memories. These memories would turn to reality when his friend in the garden returned in the spring. This brought happiness and joy to the vampire and scarecrow as they continued their friendship. Sadly, the next time the scarecrow's life was taken in a storm, he never returned, leaving the vampire to resume his old life of wandering the grounds alone, a situation only he could understand.

HONEY

+ ✦ ✦ ✦ ✦ ✦ +

Honey was a cat, a special cat, born in a rural area. Honey's mother lived her entire life in the farmer's barn; she was in charge of an elimination campaign against a large colony of mice that also lived there. The mice lived in a mountain of hay and straw, where they were quite comfortable making homes and having babies. The barn had six cats. They slept all day and hunted all night, each able to fill their stomachs full of mice. Their reward was all you could drink fresh milk from the cooler as soon as the farmer entered the barn for his morning milking. After drinking their fill, the cats would scatter to different areas of the barn where they would sleep all day, and then repeat the process all over again.

Honey was born in the hay loft. She had two brothers and two sisters, but sadly one of her sisters died at birth. The mother lovingly nurtured her new family and soon they were large enough to come out and play on the hay bales and explore the area near their den. As the weeks went by the kittens were old enough to join the other cats for their morning milk. They would then retire back home where they would play hard and sleep, often dreaming about hunting and stalking their future prey.

One morning after drinking milk, the farmer approached Honey, picked her up gently, and quickly left the barn. Because of Honey's sweet disposition, the farmer and his wife decided to keep her, making her a house cat and their pet. At first Honey had a tough time adjusting to her new role, but she was treated with love and affection and became a relaxed and comfortable cat. She usually accompanied the farmer to the barn for fresh milk and a visit with her mother and siblings. She waited every day until the farmer finished milking his cows, spending her time playing with the cows' swishing tails, biting and jumping on them. They would then return to the house where she would sleep in her favorite chair for rest of the day.

The years went by, and Honey had grown into a wise and healthy cat. The farmer had been sick and after forty years of farming was forced to give up his livelihood. They sold their farm and were moving into town to be closer to doctors and hospitals. Honey could not move with them, as their new building allowed no pets. They had to give her up which made them sad, but by the grace of God their son had two friends who took her in and give her a loving home.

Honey is well, she was not happy at first, but after learning trust she has settled in and now is enjoying her new home she shares with another cat and a dog. Honey will enjoy a long and happy life with her new owners, bringing happiness to this household as she had done for the farmer and his wife.

THE LUCKY GOSLING

✦✦✦✦✦

Once upon a time, in a swampy area in the wetlands, a mother sat on her eggs. This goose had already lost two eggs to ravens, leaving six of the original eight she laid. As hatching day arrived only four of the six eggs produced goslings, due to a problem with fertilization. The proud parents led their small brood away from the nest and taught them how to feed on vegetation, the first thing the babies learned to eat. But the parents, not realizing the danger, led the little flock out to the river where a hungry muskie lived. Muskies are large mean fish which can grow up to thirty pounds. The one in the river instantly made a quick meal of one of the little geese. Retreating into the swamp for safety did not change the geese's luck, as a large hawk swooped down and snatched up another one of their babies, a delicious snack for a hungry bird. The gander and his wife now only had two babies left.

The parents' string of bad luck did not end here, as one of the goslings swallowed a large amount of fishing line, which wrapped around his internal organs, killing him. The last gosling's life was saved, not by a stroke of luck, but by a young girl who found her alone. She had been deserted by her parents and was hungry and very unhappy. The young girl took the tiny gosling home and nurtured it back to health, becoming a surrogate mother to this bird. She named her Sally, after one of her favorite aunts. Sally would not leave the girl's side, getting jealous if anyone came near her.

As fall approached, Sally, now a full-grown bird, would go off on her own for longer periods of time. Her instincts were taking over, as she was looking for a flock that would accept her and allow her to fly south with them. One day in early November she never returned to her surrogate mother, who feared she would never see Sally again. Unlike her siblings, Sally was given a chance at life because of the love and care of a young girl and her family.

To the young girl's surprise, she did see Sally again, as the goose brought her new family to meet the young girl who saved her life. For years Sally returned for a visit, until one year she did not, her life taken by accident or disease. The little girl grew into adulthood never forgetting this pleasant memory from her childhood. The goose felt likewise, given a chance at a life it never should have had. This relationship was one of life's treasures, a lifelong bond, even though it was an unusual friendship.

GOOSE

G oose the dog was born in Watertown, New York, one of ten puppies, six boys and four girls. His mother was a busy animal feeding and caring for her babies. Luckily, her responsible owners fed the mother nutritious food, making sure she had plenty of water, and keeping her maternity area clean.

The puppies thrived, and after eight weeks there was a steady supply of people, coming in and out of the house choosing their puppies, all except Goose. Being the smallest in the family, no one thought he would grow up to be a big, strong, healthy dog. The owners, feeling sorry for Goose, decided to keep him, to the delight of their young daughter who had adored him since birth.

Goose and Melissa, who was three, were inseparable, one never without the other. Soon it was summertime, which meant going to the cottage in Canada. The summer retreat was situated on a lake near Kingston, Ontario, a short drive from Watertown. The family spent the entire summer there, fishing, boating, exploring the area, and enjoying the company of the hospitable Canadian people. Goose had grown up to be a healthy and strong dog. His favorite activity was pulling Melissa around in a cart that her father had built. They were inseparable friends until an incident that changed both of their lives.

It was time to leave Canada; the car was packed and off the family went. As they were approaching the border, a tractor-trailer cut off the car, causing it to careen off the road and into a ditch. The car hit a small tree which caused the back door to open. Goose was scared and leaped out of the car, running into the woods not knowing what happened. The car was wrecked, but the family was fine. Melisa was sobbing because Goose was gone. The family would regret not having had Goose micro-chipped.

Goose was lost and frightened, not knowing what to do next. He kept walking until he saw a farmhouse, which he approached cautiously. The farmer, who happened to see Goose, called out gently and Goose approached tail wagging. He was glad he had found someone who might be able to help him. The farmer kept Goose for a couple of days, and after consulting with his wife decided to take the dog to the animal shelter in Kingston, where they could look for his owner. After an exhausted search, with no luck, he was put up for adoption.

Because of the trauma of the car accident, losing his family, and being put in the shelter, Goose developed severe anxiety and would never be able to be left alone again. Luckily for Goose there was a young male couple looking to adopt a dog like him. They found him on the internet, made an appointment to see him, and it was love at first sight. Goose was saved and he was one happy dog.

He soon settled in his new home. It would be different living here, but he could feel the love and warmth from his new family and sensed he would be safe and comfortable. Goose adapted quickly and made friends with the two cats that lived here, Honey and Sven. He was still sad at times, but was happy to be part of this new family, and his new family was happy to have found such a nice dog, a dog named Goose.

THE LITTLE MOUSE

✦ ✦ ✦ ✦ ✦ ✦ ✦

The old farmhouse beckoned, the mother mouse anxious to get into her shelter, the cold north wind telling her winter was coming soon. She entered the house through the root cellar, where she would find a secluded place, build her nest, and have her babies. Nightly outings to the upstairs would find sufficient food, but also danger. The cat was her most lethal enemy; if this animal caught her she would be dinner. When humans sensed her presence, they would set traps which had to be avoided, it was certain death if caught in one of these devices.

The mother mouse had protected her nest well, finding a hole in the foundation big enough for her and her babies to hide in, away from their enemies that occupied the same dwelling. Childbirth for the mouse brought six new babies, one being pure white and much smaller than its siblings. It was an albino miniature mouse, able to go where no other mouse could go. He would lead the cat away to the far parts of the house, the cat never able to catch him because of his size and colour, giving the rest of the family time to come out and feel safe. Soon this became a game, as the little mouse ran all around the house with the cat in tow.

One day while running from the cat, he slipped on a newly waxed floor and ended up the cat's prisoner. He thought his end was near. But instead of eating the mouse, the cat gently held it between his paws, and purring loudly, started grooming the little mouse. The little mouse enjoyed the affection, returning the fondness by nibbling on the cat's ear. A wonderful bond was established, and these friends played daily.

The mother mouse and her babies were no longer bothered by the cat, who left them alone to enjoy the comforts of the large farmhouse. Spring came and soon it was time for the mice to leave their winter retreat, leaving behind the little white mouse. He had decided to stay with his friend the cat, who he knew would protect him from life's dangers. The little mouse remained with his friend until one morning the cat found the little mouse dead at their favorite meeting place. The cat was sad but marvelled at the friendship he had developed with the little mouse, a memory he took to his own death a brief time later, proving that sometimes enemies can become friends.

THE INDIAN BLANKET

———— ✦✦✦✦✦✦ ————

The palomino pony was the young Indian's most prized possession. The horse was given to him by his father on his sixteenth
birthday. It was his job to break the horse and train it to be
strong and loyal to its owner. The biggest asset to the early Indians who
occupied North America before the mass migration of settlers from
Europe was the horse. The natives waged a relentless war against these
new settlers, to no avail, eventually losing all of their land. The Indians
were forced to live on reservations, where they were beset by disease
brought from Europe. The white man's purpose was to break the Indians'
will, starvation and poverty their lethal weapons.

The sixteen-year-old Indian boy was now a man. His pony had
served him well, in buffalo hunts, and hit-and-run attacks against his
enemies, saving his life on numerous occasions. He was alone now, his
father killed in a raid on an army camp, and his mother dying at the
hands of the soldiers, who raided, ransacked, and burned her village,
taking no prisoners. He still had two gifts from his village, the palomino
pony his father had given him, and the beautiful blanket his mother had
made for his horse. When he was riding this animal he felt his parents
were there with him.

The years went by and the gifts he received when he was young were
his most treasured belongings. His pony finally passed of old age, and
the once strong and healthy brave succumbed to a smallpox infection,

his mother's blanket wrapped tightly around him, comforting him as he transitioned to what death had to offer. His parents met him in the afterlife, securing their bond that had followed him from birth, a love that had never died, and now never would, as their souls joined for an eternity in heaven.

THE FARM

+ + ✦ ✦ ✦ + +

The north wind was howling, blowing the snow against the old barn. The animals inside were warm and comfortable. The cattle were lined up in a row waiting for the farmer to come and feed them. The calves in the pen were nestled in their bed of warm straw, with the mother pig and her babies enjoying the same benefit. Pigeons cooed in the rafters, while field mice burrowed in the hay, their nests a warm retreat from the winter cold. Their enemy was the barn cat. If you were a rodent, you had a lot to be fearful of, as these stalkers hunted you for food.

The barn had multiple uses. The main upper building was for the storage of hay and grain, the bottom for hosting the farm animals. Large sheds were built beside the barn to store farm equipment.

Mornings came early, work usually began before daybreak. The turn of the doorknob usually set things in motion. The cows waiting to be fed were the first to break the silence, followed by noisy cats and a brood of kittens waiting for milk. The farmer entered the barn turning on the lights, the cats swarming his feet looking for attention.

Winter was the farmer's time to relax, even though his duties were still many. His fields lay empty, covered deep in winter snow, giving him a much-needed rest from the responsibilities he faced in the summer.

After feeding the cats, and much to their disapproval, Barney was let into the barn. He was the farm dog, a rambunctious collie who made it a game to chase the cats into hiding, sometimes scaring the kittens so badly they would not reveal their hiding spots all day. Barney would then drink all their leftover milk, leaving them nothing. The cats were always glad when the milking was over so the dog would leave the barn.

The farmer wrapped up his work; he would return to the barn before dinner to repeat this process all over again. He took his dog and went back to the warmth of his home and his wife, glad their lives led them in this direction and not to the corporate halls of business. The man and his dog napped, their bond unmistakable, their future inseparable, as they traveled on this path of a life they both enjoyed, living on the farm.

THE ANGEL

◆ ◆ ◆ ◆ ◆ ◆

The angel waited in the afterlife. Her job was to collect the souls of the dearly departed on earth and reunite them with their loved ones in heaven. The old woman lay in the hospital bed, her transition from her physical life to a spiritual one only a short time away.

She had lost her husband of sixty years just weeks before, and was never able to accept his death, choosing instead to join him. She had given up on life, which would lead to the early departure of her soul from earth. She lay dying, a smile on her face knowing her suffering would be ending soon, and she would be joining her husband in an eternal afterlife.

This woman had lived a happy and productive life, enjoying her ninety years with little sickness. She was the mother of four children and had eight grandchildren. She was an active member of her church, teaching Sunday school and involving herself in other children's activities. Now she lay waiting for the angel to take her soul to a place where she will be happy forever.

Her family held her close, her eyes were closed, her passing was quiet, only the weeping of her children could be heard. The angel had come for her, so the woman, who had said her goodbyes accompanied the angel to the afterlife where she was forever united with her loved ones, joining as one with the spirits in heaven.

MENTAL ILLNESS

✦✦✦✦✦✦

The elderly woman sat alone, her eyes fixated on the television, her only contact with human company. She tried talking to them, but the conversation was not returned, ignoring the woman as if she did not exist. The virus that had swept the world had left her in isolation, at home alone, the few visitors she used to have no longer came. She had no family but an estranged son, who she had not seen in years. Before the pandemic caused by the Covid virus she was healthy and self sufficient, but as the months went by and the lockdowns continued, the stress and isolation started taking its toll.

A deep depression set in, she quit eating and bathing as her mental health deteriorated. She was alone, no family to turn to, or people willing to help her. She sat in front of the TV, her stare now the stare of death as she succumbed to a situation this elderly woman did not deserve, an abandonment by her son, neighbours, and friends leaving her to die in her chair alone. The police found her, after a mail carrier reported mail not being picked up. The TV was still on, and she was still in her chair, deceased. This woman was not a victim of the virus, but of a lack of love, loneliness being the cause of death, not Covid. Another victim of circumstance, hers a life that will never be missed.

SCIENCE FICTION AND HORROR

THE HUNTER

+ + + + + +

CHAPTER ONE

The man waited for months, his instinct to kill engrained in his spirit. His quest was to witness the moment of impact as the bullet slammed into its target bringing his victim to his knees and then a certain death, as the high caliber bullet pierced his heart. The man had hatched his devious plot during a psychotic breakdown, a period of delusional thoughts that had turned violent. He waited for hunting season to start.

The deer and moose hunters were flooding the area's forests giving this man we will call Brian, the prey he so desired. Brian was a hunter, whose only prey was man. He had served in Iraq in the infantry, treated like fodder to feed the enemy. He would now have his revenge, becoming a serial killer no one would soon forget. His rifle was ready, his scope military grade, a certain kill shot at a long distance guaranteed. The excitement of the hunt thrilled him, taking him back to Iraq where he was trained to do such things. However, these men were more likely be his American brothers than the dreaded Muslim enemy he was used to killing.

He chose a secluded spot to park his truck, where it could not be easily seen. He carried his rifle, his combat experience returning to him, thinking the enemy must be terminated. His first victim was a young man who had learned to hunt with his father. The hunter walked slowly, his eyes watching intently for movement, a sign his prey might be near. Brian followed the man with his scope, waiting for the moment he would squeeze the trigger and feel the rush of adrenaline that would course through his body at the prospect of a kill. The young man had no idea he was the hunted, and his life would end at the hands of a psychotic killer, revelling in the fact he had just killed his first victim.

Brian fired and then approached the kill with caution. Many men learned the hard way when they weren't cautious, ending up dead or getting wounded themselves by a deceiving enemy. Brian picked up the man's small frame and carried him to a swampy area where he left the body in the water. Freeze-up was soon approaching and Brian was hoping for the snow and ice to conceal the body for months to come. He placed the body by the beaver dam and covered it with brush and sticks. It looked like the handiwork of the beaver preparing his home for the winter.

Brian returned home, happy with the success he felt on his first day of the hunt. He wondered if hunters felt the same elation when they watched their prey fall, lifeless and still on the cold ground. The dead hunter's wife reported her husband missing, but a search turned up nothing, only talk of another hunter gone, his family fearing the worse. The idea of not knowing why these men disappeared gripped the community, a bad situation that only seemed to be getting worse. This was the start of a mystery that the people would have to deal with, not a picture they wanted to face now, or in the future.

CHAPTER TWO

Brian was born in a small town in Maine. An only child, he became a mama's boy because of all the extra attention his mother showered on him. His father was a self-employed electrician, known around town as a dependable and trustworthy member of the community. Brian was six when his parents divorced. He did not understand the concept of Mommy and Daddy living apart and did not take the separation well. A resentful spirit he could not shed gripped his soul.

Even as a child Brian had few friends, preferring to play by himself rather than enjoy the company of other children. Because of this misunderstood attitude he portrayed, he was frowned upon as being different, which unfortunately led to consistent bullying by his schoolmates. Brian's mother worried about his social skills and the sullen and unhappy attitude he carried with him. He visited therapists who were mystified by his odd behavior, not being able to give advice to his mother that made anything better.

Brian struggled in school, his moods not making it easy for his teachers. The constant bullying had made him bitter, causing him to lash out in defense at the least provocation. Graduation from middle school was a cause for celebration. Next year was high school and a fresh start. The idea of going to high school seemed to brighten Brian's moods. He made a new friend and seemed to be a much happier person. But the dark clouds soon rolled back in, returning Brian to the state of mind there seemed to be no escape from.

His struggles in elementary and middle school paled in comparison to high school, as the trials and tribulations of the teenage years became clear. His fascination with guns and violence started at sixteen. He talked his mother into buying him a hunting rifle under the pretense that it was to hunt moose, a popular game animal in Maine. He loved to feel the power that coursed through his body when he had the rifle in his hands. He was a hunter, a stalker of man.

During hunting season in Maine, he took to the woods, reveling in his fantasy as he followed unsuspecting hunters through the forest pretending to wait for the perfect opportunity to kill his prey. Now it was a fantasy, tomorrow it could be his reality. Brian produced a plan; he would become an army sniper after he finished high school. His perverted fantasy would become a reality, with the legal authority to kill anyone he perceived as being the enemy. Nausea affected him as the excitement of this plan struck him.

Brian finished high school and enlisted in the army. He was accepted into sniper school and taught how to make the perfect kill. For once in his life, he found something he knew he would love doing. His mother was pleased with the choices her son made, not knowing the real motive behind these decisions. She never thought about him returning home as an experienced killer, returning with this talent to a small town that would never be the same.

CHAPTER THREE

Brian had done well at boot camp, his interest in becoming a sniper dulled the authoritative dialogue he had to deal with daily. He knew to become successful as a young man in the army he had to listen, obey commands, and always be respectful towards commanding officers. Following these three rules would make his new life in the service more manageable.

The plane landed in Iraq without incident, the expanse of the desert sand intrigued Brian, he wondered how so many people could call this place home. The hot desert air greeted him as he stepped off the plane. Bagram Air Force Base was abuzz with activity. The largest in Iraq, it had been taken over by the Americans to use as their main operating base in their war against Saddam Hussein loyalists, insurgents, and any other fighters who considered them invaders.

Brian had done well at sniper school, averaging a 90% kill rate on his exams. He was very excited about his new job and was looking forward to receiving his rifle. His company was taken by bus to their barracks and assigned beds. They were lectured on rules and the importance of following them. The officer stressed they were in an active war zone and death could rear its ugly head at any time, so always be prepared for any situation to develop quickly. The new recruits would be allowed to rest for the remainder of the day, giving them a chance to get accustomed to their surroundings. They would report for duty at daybreak tomorrow.

Early morning found the barracks in a state of chaos as the young men nervously got ready for their first day of active duty. They were as-signed to various companies short on men because of combat deaths or injuries. Brian was assigned to different groups, whenever a sniper was needed in the day's combat operations. He was given his rifle; the most modern high-tech weapon money could buy. He felt the power surge through his very soul, as the thought of taking another human life left him in an exhilarated state, which he hid well from others. He was sent to the gun range for the day to get use to his new weapon, and to get to know his partner who would accompany him and help with the logistics of his job.

His first duty assignment would be tomorrow. Brian liked his new partner and was sure he would prove to be more of an asset than a hindrance. They ate dinner at the mess hall together, a surprisingly good meal considering the obstacles that had to be overcome just getting the food here. They were also assigned to the same bunkhouse, the senior officers knowing a complete and trusting bond had to be developed between these men in order to make this important operation work.

Sleep was fleeting as the thoughts of men in his scope ready to be shot down like rabid dogs excited Brian greatly. The reality of combat and the realization that his death could be imminent at any time, brought focus to his situation. It made him wonder if the decisions he made were the right ones, or ones that would later take his life; a lesson Brian would learn the hard way,

CHAPTER FOUR

Darkness still prevailed as the desert sun slowly made its way up over the horizon, the new recruits awakening, getting ready for another day in this war-torn hell hole of destroyed lives and souls. Brian did not sleep well, the thought of him participating in combat now being a reality he would have to face. He got ready for the day with mixed emotions, not knowing what to expect or how he would feel in real combat. Uncertainties replaced his earlier expectations.

A force of a hundred men traveled to a small Iraqi town that had been overrun by insurgents. Their mission was to clear the town of these men, freeing the inhabitants from their rule, and eliminating a possible danger so close to their base. They reached their intended target without incident, but an uneasy silence gripped the town. No business or commerce was taking place, the civilian population staying in the only security they knew, their homes. Advance word had come through spies working at the American base, who had overheard conversations about upcoming missions. This was the enemy's main intelligence gathering method, spies on base or sympathetic civilians who hated the American occupation of their country.

The caravan stopped, smelling an ambush. Drones were called in from Bagram Air Base, sending back video of enemy movement and defensive positions. The drones remained in the area to help the Americans during the battle for the town. Armoured vehicles moved into town, soldiers filling the bellies of these machines, waiting to be dropped off in strategic areas to do battle with the insurgents. Brian proceeded to a designated spot on a rooftop that would give him a clear view of his surroundings. His partner joined him, and they set up their position together.

The insurgents held their fire, knowing they had no munitions that would puncture the thick steel the personnel carriers were clad with. Giving away their positions, and wasting their limited supply of ammunition, would not be a good battlefield tactic to take at this time. Brian's position overlooked a large strategic area. His hands shook as he prepared his rifle, adrenalin coursing through his body. He looked through the scope, noticing men running from building to building. Anyone on the streets was considered the enemy.

The US commander sent Brian a message to sight someone and try to make the first kill. This would cause the enemy to start shooting, revealing their positions. Brian found the man in his scope, an insurgent who had let his guard down and was lounging lazily against a building, providing a good chance of being successful with his first shot. The crack of the rifle and watching the man's head explode in his scope brought a feeling of euphoria Brian had never experienced before. His doubts disappeared, replaced by an appetite for killing and the overwhelming feelings it created, like food for his soul.

The battle for the town was violent and bloody resulting in casualties on both sides, the insurgents taking heavy losses and surrendering in high numbers due to a lack of ammunition. Brian had three kills, the Iraqis becoming more careful when they realized there was a sniper's nest hidden somewhere. After a hard twenty-four hours of fighting, the town fell to the Americans. Prisoners were taken and were brought back to the base where a large prison camp had been set up. The returning men were exhausted, getting no sleep since the battle had begun. They chose food and then their barracks for some much-needed sleep. Their dreams were now ingrained with battle scars, as the reality of war took away the glory of participating in it; a war not winnable in anyone's dreams, only death a possible outcome for the young men fighting this battle of little sensibilities.

CHAPTER FIVE

Brian made few friends, keeping to himself, living in a world of fantasy, death being his main object of desire. His time in Iraq would soon end, sending him back to the US where he would continue to feed his fantasies about killing, and the satisfaction it brought to his troubled spirit. One incident while performing his duties would end his career in the army.

While on a mission, his partner and only friend was shot in the head, his brain matter covering Brian with explosive force. His friend lay dead beside him, mortally wounded. He radioed for help, the situation crippling his mind, causing him to lose his sanity and experience a complete mental breakdown. Brian was evacuated and sent to a hospital in Germany where he was treated for the psychiatric disorder he was suffering from. After two weeks of treatment and therapy he was sent back to the US to continue his medical care through the Veteran's Affairs hospital. He was placed on a regiment of anti-psychotic drugs, given an honourable discharge from the army, and sent home. The drugs Brian was taking advanced his psychosis, causing him to be delusional. His mind took him back to Iraq glorifying in his kills as he squeezed the trigger and watched his prey fall dead, their lives gone, never to enjoy life's pleasures because of their sudden death.

Brian did not adapt well to being home. His desire to kill and the feeling it created in him overpowered his thinking. He came up with a diabolical plan; he tricked his mother into buying him a rifle with a high-powered scope under the pretence of using it for hunting. His mother, thinking it would be good for his health to be in the solitude of the forest, did what he asked. He was unable to buy the rifle himself because his mental health issues made him ineligible; this a result of the incidents that happened while serving in Iraq.

A feeling of familiarity gripped Brian as he studied his new rifle. He had chosen well; a gun powerful enough to take down a moose his weapon of choice to add kills to his legacy. He would pursue his career as the hunter, stalking man through the forest waiting for the opportune time to make the kill. He revelled in his fantasies, stalking his victims in his dreams, always coming out the victor. Brian's mother had noticed an uptick in his mood. She figured he was happy to get the rifle and was waiting for the hunting season to open. Little did she know that her son's interest was not in shooting deer, a most boring sport compared to the one Brian was going to participate in.

Brian had taken a job at a convenience store, his mother thinking it would be good for his mental health to have some interaction with other people. This is where he met Julie, the wayward daughter of wealthy parents who had abandoned her as a teen when she developed a drug habit, quit school, and moved in with an older boyfriend. She was now clean from drugs, but her life was a mess. Julie liked Brian and would come and visit him nightly. A relationship soon developed, dragging Julie into a world of horror and insanity she would become a willing participant in. This would change her once uneventful life into something more sinister and deadly; a future she would choose for herself.

CHAPTER SIX

Julie and Brian's relationship was blossoming. They were a perfect match for each other, supplementing one another in their equally bizarre take on reality. Julie had suffered serious mental health issues whichhad never been resolved, making her an easy target to be recruited into Brian's diabolical plan of murder and mayhem. She revealed her past to him, a well-kept secret of the torture and death she inflicted on her pets and other animals she had access to. The suffering these animals went through brought an excitement to her unmatched in any other way. Brian was sure he had found a trusted companion, someone willing to look away when a murder was committed.

The couple made numerous trips to the rock pit, a secluded area where Julie was taught to use the rifle, Brian willing to give up a kill for his girlfriend. She spent a lot of time at Brian's house much to the dismay of his mother. She did not like or trust Julie and knew she was no good for her son. A large argument broke out between Brian and his mother over his girlfriend. His mother did not want Julie in the house. Brian was forced to choose between them; he chose Julie. He would have to move.

Brian had started receiving disability payments from the service, along with a lump sum of money that was owed to him while he had waited for his claim to be processed. His part-time job at the convenience store was secure and Julie had some money coming in monthly from welfare. They rented a ramshackle house in a poor area of town. It was all they could afford, but a safe place for them to hide after they launched their plan of murder and terror in this small town. The move was successful. Brian was glad he was finally out from under his mother's controlling behaviour, and now the decisions he made would be solely his own.

Brian's wait was nearing an end. Soon the forests would be full of hunters looking for deer and moose to kill, giving Brian many targets to choose from. His rifle had been cleaned and polished many times in anticipation of his first kill, a sacred time for a serial killer just starting on his journey to hell, his future reward for taking innocent lives. Brian didn't care, he knew his soul belonged to the devil and where he ends up is where he wanted to be.

Brian packed his rifle in his truck and headed to a very secluded region that few hunters visited because of the terrain. He had been to this area previously and knew it to provide a perfect location to hide his truck and a good opportunity to hunt the rare human who ventured here. He found his stand, a cluster of rocks and trees that would provide good cover. He waited, silent and motionless, his training as a sniper returning to him.

The silence of the forest was broken by the snapping of twigs. Brian saw movement coming toward him and trained his scope on the unsuspecting young man. He followed his movements, knowing that with a squeeze of his finger the man's life would be no more. But Brian was a hunter, he would stalk his prey and would only shoot when he was assured of a kill. Brian followed him. Finally tiring of playing this game, he waited. As the man passed, Brian took aim and shot him, causing him to fall dead in a pool of his own blood. The hunter rejoiced, successful in his first mission. He hid the body, making it very hard to be found. He hoped that after a short search the authorities would quit looking, thinking the man had gotten lost and perished in the rugged terrain.

Brian collected his thoughts and left the area to return home and share the good news with Julie. It was not such good news for the worried wives of the victims. One thought she was searching for a lost and injured husband, who unbeknownst to her was spending the winter with a colony of beavers. The other was left wondering what happened to her husband as he didn't return from his hunting trip and never contacted her again. Brian's next victim would suffer a similar fate, as a never-ending lust for new victims would control his behavior and draw Julie into the hideous web of murder and torture. Not even God could save them from the path they had chosen to embark on but being saved from God was the least important thing on their minds, as horror was where their interests lay.

CHAPTER SEVEN

Brian's urge to go hunting again gnawed like an addiction at his soul, the notion of making his third kill overpowering all his thoughts, driving him to launch a plan for his next hunting trip. He would take Julie with him so he could watch her admire his great skills as a hunter. He would teach her to stalk the victim through the forest, shooting at the most opportune time, making sure the first shot was the only one needed.

They left an hour before daybreak to drive fifty miles north to a known hunting area. Brian's plan was to stalk and shoot his prey, leaving the victim exactly where he had stood. He hoped the authorities would rule it a tragic accident caused by an overzealous hunter who mistook the man's movement for that of a deer.

On the way to the site Brian was pulled over by a young cop who had been behind him, noticing his licence plate light was out. Having nothing better to do, the officer decided to pull Brian over and give him a warning. Brian was nervous as he saw the flashing lights in his rear-view mirror, knowing this cop wanted to talk with him. The police officer approached the open window telling Brian the reason he had stopped him. After some small talk and a verbal warning, the cop let the pair go, not asking for any identification or searching the truck and finding the rifle. The couple breathed a sigh of relief as they watched the cop drive off, silence overtaking the vehicle as this made them realize the seriousness of the situation they were to undertake and the penalties that would be involved if they were caught.

This incident did not change Brian's plans, as the urge to kill was an overpowering emotion he could not control. They reached the area, put the truck in a secluded spot so it could not be seen by passing traffic, readied their equipment, and struck out into the forest to hunt their elusive, but unsuspecting human prey. Brian's excitement mounted as the thought of having his scope trained on a man's head made him shake with excitement. They followed the main trail into the forest for an hour seeing no one. Coming upon a grove of thick cedars they decided to hide out of sight and wait to see if anyone would use the trail.

The wait was long, but their persistence paid off as a lone man approached. He walked past the couple, who were secure in their hiding place. The instincts Brian had gained in the service took over. He became a stealthy predator ready to expel his bloodlust upon this unsuspecting hunter. Julie watched Brian, proud she had found a man who was so brave and displayed such good character.

They stalked the man until he decided to leave the trail and go into the forest where it would be harder to follow him without being heard. Brian decided now was the best time to take his shot. He wanted to impress Julie with a long kill shot, instilling upon her his value to his country as a sniper in the Iraqi conflict. Julie watched as Brian sighted his scope, a sudden silence overtaking the forest, as if nature knew what was coming. The shot rang out, the man fell, his rifle flying out of his arms. Their victim lay still on the forest floor.

The couple left the scene certain the man was dead, not wanting to approach the body and leave unwanted evidence behind connecting them to the crime. The ride home was silent, as Brian and Julie reflected on what they had just done. Both felt a shared passion for the feelings it created, an evil so gripping it was in total control.

CHAPTER EIGHT

Brian's job at the convenience store was becoming very annoying. His boss was an arrogant man with no respect for his employees, berating and chastising them, using them as an outlet for his own grievances and personal problems. An untamed anger gripped Brian. He wanted to change the course of this man's life but doing so would probably lead to his arrest which is the last thing he wanted to have happen.

Brian finally quit his job after the owner told Julie she was no longer welcome at the store while he was working. He walked out, never to return. The owner, refusing to pay him his owed wages caused more anger to well up inside him, creating a murderous rage he was having a hard time controlling. This man would not be forgotten.

Brian had reconciled with his mother, but the loving relationship they used to enjoy was now a thing of the past. They annoyed each other greatly, most of it stemming from his relationship with Julie, whom his mother detested.

Julie wanted a dog; she felt because of the neighborhood they lived in she would feel safer with some kind of protection. Brian's friend from his army days raised pit bulls, which was exactly the dog Julie wanted. They visited his friend, and she chose a healthy year-old male that someday she thought she could use for breeding to make some extra money herself.

Brian needed money. He had no desire to get another minimum wage job and have to take orders from some overbearing superior. He had a friend who sold sizable amounts of cocaine and Brian felt keeping company with him was his best option. Brian and Julie both had dealt with cocaine addictions in the past but had been clean for many years. They agreed that personal use of any cocaine during this endeavor would be strictly forbidden.

A feeling had been gnawing at Brian, a yearning to kill; the hunter wanting another hunt, one more victim he could add to his list of trophies he kept stored in his head. He had come up with a plan. He would do one more hunt in the forest before the season ended. He would construct a tree stand, and like his days in Iraq he would wait for his human prey, shooting him or her down at the right moment, revelling in the kill and the smell of victory. Brian would go on his next hunt without Julie. He needed time on his own to try to figure out his best way forward, his choices getting fewer as his lust for the kill took precedence over everything else.

Brian built his tree stand in a dense group of hardwood trees in an isolated part of the forest, concealing it to be unrecognizable. He planned to sit there, perched above his prey below, an unsuspecting death awaiting them. He finished construction and, in the morning, he would set his plan in motion, leaving another disappearance to be solved by the, as yet unsuspecting, authorities. Brian would not sleep tonight as thoughts of the hunt tomorrow excited him, keeping him awake. His lust for horror dominated his spirit, bringing him a euphoria he could not explain, a curse that would dominate his personal life forever.

CHAPTER NINE

Brian had left the house early; sleeping very little the night before he was tired but excited. If luck was with him, he would make his third. and probably last, kill of the season in the forest today. He reached his tree stand and climbed into it, prepared for a long wait. The day passed with no activity, making Brian realize he had built his cover in a remote area that hunters didn't seem to pass through. He abandoned the stand and decided to go home, disappointment washing over him. Julie was surprised to see Brian home and in such a foul mood. He explained to her what happened and his anger at making such a mistake.

Julie had named her dog Satan, an appropriate name for a dog known for its reputation of being dangerous and unpredictable towards humans, a trait that Julie liked. She would train it to be angry and mean. She had visions of using Satan to destroy her perceived enemies, like Brian's mother.

Brian sulked around the house, trying to come up with a plan to make his life more exciting. Flashbacks from his time in Iraq haunted his thoughts. He had built up a tolerance for the medication he was taking for his PTSD, causing him to have more frequent and longer psychotic episodes of the mental illness he suffered from. His thoughts were tortured, he could wait no longer. He would go into town tonight and kidnap a prostitute, convincing her that he was just a john looking for a date. He would then take her to a secluded area, strangle her and dump her body in the forest. He would keep this killing a secret from Julie because he knew she would want to accompany him. She had been suggesting to Brian she would like to kidnap a homeless person, take him to a secluded area and allow Satan to attack him. Brian didn't agree with this plan unless Julie would allow the dog to kill, rather than maim, the victim.

Darkness fell as Brian left the house. He told Julie he was going to make a cocaine delivery. He had taken a job from the cocaine dealer ferrying large amounts of cocaine between safe houses, earning money for each delivery he made. This had become a profitable venture, but a dangerous one to pursue. Not only did he have to worry about law enforcement, but also his life was at stake from thieves willing to rob and kill for the cocaine in his possession.

Brian was nervous as he drove slowly down the street looking for a victim. He soon found a crack-addicted woman more interested in getting high than being concerned about her safety. She was quick to join Brian, thinking she would make a fast buck, not knowing it would be her last. The woman felt nervous right away, as Brian locked the doors and refused to tell her where he was taking her. He drove her to a heavily wooded, secluded area with plenty of hiding spots to dispose of a body. The woman was terrified knowing what was coming. Brian parked the truck, calmly removed his seatbelt, turned to her with a sick grin on his face, and strangled her. No one heard her screams but Brian. His lust satisfied, he dragged her body into the woods and returned to his love waiting at home, feelings of satisfaction, instead of anger, lifting his spirits.

CHAPTER TEN

The couple awoke to a pounding on the front door and the sound of Satan barking. Brian got up, pulled on clothes, and went to see who it was. It was their neighbor, an annoying alcoholic who constantly bothered them for money and about anything else he needed. The man was drunk, having been up all- night binge drinking. Brian was annoyed, slamming the door in his face, yelling at him to go home. He returned to bed angry, thinking of ways to solve this problem. He decided to lure the neighbor into the house when he was drinking and let Satan, who hated him, spend up-close and personal time with him. This episode with the dog would hopefully keep the man from ever returning.

Winter in Maine came early, ice on the windshield and an occasional dusting of snow in the mornings a warning of things to come. The old wooden house the couple rented was cold; poorly insulated it would prove to not be a comfortable place to spend the winter. Brian was happy. There had been no news reports of a missing person on his last victim, usually one of the consequences of being a prostitute; their lifestyle not stable, never missed if they disappeared. Brian knew this and it factored into his decision to continue the path he was on as far as his type of victims were concerned. He jokingly thought he was now not a hunter of man, but a hunter of prostitutes ridding society of this pestilence, making his country a more moral place to live.

Today Brian and Julie were going to the rock pit to practice handling and shooting the handguns Brian had bought from his employer. The guns were stolen in a burglary and traded for cocaine. They came to Brian at a low cost and would prove useful for his plans.

The urge to kill was now dominating his thoughts again. His lust for a kill tore at his very soul. Julie would go with him on his next mission. They would work together as a team, luring their prey into a trap there was no escape from. They cruised the alley in Julie's car, a collection of crack houses and poverty, looking for a victim. They did not have long to wait, as a woman desperate for drugs threw caution aside, accepting the dangers of her profession. She entered their car, getting in the back seat.

Julie instantly turned the handgun on her. The woman realized she had made a big mistake, wondering what the outcome of this was going to be. She would soon find out, as the car drove out of town to a pre-selected place Brian had found earlier. It was a good spot to make a body disappear. The woman sat silently as the car pulled off the main road and into a secluded area off a logging road in the forest. He took her out of the car and blindfolded her, marching her to the edge of the forest where he executed her with one bullet to the back of her head. They dragged the corpse into the forest, burying it under leaves and branches to conceal it. Brian was happy, another successful hunt, another duty done for his country. They returned home giddy with success, already talking about their next mission, only one of more to come.

CHAPTER ELEVEN

The snowstorm howled outside, the wind blowing the snow into drifts up against the house. Brian awoke, he pulled the blankets up over him, the drafty old house was cold. He pulled Julie closer, realizing how much he depended on her for emotional and moral support. She was part of his team, just like when he was in the service.

The neighbor had continued to annoy them with his constant

unannounced visits in an inebriated state. They decided they were going to lure him into the back yard where Julie would unleash Satan on him. Hopefully, a couple of bites from the dog would discourage him from ever coming back. The plan was hatched, and like clockwork the neighbor soon showed up, drunk and making no sense. He followed the couple into the back yard under the assumption that Satan had to use the bathroom. The dog was ready, always wanting a piece of this man, his hate running deep for this misguided soul.

Julie gave the command to attack; the man looked at Julie with horror as the pit bull jumped on him, knocking him to the ground. Julie was mesmerized watching her dog, so powerful and strong, showing a part of its personality she so much adored. Like in a trance she watched as the snow turned red with blood and the man's screams grew fainter. Brian's pleas to Julie to call off Satan were ignored. The dog decided when he was done, its muzzle covered in blood and its eyes like that of the devil. Like a victor he walked away from his opponent, basking in the praise Julie was heaping upon him for doing such a good job of taking care of this problem for them.

Jubilation soon turned to reality as they looked at the mangled bloody corpse laying in their back yard. They put Satan in the house, retrieved a tarp and wrapped the body in it. They would store the body in the shed where it would freeze. They would then take it to a nearby ravine where it would be dumped at a later date.

Brian was irate that Julie had let this situation get out of control. He had warned her, and her first beating by Brian followed. In order for them to survive and not end up dead, or in prison, she had to follow the rules. Julie was resentful of the beating she received from Brian, but her anger was soon forgotten as other more important issues took over her life. The man was not missed, as the neighbors were glad he had disappeared and wished he wouldn't come back. They would get their wish; the man's frozen body, in cold storage nearby, would never bother them again.

Brian's thoughts turned to his passion, an uncontrollable urge to hunt and kill his prey. It would soon be time to act. He would make his next kill more interesting by stalking his victim before he snuffed their life out forever. Tomorrow he would put his new plan in action, finally exposing the town to some of the horrors that were happening behind their backs, as the couples' murderous rage continued to haunt the area. It would be a wake-up call for the townspeople to view this as a threat from the devil himself.

CHAPTER TWELVE

The neighbor's body in Brian's shed needed to be disposed of. The police had been around the day before investigating his disappearance after someone filed a missing person report. The couple decided to load the body in the trunk of the car after dark and dump it in a ravine, where it probably would never be found. They moved him to the car around midnight, placing his frozen corpse across the back seat, as they couldn't bend his frozen body to fit in the trunk.

The place they had selected to rid themselves of the corpse was a half-hour drive from the house. The journey there was unsettling and quiet as the body in the back seat disturbed them. They would be glad to be rid of it. The highway was dark and quiet as they pulled off the road, the car coming to a stop beside some guardrails, a steep drop into a forest of trees on the other side. It was a drop of five hundred feet down an almost 90-degree slope. The body was removed from the back seat and thrown over the guardrails into the abyss below. A sense of relief swept over the couple as the successful solution of this problem ended the way it did. They returned home, went to bed, and slept soundly, exhausted from the job they had just completed.

Brian received a call from his mother, who wanted to see him. She had become very vindictive about losing her son to this other woman who she held no regard for. When Brian arrived at her house, she confronted him about the rifle; it was registered in her name, and she wanted it back. He told her it was gone, having been stolen in a burglary at his house. His mother also frowned upon Julie and her pit bull, saying that under her training the dog had become dangerous and could take the life of a person someday. Brian left angry. His personal relationship with his mother was in ruins, with no hope of any improvement; her hate for Julie overshadowing any love she felt for him.

As the days slipped by the urge that gripped Brian was becoming unmanageable. His need to hunt and kill, the rush of adrenaline he felt as his prey fell dead, and thoughts of one well placed bullet always enough to do the job were overwhelming. His next victim would be a hitchhiker, a young man seen frequently searching for a ride in and out of town. Brian would hunt for his prey, finding him on the side of the road, pick him up and take him to the forest where he would be released and hunted like an animal. The anticipation of blood and death overwhelmed Brian's senses as he worked out his plan.

Returning to the house he found Julie playing with the handguns. Her fascination with guns had become a safety issue. Brian had told her a number of times the guns were strictly for killing and not to be played with. He was afraid her lax attention and carelessness were probable cause for an accident. He now forbid her to handle the guns unless he was with her. She knew what her punishment would be for defying him.

Brian slept peacefully. His latest plan was engrained in his mind and his mission ready to be undertaken, a new challenge he was about to take. This battle was changing to include a kidnapping in an urban setting and a victim who was more visible, exposing him to a larger risk of getting caught. He would fight this battle to the end, giving up his own life to help save his country against a perceived threat he was taking care of. Psychosis was his friend, not his enemy.

CHAPTER THIRTEEN

Brian was frustrated. He had spent the last two days looking for his victim who seemed to be playing a game of cat and mouse with him. Anger gripped him as the thought of the hitchhiker getting into another car and escaping rattled his already unstable emotions. His personal lust to commit murder had taken control of his thoughts, creating a psychotic episode of horror to envelop him.

On the morning of the third day of the hunt, he was successful. He drove towards the young man who had his thumb out looking for a ride. Brian pulled over and welcomed him into his vehicle. The hitchhiker was in his twenties, a healthy young man who would make good prey. Excitement mounted as the thought of the kill made Brian shake with anticipation. He put his plan into action, first locking the doors, tipping the passenger off that something was wrong. Then the firearm came out, Brian pointed the handgun on the man telling him it was going to be alright if he followed instructions closely and didn't question him about anything. It was a lie, as murder would be the end result.

The young man was terrified, wishing that he had listened to his father, who always preached about the dangers of hitchhiking. Brian pulled down an old logging road, rarely used except during the fall hunting season. He drove his truck to a secluded spot and told his passenger to get out. Brian informed him he was giving him a short head start and then he would become his prey, he would be hunted down and shot like a prized animal. The man ran into the bush. Escape from this psychotic killer caused his adrenalin to peak, making him feel like he was being stalked, ready to be shot.

Brian retrieved his rifle from the back of the truck. He had done all the prep work the night before, so the gun was ready for the hunt. He trained his scope on the man and followed him, not wanting to lose him in the forest. Escape for this man was out of the question. Brian realized this would probably lead to his arrest, so he needed to do this now. The man was running fast, knowing he could die at any moment. Unfortunately, he could not outrun the scope that was trained on him.

Brian waited for the perfect shot, hoping to shoot his victim in the back where the bullet would travel through his heart and kill him instantly. Brian was ready, the anticipation of the kill causing a line of sweat to run down his face, even though the temperature hovered around freezing. His finger pressed the trigger, the crack of the rifle pierced the stillness of the forest air. He watched through the scope as the man went down, his death a certainty.

Brian was thrilled, another enemy killed. He was the hunter, and he would continue on his quest to rid his country of all enemies. Brian left the body in the forest and went home elated at his success. He bubbled over breakfast, as each kill brightened his spirits.

Julie was hatching her next plan to use Satan again to satisfy her sick pleasures, while Brian was already thinking about plans for his next hunt. A sicker duo could not be found, horror and murder never to be taken away from them.

CHAPTER FOURTEEN

Julie felt sorry for the neighbor's cat who had taken up residence in her back yard. She felt compassion for it, being the one responsible for the death of its owner. Julie had been feeding the cat and was being kind to it, gaining its trust. However, she had a much more sinister plan in mind, entertainment for Satan. The dog hated cats, and given the opportunity would instinctively kill the animal, tearing its body into a bloody mess of mangled flesh and fur. This was exactly what Julie wanted to see. She wanted to look into the cat's eyes and watch the look of terror on its face as it took its last breath.

She waited for Brian to leave as he would disapprove of her plan. He was against hurting any animal except Satan, who he hated and would rather see dead. He felt the dog brought the worst out in Julie, and because of its uncontrollable behavior could lead to trouble for them down the road. Julie's excitement mounted as she carried out her plan. She began by feeding the cat who was waiting in the back yard. While its attention was distracted by the food, she released Satan and sat back to enjoy the glory of the kill.

The pit bull pounced, its hatred for the cat shown in the viciousness of the attack. The cat died instantly as the jaws of the pit bull snapped the cat's neck, severing its spine. To Julie's disappointment, the cat did not suffer, as death was instantaneous. Satan did not stop there however, the cat became like a stuffed animal, and soon had all its insides torn out. The bloody muzzle of the dog and a pile of fur and flesh was all that was left. Julie's heart was racing, the excitement of watching the kill bringing back memories of when she was a teenager. She would befriend stray cats, gaining their trust, only to torture and dismember them as a thank you for being her friend.

Julie would tell Brian that she had lost control of Satan and he had attacked and killed the neighbor's cat, as she was unable to hide the mess in the back yard. Brian's patience was growing thin with Julie and this latest episode of irresponsibility was not helpful, she worried him.

Brian had two kilos of cocaine in the car that he could not drop off at the safe house because of a theft from there the previous day by some not so trustworthy help. He was to take it back to the dealer's house but had to wait a few days before doing so. The lure of the cocaine took Brian back to days gone by, when he would enjoy the escape cocaine provided him. He took a couple of grams of the drug, his urge overwhelming. He planned to use just this once, hiding it from Julie who would also start using if she knew he was indulging in this former favorite pastime.

Brian was troubled, his mental health problems growing worse instead of better. His reasoning was becoming more distorted as his problems continued to pile up, leading him down an even more dangerous path as he continued to lose his grip on reality. The result would be making decisions he would later regret, leading him to a place there was no escape from, a horror he had lost control of.

CHAPTER FIFTEEN

The cocaine sat on the table in front of Brian. He knew in his heart he was making the wrong decision, but the urge and temptation were overpowering. The first powder that went up his nose left him with a overwhelming feeling of superiority. Memories flooded his mind as the thoughts of his years dealing with a cocaine addiction returned to haunt him. He did another line, the euphoria, however temporary it might be, put him in a mood he hoped would never end.

The police were quietly investigating missing persons' reports and had concluded they were all connected and that a probable serial killer was on the loose. A special task force had been set up to try to solve these crimes. The minds of the serial killers were now controlled by their cocaine addiction. Brian had shared his relapse with Julie, and she convinced Brian to let her do the same. Psychosis reigned as the medicine he took for his mental health issues interacted with the cocaine, causing an episode that required an ambulance and a visit to the hospital. The doctor prescribed more medicine, and he was sent home. Brian's mental health was quickly unwinding, leaving him with a feeling of utter despair.

All the couple's money was spent on drugs, and they were already facing eviction. Brian called Julie to the table to discuss their situation. As she sat, he picked up the handgun from the table, pointed it at Julie and shot her in the head. She fell off her chair dying on the floor. His next victim was Satan; two bullets in the head snuffing out his life. Brian surveyed the scene. The blood and horror reawakened a sense of excitement and satisfaction as to what he created, not felt since his return to cocaine.

Brian had one more score to settle, his mother. He could never forgive her for her abandonment, and she was now going to pay the ultimate price for this. He drove to his mother's house, the lust for murder his only thought. Her dog, knowing Brian, came out to greet him tail wagging. The reward for his friendly behavior was his head almost blown off by a high caliber bullet, leaving him dead in a bloody mess on the ground. Minutes later his mother met the same fate. Her screams for mercy were not listened to. Brian then put the gun under his neck and pulled the trigger. The bullet entered his brain, killing him instantly, ending a saga of murder and horror the town would not miss; a new beginning for everyone, including the serial killers.

THE HAUNTED BARN

✦ ✦ ✦ ✦ ✦ ✦ ✦

The old farm had been abandoned after the murder of the family that had lived there, their blood-soaked bodies discovered in the well on the property. These murders had been committed while the family slept, the intruder with a knife showing no mercy as he conducted his grizzly deed. The Browns lived a quiet life with their two children in a rural setting where no one imagined such a heinous crime would be committed. But happen it did, leaving the nearby town in shock.

The Browns had not actually been farmers but had used the barn as a storage depot for the multi-ton loads of marijuana that Mr. Brown's organization smuggled in from Columbia and Mexico in the early nineteen seventies. Instead of bales of hay stacked in the barn, it was bales of pot. Mr. Brown had spent ten years in prison for his crimes, returning to the farm after his release. His wife and two young children had continued to live there after his sentence had been handed down. His wife, heir to her family's fortune made in manufacturing, was financially comfortable, and had waited patiently for her husband to be released from prison. For two years they had lived peaceful lives until they were reported missing by family members who suspected foul play, based on the conditions found in the house. A subsequent search of the property led to the discovery of the bodies.

The crime was never solved, and the house was eventually torn down, leaving only the old barn standing. This building was rented out to a man from town who planned to use it for storage and a summer thrift shop. Jack Drummond, the renter, never realized how his life would change because of this decision.

Strange events started happening almost immediately. Jack noticed an eerie silence on his first visit; there was a lack of any birds using the barn for a home, no pigeons, barn swallows or robins nesting anywhere. While moving his items to the barn an unease gripped Jack, a feeling that something was not right. The reputation of the property started to haunt him. He was no coward, but his thoughts bothered him. He would live with, and appease, whatever it was that lurked in the barn.

Opening day for his thrift shop was busy, the crowd was enjoying themselves until tragedy struck. A young girl, playing in a part of the barn where she was not supposed to be, fell through the floor to the level below. Striking her head on the concrete floor she was killed instantly, a tragic accident that would never be forgotten. Jack's business was ruined, no one would return after this incident, the people thinking the property was cursed.

Jack would have none of this. Not believing in the curse, he planned to spend the night in a small office he had built in the barn to see if his beliefs were true. There was no curse, just a terrible accident. His own foolish thoughts would be dismissed as an active imagination. Tomorrow Jack's nightmares would begin.

The rain was unrelenting as Jack pulled into the driveway of his business. As he got closer to the barn, he noticed fresh tire tracks and footprints in the mud leading to the doorway. He wondered who this visitor might have been, as few people came here since the little girl died in the tragic accident. He had prepared himself for this evening well, unloading a sleeping bag, food, water, a radio, and a propane lantern. He was determined to prove that nothing unusual was happening here, but his intuition told him otherwise.

Jack opened the barn door, silence greeting him, as he made his way to the office. With a feeling someone or something was watching he settled in, eating a sandwich, and waiting for darkness to fall, the only sound breaking the silence was the pounding rainfall on the metal roof of the barn. He turned his radio on to help settle his nerves. Suddenly he heard a loud banging. Upon investigation he found the barn door open and swinging in the wind. How could this be possible as he remembered closing and locking it?

A chill swept through him as he closed and locked his door. He realized there would be no sleep tonight as he made his way back to the office, darkness beginning to invade his spirit, a feeling of terror enveloping his soul. The blackness of the night overwhelmed him as lightning flashed through the windows, illuminating shadows he perceived as inhuman. Returning to the office he secured his door not knowing what was going to happen next.

Jack did not have long to wait as the fluttering wings and the coo of pigeons broke the silence, sending a wave of terror through him. The chirping of other birds filled the air to make the barn sound like an aviary. As suddenly as this activity began it stopped, leaving a silence that sent sheer terror to his soul. Jack was frozen in place, realizing he was trapped in a nightmare from which he could not escape.

His body was found days later sitting in his chair deceased, a heart attack taking his life. The barn was torn down ending a chapter of horror that had taken the lives of six people, leaving memories that never would be forgotten. This was a tragic ending to an unsolved mystery, only folklore and imagination left for the mind to ponder, a tale of paranormal activity that would never be explained.

THE WRATH OF KHAN

◆◆◆◆◆◆

A fter the War of twenty thirty-five there was little left of the civilized world. The war which had started between North and South Korea quickly spread to all parts of the planet, devastating the supply chains and destroying communications to all the countries in the world. The satellites which circled the earth were destroyed by major world powers, one not wanting the others to have any technologically advanced assets. However, these satellites were not destroyed in time, which allowed the countries with nuclear weapons to take part in the largest fireworks show ever displayed on the planet.

The destruction was complete, with very few survivors. Pockets of life existed outside large cities, which had been destroyed by atomic weapons leaving devastation and death. Among the survivors old scores were settled, usually ending in death for one, or both, participants. Those long standing neighborly feuds were finally put to rest, as a total breakdown of law and order prevailed. Humans were now forced to work together in order to survive. Groups of people banded together, a leader and his deputies were chosen, with the leader making all decisions for the clan, including who their allies or enemies would be.

Large structures were fortified as man's main instinct prevailed; survival from other groups whose sole purpose was to dominate and control. The most feared leader of one of these groups was a man named Khan, a violent individual who reveled in the deaths of his enemies. Usually after a takeover of another group, he would personally kill their leader by beheading him in front of a cheering audience of his followers. The remaining survivors of these raids were given one choice, pledge allegiance to Khan or suffer the same fate. Most chose to pledge allegiance to Khan, a charismatic figure in whom it was quite easy to put their trust. His promise of protection to anyone who joined him was believed, eventually leading to hundreds of thousands of devoted followers.

A new city was built in Kahn's honor, a base of operations with a plan for domination of the planet. An army was being built which would be so strong no one would challenge him. His powers were unlimited because he was Satan, an entity of great strength which was achieved by corrupting the people of earth, turning it into a hell that was irreversible. He called himself Khan, the great leader and deceiver. People believed his lies and were ready to give their lives to this false prophet. He built beautiful churches devoted to the worship of Satan, the new ruler of planet earth. He deceived the people and took their souls for his own kingdom, hoping his power would reign supreme and never return to the worship of Christ. The battle for the humans was over, but a much larger battle would ensue as the forces of darkness and light would clash in a supernatural event never seen before by humanity.

Khan's rise to power had been relentless, providing false hope to the surviving humans; he captured their souls and disposed of their lifeless bodies, leaving them to decay and return to the earth. Physical life on earth was no more, having been replaced by a spirit world run by Satan himself. It was a world of hate and suffering, not unlike the past physical realm which he had replaced.

Khan had one enemy he feared, an enemy more powerful who had cast his evil soul into the depths of hell many times. That enemy was God, his kingdom reuniting humans after death, loved ones once more together without the burdens of a physical life, sickness and suffering no longer a part of their existence. Satan would have none of this, his followers were meant to suffer, and his greatest fear was God coming and saving their souls and returning them to his kingdom.

After hundreds of years of rule on earth with no sign of God's presence, Kahn thought he would not be found, but he was wrong. God, knowing that Satan had escaped from hell where he had been cast, had sent angels from his kingdom to search out Kahn's presence. The Lord, with his army, planned to find and beat this evil, sending him back to where he belonged. God would rescue the tormented souls and return them to the Kingdom of God where they would be reunited with loved ones, never to experience again the suffering and hate that Satan stood for. Angels from all over God's kingdom were summoned, a force of power not to be reckoned with, as their combined strength was in the peace and love they projected, a power the devil could not overcome.

Satan was caught by surprise as the trumpets blaring from the heavens announced God's arrival, millions of angels in tow. This was the moment Kahn had dreaded but knew was coming. The power of the Lord and his angels overwhelmed the devil stripping him of his strength, allowing the Lord to seize control and cast this evil back to his kingdom of suffering, where he belonged. God gathered up the captured souls and returned them to his kingdom where their suffering finally ceased. The return to Heaven was a blissful event; the mission was a success, the rescue of lost and tired souls a meaningful accomplishment. The banishment of Satan to his rightful place brought peace to the spirit world and the Kingdom of God. It was an overwhelming victory in a long and never ending battle against this supernatural force.

THE ABDUCTION

- ✦✦✦✦✦ -

The boy awoke with a start, a stationary white light was shining through his bedroom window. He felt a wave of terror grip him as he realized he could not move, his mind frozen in time. He tried to yell out, but his voice was silent. This is the story about the abduction of a nine-year-old boy by extraterrestrials in an area of Northern Canada. They took him aboard their spacecraft making him incapable of thought or language. A medical examination was done on him, and his health was confirmed as being excellent. His DNA was manipulated so he would never get sick, his date with death at forty-eight was changed to be at the age of one hundred.

The aliens' plan was to alter the course of humanity, using this boy to do it. From a world that had lost hope and happiness, to a total worldwide rejuvenation of the human spirit, this boy would be the new messiah. He was taken to a room which held a machine. This machine was used to change the chemistry of his human brain, opening his mind to be able to do things he could never imagine. He was returned to his bedroom, never to remember anything about this abduction. Later in life he would make profound changes to the planet on which we live.

Chad Applegate was like any other nine-year-old boy in Sudbury, Ontario. He played hockey, loved to fish, and would often go camping at the provincial parks with his parents in the summer. His family had moved from Quebec, both parents getting office jobs in the nickel mining industry that dominated Sudbury's economy. Chad went to school, did well, and made friends. He had a stable life and loving parents.

As the years went by, he had developed into a fine young man. Chad was kind, helpful, trusted, and well-liked, but profound changes were taking place within him. He found he could understand people's thoughts and he was able to alter strangers' minds, making them never able to tell a lie. The secret alien plan was to make this boy, once he turned into an adult, the most powerful human on the planet. Chad would be able to do anything that entered his mind. He would have the power to heal the sick, change time, and cure diseases. Anyone crossing paths with Chad would be healed, releasing them from the profound struggles of human life.

For now, all of this was Chad's secret. A secret that was about to benefit humanity, change the course of history, and bring a renewed sense of hope to the human spirit which had been devastated by years of neglect. When it was time, he would announce himself as the new messiah and would perform miracles beyond human comprehension. Chad was about to launch his plan to make life a joy, not a bitter harvest of unwelcome thoughts which dominate life as we know it.

The first miracle Chad performed was the healing of his mother, who had stage four breast cancer. He arrived at the hospital with his father, to say good-bye to his mother who was expected to die that day. His father was sullen, not wanting to accept what was going to happen, the death of his loved one of forty years. He took Chad's hand and led him into the room. His mom lay sleeping, sedated, making her transition to the afterlife less painful. Chad knew what he had to do. Taking his mother's hands and placing them on his face he closed his eyes, and healing energy destroyed the cancer that once called her body home. That day he healed the sick, making the hospital disease free, and announcing to the world he was the new messiah, who was here to rid humanity of all its diseases, both mental and physical, creating a world of positive change.

He went on to remove all handguns, long guns, and ammunition from societies. All wars on the planet stopped at once when Chad removed all military hardware, including airborne and ground-based munitions. In the future, if humans wanted to fight it was to be with their hands, but the sickness called violence would be dealt with later. He travelled to Africa, cured the sick and planted large gardens capable of feeding people for generations to come. Fresh clean water was made abundant, eliminating one of Africa's largest problems. Chad had a plan; he destroyed the stigma of being black by making everyone in the world black. He taught them, like children, to work together, share, and use manners when dealing with each other.

Chad's next stop was Australia where he healed the Great Barrier Reef, bringing back the majestic glory it once had. He healed the sick and changed the weather, allowing for more food to be grown. Back in the United States, huge venues were reserved for him, where he healed the sick, and spoke to the people about how they could make their lives better.

The Messiah travelled the planet and did what he promised, leaving man to chart a new course for themselves in the new world he created. Chad's creators came and retrieved him once his job was done. He became one of them, roaming the galaxy searching for broken planets to fix, a small step taken for a large problem that plagued the galaxy. These intergalactic doctors changed the human lives which occupied these planets, taking back from Satan what originally belonged to the Messiah, a much better choice for humanity.

THE HOUSE ON THE HILL

✦✦✦✦✦✦

T he lightning flashed, illuminating the old building, an abandoned home that had seen better days. Its windows broken, its interior destroyed, it was inhabited only by the angry spirits that live there. A torture chamber in the basement was a testament to the horror that went on here twenty years ago in this dungeon of death. There was a total of thirteen victims, all women kidnapped from their comfortable lives in the city and taken to this house in the country which was decorated with the tools of a sadistic serial killer.

The man's fascination with death had started at an early age. He kept his ideas secret, locked in his head looking for a way to escape. His ultimate goal in life was to live out these fantasies that controlled his mind. The toll of mental illness, created by the beatings of an abusive father during childhood and the abandonment of his mother, drove Jerry to live his life detached from the real world. His brain damage, not noticed by his neighbors or acquaintances, a secret he harbored within himself.

His first victim was a young woman who he kidnapped off a quiet street. Pointing a gun at her, he told her to get into the car or she was dead. If she had known what she was facing, she would have gratefully accepted his second offer. He drove her to the house, not a word spoken, only horror occupying the thoughts of the woman as she realized what the outcome of this situation was going to be.

Jerry had prepared his dungeon well. He took the woman to the basement, securing her hands and feet to the wall with shackles. He returned upstairs making himself a celebratory dinner, getting ready for his first evening of entertainment. The isolation of the property meant the victim's screams could not be heard as she died a slow death at the hands of this sick man, revelling in the suffering and pain he caused this victim. The horror finally ended; the dismembered body was removed and buried in the makeshift cemetery he had readied for his victims on his property.

Jerry returned to his job the following day. He was the manager of the automotive department at the Canadian Tire store. He learned from his co-workers that a young girl out for a walk had not returned home. Her mother, sick with worry, had reported her missing. The young woman, now in pieces, was laying in an unmarked grave, never to see her mother again. A sick smile spread across Jerry's face, this secret hidden within his mind, never to be revealed. This series of murders was for his enjoyment only.

He returned home and fed his animals. Jerry had a hobby farm, a collection of animals he considered his family. He entertained children and parents alike with his friendly smile and his livestock, making his home open to anyone that wanted to come by and enjoy the farm and its welcoming atmosphere. The horrors of the basement were Jerry's secret, not to be revealed to the unsuspecting public he hoped to fool for a long time as he fulfilled his sick dreams and fantasies. His lust for torture and murder created an addiction Jerry found hard to satisfy. His soul, controlled by the evil within, was never able to enjoy true happiness, as hate captured his heart, turning him into the monster that he had become, just what he wanted to be.

Jerry awoke, the sunrise casting light through his bedroom window, the rooster giving its morning serenade. His daily routine included caring for his animals before he left for work. His perceived family included goats, sheep, and chickens which he also used for eggs, often sharing with his co-workers when he had a surplus. He also had a donkey, geese, and a happy pig with a dozen piglets. These were the animals the children came to enjoy, along with his two dogs and three friendly cats.

Jerry readied himself for work. He hated his job, the unreasonable demands from the customers and his boss were unrelenting, leaving him to stew with frustration and anger. His mind became preoccupied with the planning of his next mission, the kidnapping, rape, and torture he enjoyed so much; watching his victims die a slow death, begging for mercy they never received. His father showed no mercy while beating him as a child. He was merely continuing on with this tradition.

Jerry's latest plan included casing a local business to find a female manager who often was in charge of closing. Having found a candidate, he would sit in the parking lot of the big box store late at night watching for the woman who worked late and was left vulnerable in the parking lot, alone when she went to retrieve her car. Excitement welled in Jerry's chest as the thought of this new victim chained in his basement created a sexual excitement he could only experience through this type of behavior. Today he had left work waiting for the darkness that would come, providing him cover and lessening his chances of being seen.

Jerry sat in the deserted parking lot. He watched as all of the employees left, leaving the manager to fulfill her closing duties alone. Jerry waited, knowing that she would soon be leaving, his car parked beside hers offered cover to hide the horrible act he was about to commit. The plan was executed with precision. The kidnapped woman, terrified, beside him in his car, wondered if her life would be over, killed by this obviously psychotic man.

Upon arriving home Jerry took his victim to the basement with little resistance from the woman, who handed her life over to this sadistic killer to do with what he wanted. Her screams from the torture continued for an hour as he took his time killing her, this being the favorite part of the experience for him. He then happily dismembered her corpse and buried the remains in his cemetery, which included his graveside service before the cold dirt was thrown on her still warm body.

The rooster crowing at daybreak woke Jerry. His day would be busy as his farm animals were to be enjoyed by a visiting girl scout troop. They arrived early and loved the hospitality and accommodations their host provided them. Jerry played them for fools; his real intentions darker as he fantasized about the women leaders becoming his next victims.

Saturdays at the farm were usually like this, families coming and going, thanking the wonderful, kind man everyone counted as a friend. Jerry had provided himself with a perfect cover, allowing him time to quench his insatiable thirst for mayhem and murder. The community would be shocked when his crimes were exposed, his goal of thirteen women in his cemetery the long-range plan for this prolific serial killer.

Jerry awoke to the sound of his animals having some kind of an emergency. He looked over at his clock; it was 3 a.m. He threw on his pants, grabbed his gun, and went to investigate. Upon reaching the barn the noise had lessened, but he soon found what the issue was. A small animal, a weasel, had broken into his chicken coup going on a killing spree that ended in the deaths of half of his chickens. He was livid with anger; the death of his poultry, which he cherished, quickly took his rage to new heights.

Jerry had taken his vacation time from work, a two week rest from all the madness he perceived made his life so difficult. He especially hated the people he worked with, often fantasising about taking his co-workers and introducing them to his basement entertainment. He planned to spend his time off working on repairs to his barn and hosting a special day for the kids, with hot dogs and popcorn on the menu and donkey rides for the little ones.

His mind had been descending into darkness as thoughts of murder and torture led him to fantasies about his next victim. He drove into the city trying to come up with a plan. In Jerry's mind these unfortunate souls enjoyed the thrill of being kidnapped and placed in his dungeon, tortured, cut up, and sent to live in his cemetery. Unfortunately for Jerry, his new plans would never be executed.

The neighbour's dog had found his cemetery, dug up the latest victim's body and taken a severed arm home as a gift to its owner. This news was the talk of the town. Upon hearing this Jerry panicked knowing his gig was up and his secret would soon be revealed. He would be arrested and thrown in jail for the heinous crimes he had committed. A search for the two missing women was already underway when this latest information was revealed.

A large search party was formed and within a brief time the burial ground was found, along with the remains. The criminal investigation led to Jerry being put on the police radar. After intense questioning, he broke down, admitting his guilt and leading authorities to his makeshift dungeon. The people that knew Jerry were aghast that this criminal mind had deceived them so easily. He was convicted and sentenced to life in a mental institution, where his short life was taken by another patient who strangled him during an altercation.

Jerry's home now sits abandoned, stories of mysterious lights and ghosts of the murdered women the only inhabitants. Oh, and let us not forget Jerry, who is forever there taking care of his beloved animals and entertaining all of the neighbors' children, thankfully not in his dungeon.

DEMONS AND ANGELS

············

O n a planet that was light-years from Earth, a contingent of
rogue scientists had developed a life form that was not com-
patible with their society. These scientists had developed a new
species of life which would be used to populate barren planets in their
solar system. A few were given artificial intelligence and, if deemed fit by
the special council which overlooked this scientific project, placements
would be made and monitored.

A planet they called Alex was set up as a work-station for scientific
studies. These involved space exploration, the development of new food
sources, time travel, and many other research projects that were deemed
beneficial to the development of their own planet, as well as the many
uninhabited and desolate ones which occupied their galaxy. The most
important research done here was the development of new life forms.

Alex was run by a panel of representatives from various planets
who had formed a union to advance such research. A contingent of
alien scientists was always on duty. Unfortunately, for the leaders of this
project, a small number of these scientists went rogue and developed
a living, breathing species capable of thought, decision making, and
reproduction. Top scientists on this project, along with a few of their
co-workers, had decided their work was not challenging enough, opting
to sway from their original mission and develop a specially designed
living being they would call a human. They developed a complex brain
for this new specimen which would allow him to survive in very harsh

environments. His head was his most prominent feature. He was given eyes to see, a mouth to eat, and a nose to smell. He was given hands to work with, and with his feet he was able to run from danger. A complex intelligence was designed for his survival.

During the human's development, no safeguards were put in place for disease, as sickness was not known to these aliens, nor violence or hate. DNA from other species was integrated into this new life form, without knowing the consequences. This turned what was thought to be a harmless creature into a monster capable of doing horrific things to its own species or any other species it encountered.

A complete male and female were designed and taken secretly to a planet outside their solar system, left on their own to colonize a planet they would call Earth. The planet, already a living breathing eco-system, would serve the humans well, providing them with a livable habitat where they would thrive, reproduce, and become the dominate species in less than 100 years.

A spacecraft, using time travel, transported the humans, along with two of the scientists who helped design them, to assure they were given life. Natural instincts and programming would then take over to steer them to a successful future. The scientists would never see the outcome, as their superiors, after learning of their rogue behavior, would abandon this project, allowing human life to evolve in a way never imagined by its creators.

The vibrant colours of the earth were the first observations the aliens noted as they approached this new world. Blue was dominate, the water on the planet being its main feature. A smoking volcano could be seen, its eruption one of the many wonders this world could display at a moment's notice. This was Earth, a planet that evolved on its own over millions of years, bringing life to what was once a barren speck of dust in the universe. This planet was chosen because of its lack of carnivores, meat-eating animals which would hunt down and kill the new trans-plants, treating them as a food source. The humans faced a future of vegetarianism, which would lead them to better health both physically and mentally. The hope was the humans would become the dominate species to colonize this planet and create a new civilization, making this a livable place for intelligent life.

The spacecraft circled this new world, zeroing in on the predetermined landing site, a warm, lush part of the planet they had named Africa. It provided a year-round temperate climate capable of growing supplies of food for the new inhabitants. An area with a large cave system was selected to provide shelter for the humans. The landing was uneventful, and the aliens were met by a world unlike their own. It was a world full of sound and vibrant colours, a landscape so different it could not be imagined. They prepared the humans for activation, left them in the meadow, and then returned to their ship and home planet, never to see the results of their endeavor. A thousand years would pass, and this experiment would prove to be successful, as human life would flourish and evolve on this beautiful new world.

The humans had evolved as a peaceful species, displaying no emotions of hate or violence, only love. As the population increased clans were born. These groups increased in size, forming towns, while others chose to split apart, travelling and settling areas further afield. Because of the lack of disease and their peaceful nature, the human population flourished, eventually covering the continent of Africa. Peace, harmony, and working together was the focus of this new civilization. This was about to change.

The universe is vast and has millions of different life forms. Some are evil, most are good. These early humans would become hosts for these spirits, as they searched for life themselves. Once found, their souls would be captured, and their lives would be changed forever. The human experiment would take a devastating turn as the first wave of demonic spirits from the kingdom of Satan quickly started taking souls. A much smaller contingent of angels followed, also taking souls. These angels were sent by the kingdom of God to fight this pestilence that was set upon the humans. It was a battle that could not be won, as the power of Satan was strong, bringing misery to whoever it was able to control.

Within hours the spirits became the dominate life form on the planet, the humans now their hosts. Change was sudden as the demonic spirits infected their hosts with a range of maladies that would cause untold suffering and misery in their lives, an eternal curse brought about by the devil himself. The angels were not here to be a dominant force, but as a calming counterbalance for the humans infected with this evil.

The changes to the society happened instantly. The humans, now possessed with greed and jealousy resorted to stealing each other's possessions, committing assaults, and even killing, especially over women. An agreement was made between the demons and angels, as they met and discussed what conditions would be allowed without repercussions in this takeover by Satan of the human spirit. A special force was set up to combat these offences resulting in a new set of rules for the humans to follow. Punishment for breaking these rules could lead to confinement, and in rare cases even death. Life on earth was changed forever.

Eating meat became the norm, domesticated cattle and horses were the first to be slaughtered, followed by animals that had lived peacefully with their human company until this evil arrived and made them a food source. Rules were broken and punishment was given out, much to the pleasure of the ones appointed to do so. The age of man dominated the planet, their souls owned by the evil within.

Humanity has not been able to escape the curse that besieged them by this unrelenting spirit of evil. This has left the angels with little recourse but to wait for the return of their God, with his enormous power, to correct the wrongs and return humans to their original life form which hate, greed, and destruction were never a part of.

Will this sinister disease, passed from one generation to the next, never be defeated on its quest for domination of the human spirit? The struggle for power is ongoing, with the power of evil gaining strength with each passing year, bringing us closer to the death of our planet. Our chance for salvation is low, as evil preys on its human host helping it achieve its goal of a lifeless planet Earth.

NORTHWOOD

+‧+‧+‧+‧

CHAPTER ONE

Northwood is a small town that could be found anywhere in North America. Established in the mid-eighteen hundreds it now brags of a population of fourteen hundred people, both elderly and young families. A large sign at the entrance to the town reads, "Northwood, The Friendly Town." How fast things can change.

The town has two ponds, the Old Mill Pond, which is popular for fishing, and the other, used for recreation such as swimming, picnicking and sunbathing. Paul was ready for an early morning fish at the Mill Pond. A long-time resident of Northwood he had been fishing at the pond for years. His favorite place to fish was right above a small dam that allowed water to leave the pond so it would not overfill. As he approached his fishing spot in the early morning light, he could make out what at first appeared to be a log against the dam. Upon closer inspection he looked in horror at what was a woman's body floating in the water. The body had obviously not been there long, as little decomposition had taken place. And he knew this woman. Her name was Betty White, a divorced mother of two grown children who had developed a serious drinking problem and created problems for the townspeople. Paul surmised she had gotten drunk, wandered over to the pond, fell in and drowned. The people in town felt the same way. They were all in for a big surprise.

The police and fire department were called. The fire department arrived first and were told by the police to secure the area as a crime scene, as their arrival time was going to be much later. Northwood, being a small town, had no police force of their own, depending on outside help for such matters. Word of this incident spread rapidly and soon the whole town was at the Mill Pond watching this once in a lifetime event. Little did they know this incident would be repeated over again many times.

The body was removed from the water and taken to the morgue for an autopsy, evidence was collected, and everyone left the scene returning to their daily tasks. A chill went through the town as the results came back. It was a murder by strangulation. The common thought was that Betty had been drinking and had met a man who she brought home, a typical thing for Betty to do. A fight had ensued, and Betty was strangled, her body dumped in the pond, as there was no evidence to suggest otherwise. A search of her home suggested that no one had been there, according to the mail found in her mailbox, which had been there for at least two days.

The police conducted interviews with people close to Betty, opened a tip hotline, put out a call to look for her missing cellphone, and asked the public to report any suspicious behaviour by people in town. Life in town returned to normal, as it was thought Betty's death was an isolated incident and no harm would come to them. They were wrong.

CHAPTER TWO

The next two weeks in Northwood were quiet. The buzz about the murder had subsided, the only talk left was around the tables of the coffee shop where locals gathered to discuss the latest gossip and other town events, a tradition that went back years. This morning was different however, as there had been a fire in town and the sole occupant of the house, Mrs. Claymore, was missing, presumed to have perished in the fire. An active investigation was on going, but no body had been found. Being the second incident in two weeks, suspicion gripped the town.

Mrs. Claymore was not found in the ruins of her house and was presumed missing and deceased by the investigative team who had found evidence of foul play. A witness saw Mrs. Claymore getting into a car and leaving but thought nothing of it until she reported the house on fire. Since it was already dark, the witness was unable to give the police much information, other than Mrs. Claymore had left with a man who was driving a small car. A search was launched by the police using a helicopter, and hundreds of volunteers who came to Northwood from neighboring towns, knowing the perpetrator needed to be caught, fearing that if not this horror might come to their town next. As the search wore on without success, the search teams slowly started to disband, knowing it would only be luck that would find this eighty-year old widow. Road maintenance crews had been alerted to watch out for any signs of Mrs. Claymore, or any suspicious people they met. Little did they know they were all looking for the wrong person.

Two weeks after the fire at Mrs. Claymore's house, road crews in a small town east of Northwood were clearing blocked culverts in a rural part of the county, when one of the men looked in the drainpipe and let out a scream. A decomposed body was in there. Their thoughts turned to Mrs. Claymore. First the fire department responded, sealing off the area to protect any evidence that might have been left. The police investigative team soon arrived. A task force would now be assembled, as it looked like they were dealing with an active serial killer.

An autopsy was performed, confirming the body to be that of Mrs. Claymore, but no cause of death could be proven. It was ruled a homicide due to the other circumstances. An unease swept the area of small villages, not knowing if this killer would expand his territory to include them. Everyone in the region was under a heightened awareness and fear, not knowing how to deal with this menace. Tips flooded the hotline, but nothing became of them. The people of Northwood tried to stick with their routines, but fear now ruled. Security companies were busy installing stronger locks, outside lighting, and other security upgrades. Landscapers came and cleared brush and branches from in front of windows to eliminate hiding spots. The fire department checked on the elderly residents, securing windows, and any other entry points. The town felt under siege, not knowing when the next incident would take place. They were not ready for how fast and brutal it would be.

CHAPTER THREE

A week after Mrs. Claymore's body was found, it happened again. Only this time it was different, the killer had deviated from his first two victims, who were older women, to a young male. His name was Warren McFee, a twenty-one-year-old man born and raised in Northwood. His reputation was anything but stellar, having a long criminal record for drugs and burglary, he was an annoyance to the townspeople who did not like or trust him. His body was found in the conservation area at the north end of town by two hikers. He had been found by the creek with multiple skull fractures, a large bloody rock laying at his side. Questions were asked as to how the killer ended up here with Warren. Did he lure him here with the promise of drugs? Once again, no evidence or witnesses could be found.

The detectives investigating these crimes were stymied. Obviously, the killer was smart, leaving no clues or witnesses to his identity. The task force called an emergency meeting, where it was decided that an around-the-clock undercover operation would be instituted in Northwood. Any suspicious activity would be questioned, and all answers would be verified. After two weeks of this, with no concrete results, the men were pulled from their duties there, and the investigation went back to relying on tips. The town's inhabitants went on with their business, always doubt and fear in their minds, a new reality that they now had to live with.

As spring turned into summer, and with the investigation going nowhere, the only choice was to wait and see if the killer stumbled and left a clue which would lead to his identity. The tip came into the hotline. A suspicious truck was seen at the park. A man and a woman were heard arguing outside the truck and the witness heard the man threaten the woman if she did not get back in the truck, at which time she did, and he sped off. Was this somehow connected to the killings, or just an argument between a man and his wife?

The police investigated this tip and found a comb they felt might belong to the man in the truck. It was taken for DNA testing, but no match was found in the system. The comb was to be a valuable find as the investigation continued. The witness was unable to provide any description of the truck or people because it was late and very dark. The talk in town was abuzz with theories and conspiracies. It was like a darkness had decided to invade the people's souls and snatch all happiness from them, making them dwell on this series of events that had changed their lives. Many dreamed of waking up and all this being a nightmare. The town waited for the killer's next move, turning on their radios early each day to listen for news that might give them answers, or more horror. Soon they would get the latter.

CHAPTER FOUR

Mrs. Peabody woke with a start. She had heard something. Her dog beside her growled loudly, as if sensing danger. She lay in her bed listening, the silence deafening. Mrs. Peabody was a long- time resident of Northwood, alone since her husband died, she hated the night and now was absolutely terrified because of the recent events that had been happening in town. She had no friends, no children, and was the only one left of her siblings. The police found her, in her bed, with her dog beside her, strangled. The neighbor knowing her habits, and not seeing her for a couple of days, had called the police to check on her. A thorough examination of the crime scene revealed the killer had entered the house through an unlocked basement window, went to her bedroom, and strangled her, leaving the house through the front door, once again leaving no clues or witnesses to his identity.

A sense of terror gripped the town, now they knew no one was safe. The police, trying to control the hysteria, decided a permanent presence in town was needed, assigning police patrols around the clock. This calmed the people, but did not work well, as the future would reveal.

Mrs. Peabody's autopsy showed a strange thing, she had not died from strangulation but from a heart attack. When the killer entered her room, she was so terrorized she instantly died of a heart attack, leaving the killer to strangle her, only to leave his hallmark at the crime scene.

The summer wore on and the town prepared for their signature event in early October. The fall fair, an annual festival, was held Thanksgiving weekend and attracted thousands of people from the area. But this year was different. Because of the murders a darkness had descended on the town, not just felt by the townspeople but by visitors too. Even though there had not been any attacks in two months, this did nothing to ease the sheer terror of knowing they could be next.

The next attack came with no warning. An elderly widow, living alone, was found by her daughter after not responding to her calls. Her mother had been strangled, and found in her bed, like the earlier victim. The killer had again entered the house through an unlocked basement window and left through the front door, also leaving no clues or witnesses as to his identity. The task force called for an emergency meeting where they discussed the possibility that their killer was not a stranger, but someone who lived in town or close by. The three women killed were all widows. Was this a coincidence or did the killer know his victims?

The detectives believed the killer was at least acquainted with his victims. The crime scenes indicated he knew the area. He exhibited skill at eluding police and a very aware public, whose suspicion about strangers should surely have led to a suspect by now. The investigation secretly shifted, as to not further upset the townspeople. The police felt they were now going in the right direction and had confidence the killer would be caught soon. The killer, realizing he might be apprehended, decided to step it up and commit the most heinous crime yet, leaving the police and town's residents shocked at its brutality.

CHAPTER FIVE

It was Thanksgiving weekend, and the Northwood fair was in full swing. Thousands of people from the outlying areas had flooded the fairgrounds to attend, temporarily making the murders of the town's residents a secondary thought. However, Tuesday morning, when people from Northwood returned to work after the long weekend, the reality of the situation returned. Another body had been found dumped at the east end of town in the cedar post yard. The body was of a young woman, unknown, beaten badly, tortured, and strangled. The woman was reported missing from the fair. She ran one of the game booths and had told fellow workers she had met a man who was to take her to his place after closing for drinks and a movie night. No co-workers had seen this man, and no one had seen Lucy, the fair worker, leave with him.

This time the killer made a big mistake, letting an empty coke can fall out of his vehicle while removing the body. The can was sent to the lab for DNA testing and came back a match for the comb that had been found in the park. The detectives now knew the killer owned a small car, which Mrs. Claymore had been seen leaving in, and a black truck according to witness' descriptions. This truck had been seen the night of the latest murder by a local resident returning home from his late shift at work, passing it on the road as it was pulling out of the post yard.

The detectives acquired a list of all registered vehicle owners with both a car and a truck in the area. Looking carefully at the descriptions of the trucks shortened the list of possible suspects to under ten. A few of these could be eliminated at once, leaving only six to be called in for interviews and polygraph tests. The task force had their eyes on the least likely suspect, a man well-known and respected in town. His interview went badly. He was nervous and deceitful during his questioning and refused to take a polygraph. The detectives felt certain they had their man, but now they had to prove it.

They started by putting him under a twenty-four-hour watch and bringing his wife in for an interview. She told the detectives he had been gone in the middle of the night with no clear explanation of what he had been doing. They informed his wife he was being investigated as the main suspect in the serial killings. She shared her own suspicions but could not make herself believe he was capable of such crimes. Knowing it was just a matter of time before he was arrested, the suspect decided to turn himself in and give a complete confession. His guilt over what he had done to his wife's life and how he had let down the townspeople who respected and trusted him, overwhelmed him.

He was the fire chief. He was to save lives, not take them. Upon questioning, he told the detectives he had left the basement windows open when he went in his capacity of fire chief to secure the older people's property. He had targeted widows because he knew they were unhappy after losing their husbands, and felt he was doing them a favor by reuniting them with their loved one. The town was in shock, not believing this man they had trusted for years could do this to them.

The killer was arrested and charged with the murders, reprimanded to custody until his trial. But as fate would have it, the inmates decided to take the law into their own hands. Shortly after being incarcerated, with the guards looking the other way, he was beaten and stabbed, and left to die on the jail floor. Was this vigilante justice a suitable ending for this serial killer? The people of the town felt it to be so. They were left wondering as to what motivated the killer and hoping God would somehow heal the sadness that enveloped Northwood, bringing back its slogan, *Northwood, the Friendly Town.*

THE HARVEST

+ + + + + +

The aliens were sitting in the confines of space just outside Earth's atmosphere, watching the human civilization brought to a standstill by the virus they had released. The virus was doing its job, killing the old and the sick, leaving the young and healthy to be harvested for high quality food to fulfill its contracts with other planets. This planet was seeded, like a garden, thousands of years ago with a low-level intelligence with a high rate of reproduction. Now it was harvest time.

The youngest children were the most desirable, their meat tender and usually disease free. Anyone over fifty was considered not edible but were still collected to be ground up and fed to the aliens' pets. There were thousands of planets spread out in space specifically planted with humans, a delicacy for a variety of alien cultures. Just like a garden, harvesting had to be done before the Earthlings had a chance to destroy the planet, destroying all the food crop, humans. If the aliens had been twenty years later this might have been the case.

As the harvesting ships arrived by the hundreds and waited, the final preparations were made. A fleet of specially designed ships released gas worldwide, which killed all humans but left every other living creature intact. Human bodies froze solid shortly after death, a by-product of the gas, so as not to rot before they could be picked up. Crews were sent to the ground to enter buildings and pull bodies to areas where they could be easily retrieved.

Large grinders were placed in city centers and hundreds of thousands of workers descended from the ships to do the labor, feeding the old bodies into the grinders. The human remains were returned to the ships, which, when full, were taken to the desired planet's factories to be processed. Bodies were left in rural settings, as it was not possible to work thinly populated areas. Days after the aliens left, those bodies would thaw providing food for a variety of the Earth's species.

The harvest lasted three months, and the planet would be reseeded in about one hundred years. Before leaving, all technology was destroyed. The humans once again, with the aliens help, would start from the beginning, to try to develop a world that was peaceful, non-violent, and happy, an exceedingly rare event. If they were to succeed, the planet would be left alone, allowing life to prosper.

The aliens were done here, and the last ships pulled out, leaving a planet devoid of human life. The planet would be watched and if everything went well, another harvest would take place in a thousand years.

THE EXTINCTION – THE SECOND HARVEST

T he young boys playing on the swing set looked skyward. A strange fluorescent glow had filled the sky, changing the colour from blue to a blood red, an omen of the death and destruction that was to befall the planet. The boys were terrified, not knowing what this strange event might mean, running home to their parents for the safety they could provide. The parents had no answer either, turning on the news channel to gather more information. There were no answers, an unexplained, worldwide phenomenon had gripped the planet, creating panic among the people.

A feeling of doom and death haunted the thoughts of the dominate species on earth, humans. Was this their reward for bringing death and destruction to a planet which did nothing to deserve it? Humans would pay for the hurt they had unleashed on one another, hatred and bigotry making the true meaning of life a warped reality, something the aliens would not leave unpunished.

A slow death would come to all humans, having lost their moral way. Worldwide, vegetation was dying; the beautiful trees and plants, their flowers turned brown with death, healthy forests looking like a winter landscape as this cosmic creation slowly died. As the vegetation disappeared, it created a planet with no oxygen, causing a die-off of all air breathing occupants, leaving a planet littered with corpses, which the aliens had returned to harvest. This time they were also taking all the planet's mammals, not just humans.

The aliens altered the climate to become a deep freeze, ensuring the bodies would not decay and the harvest would not be rushed. The bounty of valuable human flesh would make this alien company wealthy, as it searched the cosmos for dysfunctional planets whose inhabitants could be harvested for their meat.

This was Earth's second harvest in one hundred thousand years. With the seeding of the planet a hundred years from now, another harvest would probably take place in the future, the cycle never-ending.

THE PUPPET

+ + + + + + +

The package arrived by mail from Vietnam; it was a gift for a six-year-old boy whose name was Mathew, a middle class kid from the suburbs of Denver, Colorado. This gift, from an uncle who worked at the American embassy, was a birthday present not well received. When Mathew opened the package, a sneering clown puppet greeted the family. It was meant to be amusing, but it was not, a feeling of unease swept over the parents. Mathew loved it and was already planning on entertaining his friends with shows he would put on with his new buddy he called Winston.

Unfortunately for Mathew his new puppet was possessed by evil. The doll was made by a craftsman in Vietnam, a wise man in his late age. He was a survivor of the American involvement in the war that killed a large number of Vietnamese civilians, including members of his own family. Because of these atrocities committed against his loved ones, the puppet maker had never forgiven those he felt were guilty. This is why he cursed the doll; knowing it was going to America; he hoped it would bring bad luck and tragedy to those who possessed it.

Mathew loved his new puppet, and it soon became his constant companion, more important to him than the new puppy he had also received as a gift for his birthday. Unbeknownst to Mathew, Winston hated the dog. He was jealous, wanting all of the boy's attention for himself. He would rid himself of this obstacle that had come between him and Matthew. Days later while playing in the front yard, the puppy got away from Mathew and darted into the street, the tires of a pickup truck taking his life. Matthew displayed little emotion over the death of his new dog, as Winston had become the primary focus of the boy's life.

Matthew's mother was becoming alarmed by his obsession with Winston. Even his young friends sensed something in his behavior had changed. The boy slept with this evil puppet, his attachment still growing. His mother was becoming less important, as Winston slowly took possession of the boy's soul.

Mathew watched as the building burned, Winston tucked under his arm, his sneering face smiling at the burning church. A neighborhood landmark was gone forever, a mysterious fire with no known cause. Mathew became more withdrawn. His teachers worried about his behavior, becoming alarmed, not understanding what was happening; his spirit was possessed, the devil wanting his soul. However, his mother understood where the problem lay.

She decided to take care of this evil doll and burn it, sending it back to hell where it belonged. She prepared a metal drum and lit a hot fire. Retrieving the doll from her sleeping child, she placed it in the hot coals, causing it to ignite. She watched as a look of horror came over the puppet's face as it knew what its future held. A long painful scream came from its mouth as this evil spirit was returned to where it belonged. A horror was waiting for the mother when she found her child dead, his soul reunited with his buddy Winston, in the fires of Hell they would share forever.

THE BASEMENT

◆◆◆◆◆◆

The cold earth of the basement floor was the first indicator that something was wrong. While standing on the floor in this abandoned building from yesteryear, a cold chill would course through the body, instilling a sense of horror not even an imagination can comprehend.

The young woman was trapped in a world she could not understand. Mary found herself standing on that floor. Looking down she screamed in horror as long snake-like creatures appeared from their underground lair, wrapping their long tenacles around Mary's legs, ensnaring her, not allowing her any movement. Frozen in horror, hundreds of large black spiders dropped from the ceiling, their webs encasing Mary in a cocoon, trapping her and ensuring no chance of escape. She would be eaten later by the lurking giant waiting in the background, its insatiable hunger soon to be satisfied. Its poison allowing for an easy kill.

Like in a hammock Mary's body swung in the air, her mind gone, the horror causing mental illness to reign supreme. Hundreds of black spiders covered her body, waiting for the spoils of the feast. Mary's mind only knew darkness, as a nether world, not known to exist, took her spirit for its own pleasure, casting Mary into a place there was no escape from.

The giant spider moved. He started to make his way toward Mary, a slow methodical walk, confident his actions would work. Mary's eyes opened in horror as she watched the menacing spider approach. She would soon be a meal fit for a king. The large spider crawled on her, moving towards her neck to inject its poison, which would guarantee a slow painful death. Mary's eyes flew open, her gaze fixated on the ceiling, her thoughts turning to her recurring nightmare, causing doubt as to her own sanity. Her phobia of spiders taken to a new height; her mind consumed by these thoughts.

They found Mary dead, the victim of a black widow spider who came to share a bed with her to help prepare her for death. The spiders would have their feast and Mary would have her peace, a sensible trade off in this real life nightmare.

THE MUMMY

The discovery had been made earlier. It was an unusual burial in the desert. This was Egypt, a graveyard of tombs dug for the Kings, Queens, and other important people who belonged to this society eons ago. This tomb was different, constructed in a way unlike the other tombs which dominated the area. It was discovered by a Bedouin watching over a flock of sheep. While looking for an animal that had appeared to vanish, he had discovered the sheep at the bottom of a shaft which had given way from its weight being placed on it. The animal now lay dead after its fall. The boy reported the incident, and the Egyptian government sealed off the area, stationing security at the site until it could be investigated further.

The lead archaeologist from the University of Cairo was to do an assessment of the discovery and decide how important it was to Egypt's history. The professor and his crew of students, who would help him, arrived first and set up camp. The labourers would arrive later, providing the backbone for this operation. The work started, the entrance was cleared of debris and widened. As the workers continued to clear the way, a set of stairs emerged leading down into the earth. Next a passage appeared, painted black with an intricate mosaic of stars that somehow illuminated the passage and led down a lighted path to the tomb's entrance.

The tomb was sealed, indicating it had never been looted, a welcome sign for any archaeologist. Men were called in to unseal the tomb. Quiet prevailed as thoughts of what or who was in there dominated their thinking. After exhausting physical labor the first hole appeared, and they soon had cleared an area large enough to enter. Excitement mounted as the professor squeezed through the opening. He was greeted by a room shaped like a globe, walls of blackness illuminated by bright shining stars and planets, a portrait of our galaxy, illustrated in detail. Never before seen objects littered the room, a collection of the mummy's belongings which were buried with him.

The opening of the tomb was witnessed by few people. It was important the news of this discovery was not leaked to the public; the promise of execution if the secret was exposed. The lid was carefully removed from the coffin, revealing something that would change the history of this ancient country. A figure not of this earth, an obvious leader by his dress, a creature not so unlike us was inside the tomb. His unwrapped body showed no signs of decay, his skin still soft to the touch. The professor marveled at the discovery, not knowing that this event would turn into a disaster for the world.

Unbeknownst to the archeologist and his crew, when the seal on the coffin was broken a virus that had been born from the corpse was released. The world would call it Covid, a genie that was let out of the bottle by man's inquisitive nature, a mistake that was made which could be the beginning of the end as we know it.

THE BEAST OF UNIONDALE

+ + + + + +

Uniondale was a small indistinct town in the mountains of British Columbia. Something or someone had been killing and mutilating the residents' pets. Fear and panic gripped the people, an unknown menace was haunting their dreams.

It started when a young girl found her beloved dog savagely brutalized, its heart ripped out and taken as a trophy or souvenir. This was followed by a number of similar incidents, cementing the fact that the town had a big problem. Many theories were discussed. Was it a psychotic teenager, or a deranged adult who had adopted the role of one his horror fantasies he took too far?

The rumor the townspeople did not want to believe was the one about the beast of Unionville, a paranormal entity that somehow escaped the confines of its imprisonment, its anger unleashed on life. Seen as a black, sulphuric smelling shadow in the forests around town, led to the abandonment of this area by the residents.

An uneasy calm settled over the town, a feeling of impending doom dominating the spirits of the people. The moments of fear turned to reality when a screaming woman's call came into the police station. It was a daughter who found her mother murdered in the bedroom next to hers. The savagery of the attack stunned the small town. Like the pets, the heart of the woman was missing. The doors to the house were found still locked, only a dead bloody corpse left to prove this incident even happened.

Then it stopped, the people waited, apprehension causing heart attacks in some of the elderly. Years went by and the beast of Unionville became a legend, having left only memories to believe and a mystery to solve, a stain on the town's past that would never be forgotten.

THE RETURN OF THE KING

‹ ✦✦✦✦✦ ›

T he skies over Israel cast an orange glow over the city. Jerusalem was on fire, the number of Jews killed in the barrage of ballistic missiles that had been delivered by Iran was many. The Jewish state felt it had no choice but to stop the destruction of its country by delivering nuclear-tipped missiles, silencing the Iranian regime forever. Silence fell over the world, the people waiting and watching as to what would happen next. They did not have long to wait.

The Syrian government, knowing it would probably be the next victim of Israel's wrath, decided to inflict as much damage as possible on the Jews before their own country was destroyed. This plan would never be carried out. Syria had angered Israel after firing Russian-made missiles into the Jewish country in support of the Iranian missile attack. A surprise awaited them when an attack by Israel involving two hundred bombers, was launched leading to a bad ending for the Syrian regime. Battered and defeated, the Syrians agreed to stop their aggression under the threat of total destruction.

Unfortunately for Russia, a number of their military personnel stationed in Syria were killed. Additionally, when the Jews launched their attack, some of Russia's equipment was destroyed due to its close proximity to Syrian assets. This angered the Russians who used this as an excuse to join a situation that was quickly spiraling out of control. Russia, bruised by the defeat of its two allies, decided to strike back launching aircraft and drones to further attack the Jewish capital. The Russians, underestimating the Israeli air defences, lost their assets which had been used against this powerful, technologically advanced country.

Jewish morale was low as they realized the shield that had been protecting them from destruction had been lifted, allowing their enemies to strike close to their heart. World leaders had brokered a ceasefire, one that would never work. The Russians were moving forces and equipment into Syria as a show of force. A long standing feud between Pakistan and India reignited, both countries deciding to end their grievances against one another once and for all. They launched nuclear weapons, destroying one another's largest cities. The casualties of the war were piling up. The Americans, with a lifetime agreement to fight alongside the Jewish state, moved military assets into Israel as a showdown with Russia loomed.

The threat of a large, destructive war materialized as the Chinese joined Russia in the fight, overwhelming numbers of their joined forces could not be stopped easily. The armies of the world gathered on the Plains of Megiddo for the final battle for the soul of the planet. Armies, a million strong on both sides, faced each other, an epic battle about to ensue.

Suddenly the sky shone with the brilliance of a hundred suns. The mortals were stripped of their weapons, their hands lifted to the sky. They begged for mercy; most would never get. The sky grew dark, the sound of galloping horses, guided by shiny apparitions, raced through the crowd of soldiers, turning many to dust. For the Jews their long awaited Messiah had arrived, saving them from their enemies, preserving their country for future generations. The power of their God, it was learned, was not to be reckoned with. A future for the Jewish state and its people was guaranteed, by a power stronger than we can comprehend, one we can only believe in.

THE ROSE GARDEN

The large home sat alone, its former glory a memory of days gone past. The home, built in the late eighteen hundreds for a rich business owner, was modern for its time. It boasted six bedrooms, a large kitchen and dining area, and a summer kitchen. The home became a gathering place for the wealthy and powerful to congregate. Large elaborate parties were held there, and the house took on a reputation, as debauchery took over and alcohol-fueled incidents became common.

During one of these parties, accusations flew about an illicit relationship between friends leading to an angry display of emotions, and a shooting which left five people dead, including the owner of the house. All activity at the home ceased, no one wanting to live there due to the horrific events that had taken place. It was boarded up and sat abandoned for seventy years, its notoriety keeping buyers away until a young couple from the city found it.

After some research, the couple located the property owners and purchased the home at a bargain price, planning on renovating it into a bed and breakfast. The couple were wealthy, having the ability to pick and choose what they wanted to do. This had been a dream for both of them, and they were certain they had selected the perfect property for this endeavor.

Researching property records to find out about the history of the property, feelings of apprehension gripped the couple when a local historian informed them of its sorted past. It was not what they expected to hear. More information about the house was volunteered by a local contractor, who came to discuss doing renovations. The couple wondered if the reputation of the property would change the outcome of their well-thought out plan.

After serious discussion, they decided to go ahead with their plans and call their business The Rose Garden. Along with keeping the house as close to its original character as possible, they would plant beautiful rose gardens around the property and offer a variety of roses for sale in their store named, The Little Shop of Roses.

However, another unpleasant surprise awaited them. While replacing a section of rotting wall in one of the bedrooms, the remains of an infant were found, bringing more bad news for the Rose Garden and another blow to the reputation of the property. After the police investigation ended, some normality briefly returned. However, the construction workers started reporting strange events, such as tools disappearing, later turning up in a different place, the faint cry of a child, and the whispers of the shamed mother who had borne the child out of wedlock only to have it die at birth. The couple felt the house was cursed and their plan to establish a bed and breakfast would not come to fruition.

They abandoned their dream, and to ensure no one else fell into this nightmare, they hatched a new plan. They would burn this evil house and its reputation to the ground; never again would it haunt the thoughts of unsuspecting home buyers such as themselves. When the fire department arrived, the old house was completely engulfed in flames, the owners nowhere to be found. The firemen let it finish burning. The rose gardens the couple planted continued to flourish, adding a bit of splendor and beauty to an otherwise tragic story.

THE STARMAN

◆ ◆ ◆ ◆ ◆ ◆ ◆

S pace is infinite, the universe an unending display of planets, moons, and stars. Unexplained phenomenon which we will never understand dominates our planet, creating a never-ending supply of mysteries to be solved. The Starman was one such mystery. He came from a galaxy far away, a manufactured robot with artificial intelligence on a mission to find new worlds, especially those capable of supporting life. He was on a one-thousand-year journey, traveling through space cataloging any life found.

The Starman was a fully functional robot, designed to work for thousands of years without food or water. He was to travel the solar system, mapping new planets and moons, searching for functioning civilizations with interesting specimens which could be taken for future study. He would eventually return to his home, his planet and people trapped in time, one year or one hundred years meaning the same. He hailed from a society of robots working together, their intelligence rivaling that of the human brain; a peaceful society cooperatively solving their problems as they arose.

The rockets exploded in a ball of fire and light, with a thunderous roar he was lifted from the launchpad into the blackness of space. His first stop was a small unexplored planet ten years away, known to have water but no life. The journey there was dark; an unending blackness known only to lost souls destined to spend eternity in such a place. It served as a dumping ground for those unsavoury characters who chose darkness over light.

The ship landed without incident in a barren area, the world containing no life, not even bacteria. He noticed the sky, a rainbow of colors not previously seen, a kaleidoscope unique to this planet. The robot determined his landing site was safe, allowing him to shut down his computers and enter rest mode. He awoke later sensing something was wrong. With an uneasy feeling, he noted the sky had turned a deep purple, and experienced a feeling of impending doom.

A thunderous noise in the distance signaled the approach of a probable sand storm, which would destroy his spacecraft if the winds reached two hundred miles per hour. He had to leave immediately or his whole mission was in danger. His ship was designed to take off or land from any kind of terrain. Within minutes his escape was secured, and he soon found himself back in the safety of space. He continued his mission gathering scientific data, recording worlds which contained life, discovering planets destroyed by their own inhabitants which littered the cosmos.

The Starman's mission soon ended, and he returned to his own planet, discovering the destruction and death of the robotic society which dwelled there. A peaceful non-warring planet, they had been attacked and conquered by space pirates with advanced weaponry, who destroyed and looted his world of all its valuables. He left, going into space, and quietly drifting in the cosmos, as no further functions could be served by this machine. He traversed the universe for thousands of years, until his fuel supply became exhausted and his support systems shut down, rendering him an historic relic that would float throughout space eternity.

THE SECRET OF DOG NOSE MOUNTAIN

A mysterious mountain cloaked in myth and legends occupies the ancestral land of the Mayans, an indigenous culture found in Mexico and Guatemala. Now just a remnant of its former power, its people struggle to survive, selling blankets and other items made to appeal to the tourists who come to view their ancient ruins. The Mayan history books are few; very little is known about this advanced culture, the ruins of their cities and temples all that is left. It is known that the Mayan were awash in gold and silver, fine stones, and precious artifacts. The Spanish arrived with their hand in friendship and disease, nothing more than a greeting to slaughter the Mayan people, steal their riches, and destroy their civilization. Large Spanish galleons loaded with tons of gold and silver returned the treasure to their King in Spain. Sometimes these vessels were lost to pirates, or to their bigger enemy, hurricanes, which sent many ships loaded with hapless men and riches to the ocean floor where some of them remain today.

Dog Nose Mountain was an extinct volcano, getting its name from the cone-shaped top formed after its last eruption. The lava cooled to create the perfect shape of a dog's face and nose, which caused the Mayan to begin worshipping the mountain. They built a large temple and an altar, where human sacrifices were carried out as offerings to the gods for prosperity. During the Spanish occupation, large amounts of riches were hidden in the lava tubes, caves, and tunnels of the mountain, never to be found by the Conquistadors.

Now a protected site, many government expeditions had examined this volcano, returning with stories of workmen dying in tragic accidents. These tales had instilled fear into the locals hired to work the dig sites, leading them to refuse further work. An American archaeologist, educated in Mayan culture, was granted permission to conduct research and excavate the site. He left Washington, D.C. with a crew of professionals and students, and set up camp in a large cave which would provide shelter from the elements, especially the heat. Armed soldiers from the Mexican army were provided to protect the excavation team from small-time criminals looking to make a quick buck.

The dig got started and a treasure trove of artifacts surfaced. Pottery and artifacts crafted by Mayan artists, mainly statues of gods and kings, were among the ancient relics found. The legend of this mountain had piqued the interest and imagination of the archaeologist. He knew of the Mayan legends and their love for gold, mindful of the treasures rumored to be hidden in the volcano.

Additional permits were needed to explore inside the volcano. Many disclaimers had to be signed, but as the work so far had been successful, the Mexican government agreed to further investigation. It was hoped the secrets of this extinct volcano would live up to its reputation and reward the search efforts with unimaginable wealth. It was wishful thinking from the mortals, from a mountain with no intentions of co-operating or revealing any of its secrets.

The American party was decimated by accidents and sickness, sending them back to their home country, discouraged by a curse which had been proven true, a spell that would not be challenged again. The sacred mountain has been left alone, its legend intact, with man never coming out the victor.

THE OLD SAFE

꘏ ✦✦✦✦✦ ꘏

The one-hundred-year-old house looked forlorn, its landscaping untouched for many years. After being purchased by a new owner, plans were made to refurbish the property to its former glory. A local landscape company was contracted to cleanup the grounds. While digging, one of the young workers discovered an old safe buried close to the house. Speculation mounted as to what the safe might hold. The owner of the property had the safe removed and delivered to a craftsman who could open it without damaging the contents. The owner would be there to oversee this venture and invited the young man who made the discovery to join him.

The day of the big reveal arrived and excitement mounted as the safe cracker readied his tools. Within a short time, the door of the safe swung open, exposing a strange, unidentifiable object inside. Upon closer inspection it looked like biological material encased in a sealed canister. Curiosity gripped the attendees as they removed it from the safe, opened the container, and released a virus so deadly, it could kill in minutes. The people in attendance were the first victims, dead after their hearts were attacked and quit beating.

This virus, once released in the air, was capable of replicating with no host, making it both dangerous and threatening. Unfortunately for this primitive life form, originating in space was its demise. While surviving initially seemed plausible, after a short exposure to the earth's atmosphere it died, its only victims being those present when the safe was opened.

Whoever buried the virus in the hopes it would never be found must have thought it to be capable of causing mass destruction. Fortunately, those who opened this Pandora's box were its only victims, unleashing a wave of death that ended as soon as it was started. Humankind was saved from a tragedy that could have caused their extinction, a lucky ending for all but the victims.

ON THE DARK SIDE
OF THE MOON

✦✦✦✦✦✦

T he unmanned American spacecraft reached the moon with little incident. The space agency's mission was to investigate reports of unexplained activity coming from the dark side of the moon. Large areas of unexplained lights, communications in an unknown language, and structures towering above the landscape required exploration. The craft achieved its orbit and was approaching its goal. At first nothing seemed out of the ordinary, but soon areas of strange lights appeared. The scientists observing this mission from Earth were mystified.

The spacecraft was programmed to land at one of the light source locations and would do so on its next circuit. The craft, when on the moon, would be able to take pictures with the advanced cameras onboard. As it was approaching the landing site, the ship's computers were taken over by a cyber attack. The scientists on Earth could only watch, hoping for the best, as they had lost control of the spaceship. This little craft, with its advanced photographic abilities, would send back surprising pictures.

The American's ship was being guided by an unknown hand to an underground base which appeared to be a research and development area. It was a hub of activity, as humanoid-like beings scurried about doing their jobs. The focus of their interest was the probe they had captured. It was taken below ground to be studied.

Alien beings who walked upright like humans, their origins dating back thousands of years, had built an underground city undetected by scientists on Earth. Mining the moon for precious minerals, such cities took root, their inhabitants flourishing till present day. Using the raw materials from the moon, they had successfully built a high-tech society, their lack of need for food allowing them to survive. However, the aliens' inability to reproduce had caused their population to dwindle, the remaining occupants ready to leave. Their leader communicated through the probe, asking to resettle on Earth, promising to share their technology. His message was received by the scientists, who were receptive to the idea, but had no way to rescue the aliens.

The alien leader said they had an old ship which was in good repair. It was capable of transporting them to Earth if they were promised a safe place to live. A deal was made for them land at Nevada's Area 51, where they would be concealed from the American public and the world. The aliens, escorted by two American F-15s, arrived without incident, and were secreted away to a remote part of the base until permanent living arrangements were made.

Over the years Americans learned from the aliens, advancing their technology in communication, computers, and advanced weapons systems, making the Americans the most powerful force on Earth. The aliens were given safe refuge, but after a short time they succumbed to an environment that was not suitable for them, leaving only folklore and legends. Stories, some true, some not, will continue to spark our imaginations as to what really happens at Area 51; the truth is out there.

THE WITCH

‣ ✦ ✦ ✦ ✦ ✦ ‣

Standing alone in the woods, the man's curiosity overwhelmed him. The remains of the old wooden house in front of him was legendary, belonging to a presumed witch who terrorized this small town. The disappearance of two small children, their whereabouts never discovered, the burning of local churches, and the remnants of pets found sacrificed in satanic rituals, led the townspeople to blame the old lady in the woods of being a witch. Against her will she was dragged from her house by an angry mob and, without a trial, taken to a clearing in the forest and hung from a lone tree. The old lady threatened the townspeople and cursed them. The people believed the death of this woman would bring normality back to their lives. This notion proved to be untrue, as a series of events made the people regret the hanging, which seemed to have brought disaster to the town.

The old woman was buried in a secluded area at the back of the town cemetery. The first signs of abnormal activity around her gravesite was the vegetation dying. This was followed by the townspeople's pets found dead at her burial site, apparently lured there by an unknown force. Strange orbs of light were often seen dancing near her grave. These events led the people to believe in the curse she had cast upon them before her death.

The town was not ready to deal with the events that followed, the first of which was a death by fire, the screaming woman unable to escape the flames. This tragedy was forever etched into the minds of the people sent to rescue her. Next a three-year-old child fell in a well, losing her life. Her family's anguish and sorrow would be with them for eternity. Residents called for the burning of the witch's house, thinking it might rid them of her curse. However, in the end calmer heads prevailed, the townspeople not wanting to tempt fate by doing something that might bring more horror into your lives.

Eventually the bodies of the two missing children were found by hunters in thick bush outside of town, not murdered, but having succumbed to natural causes after getting lost and dying of exposure. The ritual killings of the pets were proven to have been committed by a group of satanic worshippers, absolving the old woman of any blame. The townspeople were horrified they had made such a mistake, blaming an innocent old lady for these perceived crimes. A wash of shame swept over the people involved in her hanging. The townspeople wondered what could rectify the situation. They decided they must show respect for this woman they had falsely accused and put to death by moving her body from the cemetery to her old wooden house in the woods, preparing a proper resting place for her.

The whole town attended the special service and burial. Her grave site was treated with respect and well cared for. Weeks passed and calm settled over the town, terrible things quit happening, and people felt the curse had been removed. The town went back to just being a town, the curse forgotten as the years passed. The legend of the witch remained just a legend, until the burning of her house and the desecration of her gravesite unleashed retribution on the town once again. This time the horror would not stop, causing the abandonment of the town. The witch was never bothered again by the living, leaving her in peace to enjoy her afterlife, as she felt vengenance had been served.

THE CEMETERY

◆ ◆ ◆ ◆ ◆ ◆

T he cemetery is a final resting place for the dearly departed, a sanctuary for the dead. It is a place where often a presence can be felt even after death. Most cemeteries are found where large numbers of humans live, in established towns and cities. Family cemeteries are a tradition that go back two hundred years or more, as large families were buried on private land, in one final resting place. But for a small town in New England, their cemetery was about to change the town in a sinister way, a resurgence of the dead to take back the town that once belonged to them.

The first two victims were elderly women, who were found dead the morning following their daily pilgrimage to the cemetery to visit the graves of their late husbands. These deaths were followed by the widows' spirits taking over where life had left off, driving their families out of their homes.

There were tales of strange happenings reported at the cemetery. Visual recordings of tortured spirits at the entrance, beckoning people to enter were made. The souls of those who ventured in the gates were forever held in the confines of the graveyard. The spirits' personal escape from this hell, now being imminent, being free to enjoy a spiritual life on earth.

The townspeople, knowing the threat was coming from the graveyard erected a tall fence, enclosing the area, hoping this would stop people from entering and surrendering their souls to the cemetery.

This proved to be a futile attempt at stopping this horror, as the lure from the undead created an overwhelming desire to enter this now foreboding place.

Slowly the townspeople followed, sacrificing themselves to this new power that had taken over their lives, committing themselves to a burial they had not planned.

MY PARANORMAL ADVENTURE

+ +++++ +

(A True Story)

It was after midnight as we drove into Frederick, Maryland looking for a hotel. Returning from vacation we had stumbled upon this city, which we later found out was one of the most haunted towns in the state. Surrounded by large civil war battle sites, there was never a shortage of hauntings. Many of the oldest hotels were once used as field hospitals, where arms and legs were amputated, leaving a place of suffering and death which would stay with the building forever.

Not being able to find a hotel on the highway, we deviated from our course and drove into Fredrick hoping to find a place to sleep. Little choice was left as a big event in the area had filled many of the hotels, leaving few rooms for travellers like us. After checking the more desirable places with no luck, we decided at this point we would take anything, as long as it was clean. We pulled up to what looked like a decrepit hotel. A two-story building as old as the town itself. Being led down the hallway a musty odor prevailed. The room was old but clean. Having no other option, we embraced it, fatigue overtaking us.

Slumber was almost immediate, but a surprise awaited. While sleeping, I was disturbed by something, or someone, trying to pull me off the bed. Opening my eyes and being in a semi-lucid state, but fully aware of

280

my surroundings, I saw three confederate soldiers in full uniform trying to drag me from the bed. Terrified I screamed for my wife. Upon her awakening, the soldiers disappeared, and normality returned.

This story, even though it goes back twenty years, is as vivid to me today as it was back then. I will always remember the unhappy, scowling faces of the tormented soldiers as they looked for a peace they will never get. The rest of the night was spent with a feeling of unease that could be explained, an episode in my life that will never be forgotten. Was this really an event with meeting the spirits of these dead soldiers or just a cruel trick of the mind? We will never know for sure, it only sowing doubt about what to believe, as we journey through life's surprises and experiences.

THE GRAVEYARD

The black cat walked slowly across the graveyard meandering among the tombstones, heading to his meeting with the souls of the dead. He was the caretaker of the cemetery responsible for protecting the deceased against the thieves who come in the night to steal their souls. The black cat had powers unknown to the living, able to repel the entities that with stealth and speed were able to capture and flee with the souls of the departed.

The black cat reached his destination, a clearing in which all the ghosts were to congregate and let out their mournful sufferings on him. He would listen and comfort them, bringing them promises from their creator that their destinies would not be stolen from them. The black cat was loyal to the dark side, whose powers had been diminished. He was no longer able to protect these evil souls, whose biggest fear was being saved and made to worship a god unlike their own. They relished the reputations they had established on earth, as disciples of Satin, enjoying all the evils life had to offer them. Their choice, and their promise, was to enjoy the same benefits in the afterlife.

However, that promise was about to be broken, as the power of their leader had been destroyed, allowing the power of the light to strike the black cat dead, leaving the deceased souls no meaningful protection. They knew it was only a matter of time before the light would enter the cemetery, strike the evil from their souls, and leave them in a peaceful sleep with no true afterlife. This is what they were most fearful of, knowing that they would be saved but never able to enjoy the benefits of a peaceful sleep. No longer able to wander the grounds of the graveyard, they would be locked in the confines of the earth forever.

As we wander through the cemetery visiting our loved ones and friends, we never realize the dead occupy a realm unlike our own. Those uneasy feelings we get when we visit the cemetery, are the spirits of the unsaved souls reaching out for your protections, something the living cannot give them.

Be careful how you conduct your short life on earth, as your actions will be judged, and you will be put in your rightful place at death. Your destiny will be sealed with no second chances. There is no choice but to follow the path of salvation, or your afterlife will be one of damnation.

OUR WORLD OF DARKNESS

+ + + + + +

T he earthquake happened without warning. It was a worldwide event caused by an unknown celestial occurrence, ripping the planet apart, causing it to fracture but leaving it functionable except for a slight deviation in its orbit. It was soon clear that something was seriously wrong. Calculations by scientists brought the planet closer to the sun, which was apparent the first day.

Temperatures on the Earth soared, most areas of the planet recording temperatures of one hundred sixty degrees, killing anything that could not escape. Unusual lightning never seen before was caused by the Earth's new orbit, leaving the land with a never-ending heat, causing any life on the planet to be extinguished. The humans that could, tried to escape.

An underground city had been built to house the most intelligent, scientifically gifted people. This plan had been put in place years prior by world powers, hoping the citizens would be able to solve the aftermath of incidents like this. Large generators powered the city, fed by an unlimited gas source, which made these areas sustainable for life for a long time.

The humans living underground were trapped. The sun had killed all vegetation, including trees, so there was no longer air to breathe above ground. The situation was growing desperate. People who could not tolerate life below ground grew frustrated, their anger rising. The humans became polarized as trust dwindled, splitting them into two factions, each with a leader promising supremacy.

The primeval urge to survive was intact, creating a desire for domination and power. The two sides fought for control, with the ensuing war becoming more important than growing food. Soon hunger reigned with people on both sides dying of starvation. There would be few humans left alive as their quest for power had brought them total destruction. Those who survived the failed wars soon succumbed to the madness that enveloped them, causing most to die alone, never understanding what happened.

AN ASSAULT ON EARTH

+ + + + + +

The airships arrived in the night, undetectable by radar, flooding the Earth's sky with thousands of unmanned space craft equipped with deadly weapons. Their journey here was a passage through time itself. Thousands of light years away, in a galaxy unknown to man, an experiment by this war-loving planet was about to begin. They wanted to test new weapons that would allow them to conquer and control whole interplanetary systems. Our planet had been studied by this alien culture and chosen because of the total disregard by the species that lived here for the planet's health. It was an expendable, destructive culture that would never be missed.

Inhabitants on the planet would be euthanized, except for tens of thousands who would be returned to the alien's home planet and forced into slavery. Sent to work in the mines and military factories, most would live a short life, often murdered by their handlers. Thought of as low-level life forms easy to replace, galaxies were full of these types, a never-ending supply of labor was always available.

The mother ship that controlled the spacecrafts sat outside of Earth's atmosphere, waiting for orders to continue from their planet's military command. The Earth had no defensive structure to protect against this type of assault, the species living here more interested in destroying each other for personal power than in protecting the planet. The enemy assumed position, covering the planet in a net that could not be removed, waiting for orders to release their deadly cargo.

A military effort led by the United States proved worthless, as the enemy craft were protected and could not be destroyed, leaving little choice but to surrender to these intruders and hope for salvation. The aliens, knowing how naïve this species was, offered up a deal; turn over a half million of the planet's inhabitants for removal, and they would leave and spare the lives of the rest of the condemned souls. It was all a big lie, as the sole purpose of this endeavor was to strip the planet of its enemy and return it to its former glory.

The Earth's leadership was fooled, sacrificing their own people to save their pathetic selves. Shortly after the future slaves were removed, a deadly gas was released, bringing a quick end to the planet's Age of Man, a turbulent period brought on by a life form not suitable for the planet. The enemy left, their job complete, their experiment hailed as a success. Their goals had been achieved. The bodies were left for nature to dispose of, and a new beginning for a beautiful Earth left scarred by this occupation, a threat no more.

THE SECRET AT
THE CEMETARY

T he cemetery had been established in 1830. Over the years the
populace of the area had increased and aged, requiring the
cemetery to grow larger. Many of the early graves had been
lost, their markers displaced, their residents left in peace. The town,
called Bracewood, had an unpleasant history. The hamlet had dealt with
a number of personal tragedies, the latest being a local man, named
Gary, who suffered from financial problems and had shot his wife, and
then himself, in a tragic murder-suicide.

Creating tragedies and collecting bodies for the cemetery was the job
of an entity of the spirit world. He was charged with amassing an army
of the undead, who would enter the minds of humans, deceive them,
and then collect their souls for his own society, the City of the Damned.
It was a vibrant community of spirits who would rise from their underground tombs to join with others like themselves. They haunted the
grounds to protect what was theirs. These spirits were sent throughout
the town to hasten the departure of its residents, and then welcome the
newly departed to their new home.

Many of the townspeople started dying from strange accidents and
illnesses, their bodies laid to rest in what was thought to be a lasting
peace but was the beginning of a nightmare. Their souls were being
gathered. The work continued, innocent victims giving up their lives
prematurely. The town's population was dwindling, and the cemetery

was filling up with the dead. Finally, the town was no more, leaving only abandoned buildings, with no sign of the once vibrant community that existed there.

The City of the Damned had now become the dominant community, unbeknown to the people visiting Bracewood, who viewed it only as the final resting place for their loved ones. The acts by the unliving to deceive the citizens into coming and joining them in the cemetery had been accomplished. The mournful cries of the deceased souls were trapped in a life of sorrow with no chance of escape, their future was sealed.

INSANITY

⋆✦✦✦✦⋆

The Russians had complete control of America's skies. A war had broken out in space, satellites being the main target. Unfortunately for the United States, Russia and China had a shared missile program specifically designed for space warfare to attack American satellites and any other space hardware that belonged to them. The assault came as a surprise. The military satellites were the first targets, crippling the most technically powerful military force in the world, bringing it to its knees. Its weapons now useless, a counterattack was not possible. Next, the enemy disabled the satellites that were vital to humanity's existence: power grids, weather information, and utilities, including water, were all effected.

The US had been silenced along with its northern neighbour, Canada, who had been a staunch ally and had angered both China and Russia in the past. Not a single shot had been fired. The Chinese aircraft arrived first, flying low over the White House, dipping its wings as if in a mocking salute. The Russian long-range bombers were next, imposing and threatening. It was just a threat for now, as negotiations for a complete surrender would soon take place. The politicians lied to the people, telling them everything was going to be all right. The population in both countries had quit believing their governments' lies after the COVID pandemic had swept across North America and taken many lives. The ruling elite was only concerned about their own power and wealth.

The enemy was devious and cruel, hatching a plan that would kill the people, but leave the infrastructure intact for eventual inhabitation by an ever-increasing Chinese population. The Russians signed treaties with the Chinese against aggression and war. They agreed that China would take over North America in exchange for a shared wealth of the dwindling world supply of raw materials, important to keep their military strong and their people fed.

The next part of the plan was put into effect, a plot to poison the minds of the people and drive them insane. They would turn the American and Canadian residents into harmless robots, unable to care for themselves, leading to a slow and painful death. The chemical was a joint project, meant to infect millions of people in a short amount of time. The chemical's life was short-lived so it would not infect outside countries, only the areas of the world they targeted.

It worked well, doing its job across North America. The Russian and Chinese revelled in the suffering and hurt being inflicted upon their perceived enemy, relishing the fact they would never have to deal with these countries again. Unfortunately for them, this new chemical was not what they perceived it to be.

After lying dormant for a brief period, the chemical reactivated in a new form. The wind carried this now deadly chemical-turned-virus horror and released it upon the world. It was an unexpected twist for selfish powers who thought they were in control; a deserved ending to a plot that ended their goal of world domination, leaving them with only death.

It was a lesson learned the hard way. Plans may not always have the expected outcomes, ending in a bad result for everyone.

THE GRANITE ROCK

✦✦✦✦✦✦

The gray rock lay bare. It was a small island in the middle of a large northern lake; barren of life and vegetation, its purpose was never understood. As humanity races toward extinction, the earth will become that rock, devoid of life that humans have selfishly destroyed. Without the ability to work together as a global community, our species will fade away. Our planet will be nothing more than a dead shell of what it once was, another casualty of the mysterious universe we live in.

Do you think any one in this realm of mystery is going to miss us? No. Do you think in a million years there will be any sign we were ever here? No. Then what was our purpose of ever existing? We were offered life, a livable planet, a body, and a chance to experience a physical life instead of a spiritual one.

Alas, this great experiment has been a failure, resulting in a total breakdown of earth's societies as this cancer called hate spreads worldwide. The chances that we have been given are exhausted; there will be pity no more as different powers are coming together to cleanse the earth.

It will end in a great fire, as the men we will call boys finally get to push the buttons that will create the greatest and the final fireworks show in history. This spectacle will usher in the birth of a ruined planet. Man will no longer be a threat, as his demise was covered. He will never be able to reign destruction again on an innocent world. The universe will have taken back the gift that was given to us, the gift called life.

FAMILY

A DAY IN THE SNOW

◆◆◆◆◆◆

Warm air followed the large snowstorm turning the fluffy white cottony snow into a buildable material for the children who had been waiting for such a moment. The snow now can be used to build all the things a child's imagination can think of. Children build snowmen, a tradition going back hundreds of years, and will continue for hundreds more. Other children gather in large groups on these days and, like an army, build snow forts, protective structures where they can hide when the enemy attacks. The loss of their fort often leads to humiliation, the victor washing the face of the loser with a handful of icy snow.

Nearing the end of the day the kids split themselves into two groups, the ultimate battle is about to begin. Friends paired with friends; the arsenals of snowballs built up over the day. A battle cry rings out and the weapons of war fly until gone, ending the day, a cue for everyone to go home.

If given the opportunity and the right circumstances, children will play outside in the snow all day; sometimes the parents having trouble getting the children to end their play and come in for dinner. Tomorrow at school tales will be shared and hopes of this day repeating itself will be on the minds of the children. Nature will decide when to give this special gift again to all the happy kids who love to play in the snow; also providing peace for parents with their children occupied, the mothers' smiling at their children's natural curiosity towards this new world they have been born into. It is a miracle most enjoy for a long time.

A REFLECTION ON LIFE

＋ ＋◆◆◆＋ ＋

An intricate pattern of ice crystals, like mosaic tile, covered the inside of my bedroom window. On frosty winter nights as a child, I would awaken in the morning bundled in heavy blankets, the air in the bedroom cold, until my father started the woodstove, sending warm air upstairs. Looking at the window pane, it was beautiful artwork created by nature, a miracle performed by an unseen hand that cannot be explained.

The noise and activity picked up as the children awoke, creating a tsunami of events to occur. Jockeying for a space around the woodstove was a top priority for my siblings trying to get warm after a cold January night. The wood crackled in the stove causing heat to radiate outwards, warming us enough to eat breakfast. Large bowls of hot porridge ready to be devoured sat on the kitchen table, drawing everyone away from the woodstove.

Sibling rivalry took over as our mother tried to keep control. The cold and snow outside were unrelenting, keeping us inside for the day. This created a monumental task for Mom, but one she enjoyed as the love for her children took priority over everything else. The old farmhouse warmed up as the morning wore on, the children now fully awake and happy. Mother was baking, making sure there was always something special to eat for the children, adults, and company.

All of the children had jobs they were responsible for. My chore was bringing up firewood from the basement and piling it in a large wash tub that sat beside the woodstove. At this time, if any of Mom's preserves were needed they would also be brought upstairs. The basement was a scary place. As the door was opened from the kitchen, a chill would pass through your body. Was this feeling created by the spirits that called this place home, or just chilly air coming from an unheated part of the house?

After lunch, the sun shone brightly, the new snow sparkling in the light creating a winter wonderland. Only the rabbit tracks were visible in an otherwise untouched landscape. Mom shoed everyone outside to play. She appreciated the peace and quiet that followed.

My pleasure as a child growing up in the country was the freedom, not enjoyed by children who lived in the city. A never-ending feeling of peace and joy was experienced as the woods and fields were explored. These outings brought happiness to the sometimes troubled spirit of a child trying to grow up.

The daylight hours are short in the winter, darkness coming early. Bedtime was once again soon upon us. Looking out my bedroom window at the rabbits in the snow, which would visit nightly, returned to my thoughts. They would eat out of mother's compost pile below my window, never seeing me watching them. These are all cherished childhood memories, which will never be forgotten; always creating happy feelings, in this sometimes cruel and chaotic world in which we live.

THE ICE RINK

✦ ✦ ✦ ✦ ✦

T he early March weather had been warm, creating large expanses of water from the melting snow in the low areas, forming ponds. Usually this happens in early spring, guaranteeing another freeze, which creates superb habitat for young hockey players wanting to play shinny, a game typically played on an outside surface among friends making up their own teams. These gatherings are a sacred ritual for kids, who never miss this opportunity to congregate with their peers to show off their latest skills. A chance to compete in an open atmosphere free from parental oversight, allows this young culture to take care of their own problems when they arise.

These games are always fair, a set of principles and rules strictly followed by the children who govern themselves. This is not always the case in organized hockey, where parents forget the manners that they have instilled in their offspring. Outbursts by the adults on the ice is not what hockey is about. Children, when left to themselves, enjoy a camaraderie and sense of fair competition, accepting a loss as a loss, and a win as a win, accepting or celebrating each accordingly.

As dusk falls the last three children on the ice are not ready to give up, their mothers cutting them some slack, knowing for their children this was a special day that rarely happens. An early sleep ends their weekend, and prepares them for school the next day, where they will meet with friends and discuss their love of hockey and their plans for their next competition.

A hockey culture is engrained in the Canadian spirit, providing a chance for any child to become an icon. A past of playing shinney on a frozen pond may lead to one's future as a professional hockey player and memories that will never be forgotten.

THE SNOWMAN

N othing symbolizes winter more than the snowman. During a warm front, the snow becomes wet, allowing it to be rolled into large balls. This is when children and adults continue a very old tradition and build these creatures they call snowmen. Every snowman is a little different, providing a glimpse of the creative side of the people who build them, something that is rarely seen.

They are started with a large ball of snow for the base. The second ball, the midriff, is slightly smaller and stacks on top of the large ball. Loose snow is then packed where the two balls are joined together. Last is the head, a much smaller ball of snow than the previous two. After packing more loose snow around where the head connects to the snowman's body, you are now ready to put a face on him.

This is where people deviate from the norm, and with help, mostly from the kids, create outlandish characters that are only seen in a child's imagination. Crazy hats, buttons for eyes, a wild scarf, and a carrot for a nose are popular choices. The snowman stands proud, guarding its domain, until one day another warm front comes through and melts the snowman, leaving him forgotten in a pile of melted snow. This tradition will be continued as long as there are children, it is a fun-filled winter activity loved by adults and children alike.

The next time you pass a snowman, do not just think of it as an inanimate object, but a symbol of creativity and beauty built by happy people. Snowmen dot the lawns of country and city homes across our nation, reminding us of the fun that was had by all. As the winter turns to spring the snowman becomes a forgotten relic, melting into the ground along with all the rest of the snow. He will not be resurrected until the snow returns the following winter. This will start the tradition all over again. The next time winter is here, take your child, or just yourself, and build one of these mystical creations and relish the feeling of joy it brings to your spirit. It is a family tradition that is enjoyed by all.

MEMORIES

+ + + + + + +

The sound of the outboard motor dad was trying to repair sprang to life, interrupting the silence as the old motor shook the forty-five gallon drum of water to which it was attached. The sweet smile of victory replaced an earlier frown of frustration at the old motor's reluctance to run. Dad returned to his work bench to retrieve his hot tea, listening to the outboard idling in harmony, all the parts in the motor working as they should. A commotion from above caught his attention; a barn swallow's nest full of hungry babies were about to be fed by their busy parents. This was a summertime ritual, and a shared accommodation that worked out well for both parties involved.

Dad walked over to the motor, shutting it off, the quiet soon disturbed by a tractor and wagon entering the driveway. It was the owner of the property bringing hay, to be stacked in the barn for food for his cattle in the winter. This was one of the last loads of the summer, as the haying season would soon end. Dad opened the gate for him to enter the barnyard, and with two young helpers riding on top of the hay bales they made their way to the barn, being followed by hungry cattle looking for a free meal. Waves of greetings and thanks followed as the gate was shut and secured behind them.

Dad walked toward the house to get his tea refreshed. The sound of Mom's voice caught his attention, reminding him it was the day their son, Joe, would be here for lunch, a day he routinely visited as his work brought his appointments close to home. Mom was busy hanging clothes on the line, thankful it was just her and dad's laundry, and not for all the children that once lived here. Raising her children was the focal point of her life but doing laundry in an old wringer washing machine and having to hang everything to dry was not one of her favorite things.

Finishing, she returned to the house and retrieved the pie she had baked for Joe from the oven and set it out to cool. After lunch she would tend to her garden and select fresh vegetables for dinner. She loved the summers, her flowers and gardens thriving on her caring spirit towards nature. Dad would use this time to go to town and pick up things he needed, and whatever mom wanted for her baking, never knowing when visitors would arrive expecting something sweet and delicious to be waiting for them.

Supper was served early, potatoes nightly, with a vegetable and a meat, followed by a home baked dessert. Then on to the living room for the local news viewed on a black and white TV, one of only two channels their outside aerial could retrieve the signal from. Bed came early, and morning came earlier, a cup of tea and conversation at the kitchen table a morning ritual. It was a hard but happy life enjoyed by loving parents, a life not to be repeated today in our den of luxury. something never imagined in their lifetime, but also never missed, replaced with love, kindness and family.

JETHRO

+ + + + + + +

J ethro was the family dog. He was a small black dog with short legs and a longer than normal back. When I was a child, he was my companion and best friend accompanying me on my long walks through the forest areas that surrounded our home. He would bound through the deep snow, jumping like a rabbit, the only way his legs could maneuver in this fluffy obstacle. After returning from his snow bound adventures, he would curl up by the woodstove, warming himself and always falling into a peaceful sleep.

Jethro was allowed to use the inside of the old farmhouse with no restrictions. He took it upon himself to protect the house, always giving the first warning of any visitors coming up the long driveway. Jethro could always be counted on to be there when needed, a consoling friend when feeling down, a partner to share excitement with, and a relationship of shared responsibilities toward each other.

This dog was an important part of my life as I was growing up. Always a friend that could easily be found, Jethro was a dog that never felt a leash around his neck. He was allowed to freely roam the nearby fields and wooded areas, which unfortunately led to the premature death of this beloved animal. His spirit was filled with life and enthusiasm, as shown when he chased the cars down the long driveway of the farm-house, his farewell ritual when visitors left. Always returning, with a confident gait and a wagging tail.

Sadly for Jethro, the overpowering urge to mate led him to a female dog new to the area. It was on one of his escapades to visit her, that he became careless. He got too close to the busy road which ran by their property and was killed by a car, the driver having no opportunity to avoid a collision due to the dark night. Jethro was buried in a grave on the property he was raised on, a sad affair for a beloved family member that meant so much to everyone. He was a devoted friend who will never be forgotten, a faithful companion who generated happy memories in the hearts of those who loved him most. May his soul rest in peace.

OLD AGE

+ + + + + +

A baby is born, and a new life begins. The joy is celebrated by the new parents, their family and friends. At the same time, a loved one is being admitted to a nursing home, a somber event being arranged by the same family who can no longer take care of her. This woman had spent her life caring for and loving the individuals who are now deciding her fate.

As young adults we never envision becoming the old people we so easily criticized and frowned upon. These elderly people worked hard without the benefits of the life we crave today. The majority of people worked jobs that were necessary to sustain a living and feed their families but are now looked upon as the jobs of the uneducated, destroying a work ethic that had lasted for multiple generations. These old people were once parents raising large families, devoting their lives to loving their children and teaching them manners and respect. These families had nothing to make their lives easier, depending on only their children for help. As society has advanced into this new world of technology, the old people were left behind, not being able to adapt to changes, their minds having been taught otherwise. They are ridiculed by the younger people, whose cell phones have become the focus of their lives, not their grandparents.

When we are born the aging process starts, and never ends as we march toward our destiny, old age, a part of our life no one can change. Many of us will age gracefully, living to an age well beyond statistics with very few health conditions, while others will develop devastating diseases that will take their lives prematurely. Some of the elderly will be looked after at home by family members, while others will be sent to long term care and nursing homes, the last stop before their earthly adventure ends.

The old people are now largely seen as a burden on our society, as doctors devastate their ranks with pills and bad advice. Hopefully, we will be able to reflect on our lives and feel satisfied that we have done what was necessary for the next generation, who will continue this tradition, the march to old age and the end to the cycle of life.

THE TRAIL TO NOWHERE

✦ ✦✦✦✦ ✦

L ife is a long path that leads to nowhere; a journey taken by all of us, who like a hiker walking a trail, know the path we are on will eventually end. Life is a journey of one's own creation, you choose your own path. Your destiny is the product of this journey, no one else directing the route you are on.

As our children are born, our selfishness wanes as the love for our children dominates our spirit. This injects needed love into our lives, and a purpose for our existence. However, once the children are raised and gone from the family home, a sense of relief washes over us. It is as if a huge burden has been lifted, no longer having the responsibility of raising a child.

Retirement brings with it a sense of loss. Your skills no longer needed, your social contacts from work begin to disappear and eventually all that will be left is the two of you. You and your children, exist in a bubble not to be popped; your space not invaded, even by your own siblings.

Life can be measured from minutes to years, none of us knowing how long our journey will be. An acceptance that there will be an end needs to be realized; none of us capable of an escape from death. We hope that somehow life will continue in spirit, and our death will not be the end, but a beginning, the reunification with past family members our reward.

While here on this planet, respect and enjoy this gift you have been given called life. The choices you made in life will be remembered, as your body is lowered into the ground and your spirit ascends to heaven.

THE BOY AND HIS DOG

+ + ✦ ✦ ✦ ✦ +

The dog is a boy's best companion, beating out the best of human friends. To a child a dog's friendship is immeasurable, always there to comfort in difficult times, to play with when the spirit arises, and to protect you in times of danger. This pet helps the child learn about responsibility and love. Receiving his new dog as a gift from his parents, he is the one who would proudly names it, giving him a sense of pride and ownership. The benefits of giving a dog to your child are limitless. This dog will grow up with your child until one day the child can no longer protect his best friend. Nature will have taken its course and the dog has aged to the end of its lifespan.

The child, now a teenager, will mourn his friend knowing a new chapter is beginning in his life. As he progresses, his dog will never be forgotten, as only fond memories of his childhood friend will bring special joy into his heart. The boy has now grown into a man, married with a two-year-old son whose birthday is today. He is getting a special present, a puppy. The father knows happiness will be in his child's heart when he receives this special gift.

Take the best of the human spirit and use it in a positive way, and happiness will follow you through the most challenging times. Life is a lesson we learn from, and the choices we make shape our lives forever. Your destiny is the sum of your choices, so make them carefully.

THE TREEHOUSE

s a child growing up in a rural area surrounded by densely wooded forests, a treehouse was part of life. First you had to find a suitable location, usually not too far from your own house. This allowed you to easily retrieve needed items without wasting precious time walking between your two homes. Next was finding a suitable tree to build in, large enough and with a natural structure to serve as a base for the floor. It should provide easy access from the ground to the treehouse with its branches. Some structures ended up with a floor only, as building materials were at times hard to find. Most parents were reluctant to spend money on this project, forcing the kids to make do with what they could find around their homes. Because of this handicap highly creative treehouses were built using several types of building materials.

For many kids, a floor was good enough, but for the more industrious and creative, walls and even a roof were built. The roof usually had a skylight so the kids could stand up and look out for imaginary armies, friends who were going to arrive, or just to investigate what that noise was. Typically, the treehouse was a meeting place for all the neighborhood children, many of them involved in its construction. Arguments between the children broke out, as space in the treehouse was limited and no one liked being left on the ground. Sometimes these battles led splinter groups to form, who would break away from the large group and build their own treehouse, vowing to never let their adversaries enter their new domain.

In the beginning the treehouse was the most important thing in these children's lives, but as time wore on the children started to lose interest and spent less and less time there, as other activities became more important. Thirty, or even forty. years later the treehouse will still be there, and if you visit, it will spark fine childhood memories of a life we once enjoyed. In stressful times we should stop and reflect on memories like the treehouse, revisiting those carefree days as a kid. These memories will follow you for life, bringing a smile to your face and a feeling of happiness to your soul. Passing on this experience to your children will engrain thoughts in them that will never be forgotten, as they make their journey through life one day at a time.

CAMPING

‧ ✦✦✦✦✦ ‧

C amping is a leisure activity enjoyed by North Americans. Tent camping or camping with your RV are the two most popular ways to enjoy this adventure. Tent camping requires organization, outfitting your life for staying outdoors. The most important thing you will need is a tent. This is your shelter from inclement weather, where you will sleep, and store your belongings. Food is your next priority, canned food being the most practical because of its long shelf life. Sealed bags of rice and pasta are also good choices. A large cooler is needed for meats and perishables and to keep drinks cold. Unless you are wilderness camping, ice can usually be replenished easily.

When camping with children, pick a place where activities abound, like playgrounds, swimming, fishing, and even a rec hall where the older kids can congregate. As a parent this will make your life easier, as children get bored easily. Board games should also be packed in case of rain, which will confine you to your tent.

A propane stove will be needed for cooking, flashlights and battery powered lights for the tent, and a propane lantern for outside the tent. Setting up your camp, provided you have no problems putting up your tent, should take no more than two hours. After dinner and when night falls, the campfire can be started, a tradition as old as time. People gather around the fire, only the crackling of the burning wood breaking the bouts of silence. The fire, hypnotic in nature, and the silence of the forest, causes the mind to wander to days gone past, recalling a collection of thoughtful events. The fire wanes and is left to burn down to the coals, at which time it is extinguished. This signals bedtime, usually ending in a fiasco as everybody jockeys for a spot in the now crowded tent.

The lights go out, goodnights are said, and a sudden silence overwhelms the campsite. The only sounds are of nature, a hooting owl, the wind blowing through the trees, and the unexplained noises that always come from a dark forest at night. Your sleep should not be interrupted, as the darkness and silence put's your mind into a peaceful state, providing total relaxation upon awakening the next morning.

Camping is fun, but so is going home to a hot shower, and a comfortable bed amid the memories of your camping trip, luxuries we only realize after our trip. The peaceful moments we enjoyed are soon forgotten as we return to the reality of working, but the forest will always be there waiting for our return, providing us with peaceful moments that will never be duplicated.

THE TRAILER PARK

—— ✦✦✦✦✦ ——

Hundreds of recreational trailer parks dominate the shores of the lakes and rivers in North America. The seemingly unending bodies of water accessible by road, close to the US border, makes the US tourism market attractive for the South Eastern Ontario trailer parks. These factors make this a favored destination for anglers and adventure seekers alike, as an escape from the US to Canada is an escape to paradise.

These trailer parks were established as an inexpensive way for the middle class to get away from their blue collar jobs, allowing them a reprieve from the stress of trying to earn enough money to provide food and shelter for their families. The parks also allowed for socialization, often strengthening the family bond. Barbecues and campfires were the norm, as families spent their leisure time together enjoying Mother Nature's abundance of joy in the outdoors. Happy children reveled in the cool waters of the lake, swimming and splashing with their friends. Fathers, in their boats bobbing in the lake, tested their fishing expertise, sometimes leading to the reward of fish for dinner. On cool mornings, drinking coffee on the deck, watching the sun rise, listening to the birds' early morning songs, was a great start of the day. For the retired person who does not want to venture too far from home, a trailer at the park cannot be replaced. The result of years of demanding work, it offers a refuge from the boredom of retirement, your spirits lifted from the enjoyment of just being there.

Unfortunately, if you live in Canada this little piece of paradise can only be enjoyed during the summer months, its doors closing in October as the frigid winter months approach. The lake, which provides so much fun in the summer, will freeze providing only ice fisherman and snowmobilers a place to play. The return of the blue waters in the spring, leads to another awaited season for the winter weary residents of this cold environment.

A recreational trailer at the lake is a precious gem that cannot be replaced, an inexpensive treasure providing a feeling of well-being. Keep this way of life close to your heart and you will be rewarded with a lifetime of pleasure, a solitary place to renew your spirit and enjoy life. This treasured oasis of peace provides contentment not to be forgotten as you struggle with the realities of life; serenity found only in your seclusion at the trailer park where memories that will not be forgotten are made.

THE CAMPFIRE

―――――――― ✦✦✦✦✦✦ ――――――――

C ampfires are an activity that add options to the short summer in Canada. Parents, camp counselors, anglers and hunters, make up the majority of people having a campfire during the warmer months. Some enjoy campfires at home, inviting family and friends over for conversation, roasted marshmallows, and hotdogs. However, historically outdoor fires have been used for warmth.

One hundred years or more ago, homes were heated by large indoor fireplaces with chimneys, which is like a campfire only more restrained. Now campfires are typically for recreational use. A mainstay of campers, the fire is enjoyed by all ages, especially children. Spooky stories are told, and parents enjoy the company of their little ones around the fire. After the children go to bed, the adults take over. More stories are shared as the serenity and the crackling fire seems to evoke memories of the past. As the night wears on, the number of people around the fire dwindles as tiredness sets in and warm blankets beckon. Soon daylight will be approaching, and another day with the kids is coming.

The most appealing campfire for me is the one on the beach near the ocean. A clear night with a full moon's reflection on the water, the sound of the waves lapping the shore, and a roaring fire cannot be beat. Fires are a mesmerizing thing, causing the mind to reflect on events from the past, the time you first met your mate, or when you first became a grandparent, or even memories of being a child and sitting around a similar fire doing the same thing.

Campfires are found in every country in the world, going back to the days of early humans who cooked their food over them and used fire to keep warm. But fires also have a dark side, such as causing large forest fires when a camper leaves a site with the fire not extinguished. Also, children have been burned when their non-attentive parents were looking the other way and they ventured too close. An avoidable accident around a fire is when a drinker, who has passed his limit and lost his balance, trips and falls into the flames. A majority of these accidents do not result in injury, only laughter at the person's misfortune.

Campfires will be with us until the end of time, the smell of the smoke and the warmth of the flame evoking memories of time spent around a fire pit. Do not forget when the opportunity arises, grab your family and friends and enjoy a good tradition that all people should experience at least once in their lifetime.

Happy Camping.

A CHRISTMAS STORY

——————— ✦✦✦✦✦ ———————

The little house sat decorated, its Christmas lights were shining, sending a message of hope to all who laid eyes upon them. It was Christmas eve and inside the house, a calm prevailed after a chaotic day of shopping, and trying to keep control of three small children. After much drama, the children were finally in bed sleeping, leaving the parents to fill the stockings and put the gifts under the tree. The milk and cookies on the table magically disappeared, delighting the children upon their awakening. The parents exhausted, went to bed, only to be awakened at first light by their little ones climbing all over them.

The children were excited and wanted to open their presents. Everyone went to the living room and soon happy faces prevailed as the children opened the gifts they had under the tree. Today was a day for parents, as the children, obsessed with their new toys and games, needed little attention. Their friends would come over and bring their toys, sharing in the joy of Christmas.

After a busy day and a big dinner, which included friends and other family members, this beautiful day of love and friendship ended. A calm prevailed making the chaos of the Christmas season already a memory. To a happy child everyday is Christmas, growing with the help of their parents to become responsible adults, to continue this tradition for generations to come. Merry Christmas and a happy New Year to all.

A SPECIAL CHRISTMAS

＊＋＋✦✦＋＋＊

T he young couple pulled onto the road that led to the cottage they had rented for the Christmas holiday. They had left the city and headed north to a lake in Algonquin Park, where they rented a winterized cottage. As they turned into the driveway they noticed a large pile of dried firewood stacked in front of the building. The cottage was cold, making their first task getting a blazing fire going in the fireplace, after which they would unload the car. The warm fire brought a comfortable atmosphere to the inside of the building, leaving the cold outside for nature to enjoy. They brought in the supplies they had brought for this trip. The bottles of champagne would serve a special purpose after dinner. Soon Christmas Eve was upon them.

The darkness came early, the shortest day of the year having just passed. The evening was enchanting with a cloudless sky; the full moon and twinkling stars reflected light off the snow. This illuminated the frozen lake as if it were under a giant spotlight. The silence of the moment sent a feeling of peace through their tired souls.

They went inside the cottage and enjoyed a dinner of chicken and salads, topped off with a piece of berry pie. They opened the champagne and retired to the front of the fireplace where they were going to exchange gifts. A surprise awaited as John and Rebecca enjoyed the evening and finished the champagne.

John told his girlfriend to close her eyes, and to not open them until he told her to. He took the ring case out, opened it, and told Rebecca to open her eyes. She did and let out a gasp, a beautiful diamond engagement ring was looking back at her. No words were exchanged as the hugs and tears said it all. A most beautiful Christmas that would never be forgotten, even fifty years later as their love for each other was never extinguished; a moment they both would cherish forever.

THE HOLIDAY TREE

⋆ ⟡⟡⟡⟡ ⋆

Today is the start of the Christmas season which means it is time to get our Christmas tree. My father got our tree saw, and since we live on a farm we head off to the woods behind our house. We dress in our warmest clothes because it is winter, and it is very cold outside with snow on the ground.

First, we head to the barn to feed the animals. We have a pig named Arnold, a cow named Betsy, a goat named Theodore, and a sheep named Ruby. We also have four cats who love to chase and catch the mice that live in the barn. Our dog Bernie is also going with us. Off we go, with Bernie leading the way, jumping in the snow and barking loudly. We see rabbit tracks, and an animal track that goes in a straight line, which my father says was made by a fox. The fox was following the rabbit, I thought.

There are many Christmas trees, and I am careful to pick just the right one. Bernie also gets to help pick the tree. He runs to the tree barking and running around the one he really likes. Finally, my dad says it is time to pick the tree and go home as he is getting cold, and it is starting to snow. Suddenly there is a rustle, and then the sound of a chickadee singing in the very tree I am picking. The chickadee picked our tree this year. Father gets to work sawing down the tree, and with only three cuts the tree falls into the deep snow. We tie a rope around the bottom of it and are ready to drag it home.

Off we go, Bernie leading the way barking and running all the way back to our house. Finally, after pulling and walking we are home. We leave the tree outside and go into the house for hot chocolate, which mother has ready for us.

My favorite part of the holiday season is smelling the fresh evergreen scent of the Christmas tree, the decorations, and especially all the wrapped presents under it. The snow is falling, and I am glad our job is done. I hope every kid has a Christmas as happy as me.

A CHRISTMAS PAST

❖❖❖❖❖❖

I t is past midnight, and another Christmas has passed. The children and parents, both exhausted from their early morning start, are sleeping peacefully in their warm beds while the frigid winter wind blows outside. The excitement of Christmas morning with the children is a memory treasured forever. Sleep prevails, a time for the mind to rest after a day of constant stimulation and excitement brought on by this special holiday. Now it is over, becoming another recollection of the happiest day of the year.

The Christmas tree lights will shine brightly for another week. Then they will be packed away, slowly making this festive season just a memory like the ones gone by. The mother sleeping peacefully, dreams of her childhood Christmases, waking early to Santa's gifts for her and her siblings. The stockings full of surprises and candy, as her mother always tried to make this holiday as enjoyable as possible. The presents placed under the tree, the ones from Santa always at the forefront waiting to be opened; the new doll from him her favorite gift.

The father dreams of his Christmases past, part of a large family that displayed love over wealth. Small gifts, only what the parents could provide, given with unlimited love from the heart for their large brood of children. Love and kindness that will always be on display.

Let us think about the Christmases from our childhood and bring back forgotten memories we should cherish in our hearts forever. Memories that will never be forgotten and will always be treasured. There will always be a special place in our heart for this gift called Christmas.

THE REINDEER FARM

＋＋＋＋＋＋＋

Did you know that Santa has a reindeer farm? Staffed by his elves, it plays an important part in the spirit of Christmas. Without a healthy supply of reindeer, gifts could not be delivered, leading to the disappointment of millions of children all over the world. The farm, found close to Santa's workshop, has been raising and caring for these animals for a millennium, providing a healthy supply of reindeer when needed.

It was the night before Christmas and Santa's workshop was buzzing with activity. The gifts were being packed on the sled, a magical platform that could carry enough toys to provide every child in the world an offering of one for peace and happiness. This was Santa's purpose, to put smiles on the faces of children all at the same time, everyone taking part in this offering of love that happens but once a year.

The farm was also buzzing with excitement as the reindeer were prepped for the long journey. Rudolph's nose shone red with excitement as he knew he would be leading this party through all kinds of weather, Santa depending on him to show way. The time was drawing near; the excited reindeer were brought to the workshop to be hooked to the sleigh to begin their long magical journey around the world. Everyone gathered to see them off. Mrs. Claus gave her jolly old man a big hug and kiss goodbye. With a wave and shouts of "Merry Christmas to all", the sleigh flew off. The full moon and stars illuminated the way as another Christmas was about to be enjoyed, the reindeer being the happiest of all.

THE SPIRIT OF CHRISTMAS

·✦✦✦✦✦·

The sound of the sleigh bells ringing broke the silence of Christmas eve morning. Two horses pulled the sleigh down the long driveway for an early warm-up, getting ready for an afternoon of work giving sleigh rides to family and friends who congregate here every year for pre-Christmas celebrations. A fresh layer of snow covered the trail the sleigh would take on its journey around the farm, with the family dog running in tow.

The guests started arriving after lunch, family members with children, friends, and neighbors, all gathering together to celebrate this special holiday. The hosts of the party were offering sleigh and pony rides, to the delight of the children, and hot chocolate afterwards to warm their cold little souls. The afternoon was waning as the party retired to the house for a buffet style dinner of cold meats and salads, a Christmas eve tradition and a way to feed a large number of guests.

The sound of old time Christmas carols filled the air creating a festive and happy mood. The twinkling lights on the Christmas tree reminded everyone why they were here. Announcements were made as a way to convey notable events that had been kept secret during the year. These events included an upcoming marriage and a new pregnancy, two nieces sharing their big news. Unfortunately, there would also be a divorce; an uncle having been caught running around by a not too happy wife.

Some of the older adults continued the party outside around the campfire, reminiscing of days gone by when their children were small, like their grandchildren of today. They talked about how time slips by and how old age has suddenly been bestowed upon them. A silence ensued as they thought of times gone past, igniting an emotional state not experienced for years, wonderful memories of Christmas flooding their thoughts. The star-filled night shone brightly as the fire's coals glowed with dimly, signalling the night would soon turn to sleep for this older generation hoping to enjoy the celebration of Christmas for years to come.

CHRISTMAS

+ + ♦ ♦ ♦ + +

The outside lights shone brightly, the snow reflecting their glow, illuminating a landscape that beautified the outside world. The gift of the holiday season dominated the young couple's spirit as they relaxed around the Christmas tree, enjoying carols, and the peace of mind of getting the children to bed. The tree stood proudly, decorated with ornaments of years gone past, a reminder of childhood Christmases spent at the family farm. Carrying on family traditions, children decorating the tree with ornaments made at school or with mother around the kitchen table. These decorative items are kept forever, hanging on the tree for generations as a quiet reminder of days gone past.

The fireplace crackled, casting a warm glow over the room, as lightly falling snow outside joined put on a beautiful show of peace and tranquility, the true meaning of Christmas. Thoughts of being thankful filled the minds of the happy couple. Their two beautiful young children who had brought so much joy into their lives, were now sleeping safely in their warm beds dreaming about Santa and all the presents about to be bestowed upon them.

As midnight approached the stockings were filled, the exhausted parents retiring to bed to get rested for the big day, Christmas; a forever celebration that will never lose its luster as the world's Christians celebrate the birth of God's son. There is hope that this saviour will bring peace to a troubled planet and the unhappy spirits that dominate it.

SANTA'S WORKSHOP

+ + + + + +

A long way away, where the snow never melts, there is a special place; a workshop where elves make toys for children. Santa's workshop is a magical place, nestled in the white snows of the North Pole, it has been producing toys for children for hundreds of years. Santa has been delivering these toys to children in a special sleigh pulled by nine reindeer for equally as long.

This year, Santa directed his elves to make toys the way they have been made for a millennium. He banned all electronics in his workshop, branding them as a bad influence on children. His elves tried to convince him this is what the children were asking for, but Santa would have none of it. He instructed his elves to make wooden toys, trains, cars, and trucks painted with bright colors, as well as stuffed animals of every size and color, and dolls dressed in Christmas clothing. He also asked them to make army toys and men for the imaginary wars the boys would always fight. The elves shook their heads at Santa and his stubborn attitude towards their advice. But Santa had a plan; he was tired of losing children to technology and was ready to fight back.

The excitement of Christmas eve was upon them. The workshop buzzed with enthusiasm as the sleigh was filled with toys, the reindeer harnessed and ready to go. With a "Merry Christmas to all!" Santa streaked across the sky, the full moon lighting his way. The spirit of Christmas filled his soul, launching him into a magical time of going down chimneys and leaving toys for all the children under the brightly lit and decorated Christmas trees.

But his plan for this year was slightly different. Santa would leave his toys but take all the electronics parents had bought. The children, disappointed they never received what they asked for, were overjoyed by the bright colors and the uniqueness of the toys they had never seen before. Eventually the children would get their electronic devices, just not on Christmas day this year. Happy with the toys they received and filled with the joy of Christmas, they were thankful for a wonderful holiday.

THERE'S A MONSTER
IN THE CLOSET

————— ✦✦✦✦✦ —————

The little boy yelled out, "There's a monster in my closet!" His mother came running. She had just tucked the sleepy boy in his bed and kissed him goodnight, giving a sigh of relief, as she was looking for a few moments of peace and quiet for herself. Entering the room, she saw her son sitting up in bed pointing at his closet door, telling her there was a monster in his closet and he had seen it. He said it had a large head with warts all over its face and two eyes that glowed red.

The mother went to the closet, checked it thoroughly, and assured the boy that there was no monster in the closet. The boy said, "Maybe he went under my bed." The mother checked under the bed, still no monster. The boy would not believe her, as he was certain what he had seen. The only solution was to set traps and try to catch this monster.

The boy agreed that if his mother placed traps in his closet and under his bed he would go to sleep for the night. She seized on this opportunity and went about setting imaginary traps until the boy was satisfied. When finished to his satisfaction, the mother tucked him in, gave him a kiss goodnight and within minutes he was sound asleep. She retired to the living room where she picked up her book and was just getting ready to open it, when she heard, "Mommy, help me! There's a monster in my closet!"

THE CABIN

+ + + + + + +

In the woods behind Reece and Wesley's house, stood the remains of an old log cabin rumoured to have been built in the middle of the last century. There were tall tales and rumours about this place. Reece and Wes's mother had done research on the property and learned unusual things about the person who had built it. The man was a wealthy recluse from New York City who had come to Canada to get away from his family, whom he disliked. He felt they only tolerated him because he was rich, always asking him for money or wanting him to buy them things.

This got Reece and Wes thinking. If he had been well-off, what had he done with his fortune? They were not the first to think of this, as historic accounts said that people had tried, unsuccessfully, to find his valuables. Had any one ever thought to look inside the logs of the cabin? The boys knew some of the logs were strewn about, and perhaps the owner of the cabin had hollowed out one of these timbers as a hiding place for his money.

Early the next morning the boys left their house and made their way to the cabin, certain they were going to find what would amount to treasure. Armed with a hatchet and a hammer, they got to work checking the ends of the logs, knowing that finding a soft end would tell them to investigate further. Wes let out a scream, startling Reece. He had found something that looked suspicious and wanted his older brother's opinion. Reece took his hatchet and chopped the end of the log. He soon broke through and was able to pull all the filling out of the middle. Reece reached in the cavity, feeling a canvas bag. He pulled it out of the hollow log. Wes took the bag from Reece and looked inside. It was full of gold coins! They had found the treasure that for so long had stymied others.

The coins are now sitting in a safety deposit box in the bank. The boy's father says when they reach the age of eighteen he will have their find appraised, cash it in, and deposit the funds in a bank account for Reece and Wes. This proves that imagination and intuition can sometimes lead to an almost unimaginable find, making one rich beyond belief.

MY SPECIAL PRESENT

◆ ◆ ◆ ◆ ◆ ◆

Today is my birthday and Mommy and Daddy have told me they have a very special present for me. It's Saturday and my party, which I have been waiting for, is about to start. We have decorations up and we have hot dogs, lots of good treats, and ice cream. My best friend, Dylan, arrived early to help set up the games we are going to play. After lots of hard work we are finally ready. My mommy has the party table set and I love my birthday cake with seven candles on it. I am so excited about my party, I almost forgot about my special present. I wonder what it is!

All my friends are here, and we play a lot of different games. It is a warm spring day, but there is still quite a bit of snow on the ground. We build a big snowman, have a snowball fight, and make snow angels. Mommy yells at us to come inside, as it was time to eat, sing Happy Birthday, and have cake. After these festivities, it is finally time to open my presents.

My best friend, Dylan, bought me a new helmet for when we would ride our bikes together after the snow melts. My other friends bought me games and I even got a new fishing pole. Where was my present from Mommy and Daddy?

All of a sudden, the front door opened, and I heard little feet scratching on the hard floor. It was a little puppy with very short legs and a tiny little nose. Was this my special present? I was so excited! My daddy handed me the leash and said, "Happy birthday Timmy!" My mommy was crying because I was so happy. I called my dog Blue, and he became my best friend. This was the best birthday any kid could ever have!

THE GARDEN FAIRIES

+ + + + + + +

Who believes in garden fairies? Children of all ages not only believe in the fairies but also in a magical world of talking insects and families of beautiful butterflies fluttering about the garden flowers. Joey loved the garden, he loved all the different smells and activities of his garden friends, but most of all he loved the garden fairies. These fairies were the caretakers of the garden, keeping all of the garden life in a happy balance of love and mutual respect. As they flew around the garden, they would visit their friends, the insects, flowers, and other creatures. Their best friends were the dragonflies, who they would race around the garden stopping occasionally to drink at the feeders of sweet sugar water that Joey and his mother placed throughout the yard.

Today was a special day in the garden. It was early spring and time to plant the vegetables. Joey, Davey, his mommy, and his daddy all took part. Under the watchful eyes of the fairies they made the rows for the carrots and the mounds for the potatoes. They also planted beautiful sunflowers, which would grow tall. Their yellow colour would attract other fairies and visitors from nearby gardens, becoming a gathering place for the special life in this part of the earth.

Joey could hardly wait until the vegetables were ready to pick and eat. The fairies would watch over this beautiful garden daily, until it was time to go to sleep for the night. Then the fairies would fly home to their special sleeping place but would return the next morning with the warm sunshine. Joey would come out to the garden and enjoy his friends and all of the fragrant odors of this enchanted place.

"Joey", his mother yelled, "it is time to get up. Remember we are going to plant the garden today."

PETE'S DRAGON

✦✦✦✦✦✦

"Pete!" his mother yelled, "you need to get out of bed right now and feed your hungry dragon, he is breathing fire all over the place!" Pete did not want to get out of bed. He was so tired, but he knew it was his responsibility to take care of his pets. He went to the freezer and grabbed a large piece of dragon food. His dragon, whose name was Good Guy, cooked all his own food with his fiery breath. Good Guy was Pete's favorite pet. He could fly, breathe fire, and swoosh his wings playfully, blowing Pete into a round ball sending him rolling down their favorite hill. Good Guy was a friendly dragon who loved to play with all the children in the neighborhood.

After eating, Good Guy gave all of Pete's friends dragon rides. They flew over their homes, their parents coming out and waving to them, telling them to hang on tight. Good guy was tired after giving everyone rides, so he decided to go home and have a nap. He had a wonderful dragon house with a nice, big, comfortable bed. He laid down and soon fell asleep. He started dreaming about flying, swooshing his wings, and doing summersaults all while breathing fire.

Suddenly Good Guy's eyes opened, and he realized he was not really flying but was in his bed. He got up and went to find Pete, as they were planning to go to the dragon park where there were special things for dragons to play with. A trip here was Pete's special treat to Good Guy for being such a good dragon. Pete was so lucky to have such a magical pet and Good Guy loved Pete with all his heart.

THE SCHOOL HOUSE

✦ ✦ ✦◆✦ ✦ ✦

When I went to school it was not like going to the schools of today. I attended a one room schoolhouse called the Daisy Dee. The school had one large room with eight rows of seats. Each row stood for a grade, one through eight, with no kindergarten class. This small school was in a rural area offering children the opportunity to learn how to read and write, the two most important subjects taught at that time. All work was completed on paper, the only technology was the teacher's manual typewriter.

The Daisy Dee's enrollment was no more than fifty students, with siblings attending together. Transportation to school was not included, which meant a long walk, in all kinds of weather. Arriving in the morning the children had to wait for the teacher to come out and ring the hand bell announcing school was about to start. We then went to our designated cloak rooms, the girls on one side of the classroom, the boys on the other. This was where you would take off any coats, sweaters, or boots that were not needed for class. Any time you went into or outside the building you were expected to use this entrance.

Our teacher was strict, like most one room school house teachers. She was alone, with no other adult to help her, with what were usually active children of various ages, and plenty of sibling rivalry. The teacher had the authority to dish out punishment to any child who misbehaved or broke the rules. One form of punishment was a strap that was a real beaver's tail. I had the privilege of feeling this strap once, when I kept dragging leaves and debris into the school, making extra work for the teacher to clean up.

When school was in session the teacher worked with students in each row, which was one grade. She checked homework, projects, and handed out new assignments. She went down each of the rows, working with individual students, answering their questions. In this environment, it was not unusual for children to learn an upper grade's work while in a lower grade. That was how I was promoted from grade one to grade three. Over the course of the day we were allowed two recesses of fifteen minutes each and one hour for lunch.

My favorite entertainment at school was on Thursday's when Mr. Fife would bring his fiddle. We would put all the chairs around the edges of the room and have a square dance. An old phonograph player supplied the calling, and Mr. Fife's fiddle supplied the music. This also helped with the socialization between the boys and girls, as everyone had to pick a partner.

Our bathrooms were modern for the time. We had his and hers outhouses with double seats. The teacher never had to worry about the kids spending too much time in the bathroom, especially in the winter. The school was heated by a big, old woodstove, which the eighth grade boys were responsible for keeping the fire burning. Most of the boys were familiar with woodstoves, as they usually had one at home.

A favorite event was show and tell, where each child had the opportunity to bring an item to share with the class. The children enjoyed seeing the interesting things brought in to show. It was an added bonus if my father were home on these days, as I could get a ride to and from school, not having to carry my item. It was a simple life but one of great satisfaction and happiness.

HALLOWEEN HOUSE

--- ✦✦✦✦✦ ---

My father had the job of decorating houses for Halloween and today I was going to help him. He was hired to perform his Halloween magic decorating the historic estate of the Peterson family. After a breakfast of pancakes that mommy made shaped like ghosts, we loaded the Halloween decorations from the garage into the truck. There were ghosts, werewolves, spooky animated characters, tape recordings of spooky sounds, and colored lights. We set off in the truck, but little did we know about the surprise that awaited us.

As we were pulling up to the mansion, I saw someone looking out the upstairs bedroom window. I thought this was strange, as my father had told me we were going to be the only ones at the house. When we approached the house I felt a shiver go up my spine. As I looked at the old porch, there were cobwebs everywhere and big spiders crawling around, wrapping their catches of food in their webs to be stored and eaten later. We opened the creaky front door and entered the house. I was so scared I was ready to go home.

All of a sudden, we heard a loud crash coming from upstairs, followed by what sounded like a loud voice that said "Get out now while you can, you are not welcome here." This was followed by footsteps coming down the creaky old stairs and the sound of chains being pulled across the floor. My father and I looked at each other and ran out the front door to the truck. We jumped in the cab and sped all the way home. We could not believe what had just happened.

William Stanley

Then the phone rang. It was daddy's friend laughing loudly at us. It was all a hoax; a Halloween joke they had played on us to scare us. With relief we turned the truck around and went back to the old house. After a day of challenging work, we set up the spooky decorations and made it ready for all the children to enjoy on Halloween.

Happy Halloween and enjoy the haunted house!

WESLEY

✦✦✦✦✦✦

The day was getting close for the birth of our new baby. Mommy woke up one morning with a funny feeling in her stomach. She woke up Daddy and said, "I think it's baby time." Daddy jumped out of bed and activated his plan of action; phone Grandma and Grandpa to get me in case they had to go to the hospital fast. Mommy was feeling fine, but apprehensive about what the day would bring.

After a breakfast of toast and cereal, Mommy thought it would be best if she phoned the midwife to ask her advice. The midwife told her to relax on the couch and wait to see what happens. Daddy was nervous. The phone rang, it was Grandma checking to see how things were going. She was excited about the new baby. As the day wore on Mommy thought that just maybe it was not time yet for the baby to come into this new world. After again talking to the midwife, she was told to go to bed and see what happens tomorrow. Grandma and Grandpa brought me home, and everybody went to bed.

In the middle of the night, Daddy was awakened from a deep sleep by Mommy yelling, "The baby is coming!" He grabbed the phone, dialed 911, and told them to send help as soon as possible, as a baby was being born. Then Daddy helped Mommy bring the new baby into the world. Everyone was so excited no one thought to see if the new baby was a boy or a girl. It was BABY WESLEY, a beautiful healthy boy. Daddy and Mommy were so happy! Soon help came, but Daddy had things all under control. He phoned Grandma to get me, as they were going to the hospital.

When Grandma and Grandpa got to the house there was so much excitement. The paramedics and their supervisor were there, and he told Grandpa that in thirty years of working he had only seen this kind of birth happen twice. One of the paramedics handed Grandma the new baby and asked her to get him ready to go to the hospital. Grandma dressed the newborn baby very warmly, as it was winter and cold outside. But wait where was I? I had slept through the whole ordeal. Was this divine intervention?

Soon Mommy, Daddy, and Wesley were ready and off they went to the hospital. As soon as Grandma and Grandpa heard the front door shut, they heard the door knob on my bedroom door turn. I came out, oblivious as to what had just happened. What a miracle birth, an event that will never be forgotten by anyone involved. A happy ending to a wonderful baby story.

THE GRANDCHILDREN

❖❖❖❖❖❖

Being the grandparents of two active children, now eighteen months and five years old, has been like a summer camp experience. Being guardians of these children three days a week for ten weeks while their parents worked, there was rarely a dull moment. The days start at 8 a.m., with Reece, the oldest, in the door first, immediately telling us about his adventurous plans for the day. Next comes Wes and his mommy, Wes usually having a big grin on his face, while his mother has a more serious look as she contemplates her day. After pleasant greetings and fanfare when Mommy leaves, the kids get down to what they know best, playing.

They head for the toy section and select things they think will hold their attention. It seems children like the same toys, as battles usually ensue, along with loud screaming and aggressive baby behaviour trying to get the toy one feels he is entitled to. Grandma is the judge and usually, with some kind talk, defuses these situations easily. As the day progresses, snacks are served, and T.V. is watched. Reece and Wes play well together but can be rough. Wes, being much smaller, usually coming out on the losing end.

Wes loves to chase the cat, getting great enjoyment out of this activity. Soon its time for his nap. Grandma reads books, rocks him, and soon he is sleeping soundly. Sometimes Grandpa and Reece walk down to the dollar store so Reece can buy something for himself. This trip is always enjoyed by both the grandfather and grandson. After Wes wakes up, lunch is served. Reece usually eats a grilled cheese or peanut butter sandwich, while Wes likes to eat leftovers from the refrigerator.

After lunch, plans are usually made to either play in the back yard or go somewhere in the car, typically the park or to lake to feed the ducks, where the kids can run on the spacious grass, Grandma and Grandpa hoping they will burn off excess energy. That idea never seems to work.

Soon its time to get back in the car and go home. Upon arrival another snack is served, and they both enjoy a freeze pop to cool off. Shortly thereafter, Mommy arrives with much excitement as the children have not seen her all day. After a short visit, she manages to corral them, and after hugs and kisses they leave us promising the same for tomorrow. A calmness envelops the house, as the spirits of these children move on to brighten the day of someone else. We will never tire of our grandchildren, always finding pleasure in their company and their innocent views of life, knowing we only have the opportunity to experience this once and enjoy it we will.

RED

◆ ◆ ◆ ◆ ◆ ◆

They called her Red. She was born into a large, poor family and taken out of school early to help her exhausted and often sick mother with the household chores. Red helped with the cooking, and she helped her mother create a stable environment in this large household of children. She was one of seven siblings and one nephew, with sibling status, raised in a large one-hundred-and-fifty-year-old country farmhouse, with a dirt floor basement and no indoor plumbing. Red, her nickname for being the only family member with red hair, which was an asset as she became her father's favorite child.

She was known to have an industrious spirit, going beyond her assigned responsibilities. Because of a lack of discipline by other family members to fulfill their obligations, she took on their chores as well. She was always the one to step up and help Mom with sickness in the family and became Mom's caregiver when she was sick. With her mother as her teacher, Red grew up to be a caring person, making her goal in life to work and care for the sick; volunteering in long-term care homes and caring for family members until the end.

Red married early. Her husband of fifty-four years had a successful career in the field of finance and provided his wife and two children with a comfortable life. He was a stalwart supporter of Red's, as she went on to become a loving mother, always putting herself last, never learning what selfishness meant. She had a good life, travelling extensively with her husband visiting foreign countries and many tropical islands for leisure, and taking part in their special hobby, bird watching. They were also members of the lawn bowling club for years, where her husband was instrumental in having a beautiful new clubhouse built, replacing an old structure that had become obsolete.

Red has spent her life helping people who were less fortunate, never saying no to running an errand, taking someone to the doctor, or picking up prescriptions and delivering them to their home, asking for nothing in return. Now in her seventies, being a cancer survivor, and suffering from a lifetime of severe arthritis, her physical capabilities have slowed but her spirit has not. She is the same Red, only an older version.

Because of her actions while here on earth I am sure Red will be blessed in the afterlife, with her past charges meeting her in heaven. Now she is enjoying her two hobbies, growing flowers in the summertime and shoveling snow in the winter.

May Red enjoy a long, happy, and healthy life, which I am sure she will. And we hope people will follow her example, making this world a better place for all of us to live in, like she has.

A CHILD'S FIRST YEAR

━━━━━━━━━━ ✦✦✦✦✦✦ ━━━━━━━━━━

The excited mother is in the hospital, in labor with her first child. After the baby is born, her life will take on new meaning. The baby will become the focal point in her new world, more important than her husband, mother and anyone else in her life. Suddenly the selfishness and her self worth changes to just love for her child. The father, who is also an important part of this new life, sometimes feels neglected by his wife as all her attention is directed towards the new baby. This soon changes as the baby is brought home from the hospital and the father takes a more active role in the baby's care, as the first months of life are a busy time for both parents, often leading to their exhaustion.

As the baby grows, so does the love for their child. A child's emotional and physical health depends more on the love it receives from the parents than the food it eats. Nursing the baby is important, as it forms a special bond between mother and child. Breast milk also provides important nutrients and disease-fighting antibodies that cannot be found on a market shelf. As the months go by, the baby starts to coo, smile and make eye contact with the parents, bringing a special joy to their hearts. The baby's world is expanding at a fast pace, now reacting to color, touch, and beginning to play. Next comes crawling, followed by the ability to pull himself up to a standing position, hanging on to furniture, or just about anything else that is stable enough to support him. One day the baby lets go of what he is hanging onto and takes his first steps on his own. This is a milestone for the parents and also an important point in the baby's life. It gives the baby more access to the things it sees and wants, which is usually almost everything, much to the dismay of the parents. This is a time of constant supervision, as the baby, if not watched carefully, can get into serious trouble and suffer injuries that sometimes require medical care.

Soon the baby's first birthday is here, and a big celebration is in order. This event is attended by happy family members and a big cake is usually served. The baby enjoys eating the cake with his hands while making a huge mess, much to the enjoyment of the adults. Many pictures are taken to mark this milestone and the proud parents are happy to have crossed this threshold, looking forward to a happy and healthy future for their baby who is now a toddler. The future looks bright for this baby, as it has been raised to this point by a very loving family with a good support structure from the grandparents.

May the second year of this baby's life be as loving and warm as its first, and the parents coping skills survive the raising of this child to become a productive member of society. Raising a healthy child in a loving stable environment is one of life's most intense pleasures enjoyed by humans. Good luck in round two!

ACKNOWLEDGEMENTS

I would like to thank my brother, Joe, and his wife, Jan, for supporting my writing endeavours. Also my wife, Ruth Ann, who listened to each of my stories and worked tirelessly in helping me organize them into this collection.

Printed in the United States
by Baker & Taylor Publisher Services